Pairing Up

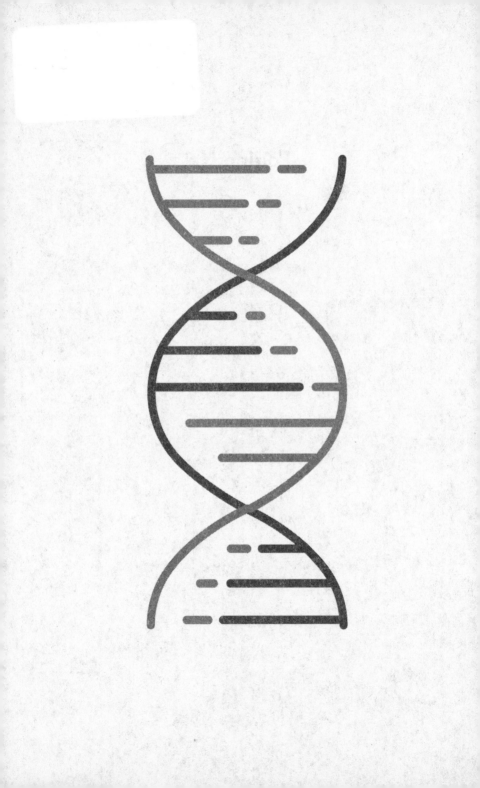

GEORGE R. R. MARTIN

Presents

Wild Cards: Pairing Up

EDITED BY GEORGE R. R. MARTIN

assisted by

Melinda M. Snodgrass

and written by

Kevin Andrew Murphy   Walton Simons

Christopher Rowe   Gwenda Bond

Marko Kloos   Peter Newman

Melinda M. Snodgrass   David Anthony Durham

Bradley Denton

Bantam

New York

2024 Bantam Books Trade Paperback Edition

Copyright © 2023 by the Wild Cards Trust
"Trudy of the Apes" copyright © 2023 by Kevin Andrew Murphy
"Cyrano d'Escargot" copyright © 2023 by Christopher Rowe
"In the Forests of the Night" copyright © 2023 by Marko Kloos
"The Wounded Heart" copyright © 2023 by Melinda M. Snodgrass
"Echoes from a Canyon Wall" copyright © 2023 by Bradley Denton
"The Long Goodbye" copyright © 2023 by Walton Simons
"What's Your Sign?" copyright © 2023 by Gwenda Bond and Peter Newman
"The Wolf and the Butterfly" copyright © 2023 by David Anthony Durham

Published in the United States by Bantam Books, an imprint of Random House, a division of Penguin Random House LLC, New York.

BANTAM & B colophon is a registered trademark of Penguin Random House LLC.

Originally published in hardcover in the United States by Bantam Books, an imprint of Random House, a division of Penguin Random House LLC, in 2023.

All characters featured in this book, and the distinctive names and likenesses thereof, and all related indicia are trademarks of George R. R. Martin.

LIBRARY OF CONGRESS CATALOGING-IN-PUBLICATION DATA

Names: Martin, George R. R., editor. | Snodgrass, Melinda M., contributor. |
Murphy, Kevin (Kevin Andrew), author. | Rowe, Christopher, author. |
Kloos, Marko, author.
Title: George R. R. Martin presents Wild Cards: Pairing up: tales of love & lust
from the world of the Wild Cards / edited by George R.R. Martin; assisted by
Melinda M. Snodgrass and written by Kevin Andrew Murphy, Christopher Rowe,
Marko Kloos [and others].
Other titles: Pairing up
Description: New York: Bantam Books, [2022]
Identifiers: LCCN 2022038255 (print) | LCCN 2022038256 (ebook) |
ISBN 9780593357880 (trade paperback) | ISBN 9780593357873 (ebook)
Subjects: LCSH: Science fiction, American.
Classification: LCC PS648.S3 G46 2022 (print) | LCC PS648.S3 (ebook) |
DDC 813/.0876208—dc23/eng/20221014
LC record available at https://lccn.loc.gov/2022038255
LC ebook record available at https://lccn.loc.gov/2022038256

Printed in the United States of America on acid-free paper

randomhousebooks.com

1st Printing

Book design by Virginia Norey
Helix art: bsd studio/stock.adobe.com

this one is for
KATYA
the Potato Princess

Contents

Wild Cards

The virus was created on TAKIS, hundreds of light-years from Earth. The ruling mentats of the great Takisian Houses were looking for a way to enhance their formidable psionic abilities and augment them with physical powers. The retrovirus they devised showed enough promise that the psi lords decided to field-test it on Earth, whose inhabitants were genetically identical to Takisians.

Prince Tisianne of House Ilkazam opposed the experiment and raced to Earth in his own living starship to stop it. The alien ships fought high above the atmosphere. The ship carrying the virus was torn apart, the virus itself lost. Prince Tisianne landed his own damaged ship at White Sands, where his talk of tachyon drives prompted the military to dub him **DR. TACHYON.**

Across the continent, the virus fell into the hands of **DR. TOD,** a crime boss and war criminal, who resolved to use it to extort wealth and power from the cities of America. He lashed five blimps together and set out for New York City. President Harry S. Truman reached out to Robert Tomlin, **JETBOY,** the teenage fighter ace of World War II, to stop him. Flying his experimental jet, the JB-1, Jetboy reached Tod's blimps and crashed into the gondola. The young hero and his old foe met for the last time as the bomb containing the virus fell to Earth. "*Die, Jetboy, die,*" Tod shouted as he shot Tomlin again and again. "I can't die yet, I haven't seen *The Jolson Story,*" Jetboy replied as the bomb exploded.

Thousands of microscopic spores rained down upon Manhattan. Thousands more were dispersed into the atmosphere and swept up by the jet stream, to spread all across the Earth. But New York City got the worst of it.

It was **September 15, 1946.** The first Wild Card Day.

Ten thousand died that first day in Manhattan alone. Thousands more were transformed, their DNA rewritten in terrible and unpredictable ways. Every case was unique. No two victims were affected in the same way. For that reason, the press dubbed xenovirus *Takis-A* (its scientific name) the *wild card.*

Ninety percent of those infected died, unable to withstand the violent bodily changes the virus unleashed upon them. Those victims were said to have drawn the *black queen.*

Of those who survived, nine of every ten were twisted and mutated in ways great and small. They were called *jokers* (or *jacks, knaves,* or *joker-aces* if they also gained powers). Shunned, outcast, and feared, they began to gather in the Bowery, in a neighborhood that soon became known as **Jokertown.**

Only one in a hundred of those infected emerged with superhuman powers: telepathy, telekinesis, enhanced strength, superspeed, invulnerability, flight, and a thousand other strange and wondrous abilities. These were the *aces,* the celebrities of the dawning new age. Unlike the heroes of the comic book, very few of them chose to don spandex costumes and fight crime, but they would soon begin to rewrite history all the same.

These are their stories.

Pairing Up

1957

Trudy of the Apes

by Kevin Andrew Murphy

The Garden of Allah was found, not in the Prophet's Paradise, but in Hollywood, at the intersection of Sunset Boulevard and Havenhurst Drive. But instead of flying there on the back of the Buraq like Muhammad, Trudy Pirandello had taken Pan Am.

She checked her bags at the front desk, checked her makeup with her compact, and in the reflection, checked out the jewels and jewelry on display on the other guests—a nice watch here, a pretty ring there, but nothing that wouldn't be missed and nothing worth risking, especially with her eyes on a greater prize. Trudy slipped her compact back in her handbag, slipped the bellman a generous but not lavish tip, and slipped off into the interior of the Garden of Allah.

She had expected paradise to look a bit more Arabian, with fanciful fountains and arabesques, not a couple dozen Spanish Mission–style bungalows, all terra-cotta tiles and stucco. At least the landscaping was pretty and tropical enough, with bougainvillea vines and night-blooming jasmine, the dark shiny leaves glittering in the sun. The houris were there, too, or at least starlets, many of them taking advantage of a swimming pool in the shape of the Black Sea, the legacy of Alla Nazimova, silent-screen Salomé turned hotelier.

Rumor also had it that Nazimova coined the term *sewing circle* for ladies who liked ladies, though as Trudy understood, Alla liked *everyone*. Her tradition had continued—the Garden of Allah, as the hotel had been renamed with an added *h,* was the swinging place to go if you were a Hollywood creative. F. Scott Fitzgerald had stayed there, as had Errol Flynn. It-girl Clara Bow, Ernest Hemingway, Ginger Rogers, D. W. Griffith, Laurence Olivier, Frank Sinatra, and Dorothy Parker. Even Marlene Dietrich, who'd starred in the movie *The Garden of Allah.*

Of course, the hotel had seen better days. Alla Nazimova had died in '44—two years before the wild card—and it was now 1957. Errol Flynn had swashbuckled away. Trudy thought she glimpsed the dark-haired head of Ronald Reagan in the pool, surrounded by a bevy of bathing beauties—a definite trade-up from Bonzo the chimp—but a B-movie star wasn't what Trudy needed. What she needed was an ace: a blonde, to be specific.

She spied a very small one: A little blond girl, no more than six, sat poolside sipping a pink lemonade. She wore a white blouse, a black skirt with suspenders, matching white socks and black Mary Janes, with a shocking-pink bow in her hair, and a supercilious expression as she watched the adults.

"Hello, Eloise." Trudy sat down next to her. "I was hoping to see Kay."

"She's taking a nap . . ." Eloise told her.

"I expected she might," Trudy said, keeping the secret unspoken. Kay was taking a nap because Eloise was her alter ego. Kay was Kay Thompson, star of stage and screen—singer, dancer, multi-talented everywoman—who three years ago had gone to New York for a singing gig and taken ill. There were rumors that it might have been the wild card, but Thompson brushed them off, saying it was nothing more remarkable than menopause, then went on with her show.

No one else had noticed a little girl from time to time slipping out of Thompson's suite at the Plaza Hotel, going off to make mischief or spy on guests. No one else except Trudy.

Trudy was an ace herself, but she was also smart enough to keep her wild card up her sleeve . . . and not just because she was also a thief who specialized in teleporting small objects—particularly jewelry—into her hands. Aces who got caught ended up in government service, doing far more dangerous and less rewarding jobs than going to nightclubs and musical revues and, in the dimness, teleporting this diamond earring or that gold watch to the inside of an evening bag.

Hotel lobbies were also good places to spy valuable jewels, particularly hotels as swanky as the Plaza—although Trudy hadn't expected that the sharp-eyed little girl would be the same person as the popular songstress whose shows Trudy had pick-teleported one too many times. But Eloise was a touch too fashion-conscious for the average little girl, sharing a few too many tastes in common with Kay Thompson, which Trudy had remarked upon. Soon an uneasy truce sparked an unlikely friendship.

The fact was, Trudy liked Kay, and Kay liked Trudy, and two lady aces up the sleeve could cover for each other better than either could alone. Plus, Kay owed Trudy. Kay's ace wasn't fully under her control, tied, Trudy suspected, to menopause and hot flashes, and last year there'd been an overly suspicious hotel detective at the Plaza, asking a few too many questions about Kay's occasional young guest, Eloise. After Trudy had arranged for the police to find him with a stolen string of pearls in his pocket, he'd gone away, and Trudy had let his successor think that Eloise was her own daughter, going off and getting into mischief while Trudy visited with Kay.

"So, what brings you to Hollywood, Trudy?" Eloise glanced up over her lemonade, holding it the way an older sophisticated woman would handle a cocktail. "Something I could help with? Or do you need Kay?"

"Well," Trudy admitted, "Kay mentioned in her last postcard that Jack Braun had a bungalow here. I was hoping for an introduction . . ."

"What sort of introduction?"

Trudy cocked her head, gazing at the pool with Ronnie and his bevy of beauties, then gave Eloise a sidelong glance. "Not the sort of introduction it would be proper for a little girl to give . . ."

"Wait here." Eloise gave her a knowing look and a wink. "I'll manage it." With that she downed the last of her lemonade like a hard-drinking woman would a cocktail, then skipped off down the tiles beside the pool with all the skill of a dancer with forty-plus years of training.

Trudy was a bit bemused. The parties at the Garden of Allah were legendary; she'd planned to find her way to them at night, try to work her charms on Jack, and see where that led. Instead, she looked at the poolside menu and ordered a limeade and an avocado-and-bacon sandwich, feeling very Californian in her choice. She wondered how many stories about the Garden were true.

The best she'd heard was the one about the naked actress, her pet monkey, and the telegram boy, which sounded like a bawdy tale from *The Arabian Nights* lightly retold for the Silent Era. But then Trudy heard the actual screeching of the remembered monkey, or at least a little girl screeching like a monkey: Eloise careening back into the pool area in her Mary Janes. Somewhere she'd acquired a fruit basket the size of one of Carmen Miranda's headdresses. "Ook! Ook!" Eloise shrieked, hurling an orange with startling accuracy at a blond man chasing her. He was tall, handsome, and barefoot, wearing only shorts, and the orange hit him right in the middle of his broad bare chest. Or almost did, because there was a golden flash of light as it splatted on the air half an inch from his skin. "Eloise!" he roared.

"Ook!" cried Eloise. "You Tarzan, me monkey!" She danced around the pool to the amusement of minor stars and starlets, lobbing tangerines and apples at Jack Braun, Golden Boy of the Four Aces, the strongest man in the world . . . and also, incidentally, the actor playing Tarzan on television for NBC, coming off his first season in the role and almost ready to start his second. Eloise's game would have been dangerous for anyone else to play, but the strongest man in the world didn't mean the most agile, Jack Braun looked hungover, and Eloise had all the training of a dancer in her forties packed into the body of a six-year-old girl.

She also had a fruit basket with a bunch of bananas inserted randomly for color, so Trudy made a decision. One of the bananas disappeared from the basket and reappeared in Trudy's hand underneath the napkin in her lap. Trudy produced the banana, as if she'd had it all along, and idly began to eat it as Eloise continued to pelt Golden Boy with fruit, dancing and laughing and crying, "Ook!" until she got him to chase her at just the right angle, headed straight toward Trudy.

The old slapstick trick had worked for Harold Lloyd in *The Flirt*, but rather than toss her banana peel under Golden Boy's foot, Trudy teleported it there, with the desired effect—he skidded out. Rather than run past her after Eloise, he slid straight into her, knocking her, her chair, and himself into the pool. Trudy yelped, feigning surprise as best she could, and then they were tumbling into the water with a flailing of arms and a flashing of golden light.

Ladies falling clothed into the pool was something of a tradition at the Garden of Allah, and while it wasn't quite the Hollywood meet-cute she'd planned—she'd learned the screenwriters' term when she saw *Will Success Spoil Rock Hunter?* last year on Broadway—it more than worked, allowing Trudy to put her arms around Jack's neck and play the frightened soggy young thing while Jack played the gentleman. "Are you okay?" he asked, sweeping her up in his arms and dumping her on the side of the pool, then clambering out himself. "That kid is a menace!"

"I'm okay," Trudy said, "just wet. Oh, I must look a fright . . ." Trudy considered feigning tears, but the waterworks weren't really warranted, just a bit of vanity, because she knew she looked like a very attractive brunette with a wet blouse and nice tits.

"You just need to get dried off," Jack Braun told her. "Are you staying here? Do you have dry clothes?"

"In my bags at the front desk," Trudy told him. "I'm visiting a friend, but she's not home yet."

"Well, you're welcome to change at my place . . ."

Trudy smiled. "Thank you," she said, half to Jack, half to Eloise, who'd made her escape.

Kay Thompson had more than repaid her debt.

Getting Jack into bed wasn't that hard. He was reasonably good in it, and so was Trudy, plus Jack was easy on the eyes, which helped. Besides, they were around the same age, so they had that in common—although, unfairly, he looked younger than her, even though Trudy was pretty certain he was actually older. She had thought that blonds wrinkled early, but somehow Jack's body hadn't gotten the memo. But he was also coming off a painful and expensive divorce and made it clear that he wasn't looking for a new Mrs. Braun. "I may be Golden Boy," he told her, "but the only gold I've got left is my hair—and this." He clenched his fist, making it glow with golden light, the power of his force field.

Trudy considered. While she wasn't without her charms, they were also in Hollywood, and hotties were nothing special, especially for a handsome famous ace. She needed to up her ante if she wanted to stay in the game. "Well, I won't say I'm no gold digger, but I dug my gold years ago and I've got more than enough to last me." Trudy laughed what she hoped was the right amount. "Now I'm just out for a good time. Don't believe me? Here, let me show you my rocks."

Trudy got up from bed, naked, and went to her luggage, leaning over it long enough for Jack to get a nice view of her ass while she got into her jewel case. The rocks were a couple of diamonds and an emerald, and rocks indeed—a thirty-three-carat diamond pendant, a twenty-one-carat emerald flanked by baguette diamonds, and an almost forty-two-carat diamond ring. The diamond pendant was greenish yellow, but pretty, in a Second Empire setting with three tulips and three teardrops; the diamond ring was a bluish-white stunner, in a newer setting by Cartier; and the emerald had a Cartier setting, too. Trudy put on all three. "Ta-da!" She turned around, wearing nothing but them and her birthday suit. "Like I said—rocks."

Jack Braun stared at her slack-jawed, but mostly at the rings on her fingers and the pendant between her tits. "Where did you get those?"

Trudy sat down next to him on the bed so he could admire them closer. "Well, like I said, I was in New York on Wild Card Day, too." The rings winked art deco seduction while the pendant glittered, old-fashioned but classy. "There was this old guy I was involved with." She'd stolen the diamond ring from Harry Winston and gotten the pendant from a less reputable jeweler when she'd fenced a bunch of random baubles she didn't want to hang on to. "He was good to me, but he wasn't a nice man." The emerald had necessitated a vacation to Palm Beach, Florida, to Mar-a-Lago, the estate of breakfast cereal heiress Marjorie Merriweather Post, who'd swanned around with a full emerald parure at a ball, declaring herself Juliet, until Trudy plucked the ring from her finger in the middle of "Begin the Beguine." "He died. I didn't." A fourth heist, before all the others, netted her a dozen Georgian diamond buttons that had once belonged to Hetty Green, the Witch of Wall Street, along with some documentation that tied all the jewels Trudy was wearing together and set her on her ongoing scavenger hunt for the remainder of the prize. "But hey, he still left me something for my trouble."

She gestured to the pendant with the hand with the diamond

ring and let Jack stare at both diamonds along with her tits, not explaining that what she'd gotten from the old man wasn't the rocks, but an ace power. Trudy also skipped the fact that the unnamed old guy wasn't her sugar daddy, but the infamous Dr. Tod, who had released the wild card over Manhattan and died with Jetboy on that fateful September day over ten years ago.

"You said you shot *Tarzan* last year in Brazil?" Trudy asked, making conversation. "Well, these are Brazilian, too." She waved the rings and dandled the pendant, letting them glitter. "Guess who found them there?"

Jack shook his head. "I couldn't even begin . . ."

"Emperor Maximilian," Trudy told him. "Well, he wasn't emperor yet, he was on a botany trip, but he bought the diamonds. He had the pendant made for his wife, Carlota, and kept the diamond ring for himself. When he became emperor of Mexico, he picked up the emerald. Supposedly it once belonged to Cuauhtémoc, the last king of the Aztecs, who ended up getting tortured to death by Cortés." She grimaced. "Then Maximilian got shot by a firing squad and Carlota ended up in a nuthouse, and she hocked the rings to pay for doctors. But hey, everything comes with a history."

Jack looked glum then, like something she'd said brought up a memory more painful than just watching Bette Davis chew the scenery as Empress Carlota in *Juarez,* so Trudy suggested, "Wanna make a little more history of our own?"

Jack did and Trudy fell back in bed, wearing nothing more than her diamonds and one emerald.

As Trudy had read in *Variety,* NBC had moved production of *Tarzan* from Brazil to Mexico, specifically to the state of Durango. They were shooting out of John Wayne's ranch in the little town of Chupaderos, just seven miles north of the city of Durango itself, while the Duke was off in actual Africa with Sophia Loren, filming

Legend of the Lost—except there, Libya was being shot as Timbuktu. And that wasn't the only change. *Tarzan* still hadn't gotten a Jane, but they did have a new Cheetah, Tarzan's chimpanzee buddy—and one who could act.

Trudy smiled at the joker, hoping he wouldn't recognize her, but no such luck. "Hey, wait a minute, I know you." He pointed a chimpanzee finger at her. "You're that hotsy-totsy nat broad who likes slumming it at Biff's."

Ace broad, Trudy thought, but she didn't say it. She usually went masked to Jokertown, both for anonymity and to better blend in with the jokers, but you couldn't eat with a full mask. "So sue me," she told him. "Biff makes the best patty melt in Manhattan." Biff was a joker who was a man-sized chipmunk from the waist up. Cheetah was the same, except the wild card had given him the upper body of a chimp. "You hung out with that tall kid, Troll, right?"

"Tall kid." Cheetah laughed. "Yeah, like nine feet! Strong, too. Stronger than Golden Boy here."

Jack's expression was somewhere between incredulous and annoyed, but he just ignored Cheetah and went over to the grill on the rancheria's back patio where they'd set up craft services, apparently trying to find something that fit with midwestern tastes.

Trudy took a seat opposite Cheetah at his picnic table. It was hot in Durango, the nat guest actors were all crowded at the other tables, and Cheetah's umbrella offered the one free bit of shade. Besides, it's not like she had to worry about catching anything from jokers, even if the wild card was contagious, which it wasn't. You only got it from Takisian spores, like the ones in the canister Dr. Tod found then later took up in a blimp as a bomb; Trudy had learned that the hard way, and before any other earthling, too. "So," she asked, "what's your story? Long way to go for a kid from Jokertown." Left unsaid was Trudy's knowledge that Cheetah had run on the wrong side of the law like she did, if far less successfully.

"Hey, I only went to Jokertown for high school. I'm from Flatbush. But you're asking how my card turned? Guess."

"You made the mistake of seeing a Ronald Reagan movie?"

"Close!" Cheetah laughed, showing far more of his gums than any nat could. "You know we've got Bonzo here as one of the other Cheetahs, for when we need to do leg shots? But my dad works for the Brooklyn Zoo. Primatologist, really loves working with chimps. I wanted him to pay more attention to me . . . then hey, look what the damn virus did." Cheetah shrugged his chimp shoulders beneath an ordinary human polo shirt. "But it let me get closer to my old man and gave me my first acting experience. Before this, I mean."

"Oh?" Trudy asked.

"Yeah," Cheetah told her. "Like I said, my old man works for the zoo. After I got like this, he took me to work, and one day the chimp—the real one—got sick. Big favorite with the kids. So I thought, what the hell—took my shirt off, left my pants and shoes on, crouched down, and went out into the chimp house and started doing monkeyshines for the kids. They loved it. So I got up on the ropes and started swinging back and forth, and the kid were cheering, and it was great. So then I start really getting into it, doing acrobatic flips, the whole flying trapeze number, then the next thing I know, I flip out of the chimp enclosure and land in the lion's den, right next to the big lion. I start screaming, 'Help! Help! Get me out of here!' Then the lion opens his huge jaws and snarls, 'Shut up, you fool, before you give us all away!'"

Trudy laughed lightly but Jack laughed more. "That's what he told for his audition." He came over to the table with a couple of plates of grilled skirt steak and tortillas. "Carne asada?"

Trudy took a plate. "Thanks, Jack." She glanced to the chimp joker. "So you go by Cheetah?"

"Yeah," he said, "never liked my nat name, so I ain't telling no one."

"Except payroll," said Jack, taking a bite of the carne asada sandwich he'd made with a tortilla.

Cheetah laughed, asking Trudy, "So who are you? Do we finally get a Jane?"

"If I play my cards right," Trudy told him. "Right now, I'm just script girl."

Cheetah glanced from her to Jack and grinned like a mad chimp. "What's the script? I haven't seen any pages yet."

"Does it matter?" Jack asked. "Your lines are just saying, 'Ook' a lot."

"Hey, I wanna find my motivation . . ."

Trudy took pity on him. "We're going to be shooting out of order anyway. The first couple of episodes need tigers and elephants, and they're not here yet, so we're skipping to episodes four and five. It's a two-parter titled 'The Blue Stone of Heaven,' loosely based on *Tarzan and the Jewels of Opar*—" Trudy got out the script, laying it on the table. "—and yes, the John Wayne pic's ripping Burroughs off, so we're ripping them right back. But instead of looking for rubies and emeralds in the Lost City of Ophir like Wayne and Loren, Tarzan's going to the City of Death and the jewel's a sapphire."

"Like Queen Azura's from *Flash Gordon*?"

"Pretty much the same prop," Trudy admitted, taking it out of her blouse. It was as big as the Daria-i-Noor, the "sea of light," once part of the Great Table diamond—a jewel Trudy would have loved to get her hands on—but instead of the priceless pink diamond, it was flashy but cheap blue quartz. "I don't know where wardrobe found this, but it's very nice." It also nicely hid Carlota and Maximilian's diamonds and Max's emerald, which Trudy was wearing underneath, inside her blouse, trusting the maids here less than back at the Garden of Allah. As for the dozen diamond buttons and Hetty Green's other treasures, she'd teleported them behind the lining of her purse.

Cheetah reached out with his long chimp arms and touched the script covetously. "Is this for me?"

"That's Jack's copy," Trudy told him, and he flinched back with an apologetic chimp grin for the big ace. "I've got your pages here." She reached into the leather map case she'd grabbed from wardrobe and took out a thinner sheaf.

"Thanks," said Cheetah, taking them.

Trudy let the other actors get over their fear of joker cooties long enough to come over and snatch their pages. She found it frankly ridiculous. She'd seen the horror of what the virus could do *before* Wild Card Day, and on it, too, and while there was always a chance of a new cache of spores surfacing somewhere, there wasn't much possibility outside of Manhattan.

But these were actors, not botanists, archaeologists, or African colonels, no matter what they looked like or were costumed as. Dr. Tod's gang, despite their many other failings, had been made of sterner stuff.

They finished their late lunch, then Jack smiled down at her. "Care to go see the town?"

"I'd thought you'd never ask."

They took a jeep, rumbling over the tracks of the private railway spur John Wayne had installed directly to his ranch. Trudy noted with interest the new railway switch and the spot where it joined up with the older tracks, which looked a century old. She wondered if the elephants and tigers would be brought in by train, like the circus coming to town, and wondered which direction they'd be coming from.

Jack drove the jeep with all the skill of a man who'd done army service, and Trudy took in the rest of the sights. The sky was a pure sort of blue she'd never seen in New York and a match for the Blue Stone of Heaven prop she wore around her neck. The vistas were both spare and majestic, the Mexican brushland being a reasonable replacement for the African veldt, or for that matter the Wild West, as Jack drove them through an Old West town that looked like the set from half a dozen westerns and probably was. Then he rounded a corner and the Old West became an African village, the set designers having done a remarkable job of reproducing the look of Africa, or at least the look of Brazil shot for Africa from last season's *Tarzan*.

Then they rounded the next corner and Trudy spied what could only be the City of Death, or at least a façade of grand African gates, like the entrance to King Solomon's Mines. "Well, that's impressive," she remarked.

"Yeah," Jack agreed. "Doesn't get old." He stopped the jeep and stood up, shining in the light of sunset and just a little bit of his own, looking like a young god—a young god with a particularly nice ass. Trudy reached up and pinched it, watching the golden light sparkle around her fingers, then while Jack was distracted, teleported the key from the ignition to her other hand, slipping it into her pocket. "Sorry," she said, "I just couldn't resist." She smiled at her secret double entendre, since it applied to both pinching his ass and the key, and having him search for the latter would provide cover for any small props she might want to appropriate from the faux City of Death. Dr. Tod had taught her to think ahead. "Can we look around?"

"Of course." Jack hopped out of the jeep, then, as she expected, glanced at the empty ignition, then to her. Trudy responded with a blank expression and did the math herself. A forward woman always just slightly unnerved even the most cocksure man, so since Jack didn't know about her ace, the simple math was that he must have slipped the keys in his own pocket after turning the jeep off, then forgot about it when she'd pinched his ass.

He was enough of a gentleman to come around to her side of the jeep, and enough of a cad that, rather than opening the door, he lifted her out of it, his aura glowing as he did while he smiled. It didn't seem a threat so much as being forward himself, since as he set her down, his hands gently brushed her breasts. "You can't resist either, Mr. Braun."

"I could," he confessed. "I just decided not to."

It was a romantic moment, made less romantic by a voice calling, "Señor Braun!"

Trudy turned. A middle-aged Mexican man with an unusually lush mustache and an immaculate but sensible light linen suit walked up the street toward them, looking especially out of place against the gates of the City of Death.

Jack looked as mystified as Trudy was. "Hello?" he asked. "I'm sorry, I'm not certain we've met."

"My apologies." The man laughed. "You are unmistakable, but we have been in contact, after a fashion." The man's English was good, which Trudy was grateful for. "I am Tiburcio Aguilar, the landowner here. Your NBC leased these lots to build your African village and your . . . Xibalba?" He lapsed into Spanish or some other language at the end, looking at the grand gates ornamented with African-style skulls and devil masks.

"The City of Death," Trudy supplied. "*La Ciudad de los Muertos.*"

"Ah, you speak Spanish!"

"*Un poquito,*" Trudy said. "Mostly what I picked up at Puerto Rican bodegas." While shoplifting and practicing with her ace ten years ago, though Trudy didn't add that. She saw a telltale bulge under the linen of the landowner's coat and knew he was packing heat, and a certain woman's intuition that came from experience rather than the wild card made her suspect that Señor Aguilar, Mr. Eagle, likely made his dinero from less legal operations on the days when Hollywood wasn't dumping a dump truck of money on his doorstep for property leases.

"Well then, we shall speak English," he said. "Welcome to Chupaderos!" He smiled at her especially.

Trudy knew she was pretty enough to be an actress, so defused the obvious question. "Trudy," she told him, "not Jane—yet—just script girl and Tarzan's personal secretary." She winked at Jack.

Aguilar looked askance toward the City of Death, so Jack told him, "The gates to the Lost City. Tarzan's going to find the Blue

Stone of Heaven." He gestured to Trudy and she held up the prop pendant.

"Ah, a treasure hunt! There are many treasures in Durango, both found and lost. Durango is known for its silver mines, and gold as well."

"Any with a waterfall?" Trudy inquired.

"Ah, then you know the legend?"

"Legend?" Jack looked puzzled. "No, it's just one of the locations in the script. Trudy helped doctor it. She had some really great ideas the writers were able to incorporate."

"The legend of Maximilian's treasure," Aguilar explained, prompting Jack to give Trudy a quizzical look. "Before Benito Juárez executed Emperor Maximilian, the European interloper packed forty-five barrels with gold and jewels plundered from Mexico, which he sent with Austrian soldiers up past the Rio Grande. But after they hired some former Confederate soldiers and were double-crossed, then suffered a Comanche attack, all that loot ended up lost, buried somewhere in Texas. Supposedly one survivor left a treasure map before he died, but it is yet to be found." He stroked his lavish mustache sagaciously. "Señor Wayne is thinking about making a movie about it."

"That does sound like Wayne's sort of story," Jack agreed, still eyeing Trudy.

"But that is only half the story!" Aguilar exclaimed. "Durango is far richer in silver than it is in gold, so Maximilian's loyalists left all the silver behind, four hundred barrels, secreted, they say, in a cave or an old mine shaft, sealed by dynamite, along with Carlota's choicest jewels, including her crown. Treasure hunters have been searching these hills for years. But the location was buried along with Maximilian's loyalists, who took the secret to their grave."

Trudy readjusted her purse, the dozen diamond buttons lumpy in the lining, along with the sheaf of notes from Hetty Green, who in 1900 had paid a couple of Maximilian's old loyalists for them, as well as the ciphered map to the location of the treasure. However, unlocking the cipher required not just the diamond buttons from Maximilian's coat, but also Carlota's pendant and Maximilian's rings.

Unfortunately, both the diamond and the emerald had been reset by Cartier and the old settings melted down before Trudy acquired the gems, making the key incomplete. "Do you have any idea where it is?" Trudy asked.

Aguilar gestured expansively. "Ah, señorita, if I knew that, I would be a far richer man than I already am. The state is riddled with old mine shafts, the countryside is overflowing with waterfalls, and treasure legends go back to the days of the Aztecs; Maximilian's is only the most recent. Besides which, Maximilian's loyalists only planned to retrieve his treasure after the French had retaken Mexico and reinstalled Carlota as empress, which they never did. Even if one knew where it was, one would need mining equipment to excavate the tunnel."

Mining equipment, or the right ace power. Trudy could teleport things, including rocks, but she liked to stick to small ones, like gemstones. Big items tended to make her feel sick. But Jack Braun could lift a tank, so she was certain he could toss around a few pesky boulders.

"Not that folk haven't looked," Aguilar continued. "There are countless mine shafts, as I said, going back to the days of the Aztecs, and many that were played out or collapsed on their own. The only difference is, the one with Maximilian's treasure, if it exists, was collapsed almost a hundred years ago."

Ninety years, to be precise. Trudy had made careful study of Hetty Green's notes, which were meticulous, as was to be expected of the famous miser and female finance wizard. Maximilian of Mexico had died on June 19, 1867, and his loyalists had tried to smuggle some of his loot and hide the rest shortly thereafter. "What a pity," Trudy said with a sigh, "I am so fond of gems." She held the faux Blue Stone of Heaven fondly while touching Maximilian's rings and Carlota's pendant behind it. "I'd love to have Carlota's crown." She smiled coquettishly at Jack. "Four hundred barrels of silver would be nice, too."

"Yeah, wouldn't they," Jack agreed. Given the terms of his divorce, Trudy knew exactly what he'd be using them for, or at least a large chunk of them . . . assuming the treasure fell into his hands.

"But lost treasures aside," Trudy said lightly, "do you know of any good caves or mine shafts where we could film, especially near a waterfall? As Jack said, we're looking for sites for the script. Production found a few already, but it's always nice to have other options."

"That it is," Aguilar agreed, "but I would advise you not to go poking around in most of the mine shafts here. They are very old and the true City of Death." He paused while she smiled, then he conceded, "But I can give you a list of the safer ones that are already closed off. The waterfalls as well."

"Editing can put the best waterfall together with the best cave," Jack pointed out.

"Of course," Trudy agreed.

"Would you like to come to my hacienda?" Aguilar pointed far up the road to an old Spanish Colonial–style dwelling, surrounded by the weeping branches of pepper trees—an original, of which the bungalows at the Garden of Allah were but a pale imitation.

"Sure," Jack said. "Can we offer you a ride?" He reached for his back pocket, and Trudy reached into her own pocket. It was a bit tricky and required some finesse, but she was able to teleport the key in just as Jack slipped his hand inside, leaving just enough of a gap. There was a flash of golden light from his palm that only she noticed, then Jack withdrew the key, slightly bent. "Sometimes forget my own strength," he remarked, then casually pulled it straight with another glitter of golden light.

Trudy hopped into the back with one hand on the roll bar while

Jack offered Aguilar the passenger seat. It was just a quick jaunt up the road in the jeep but would have been a long if pretty walk in the light of sunset. There were long low verandas along the front and what looked to be a tennis court in back. And inside, there were also far too many ranch hands about for what didn't seem a working ranch, but exactly as many as Trudy would expect for a local crime lord, especially one playing the part of being the grand man, completely willing to turn his hand to legitimate enterprise if it paid more.

He was also a generous pour with the tequila and mezcal, filling handblown pale-blue shot glasses with dark-cobalt rims, the colors echoing the sky and the Blue Stone of Heaven. "Do you know where the tequila comes from?" he asked, holding up a shot and regarding it with almost divine reverence.

"The bottle?" guessed Jack.

"I was going to say the distillery, but I'll go with his answer," said Trudy.

Everyone laughed, then Señor Aguilar said, "True and true, but it comes from the agave plant. It is said that the Aztec goddess of the agave, Mayahuel, got drunk on it one night and got together with her husband, Patecatl, god of the agave, who also got drunk, and soon she gave birth to four hundred drunken rabbits—and this long before the wild card!"

Everyone laughed more, and the shots were handed out, then Señor Aguilar raised a toast. "To Mayahuel and her four hundred drunken rabbits!"

Trudy slammed her shot for politeness, but it was strong. Delicious, but strong. Señor Aguilar poured a second round. "To Patecatl and his four hundred drunken rabbits!" Trudy sipped her second, because it was delicious, but held her hand up to beg off a refill. She wanting to keep her wits about her, especially since she wasn't invulnerable like Jack.

"To the firstborn of the four hundred drunken rabbits!" Señor

Aguilar cried, raising the third round of shots. All the men drank again, Trudy realizing with something between awe and horror that he intended to make it through all four hundred rabbits, like some hellish Aztec version of "99 Bottles of Beer on the Wall," only times four and plus four.

At least, being a lady, she wasn't expected to play machismo drinking games like Jack. Aguilar signaled to one of his boys, who made a margarita and presented it to her with great ceremony. She accepted and sipped it idly as she wandered away from the drinking game and took in the rest of the place.

Aguilar's hacienda was old and grand. Eighteenth century from the look of it, or at most very early nineteenth—Spanish Colonial in any case, long low adobe with glazed terra-cotta tiles and an interesting mixture of Spanish and French antiques. Maximilian probably hadn't stayed here, but likely one of his supporters had, or at least someone who liked Empire furnishings. Atop the marble mantel was a French mantel clock with what looked to be figures of Cupid and Psyche—a golden girl with butterfly wings placing victor's laurels atop the head of a golden boy with swan wings, who looked an awful lot like a shirtless gilded Jack Braun.

Trudy would have liked to take the clock with her back to New York, but it was too hefty to easily lug around in a suitcase, not to mention the trouble of Aguilar and all his men, many of whom she started to recognize as locals from the production crew.

But then came the main reason for their visit, as Aguilar paused the drinking after toasting the thirdborn drunken rabbit, then gathered them around an ancient oak table and laid out maps of Chupaderos and the surrounding countryside of Durango. Trudy paid special attention to the railway lines, asking about how close they were to certain waterfalls, caves, and mine shafts, almost all of which had fanciful poetic names, like *la Gruta de la Sirena*, the Grotto of the Mermaid; *la Calavera Llorando*, the Weeping Skull; and *el Eje del Diablo*, the Devil's Shaft, the last of which was cause for a lot of giggling and bawdy jokes. "We've got use of a small locomotive," she explained, "which will be useful for transporting the cameras and crew for location shots."

"Ah, Señor Wayne's train? He made a very grand entrance when he first came to town."

"Wayne does that." Jack chuckled. "But it was nice of him to let me use his private car when he leased us the train. Much nicer than the trailer I had in Brazil."

Drinking continued, Trudy still sipping her margarita idly while Jack showed off his ace for Aguilar and his men, glowing gold as he casually lifted the enormous oak table with one hand as it creaked and groaned. Trudy was reassured: Jack could move boulders easily—the trick was just getting him to do it. She hadn't planned to tip her hand quite so soon, but one thing Dr. Tod had taught her about the crime biz is you made your plans, and then when everything fell to shit, you readjusted on the fly. That advice had served her well so far.

Also, when an opportunity presented itself, you took advantage of it.

Someone opened one of the windows to let in the cooler night air. The hacienda was well regulated for temperature, but the old-fashioned way, with adobe and tile, and still required ventilation. Trudy moved closer to the delicious cool, then smelled something even more delicious: the scent of marijuana.

It was as illegal in Mexico as the US, but that was of course a way to say it was well known and generally something the police didn't bother with unless some DA needed reelection, at which point it became the weed with its roots in hell. Trudy slipped out the back door and followed her nose down to the tennis court where three young men were taking in the cool night air and polluting it with a haze of pot smoke.

Trudy's Spanish was not good enough to understand what they were saying, especially with the thick Norteño accent, and they stopped speaking completely as soon as she appeared anyway, standing there with her mostly full margarita. But the verses of "La Cucaracha" provided the proper phrase. *"Marihuana para fumar?"* Trudy inquired, gesturing with her free hand, then miming a toke with an invisible joint when they didn't immediately offer to share.

Chivalry was not dead, thankfully, and neither was the pot: It was very good, very fresh, and very clear proof that Señor Aguilar was not just the local crime lord but the local drug lord as well. "Gracias," Trudy thanked them, hoping her secondhand Puerto Rican Spanish didn't sound too barbaric.

"De nada," they said, then a garble of Spanish that was too quick and too thickly accented for her to understand. She smiled apologetically, but she was a pretty woman, flirting was a universal language, and she realized that, rather than talking about *marihuana*, the word that they were instead saying repeatedly was *Juana*, which was Spanish for "Jane."

It was an easy and obvious guess, the same one that Cheetah made earlier, but Trudy was willing to run with it if it got her more joints. *"Sí,* Juana," she agreed, gesturing for more marijuana.

One proffered not just a joint, but a pretty silver cigarette case, the cover worked in an Aztec design with a hummingbird. Inside were almost a dozen fat joints. Trudy wanted to take them all, and the case, too, but just plucked one, and then hesitantly and coquettishly inquired, *"Para mañana?"* and plucked three more. Being Jane had its perks.

She toked a bit more and smiled and nodded for politeness, then finally said, "Gracias" again and waved her goodbyes, going back to the house. She stubbed out the quarter-smoked joint on one of the doorposts before she went in, adding it and the fresh joints to the cigarette case in her purse—a nice bit of Kuppenheim silverwork and Usabal enamel she'd lifted from a German diplomat at last year's Met Gala—then went back inside to find Jack doing more shots with Aguilar, toasting even more ridiculous numbers of drunken rabbits, and beginning to lose the machismo contest. Rather than risk a teleport and a lie, Trudy just leaned over to hug Jack, took it as another excuse to pat his ass, then picked his pocket the old-fashioned way and showed him the keys. "I may not be one of the Four Aces," she told him, taking pride in the fact that she was in fact the First Ace, hidden up her sleeve the whole time, "but Jane's sober, Tarzan's not, and I'm driving us back."

"But we're still drinking!" Jack pointed out.

"And you still can," Trudy pointed back, "I'm just saying this lady's not unbreakable, so I'd rather drive. Could I get some water, please?" Trudy set down her margarita, still half full.

"Of course," said Aguilar. "*Agua, para la señorita!*" Three of his men stepped to, one with a handblown amber tumbler fitted with a pierced iron sleeve it had been blown through, the other with the carafe from the same service, pouring it mostly full before handing it to her, and the third offering her the matching ice bucket filled with chipped ice and a set of abalone-handled tongs.

"Gracias." Trudy selected three large diamond-like chips and added them to her glass.

"To women who know what they want!" proclaimed Aguilar, raising his shot of tequila and nodding to her in salute. All his men did as well, and so did Jack.

"I'll drink to that!" Trudy raised her glass in return, but merely sipped it while the men slammed theirs.

It took three more shots and toasts to the drunken rabbits to put Golden Boy under the table, but under he went, flashing gold briefly as he hit the floor. Aguilar had to be propped up by his men, but he laughed and held up his empty shot glass in triumph while his men quickly poured him glasses of water so he didn't die of alcohol poisoning. Trudy had seen such antics with Dr. Tod's gang before—minus Dr. Tod, who was a badass with half his face shot off who didn't like fraternizing with his men—but Tod also didn't much care what they did on their own time so long as they were sober when he needed them.

Aguilar obviously had a different touch, and some of the men were doubtless his relatives—possibly sons, definitely nephews. Trudy had seen similar dynamics in the Italian mob, the Irish, the Puerto Ricans—pretty much every family gang—so it came as little surprise that the Mexicans followed the same pattern. Dr. Tod had been a lot more hardcore, and it was more than a bit of a relief that he was dead. Trudy laid flowers at Jetboy's Tomb every Wild Card Day for that alone.

The fact that she'd known about the virus beforehand?

Well, she could have possibly told someone—should have told someone—but Trudy was a pretty girl with an almost magical alien power, and if she'd told anyone, she would have ended up a lab rat before Wild Card Day and a government slave after it, so she was smart to keep her trap shut.

Dr. Tod had taught her that, too.

Trudy's own experience with mobs told her that Aguilar had won respect and loyalty by drinking the big ace under the table, but the time had now come to get Jack home. She'd set herself up as his personal secretary, and this is what came with that paycheck. "Could some of your boys help me get him to the car?" Trudy asked politely. "Jack's a bit big for me to lift."

Laughing and whooping and peppering their talk with assorted good-natured Mexican insults—Trudy overheard *cabrón, pendejo,* and *puto,* among others—a small gang of six men lifted Jack off the ground and carried him out to the car, laughing again as his head flashed gold when they whacked it on one of the doorposts. They were rather drunk themselves, so Trudy didn't know whether this was accidental or on purpose.

Trudy followed, taking the maps and notes Aguilar had gifted her with. These would be extremely useful in combination with Hetty Green's notes.

She buckled Jack in because no matter how unharmed he'd be if he fell out, there was no way she was lifting him back in herself. His force field stopped any attempts to slap him awake, and nudging and poking did little good, either, which was especially annoying because the lane to John Wayne's ranch was hard to find in the dark. But finally, after going up and down the same section of road, the jeep's headlights caught the glitter of the shiny new railway switch to Wayne's private lane.

Trudy pulled into the ranch and parked, right beside Wayne's private train car, a beautiful Pullman number constructed from varnished wood. Knowing Wayne, it had probably once carried Lincoln, or at least Chester A. Arthur—or in any case someone else similarly flashy and important.

Trudy looked up, taking a moment to admire the desert sky. Just as the day was a blue she'd never seen in New York City, the night glittered with more stars than she'd ever seen in her life, like a dome of polished lapis lazuli. Breathtaking. But she still needed to get in and get to bed, and she needed to get Jack into his bed, too. Leaving him out overnight wouldn't do, and not just because she liked him—she needed his ace if there was any chance of this scheme working.

Jack still didn't shake awake, so she looked around, hoping to see someone up and out who could help her get Jack out of the jeep and into Wayne's private railway car. Everyone seemed to have gone in. But then, in silhouette, Trudy noticed someone still out in the darkness of the back patio, leaning back and looking up at the stars. From the waist down, the silhouette was the unremarkable and indistinguishable legs and shoes of a young man, but from the waist up the body was that of a chimp. Cheetah.

Trudy got out of the jeep and went over to the joker. "Hey, Cheetah. I was hoping you might help me with something."

The joker grinned at her, his yellowy chimp teeth white in the light of the starry sky. "What do you need, Not-Jane?"

"Call me Trudy," she told him, then pointed back to the jeep. "Jack tied a few too many on, so I want to get him back in his train car so he can sleep it off without alerting everyone else."

"Always good to get on the boss's good side." Cheetah grinned wider. "Sure." He got up and ambled over with her, taking a look at Jack Braun still passed out drunk in the jeep, slightly snoring. "He's awfully big. I don't want him to suddenly wake up and start fighting me if we drag him."

"Aren't chimps a lot stronger than humans anyway?"

Cheetah waved one long chimp arm, gesturing to Jack. "Yeah, but chimp-strong ain't ace-strong, and he's Golden Boy! I once surprised my friend Troll and he nearly ripped my arm out of its socket. I may hate having ape arms, but I still like having two of them." He massaged his jaw with one chimp hand a lot like Aguilar had stroked his mustache. "Let me go get some help. But trust me, the guys I know are discreet—they won't tell no one about Jack's little indiscretion . . ."

Before Trudy could object, Cheetah ran off, except not for the ranch, but the barn. He disappeared inside, then came back leading a gang of identically disfigured jokers, all of them looking like chimps, including one tragic joker woman wearing a polka-dotted dress that looked like she'd gotten it by mugging Minnie Mouse. Then, a second later, Trudy realized they weren't jokers at all; they were actual chimpanzees—all the chimp Cheetahs they'd used last season before they'd hired the joker Cheetah for close-ups.

Cheetah gestured to the chimp in the Minnie Mouse getup. "Trudy, meet Bonzo. Her real name is Peggy. Peggy, meet Trudy." Cheetah waved his arms then, thumping his chest and moving his chimp fingers through the complex gestures of sign language. Peggy grinned, then took the sides of her skirt and dropped a curtsy, as neat as Alice greeting the Queen of Hearts. Then she turned to Cheetah and distended her lips in a grotesque pucker, and he responded in turn by doing the same and giving her a kiss.

Trudy had seen chimps dressed as humans kissing on *The Ed Sullivan Show,* and sometimes even kissing human trainers, or Ronald Reagan, but seeing Cheetah kissing Peggy seemed deeply wrong. But the moment the kiss was done, Cheetah began wildly signing to the chimp gang, who grinned and capered maniacally, then a second later all of them went and hopped in the jeep, including Peggy, unbuckling Jack from his seatbelt, then carrying him overhead like a high school football hero being borne aloft by his team after the big game.

"Is the railway car unlocked?" Cheetah asked.

"I don't think so," said Trudy, then checked the jeep keys and thankfully found a second key attached to the ring. She took it over to the door of the Pullman car and inserted it. It turned smoothly, and a moment later she had it open. A cavalcade of apes pushed by her, followed by half-ape Cheetah, bearing Jack into the interior of the Pullman car.

Trudy followed, fumbling for a button to get the lights on. They sparkled to life, converted Victorian oil lamps or gas brackets with handblown shades, revealing that the train car was indeed lavish: gleaming brass fittings, rich burgundy leather and velvet upholstery, and everywhere pictures of US cowboys and Mexican caballeros.

Cheetah's chimp squad found the bed, done up for the Duke with a Grandmother's Fan quilt and pillowcases embroidered with wagon wheels and cowpoke whatnot, and dumped Golden Boy there, still snoring, with a flash of golden light. Cheetah screeched for attention, signing wildly, then all of the chimps filed out. Bonzo/Peggy brought up the rear, dropping a curtsy to Trudy unprompted, then puckered up for a kiss from Cheetah, which he gave her, followed by a fond pat on the ass—a bare bright-pink chimp ass, since Peggy wasn't wearing any panties under the Minnie Mouse skirt, because she wasn't human.

"So you're an ace who can talk to chimps?" Trudy asked.

"Nah," Cheetah told her. "Like I said, my dad's a primatologist. He taught me sign language, and I've been signing to chimps since I was five. They're a lot smarter than people think, but it's still like talking to toddlers. But since I got like this, they like me a lot more."

Thinking of chimps as toddlers felt even creepier to Trudy than thinking of them as animals, but it's not like she was puckering up to kiss Cheetah, so she could adjust her scruples, as she had so many times before. "Thanks. I owe you." She sighed, glancing at Jack. "Golden Boy will, too, once he sobers up. Mum's the word?"

"Mum," said the half-chimp joker, bringing one long chimp finger to his chimp lips in the very human sign for silence. Then he lowered it, cocked his head, and grinned at her as his nostrils flared. "But so far as favors go, I've got a chimp's nose, too, and I can smell that you scored some Mary Jane, Not-Jane—I mean Trudy. Set a fellow up?"

"Of course," Trudy said, taking out her cigarette case, "I only got a few, but I know where I can get more." She took out one, then on second thought handed him two, flashing him the inside of the case so he knew she wasn't holding out on him.

"Thanks, Trudy," he said, placing one joint behind his chimp ear and putting the other in his lips as he reached into his pocket and took out a Zippo. "You're a peach."

"You too," Trudy told him.

He lit up before he went out the door, took an appreciative toke, then waved as he hopped out of the private train car and shut the door behind him.

Trudy looked at Jack, lying there passed out atop John Wayne's quilt, then began to untie his shoes before taking off his clothes.

Trudy woke up to Jack shaking her awake, but gently. She didn't have an invulnerable force field, so she appreciated the care. "Ow," moaned Jack. "What hit me?"

"Four hundred drunken rabbits," Trudy told him. "Also, some tequila and mezcal. Bugs Bunny, Harvey, and Oswald the Lucky Rabbit all went to visit Mom in your head." Jack stared at her blankly, so she explained, "You got into a drinking contest with Señor Aguilar."

"Did I win?"

"No," Trudy told him truthfully, "and yes. You let the local mob boss beat the strongest man in the world in a drinking game, giving him loads of credit with his men and giving you a friend you're going to need if you'll be shooting here for any length of time."

Jack had been burned too badly by life to properly sound like an ingénue, but he did sound a bit surprised. "He's a mob boss? How—"

"My name's Trudy Pirandello. *Pirandello.* I grew up on Arthur Avenue. You know the Gambiones? Not a nice family. I know how to spot a mobster when I see one. Besides, there's this." Trudy reached over for her purse. They were both naked in bed except for the chain around her neck with Carlota's pendant and Maximilian's rings.

Trudy slipped out her cigarette case, formerly the German diplomat's cigarette case. It was a pretty thing with an erotic enameled portrait of a rich woman in a pink-and-gray gown being kissed in the middle of her back by her rakish tuxedoed lover. The portrait was signed **Luis Usabal, 10,** which would be 1910, which matched the clothing and furniture—and while it was from Grandma's day, it was a nice bauble to show your lover in bed. Even nicer when you popped it open and revealed a couple of fresh joints.

Trudy took the stubbed-out one for herself, then offered the remaining fresh one to Jack, who accepted. "I think they thought you a little straitlaced," Trudy told him, "but it's Jane's job to take care of Tarzan, and these should help with the hangover."

She got out her lighter, which was silver as well, with a Siamese temple dancer on it. She'd picked it up from a shop window in Chinatown and kept it because it worked well. She lit Jack's joint, then her own.

"Damn," he said. "This is good. Where—"

"Some of Aguilar's men were smoking out by the tennis court," she told him plain. "They asked if I was Jane, so I said yes." She took a drag, then gave him a sidelong glance. "You open to that?"

"Maybe," Jack told her, then took a deep drag. "Depends on NBC, too. I'm not my own man right now, and the writers weren't planning to bring Jane in until third season. But we can see." He glanced over at the sparkling rocks between Trudy's tits. "So are you after Max's silver to go with his diamonds and emeralds?"

"Hey, who doesn't like a treasure hunt? And who couldn't use four hundred barrels of silver?" Trudy took another toke, wondering how much of the truth to tell him. Dr. Tod had taught her that a partial truth was always more effective than an outright lie, especially when part of the truth had already been uncovered. "The old man I inherited it from told me that it had been smuggled into the US in 1900 by a couple guys from Durango. They got arrested and it got auctioned off to some senator, then when it came up for sale again, he got it, along with the story of what Maximilian's former loyalists said. Supposedly the mine shaft with the treasure is at the back of a cave behind a waterfall, and it's also close to railway tracks for an old mine spur." She shrugged. "That's all I know."

She wasn't sure if he trusted her, since his expression was hard to read, bespeaking mostly hangover and pot, along with whatever the wild card had done to boost his metabolism. But thinking about it must have made his head hurt, judging by his pained expression. "All I know, Trudy, is that I've got to take a leak then get some breakfast. It would be great if you could join me, and we can talk about this later when I'm not hungover."

"Okay, Tarzan," Trudy said, watching as he got out of bed. His nice ass looked nicer than ever, and his abs looked even more chiseled, which spoke to him being dehydrated. But she could still admire the view while it lasted.

Breakfast was beans and rice and tortillas, which didn't feel that breakfasty to Trudy but seemed pretty standard to the extras. Jack didn't care, either since he'd been to Latin America before or because he had a hangover. Probably both. Trudy tried it and found that she liked it. She'd eaten a lot worse as a kid and during the war anyway, and while wealth was great, her ace and the money it could literally put in her hands had taught her that while unlimited caviar and champagne were fine, sometimes all you wanted was a good patty melt. And if the best ones were at Biff's in Jokertown? That's where you went.

She didn't know if these were the best beans in Durango, but they were pretty good, and she recognized the kid slinging them as one of the youths from Aguilar's tennis court last night. "Gracias," she told him as she went back for a second helping and winked.

"De nada, Juana," he told her with a knowing smile as Jack staggered in, looking rode hard and put away wet; Trudy thought the kid might be one of the ones who'd carried the big ace to the car.

The rest of the crew was definitely amused around Jack, too, at least all the gaffers and extras and other folk, especially once they got to the set and more of the gang from Aguilar's hacienda showed up. Jack sobered up in the makeup chair then walked around with his shirt off while they started filming the scene with the gates of the City of Death, which consisted of blue-eyed Britt Lomond playing a dashing archaeologist while David Niven, Method-acting for his life to play the botanist, tried to convince everyone that an ordinary potted bromeliad was some rare African plant that the natives thought had supernatural properties. Newcomer Ivan Dixon, playing Colonel Takakombi, looked incredulous, while Tarzan just looked stoned and hungover—but his abs looked awesome, so the director told the cameraman to focus on those.

Trudy was at loose ends. Since they didn't need the Blue Stone of Heaven today, she was allowed to hang on to it for safekeeping. When Trudy asked where they'd found such a nice prop, the wardrobe mistress told her that there was a silversmith in town who'd made it. Trudy thanked her and strolled off. She always loved window-shopping.

A couple of streets over from the false Wild West main street was the actual main street of Chupaderos. A dressmaker sold frilly quinceañera dresses, bridal gowns, and christening gowns so ornate and lacy they could have doubled as bordello lampshades. The next shop was an undertaker, with a full window display of coffins. But next door was the silversmith.

Trudy went over, gazing at the various rings and necklaces in the window, wondering if there were any trinkets worthy of being plucked with her ace and its five-finger discount, especially since everything here was silver rather than gold and semiprecious rather than precious gemstones.

Then her eyes strayed past a mannequin bust wearing a familiar necklace and an ornate tiara to a couple standing at the back of the shop, behind the jeweler. Standing life-sized but suspiciously still, because Trudy realized the couple was in fact a full-sized portrait of Empress Carlota and her husband, Maximilian.

Trudy stepped into the silver shop. She had not imagined it. Maximilian and Carlota were standing there, with their full regalia and ornaments of state, in what could only be a coronation portrait once owned by some loyalist royalist. It hadn't been destroyed in any of the revolutions to follow but instead ended up as the eye-catching display of a small-town silversmith in the Mexican hinterlands. The silversmith smiled and nodded, then his eyes fixated on the Blue Stone of Heaven around Trudy's neck. He beamed with pride. "Ah, you are Tarzan's new Juana!"

It seemed that a small lie got around quickly in a small town. "Why yes," said Trudy, running with it, clutching the Blue Stone of Heaven proudly and hiding the lump of Maximilian's rings and Carlota's pendant nestled into her bra.

"I am Diego Barriopedro. Welcome to my shop."

Trudy smiled. It wasn't hard because she was noticing that the mannequin in the window was wearing an exact copy of Carlota's lost crown from the portrait, only reproduced in silver and rhine-stones, making for a particularly lavish quinceañera crown, and her pendant as well, only in silver and citrine instead of gold and greenish-yellow diamond like the original Trudy was hiding.

She went farther into the shop, walking up to Maximilian, or at least his painted effigy. She recognized the dozen diamond but-tons on his coat, which looked the same as the ones hidden in the lining of her purse, and the huge bluish-white diamond on his ring finger and the smaller but no less precious emerald on his middle finger—however, both gems, rather than Cartier's art deco elegance, had their original Second Empire settings. Maximilian also, on the other side of the diamond, wore a third ring on his pinkie, a carved red gem, perhaps ruby or spinel, engraved with the initials **MIM** underneath an imperial crown ringed with more than a dozen tiny diamonds. Together, the gems of the three rings formed the green, white, and red of the Mexican flag.

"MIM?" Trudy asked, pointing to the signet ring.

"*Maximilian Imperator Mexico*," the jeweler proudly supplied in flawless Spanish-accented Latin. "His royal seal. The diamond of course is the Emperor Maximilian diamond, his wedding band with his wife, Carlota. But the emerald you see there is the most special of all, for Maximilian claimed it belonged to Cuauhtémoc, last king of the Aztecs." The jeweler leaned in then and whispered conspiratorially. "I do not believe that, of course. I think it was just a third gem he obtained in Brazil, to secure his claim to the throne, for even Cortés could not torture the location of his treasures out of Cuauhtémoc. How could Maximilian centuries after his death?"

"Maybe the wild card?" Trudy speculated and they both laughed.

Diego Barriopedro then said, "But you do not need the wild card to obtain these lost jewels—only the jeweler's art." With that he removed the cover of a jeweler's tray he slid onto the counter in front of her, revealing an assortment of duplicates of Maximilian's rings—duplicates with the original setting, only in silver instead of gold and with semiprecious stones instead of precious. "Peri-dot, quartz, and red citrine, the same as Maximilian's original sig-net."

Trudy's eyes went wide. "How much for all three?"

"In what size?"

Trudy mused. "What size did Maximilian wear?"

Trudy locked herself in John Wayne's Pullman car. Hetty Green would have haggled better, but then again Hetty Green was a famous miser who'd never actually gone on a treasure hunt, deciding it was a bad risk. But Hetty had also left meticulous notes on the other treasure she'd bought from the former loyalists along with Max's diamond buttons: an unsent farewell letter from Maximilian to Carlota, in German.

Having worked for Dr. Tod, Trudy's German was far better than her Spanish, though that didn't particularly help—aside from being understandably sad and weepy, written by a doomed man to his bride, whom he was actually in love with, it had weird turns of phrase and odd word choices, poetic instructions to *count the stars around my crown*, and assorted strangeness that made more sense once you realized that it contained a coded message and the keys to that code were the dozen diamond buttons, the diamond ring, the emerald ring, the red citrine signet, and most of all, Carlota's pendant.

Hetty Green had puzzled much of it out but she hadn't found the last clues, which simply required the luck of walking into the right silversmith's in Chupaderos. Count the stars around the crown? There was a crown on the reproduction signet ring, surrounded by eighteen rhinestones exactly. Trudy counted them twice, just to make sure. The gold backs of the original buttons could be removed, allowing them to be worn as diamond pendants instead, but a careful inspection revealed that they were numbered by the goldsmith and there was a way to place them atop Maximilian's letter to align with tiny dots of ink that looked like quill flecks until you realized that they perfectly aligned with the points on the star-shaped buttons. Placing them there, the central facet of each covered and magnified a single letter: **DER-WEINENDES.**

The next character required Maximilian's diamond, but not in its Cartier setting. Trudy inspected it, then the silver and quartz reproduction made by Diego. The faceting was slightly different, but then again, Diego had been making a reproduction from an almost century-old painting. But ace powers could help, or at least *her* ace power. Trudy plucked the rhinestone from its silver setting via teleportation, quick as a magpie snatching a shiny bauble from the ground, then she took the empty silver setting and watched as the blue-white diamond disappeared from the gold Cartier ring and reappeared in the bezel of the silver ring as if it had been made for it. Aligning that with dots drawn on the letter had the letter **C** appear in the back of the diamond like a fortune surfacing in the window of a Magic 8 Ball.

The emerald came next, the one that supposedly once belonged to Cuauhtémoc, in a classic emerald cut that accentuated the gem's natural crystalline shape. Like most emeralds, it had flaws, but was beautiful despite them. Trudy held her breath as she popped the peridot out of its silver setting and then popped in the emerald. There was a click, but not a crack, and then she exhaled, placing the ring onto the farewell love letter. The letter framed precisely by the emerald green was an **H.**

Then came the seal ring . . . except not. Hetty hadn't seemed to find it important in her notes, despite it having a clue to the number of letters Trudy was looking for, but she then realized that the gem was engraved and the back was solid. But that wasn't the case with Carlota's pendant, Maximilian's betrothal gift for Princess Charlotte of Belgium before she became Carlota of Mexico. Trudy unthreaded it from its chain and aligned it with the last three ink flecks on the letter. The yellow-green diamond perfectly illuminated and framed the letter **Ä**.

Three letters left, but there were no more gems to place atop them.

Trudy reread Hetty's notes, then Maximilian's letter, grateful for Dr. Tod's German lessons. Maximilian ended the letter with a maudlin *I would like tulips for my funeral.* Except instead of *funeral* in German, which was *Beerdigung,* Maximilian had written *Beendigung,* one letter different, a slightly unusual word that meant "ending."

Tulips. Carlota's pendant was ornamented with three diamond tulips and the three, in order, pointed precisely to **DEL**.

Trudy transcribed all eighteen letters: **DERWEINENDE-SCHÄDEL**.

Der Weinende Schädel. The Weeping Skull. *La Calavera Llorando.*

"Oh, Dr. Tod," Trudy breathed, "I could just kiss you . . ."

Trudy immediately took the thought back. She'd rather kiss Bonzo. And Cheetah. At the same time.

But regardless, German lessons were German lessons, even when they came from a Nazi war criminal who later released the wild card virus into the world.

"The Weeping Skull?" Jack asked over dinner that evening in his private car, or at least John Wayne's private railcar. "Are you sure? Norm thinks the Mermaid's Grotto and the Devil's Shaft are much better bets, especially if we use both."

Norm was Norman Foster, the director, who'd done *Mr. Moto Takes a Vacation* with Peter Lorre, so he didn't have the best decision making, not that it was the best idea to say so.

Trudy took another tack: "Call it women's intuition."

"But have you seen the spots?"

Trudy had. While Jack was shooting the gates of the City of Death scene, and Trudy was jewelry shopping then deciphering Hetty Green's notes and Maximilian's last letter to Carlota, the location scouts had been out to all the spots suggested by Señor Aguilar and come back with reports and photos.

The Mermaid's Grotto was stunning, a valley with a waterfall that arced down into a small pool with a grotto undercut into the cliff face below. There were even rainbows formed by the waterfall spray when the sun was at the right angle. The Devil's Shaft was a mine shaft that went deep into the ground, both forbidding and eerie, with horrific whispering echoes the deeper you went. But the scouts had pronounced the entrance at least safe enough for shooting.

The Weeping Skull, the third option, was high up a mountain, and the only thing that made it remotely filmable was the fact that an old railway spur led there. It would take some time to clear that, unless Jack used his strength, but he was billed as star, not heavy equipment.

But once there, there was a cave that looked like a yawning skull with twin waterfalls above it that formed the weeping eyes. Inside there were even mine-cart tracks that led to a cave-in.

Trudy looked as plaintive as she could, considered pouting, then kicked herself mentally. The whole *Lysistrata* gambit only worked if you were married, in a culture without any divorce, and with a man who would never consider infidelity. Jack Braun was divorced at least twice, famous for his cheating, and had made it explicitly clear at the start of their relationship that this was just an extended fling. *Ha-ha, you're not getting any!* was not going to work.

But greed might. "Like I said, a woman's *intuition*," Trudy stressed, giving him a knowing glance, then touching the Blue Stone of Heaven.

"You know something you're not telling me."

"Yes," Trudy admitted. "We've all done things we're not proud of, Jack. I'm no different. The only difference is, I'm going to keep my secrets. So just trust me on this one, okay?"

"I can respect that," said Jack at last. "But what are we going to tell Norm? He's the director."

"Tell him I want to direct?" Trudy suggested, then took another bite of chicken mole, chewing as she watched Jack's face for his reaction. "Tell him we shoot all three locations, then whatever we can't use for 'The Blue Stone of Heaven' we recycle later on in the season? The elephants and tigers still haven't shown up, so why not get some stock footage?"

"Not bad for a script girl. You might even make director one day."

"Why, thank you, Mr. Braun."

Norm not only bought it, he thought it was brilliant, mostly because Trudy had convinced Jack to clear the tracks leading to the Weeping Skull.

"I honestly couldn't ask for anything better than that rock formation, but there was no way I was asking the star to spend half a day clearing brush and lumber," Norman Foster told her as they rode up the mountain slowly in Wayne's private railcar. It was hitched directly behind the engine with a few boxcars and a caboose behind it, loaded with equipment, a few extras, plus the chimp wrangler, the chimps, and Cheetah, who'd all but replaced the chimp wrangler in their simian hearts. "Thanks."

"Jack's got incentive." Trudy let Norm think the incentive was her, rather than the possibility of four hundred barrels of silver. The track slightly curved up the mountainside, letting them watch Jack walk along the abandoned rail spur and pick up fallen pine trees and toss them to one side or fallen boulders and toss them to the other. Occasionally he paused to inspect the tracks and hammer down a raised railway spike with his fist, flashing gold as he did it. The locomotive inched on after him, the engine driver going very carefully over the cleared and repaired tracks.

Eventually they got there—a railway turnaround loop on the mountainside just before the cave. A further spur led into the cave, except it was meant not for locomotives but for mine carts, a few of which lay abandoned outside the mouth of the cave. "Perfect," Norm said, dismounting the Pullman car once they were stopped and pointing them out to Jack. "Don't touch those. Nothing says King Solomon's Mines like mine carts."

"Wasn't King Solomon a long time before these?"

"We've got a Tarzan who lights up gold when he pounds his chest too hard. If it looks good, who cares?" Norm shrugged. "Most kids won't mind and those who do will feel smart and keep watching anyway. Win-win."

Being a director was a lot like being a crime boss, only without threatening to shoot people. Trudy got off the train and looked around. The engine and train cars had gone in a circle, snaking back and ready to head back down the mountain when they needed, but Norm had made sure there was also enough camping gear to set up tents so the crew could stay for a day or two of shooting. Trudy was all for that. The Durango heat was much lighter here up in the mountains, which could almost have doubled for someplace up in the Poconos, at least one with a lot of pines.

But what was truly spectacular was the Weeping Skull. The mouth of the cave yawned like the mouth of a skull and the railway tracks leading in snaked like a lolling tongue sticking out to the left. But it was the waterfalls that sold it—twin falls sprayed small plumes of water down past the mouth of the cave and off over a sheer cliff that led down the backside of the mountain.

"Better than any matte painting," Norm remarked, then turned to the rest of the gang who'd gathered behind him. "Care to check out where we'll be shooting the next couple of days?"

Besides Jack and Trudy, there was David Niven, Ivan Dixon,

and Britt Lomond, plus crew. Niven was already in costume as a botanist, so Dixon and Lomond had followed suit as the young African colonel and the dashing archaeologist, while the gaffers and lighting techs brought battery-powered lanterns. They shone them around while Jack provided even more illumination by punching a fist into his hand, causing his force field to pulse. The cave was huge, going back a long way, until the mine-cart tracks disappeared in a pile of boulders.

"Coatepec!" one of the lighting techs exclaimed.

Trudy thought she knew most Spanish profanities, but this was a new one on her. Then David Niven provided a helpful explanation: "Snakes!"

Trudy looked and realized that what she thought was a pile of gray and brown rocks and loose stones strewn across the railroad tracks was in fact a pile of dust-gray and sepia-toned rattlesnakes. Snakes up to five or six feet long, some looking even longer, all coming awake in the sudden light and beginning to rattle.

Trudy had only seen rattlers in movies before, black-and-white westerns, but the snakes were the same color as the films, and almost as long and terrible.

Britt Lomond moved first. His archaeologist was also an expert fencer because Lomond was, and that had been written into the part at his request. He had his cavalry saber out in a trice and a second later a too-close rattler's head separated from its body. The body twitched and writhed, and the head snapped open and closed and open again, sideways on the ground, still trying to bite.

Jack stepped toward the mass of serpents, punching his hand to get their attention, causing his force field to flare, four rattlers leaping to strike. Three impacted on the force field, causing it to flash, and one leapt past Jack to Trudy.

It was half instinct, half careful training, but Trudy used her ace to grab the severed snapping snake's head, careful to grasp it from the back like a bloody venomous baseball, then launched it forth by teleportation to catch the striking serpent jaw-to-jaw: screwball-style, twisted upside down, fangs locked in a deadly kiss. The rattlers stared at each other's chins as the striking snake hit Trudy's bare leg, but—rather than its deadly fangs—with the backward bloody stump of the severed neck of the other snake.

Why had she worn a skirt? Trudy ran, panicking, wondering if anyone had seen her use her ace, but everyone was running for the entrance of the cave, too, except Jack. "Coatepec!" the lighting tech exclaimed again once they were outside the cave. "The Mountain of Snakes!"

"Well, maybe not a mountain," Ivan Dixon said, "but that was sure a whole pile of them."

"No, a whole mountain," Lomond corrected. "It's an Aztec legend." Everyone stared at him until he said, "What? My character's an archaeologist. I read a few books."

"Makes sense to me," said David Niven.

"*Sí*," the lighting tech agreed, "the Mountain of Snakes, Coatepec, where Coatlicue, the goddess of the serpent skirts, gave birth to Huitzilopochtli, the sun god."

The business about the sun god, whose name Trudy was not even going to try to pronounce, seemed more than a little non sequitur, except for seeing Jack still inside the cave, limned in golden light like a saint from the front of a votive candle as he strangled snakes longer than him. Blood still dripped from Lomond's sword and was all over Trudy's right leg from the neck of the same snake, after she'd teleported it to use as a shield against the one that came after her. But no one seemed to have noticed, so she was not going to bring it up.

"I need to get cameras on this," Norm declared and went off to enlist some crew members.

Trudy gave him a sidelong glance. Directors were really close to crime bosses; she hadn't heard anyone so coldly practical since Dr. Tod.

The unpronounceable sun god continued to beat his mother's skirts, or at least Jack was beating a giant nest of rattlers like Trudy's nana used to beat a carpet, only with weird flashes of golden light. The snakes couldn't get their fangs on Jack, and Trudy glanced to the lighting tech, whom she thought she recognized from Señor Aguilar's tequila party. "So does this have anything to do with the four hundred drunk rabbits?"

"No," he said, "but Huitzilopochtli's sister, the moon goddess Coyolxauhqui, led the four hundred stars to kill their mother, Coatlicue, and after that Huitzilopochtli cut Coyolxauhqui's head off."

Probably with something more old-fashioned than Lomond's cavalry saber, but one never knew. Trudy suspected the four hundred stars weren't the Hollywood type, but four hundred stars, four hundred drunken rabbits, four hundred barrels of silver? "What's with the 'four hundred' everything?" Trudy asked.

"It's Aztec for 'more than you can count.'"

"That makes sense." If that extended to the barrels of silver, Trudy liked the sound of it. Rattlesnakes? Not so much. But her leg was spattered with snake blood and she wanted to get cleaned off, so she headed back to the train.

Jack did not return to Wayne's Pullman car until well past nightfall. Trudy had made sure the cooks made extra burritos for him, which were almost as good cold as they were hot, but they were very cold now. Jack didn't seem to care, staggering in, and sat down heavily with a flash of light, grabbing a burrito and stuffing it into his face.

"Are you okay?" Trudy asked. He was covered in dust and blood.

Jack nodded, wolfing down half the burrito then reaching for the glass of water she offered him. He gulped half that down, too, then told her, "I found it."

Trudy had been tired but was fully awake in an eyeblink. "Found what?"

"Maximilian's treasure," Jack told her, looking like a kid on Christmas morning or, more than that, a tired star who'd suddenly found the answer to his divorce settlement, "and it's way more than four hundred barrels."

More than you can count, Trudy thought, but only asked, "Does anyone else know?"

Jack shook his head and Trudy had a chill down her spine. This was the part of every noir pic where the dumb broad gets her neck snapped, but evidently, she'd picked the right hero. Jack might be a bit of a cad, but only enough to be exciting, because Trudy knew bad guys and he was not a bad guy. "Is it safe to see?"

Jack grinned. "As safe as I could make it."

Trudy glanced around. John Wayne had attached a cavalry saber to the wall as decoration. "Hand me that," Trudy said. "Britt used his to lop the head off a snake."

"You know how to use one?"

"You might be surprised," said Trudy. Honestly, she was much better with a gun, but it was enough trouble smuggling jewels and rare documents past customs officials, even with her ace, without having to worry about a gun, too. Still, Dr. Tod had made sure everyone in his gang knew how to handle weaponry, Trudy included. That involved basic fencing lessons.

Aside from the cavalry saber, Trudy also took a cobalt glass oil lantern with a hurricane shade. It would have been nicer to have one of the electric lanterns, but not worth the risk of waking any of the film crew.

The stars glittered above them, the four-hundred-plus along with their sister, the decapitated moon, who'd decapitated their mom, the goddess of the serpent skirts. Mom's skirts were everywhere in the cave, too: torn to ribbons or at least smashed snakes. Jack had cleared a ton of the cave-in as well, but there were still tons more rock blocking the passageway. Then Jack smiled and pointed to one huge boulder near the edge. He went and lifted it, glowing gold as he did, and set it to one side as casually as someone might move a dressing room screen.

Behind it was a tunnel cleared from the rocks, leading into the heart of the mountain.

Trudy raised the oil lantern, looking at the tunnel before them. It was old and dusty, half of it the wall of the former mine shaft, but had been left clear and reinforced, part of a planned demolition, a secret passage leading in and on.

Before long they came to a barrel, looking at least a hundred years old, but with the top recently removed, ripped off not by a crowbar but by the hands of an incredibly strong man. Jack lifted it, let Trudy see the blue-white corrosion of old silver coins, then put it back and proceeded on.

Barrels lined the way: one, two, three, and then Trudy lost count, like the four hundred drunken rabbits or matricidal stars, *four hundred* just another phrase for too many to count. The air got cooler the deeper they got into the mountain, and drier farther away from the waterfall at the mouth of the cave, and Jack popped the lid of another barrel to show that the coins were bright and silver. Trudy picked a peso up. Big as an American silver dollar, with the profile of Maximilian and the legend **MAXIMILIANO EMPERADOR,** the obverse bearing the eagle on the cactus eating the serpent from the Mexican flag, only crowned and supported by griffins. Trudy pocketed it.

They went on farther, passages snaking left and right, both stacked with barrels, and still farther down a staircase chiseled into the stone of the mountain. "How far down does it go?" Trudy asked.

"I don't know," said Jack, "this is farther than I got to begin with."

Trudy nodded and went down the stairs, which were carved but short, even for a woman's foot. Jack had to walk down crisscrossing to keep his balance. Then they came out into the cavern below and saw the rest of the barrels as well as Aztec effigies of what could only be the goddess of the serpent skirts and her kids, the sun and moon goddess, except the moon goddess was just her giant moonlike head. Except atop her moonlike head was a crown, and not an Aztec one, either, or a knockoff made of crystal and silver for an overly fancy quinceañera, but one identical to the one worn by Empress Carlota in the portrait in town.

"Well," Trudy told Jack, letting out her held breath, "I think we know where Maximilian got Cuauhtémoc's emerald . . ."

"What are you talking about?" asked Jack. "Didn't you notice the snakes?"

Trudy looked again where Jack was pointing. The goddess of the serpent skirts did indeed have serpent skirts, artfully sculpted out of gray-brown stone, flowing down and covering the dais and the ground around it, like the most festive albeit creepy quinceañera gown ever, except then Trudy realized that only the skirt itself was stone and the whole elaborate train was four hundred hibernating rattlesnakes—four hundred in the Aztec sense of too many to count.

Trudy then heard a sound, a sound more dangerous than a rattlesnake's rattle or a serpent's hiss: the sound of the hammer of a gun being cocked.

Trudy whirled.

"Hello," said Señor Aguilar, standing there holding his gun, no longer in his hidden holster, flanked by two of his men, one of them the lighting tech from before, still holding the same lamp. "I see you have found what I have been after for so many years—not just the treasure of Maximilian but the treasure of Cuauhtémoc, two for the price of one!"

"There's more than enough to share, Aguilar," Jack pointed out.

"I think not," said Aguilar in a voice as deadly as any ever used by Dr. Tod, pointing his gun directly at Trudy. "Señora Juana, put down the sword. Señor Tarzan, I would like you to swing or jump or wade over to Huitzilopochtli there and bring me his jeweled atlatl." He pointed to the statue of the sun god and a spear thrower shaped like a snake made of gold and studded with emeralds, except for one ring-sized one missing from the serpent's forehead.

Trudy set down her sword slowly, and the oil lamp as well.

"Very good, Juana." Aguilar stepped close, putting the gun to Trudy's head and holding her in his arms from behind while turning her to look down the steps at Jack.

Jack looked horrified but said bravely, "You won't get away with this, Aguilar. There's nowhere you can hide."

"Oh, there are a great number of places to hide if one has the means."

Jack gave a couple of glances back, but Trudy looked at him with pleading eyes and he went down the steps, wading into the snakes of the goddess's serpent skirts. The snakes were deeper than they looked, and Jack fell forward into the writhing mass, flashing gold in spots as their fangs tried to pierce his force field.

Trudy forced her eyes away from the horrid spectacle and to the more pressing danger of the gun Señor Aguilar had pointed at her forehead right where she could see it. "Your Tarzan is very brave, isn't he, Juana?" he whispered in her ear.

That was a mistake. That let Trudy know exactly where Aguilar's forehead was. His gun disappeared from his hand and reappeared in hers as she pulled the trigger.

¡BANG! Trudy was deafened by the explosion and spattered by Aguilar's brains, but there was no time to think, only react. Aguilar's second henchman was armed, too, but he wasn't expecting the oil lamp to disappear from the step and reappear falling onto his head, shattering and covering him with flaming kerosene.

Trudy plugged him full of lead till he stopped moving, then turned and shot at the third henchman, the lighting tech, with her last bullet. He dodged, and then Aguilar's gun clicked and clicked, the hammer finding empty chambers. Trudy threw it away and reached for the battery-powered lantern in the man's hand.

It disappeared from his hand and reappeared in hers. She used the second of shock as he realized she was an ace to reach for the saber, only to realize herself that she couldn't see it—it was behind him. Instead, she snatched one of his boots, then the other, flinging them at him like Eloise had hurled the fruit at Jack—except the man didn't have a force field, they were heavy boots, and his big stockinged feet were balanced on the edge of an overly narrow ancient Aztec stone stair. After both boots, he was overbalanced to the point that a roundhouse kick, even from a lady's foot, was enough to topple him backward and send him rolling down the stone stairs, barefoot, past the cavalry saber, which Trudy teleported to her hand.

The man screamed, clawing for the steps to save himself from sliding into the snake pit. He slid, a silver cigarette case falling out of his pocket along the way, until he stopped just short of the mass of waking snakes, his feet pointed straight toward them.

The rattlesnakes found this irresistible and struck. The man screamed more, then even more as he turned to face the snakes biting his feet and fell in with Jack, still fighting with the writhing mass. The snakes had much more success biting the screaming man, but he didn't scream very long. Then more rattlesnakes began to wake and slither up the steps toward Trudy.

She considered waiting for them with the saber, to behead them like Britt Lomond had earlier, then had a better idea, using the blade as a pry bar to overbalance one of Maximilian's barrels of silver at the edge of the stairs.

It tipped on its side and rolled down the stone steps, like something from a German beer hall song, gathering momentum, flattening several of the serpents in the lead and a whole line of them going down before bouncing and bursting as it impacted on the edge of Coatlicue's dais, scattering her serpent skirts with silver pesos like sequins for a grotesquely lavish quinceañera.

But there were four hundred snakes, in the Aztec sense, more than Trudy could count, and more and more kept coming, so she gave up on the barrels of silver and went on the quickest window-shopping spree of her life: Carlota's crown appeared atop her head, the sun god's emerald-studded atlatl appeared on her shoulder, and the shoeless corpse's silver cigarette case appeared in her hand beside the hilt of the sword, the silver decorated with an Aztec hummingbird. Trudy realized he had been one of the youths who'd been kind to her at the tennis court a couple days before.

But regrets were something for later. Trudy teleported the cigarette case into her purse and ran for her life up the steps, down the tunnels lined with barrels of silver pesos, and out into the main cave, waving her slightly bent saber, ready for anyone, only to find it empty. She ran, out under the murderous moon and stars.

The camp was not completely dark, but the locomotive was, pointed down the track for the return trip back to Chupaderos. It was not a getaway car, but Trudy was again grateful that Dr. Tod had effectively run a finishing school for crooks, making sure everyone in his gang, even the girl who fetched coffee, had not only combat training but also basic working knowledge of how to operate most vehicles.

But there were people all over the train, hanging out in the boxcars and using the caboose. Trudy went to where Wayne's Pullman was coupled to the boxcar behind it, the menagerie car for all the chimpanzees, and teleported the pin to the ground. She then went and got into the locomotive, hoping no one would notice as she started it up.

Mercifully, the boiler was still warm, but it was still an agonizing wait as it slowly got to steam. Trudy kept watch, expecting more of Aguilar's gang to appear at any second, but they didn't. As Trudy knew from personal experience, organized crime was more often disorganized crime. Apparently, no one else knew yet that the boss was dead. She wondered about Jack. But Jack was invulnerable and had already dealt with one pile of snakes; he could deal with another. She hoped.

At last the boiler was hot enough. Trudy released the brake and began to pull away, and that was when all hell broke loose, or at least a great deal of screaming in Spanish, people running for the train like they were late for a commute at Grand Central Station.

None of them made it, except for the gang of chimps, who jumped the gap from the uncoupled menagerie car, clambering and swinging along the roof of Wayne's Pullman while the one chimp with human legs called back to Aguilar's gang in flawless Puerto Rican Spanish. Of course Cheetah was Puerto Rican. It made perfect sense.

Trudy ran to the back of the locomotive with the electric lantern and shone it at the coupling, teleporting the pin to her hand with the bent saber as Cheetah ran to the front of the roof of the Pullman and stared at her as she stood there, saber in one hand, lantern in the other, wearing Carlota's crown and an emerald-studded ancient Aztec atlatl. "What the hell, Trudy?" he screeched. "What the hell?"

"Say goodbye to Jack for me!" Trudy called and waved the bent saber as the distance between them grew and the locomotive began to speed up down the mountainside.

Trudy ran back to the front to get control but regained it soon enough. Dr. Tod had taught her well.

She took stock of her possessions. She'd lost her luggage and clothes, but still had all her jewels and more, even the damn Blue Stone of Heaven prop, plus that poor kid's hummingbird cigarette case.

Trudy opened it. Half full, with ten hand-rolled joints. She had a feeling she'd smoke all of them by the time she got to the border.

How was she going to smuggle out Carlota's crown? Maybe grab a quinceañera gown from that shop window and try to brazen it out? Everyone loved a quinceañera, right? Except how would she explain an emerald-studded gold atlatl? Really old-fashioned party favors?

Trudy teleported her temple-dancer cigarette lighter out of her purse and lit a joint. She had time to figure this out. She'd had a more-than-successful heist, even with the messy bits, because there were always messy bits, just like Dr. Tod had taught her.

And Jack? Well, he'd wanted a fling. She didn't expect him to fling himself into a snake pit for her, but love was a lot like crime: You made plans, you saw everything turn to shit, then you re-adjusted on the fly.

She hoped Jack would get to keep enough silver to pay off his ex. He deserved that at least.

Trudy took another toke of Mary Jane and rode John Wayne's locomotive off into the Mexican night.

1981

Cyrano d'Escargot

by Christopher Rowe

This is the story of the time I had a gig try-ing and failing to seduce the most famous fashion model in the world on behalf of a wealthy fourteen-year-old kid who was also an enormous snail.

My name is Trevor Fitzgerald. I am an actor. You may have seen me as Mr. Paravicini in the Charleston Dinner Theater's production of *The Mousetrap* or as Lord Capulet at the Derby Dinner Playhouse in Clarksville, Indiana, which of course isn't where they have the Derby but *is* right across the Ohio River from Louisville, with a really nice view of the skyline.

Or maybe you saw me at the height of my fame—a two-week stint as a hit man on *General Hospital* who was eventually killed by the Australian guy on that show.

I should remember his name. We went out for drinks once with a couple of the regulars and he paid for everybody. I can't think of it at all now, but of course that was almost forty years ago.

On the other hand, everything that happened with Theodorus Witherspoon—that's the giant snail kid—and with Peregrine—

who was already famous as the "Flying Cheerleader" and for her *Playboy* spread a few years after that, but who wasn't yet the host of *Peregrine's Perch* and then *American Hero*—everything about *that* screwed-up situation, I remember clear as day.

I had just finished a job at the aforementioned Charleston Dinner Playhouse. It wasn't the Christie play, though, it was . . . it was in the same category as the Australian guy, something I should remember but don't.

It's funny. I remember lines, speeches, soliloquies, even enough fight choreography to make an impressive show of it if my back doesn't go out on me. But scenes and plots escape me. Except, as I have mentioned, the plot hatched by Theodorus Witherspoon, then still young, and already rich.

I was the last person still staying at the apartment near downtown that somebody had arranged for us out-of-town Equity types, waiting for my agent to call with word of an audition for another play, or a commercial, or anything really, because dinner theater gigs aren't exactly the road to riches, though you do get to go through the buffet line as often as you like without paying, even if the guys carving the roast at the end would sometimes grumble a little bit on your second time through.

I never understood that. It's not like they got paid any different depending on how much free beef they carved.

So I was packed up, living out of my suitcase and assuming I'd soon be headed to the airport to make a three-transfer flight to Kansas City or Tallahassee or some other exotic location where the services of a blandly good-looking white guy were required for an exhibition of the dramatic arts. Dramatic or comedic—I'm actually pretty versatile.

That makes me think of something I should have said from the beginning. I am quite a *good* actor. I just never caught any breaks. Except for *General Hospital*.

Anyway, the call wasn't coming as fast as my money was running out and access to the buffet line had ended when the show went dark. I was just about to place a call or two myself, to maybe check around and see if anybody had gotten sick or injured or otherwise made unavailable at an outdoor historical drama, as often happens because acting outdoors is surprisingly hazardous. I knew a guy who was bitten by a rattlesnake during a performance on Roanoke Island where he was playing Ananias Dare. His English accent was pathetic, but nobody deserves that.

I keep getting off track, sorry. I'm better with scripts.

No calls, then, but one morning there was a knock at the door. I was drinking coffee and watching a local morning news show being remotely broadcast from a nearby beach. See, I told you I could remember everything about the situation in detail.

I was in my boxers and the T-shirt I slept in—I wear pajamas these days because it seems like I'm always cold at night—so I pulled on a pair of pants and went to open up. I didn't know what to expect, but I would have had to hazard a whole lot of guesses before I landed on a middle-aged black man dressed like a chauffeur in a Preston Sturges movie.

"Mr. Fitzgerald?" he said. Drawled, really. That South Carolina accent, man.

"That's me," I said. "I, um, I didn't order a car."

"No, sir," he said. "I am in private employment. It is my employer, in fact, who sent me. He read the reviews of your performance in *Our Town* and would greatly appreciate the opportunity to meet you."

Our Town! Right! I even played the Stage Manager; how did I forget that until just now? "That's great," I said. "Great that he liked the show, I mean."

"Oh, Mr. Witherspoon didn't see the show, just read the notices. His condition makes it difficult for him to attend theatrical events."

He stressed "theatrical events" in a way that made me suspect he didn't think much of theater. Then I thought maybe he just didn't think much of actors, which is kind of a subtle difference but something you run into a lot in this business we call show.

Then something occurred to me. *Witherspoon.* There was a Witherspoon Street in Charleston. There was a Witherspoon Auditorium at one of the local universities and a Witherspoon Foundation that provided grant money for local arts organizations. These are the kinds of details you pick up when you're on the fringes of a local scene.

So here was a chauffeur who certainly worked for some South Carolina old-money family, a scion of which, for some reason, wanted to meet me.

Other than wait by the phone, I had literally nothing else to do that day.

"Let me put on some shoes," I said.

The car was something else.

It was longer than your typical sedan, if not as long as a true stretch limousine. In fact, when I said, "Nice limo," the driver—who still hadn't offered his name—told me in no uncertain terms that the car was *not* a limo but a Duesenberg Model J luxury cabriolet.

It looked like a limo to me, if an old-fashioned one. It had running boards, for God's sake. And the enormous round headlights looked like the overheads in a Broadway theater. Not that I'd ever played onstage in a Broadway theater, but I'd seen them when I was reading for parts.

The car was deep green and polished to a high sheen. The driver opened the door for me, and I made myself comfortable. To describe the interior as luxuriously appointed would be a massive understatement. The leather covering the seats was cream-colored and so soft. I sank back in my seat and waited to be whisked away to my appointment with destiny or whatever, but the minute Mr. Uniform got in behind the wheel, he got right back out again, saying, "Excuse me, sir. Just a moment."

I leaned forward to see what he was doing. He'd taken a small spritzer of some liquid out of one pocket and a cotton handkerchief out of another. He leaned over the hood, bending down so that his nose almost touched the windshield. Maybe I was supposed to say *windscreen,* but I wasn't planning on asking him.

He sprayed a spot on the glass and carefully ran the handkerchief over it in precise circular movements, eight times clockwise, eight times counterclockwise. It may seem weird that I counted, but this guy was fascinating me. I'm always impressed when somebody fully commits to a role.

He was getting back into the luxury cabriolet when a siren blared briefly behind us. I turned around and strained to look through the comparatively small rectangle of glass behind me. Yeah, it was a cop car, and I started to get uncomfortable. This was the early eighties, remember, and Charleston was about as Old South as Old South gets. And my chauffeur pal was a Black man driving a *very* fancy car.

I was rehearsing what I would say to the cop if he gave us any hassle. *See here, my good man, do you know who I am?*

But instead of asking the driver to get out of the car or show his license, the big, beefy, red-faced, and—of course—white cop stood a respectful three or four feet back from the driver's window, which was rolled down in, again, precise circular motions.

"Officer Shoemaker," said the driver.

"Mr. Bomar," said the cop. *Aha,* I thought. *Bomar. Got it.* Officer Shoemaker kept talking. "It's rush hour. Would you like me to go ahead and save you the trouble of waiting in the traffic?"

"I'm sure that won't be necessary."

Those southern drawls. It seemed like it had taken them about five minutes to exchange four sentences.

The cop smiled. "Straight eight," he said, sounding sort of wistful.

Mr. Bomar smiled back. "Supercharged," he said.

I was mystified. I didn't drive then—I rarely do now—and didn't know anything about cars, especially not luxury cabriolets that, by all appearances, had been hand-built by elves in the mountains of Bavaria sometime between the wars.

It turned out that straight eight was the type of engine the Duesenberg Model J luxury cabriolet had. It turned out that supercharged meant that it could go really, really fast.

Like the car, the house was something else. I would have called it a mansion, but I was afraid Mr. Bomar would correct me, as he had on *limo*. Maybe it was a chalet. I'm no more a student of architecture than I am of automobiles, even though architecture is at least one of the humanities, like drama. Or so I seemed to remember. I spent most of my time in college in the theater department and barely scraped by in all my other classes.

Mr. Bomar came to what was not quite a screeching stop after the—really terrifying—drive from central Charleston. At that point I couldn't see the house/mansion/chalet behind the high hedgerows either side of the closed wrought-iron gates. The gates were all elaborate swoops and circles, leading inward to stylized W's at the center of each. They must have cost a small fortune, but as I was shortly to learn, small fortunes were what the Witherspoons spent on, I don't know, catering for their New Year's Eve parties.

One honk of the horn and a head popped out from around the corner of the left-hand hedge. This guy—an elderly white man wearing a sort of policeman's uniform like I'd worn in regional productions before, but more expensive looking—waved at the car then tottered over to the center of the gates. He lifted a bar—it looked like it was quite an effort—and the gates swung smoothly open.

Mr. Bomar waved as we drove by and I saw what I guessed was a guardhouse tucked out of view behind the hedge. I also saw that the old guard was wearing a pistol on his belt.

The driveway was white pea gravel and Mr. Bomar took it in

pretty much the opposite manner than he had driven along the highway, slowly and carefully. The crunching noise under the tires was oddly pleasant, if barely discernible under the low growl of the straight-eight supercharged engine.

Through a stand of trees, around a low hill, and there was the house. As I said, it was something else. Sort of a combination of Tara, the White House, and a drawing by a very talented kid who'd been told to draw a rich person's house. Three stories, two wings off a large rectangular central section, and a wide set of stairs leading up to a porch that must have been fifty feet wide and twenty feet deep.

The first time my agent had ever set me up with a job in the South—it was in Savannah—he had given me what he imagined would be useful advice about southerners. This from a man who I'm pretty sure had never traveled farther south than Houston Street. He'd said: "In the South, you can safely subtract ten points of IQ for every column on the front porch."

If that was true, I was about to meet somebody very, very stupid.

It wasn't true, though. Boy, was it not true.

Mr. Bomar didn't stop the car in front of the house but drove on around the back. There were various outbuildings, including a greenhouse and what must have once been a barn of some kind but was now a garage. Mr. Bomar drove past one of the wide-open doors on the second building and then backed in.

"We're going in through the kitchen," he said.

This time he didn't open the door for me, and I wondered what had changed my status. Fair enough, though. I once had a job in Chicago starring a past-his-prime Hollywood guy taking all the work he could find to pay a huge IRS fine. He had people carry his luggage for him. I can carry my own luggage, and I can open my own doors.

The kitchen was a large, well-lit room that looked like it was better equipped than the kitchen at the Charleston Dinner Theater. There was a short, middle-aged Black woman standing at a marble-topped counter, rolling out dough. There was a lingering smell of something delicious and no doubt spectacularly unhealthy in the air.

The woman looked me up and down. "This him, then?" she asked.

"Who I was sent to fetch, yes," said Mr. Bomar.

The cook didn't look like she much cared for actors, either. But then she nodded and gave me a big smile.

"You're going to have to wait a little while, they're still eating dinner." There are a lot of people in the South who call the midday meal dinner and the evening meal supper. I think *lunch* was a little informal for this particular subset of southerners.

I shrugged. I still hadn't a clue what was going on, but at least it was interesting.

"Do you want something to eat? I've got chicken from last night, and a mess of greens."

"Sounds good," I said. I hadn't realized I was hungry until I walked into the kitchen.

It was better than good; it was fantastic. She pulled out some fried chicken from an industrial-sized refrigerator and spooned out some greens from a covered iron skillet on the stove. She plated this up, not bothering to heat the chicken. "Fried chicken is best cold," she said, and it turned out she was right.

Mr. Bomar got a plate, too, and a tall glass of milk. I asked for water and got fresh-squeezed lemonade. Not my kitchen, not my rules.

The cook, who had not introduced herself by name, either, went back to rolling out the dough. Mr. Bomar and I sat at a big cedar chopping block, eating, and when I was done with the greens—I had no idea what kind they were specifically, but they had been cooked in bacon fat, so they were okay by me—I drained my lemonade and decided to take some initiative. "So, Mr. Bomar. What's up?"

"Just eating my dinner," he said.

Heh. "Yeah, me too. It was great. Thank you, ma'am!" I called over to the cook.

"You don't have to ma'am me," she said. "I'm Loretta."

"Thank you, Loretta."

"You're welcome. You just do good by Theodorus and you can come here and eat whenever you like."

I nodded. "Is Theodorus the drama fan?" I asked, directing the question to Mr. Bomar.

"Mr. Witherspoon," he said.

"Is Mr. Theodorus Witherspoon the drama fan?" I asked.

"Mr. Theodorus Witherspoon is who sent for you," he answered.

Mixed signals, there in the kitchen of Chez Witherspoon.

"So, I'll get to meet him after he's finished eating?"

"You'll get to meet him when he rings for you."

Wow. "Is there really a bell? He pulls a rope and everybody comes running?"

Mr. Bomar pointed at a telephone on the wall. "He'll call down."

That actually kind of disappointed me.

"And you don't know what Mr. Theodorus Witherspoon wants with me?"

Mr. Bomar gave me an arch look. "I do," he said.

I smiled. I was liking him more all the time. "But you're not going to tell me, are you?"

"I am not," he said.

The phone rang.

There might not have been ropes to pull summoning the servants—or temporarily-out-of-work actors—but there *was* a back staircase. Mr. Bomar led me up it, stopping at the landing halfway up to the second floor and turning to say, in a low voice, "Don't speak, please."

I gave him a bewildered look.

"It's important that Mr. and Mrs. Witherspoon not know you're here."

I risked whispering. "I thought I was going to see Mr. Witherspoon."

"You are going to see the younger Mr. Witherspoon."

I nodded. "Brother or son?" I asked.

For once, Mr. Bomar was forthcoming with a little information. "Son," he said.

"Not a little kid, I hope."

A troubled expression crossed his face. "No," he whispered. "No, not little."

The situation remained interesting, so I followed him on up the steps.

The door at the top of the stairs opened into a very long hallway. I don't know what I was expecting by way of carpeting and furnishings, but heavy sheets of plastic along the floor the whole length of the hall wasn't it. There was a sizable teak elephant, though. That was close enough to what I might have been imagining, furnishings-wise.

Mr. Bomar looked left and right, then gestured for me to follow him. "Careful," he said. "It's slippery."

I looked down at the plastic. There was some sort of translucent substance pooled here and there. I avoided it.

We walked—being careful—past two or three doors, to one just beyond the teak elephant. This door was different from all the others. It was twice as wide and half again as tall, and these were clearly recent modifications.

Mr. Bomar knocked. "I've brought him," he said. And with that, he turned on his heel and headed back to the staircase.

A voice came from the other side of the door. "Come on in." It was an odd-sounding voice. Like a teenage boy just hitting puberty who was swallowing something thick and liquid.

I opened the door, and there, in the center of the room, was Theodorus Witherspoon.

I am not going to be one of those people who says that some of his best friends are jokers. Especially not while relating events from 1981, when it wasn't even a little bit true—and not even now, though I do have good friends who are jokers.

But for a while, and intermittently for decades thereafter, Theodorus probably *was* my best friend. And I like to believe I was at least *one* of his best friends. His actual best friend was another joker, Mathilde, but I didn't meet her until years later.

Of course, I *knew* jokers and had worked with them a lot. My best reviews up to that point had come when I somehow landed a job playing Caliban at the Stratford Festival in Ontario, in a production that cross-cast jokers in most of the parts but nats as the non-humans. It was a wild success, mainly because the woman playing Prospero was absolutely astonishing. The production values were great, too. At "I'll drown my book," Prospero caused this column of water to rise from the stage and fountain down over everyone, the book floating at the top. Actually, I'm not sure that counts as a production value because she was doing that herself with her wild card power.

So, while I was surprised when I saw Theodorus for the first time, I'm not sure I would say I was shocked. I was born in 1953, so I don't remember a world without aces and jokers. I had also lived in New York in my twenties when I was still trying to land the big gigs and had been poor enough to live, at one point, on the fringes of Jokertown. I'd seen what I guess you would call a pretty broad range of phenotypes. (I admit that I looked that word up just now.)

Theodorus is known worldwide now, of course—or maybe I should say worlds wide. Covers of magazines, profiles on cable news, even a couple of documentaries. When I met him, his card had turned only a year or so earlier. Very few people outside the Witherspoon household had seen him since, or even knew about his "condition."

And now I joined that exclusive club. Now I knew that Theodorus Witherspoon had become, as I said at the very beginning of this extended recollection, an enormous snail. And I mean *enormous*. He told me once he weighed over three thousand pounds. The upper curve of his shell topped eight feet. The human-shaped chest and arms and head extending out from his snail body leaned down from well above me, and I'm not a short man.

He was looking at me expectantly. Out of the corner of my eye I could see crammed bookshelves. There were models of spaceships and airplanes hanging from the ceiling. There was no plastic sheeting on the floor, but it had been covered with surprisingly cheap-looking linoleum.

There was no bed.

I suddenly felt unaccountably sad. I tried to not let that sound in my voice.

"Hey there, Mr. Theodorus Witherspoon," I said.

This seemed to disarm him. He bobbed his head, then said, shyly, "Hey there, Mr. Trevor Fitzgerald."

He moved—he *glided*—toward me and I took two steps to one side to give him room. He closed the door. Now that he had moved, I could see that there was, for some reason, a Xerox machine against one wood-paneled wall. Above the Xerox, taped to the paneling, was a poster of a winged girl wearing a cheerleader's costume.

"Did Clovis tell you why you're here?"

It took me a minute. "Mr. Bomar's first name is Clovis? That's a pretty great name. And no, he didn't."

"I told him he could, but he said he shouldn't."

"Well," I said, "he went with his gut."

Theodorus laughed. This time there was no glottal noise. He sounded like the fourteen-year-old boy when he was giggling. It was delightful, really.

"He usually does," he said. "Well, should I tell you? Or do you want to guess?"

I tried to come up with reasons a rich kid might want to have his chauffeur bring an actor to his house and keep it a secret from his parents.

"You want to hire me for elocution lessons?"

Theodorus snorted—also delightful.

"Strike one," I said. "Okay, I'm here because you've decided to fund your own production of *Rosencrantz and Guildenstern Are Dead* and the two of us are going to be the stars."

"There *is* funding," he said. "I have money and I'll give you some of it."

I let that pass. "I take it that means *Rosencrantz and Guildenstern Are Dead* is strike two."

"I've never even heard of it. I mean, I know who Rosencrantz and Guildenstern are." He raised one hand and drew a finger across his throat, made a gurgling sound.

"You have the gist of it," I said. "Okay, one more try. I'm here because you're planning to take some of that money, get Clovis to rent a moving truck for you to ride in, then light out on a cross-country adventure during which you pretend to be a Romanian prince on the run from the KGB. You need me to coach you in the role."

He just smiled this time, no laugh. "You're here," he said, "because I'm in love."

The Xerox was for his side of the correspondence. He kept copies of everything he'd sent her inside plastic covers, filed by date in a locked cabinet next to the machine.

As for everything she'd sent him—starting with a signed eight-by-ten glossy, then progressing through what were clearly form letters, then through handwritten notes and finally on to full-fledged cards and page upon page of cream stationery covered in loopy purple-ink cursive—as for all that, well. Theodorus treated that thick stack of paper like pirate treasure. Literally.

Somehow, he had arranged for a trapdoor to be installed at the center of the room, its outline cleverly concealed by the seams in the linoleum. It opened up to reveal a shallow compartment holding a small rosewood trunk. This was, like the filing cabinet, locked, but in the case of the trunk, the lock was an ornate, brass, antique-looking mechanism, the key to which he somehow kept hidden back beneath his shell.

He put on gloves before he opened the trunk. Oh-so-delicately, he took out the sheaf of papers and spread them out in a fan on his desk, like a close-up magician asking me to pick a card. All of that operation complete, he smiled once more and, finally, spoke again. "She loves me, too."

"She" was the girl in the cheerleader poster—the woman, I should say, because she was well into her twenties by the time all this happened. I recognized her, of course. Peregrine, the gorgeous flying ace supermodel who had first come to the attention of the world as "the Flying Cheerleader" and then grew up fast, launching her modeling career straight out of high school and taking what was rumored to be a ridiculous amount of Hugh Hefner's money for the famous *Playboy* spread a year or two back.

I took a surreptitious glance at the bookshelves but didn't see any magazines. I didn't ask Theodorus if he had a copy, then. Never did, in fact.

His pronouncements made and the stage business finished with, he looked at me expectantly.

I cleared my throat. "Isn't she a little old for you?" I asked.

"She's pretty young," he said.

"How old are you?" I asked.

"Fourteen," he said.

"She's too old for you." I was avoiding the real issue, of course.

"I think you're avoiding the real issue," he said.

I told you he was smart.

"How long have you been writing her?" I asked.

"Almost two years. Well, she's been writing me for almost two years. I've been writing her for . . . longer than that." He gestured at the filing cabinet.

These were deep waters, but I decided to skirt around that. "I don't see an acting angle here, Theodorus."

"Oh!" he said, honestly excited. "Wait!"

He glided over to one bookcase, peeling off his gloves as he went, then producing another, dry pair from somewhere. He pulled a thick volume off a shelf and came back to me. He handed over the book.

It was an old book, heavy in my hand. The title was written in gold leaf. *L'œuvre complet d'Edmond Rostand.*

I didn't read French, but I knew the name of the writer. Of the *playwright.*

"Oh," I said. "Oh, you poor kid."

Edmond Rostand. Author of *Cyrano de Bergerac.*

In my opinion, you should already know the story. In my experience, you may very well not. It's a story from a play, and a French play at that. There have, however, been at least a dozen translations into English of it since it premiered in Paris in 1897. The curtain calls for that first staging lasted for over an hour.

Like I said, I spent most of my time in college in the theater department.

Cyrano de Bergerac was a real man from France. He lived—for a relatively brief span, dying at thirty-six—in the first half of the seventeenth century. A lot of people have done a lot of work trying to develop some kind of detailed biography of him, which has proven difficult, but it's pretty clear that he was himself a play-wright, as well as a novelist (he wrote an early science-fiction book) and a duelist. There are different versions of his death, but the most popular theory is that he died of wounds from a botched assassination attempt.

Interesting guy, in other words.

It's an open question whether or not he would be widely re-membered if it weren't for Edmond Rostand. Rostand wrote other plays—some of them quite good, if not often staged—but his *Cyrano* is the one people know about. A few people anyway.

Forgive my tone. I'm not exactly bitter about how well plays other than the Bard's are known to the general public, but I'm not exactly happy about it, either.

But I was telling you about *Cyrano* the play, not about Cyrano the man—and certainly not about general knowledge of the dra-matic arts.

In the play, a fictionalized Cyrano de Bergerac falls in love with a beautiful woman named Roxane, a distant cousin of his. He doesn't like his chances, though, because he's insecure about his huge nose (there's a great bit in the play where Cyrano himself disparages his own appearance when another courtier makes an obvious joke about his nose, and Cyrano replies by listing ever more colorful and clever schnoz-related insults, all in rhyming couplets of twelve-syllable lines).

In addition to his anxiety over his appearance, there's a second problem. At a meeting with Roxane, she tells Cyrano that she's fallen in love with Christian de Neuvillette, a handsome young cadet. She asks Cyrano to befriend his rival and protect him. Cyrano, disheartened, agrees.

It turns out that Christian is in love with Roxane, too, but *his* anxiety about the situation is that he doesn't think he's clever enough to woo someone of her wit and charm. Various incidents ensue, the applicable ones to the Theodorus situation being that Cyrano writes what is apparently a knock-her-dead love letter on

Christian's behalf, and then, after Christian has made a fool of himself in a conversation with Roxane, Cyrano parks the cadet under her balcony and feeds his rival lines.

So the parallels weren't exact. But I knew as soon as I saw the book what was up. Theodorus had been exchanging love letters with the famous and beautiful Peregrine, and now apparently things had come to a head, and it was time to meet her in person.

Gigantic nose, gigantic snail.

I was being considered for the part of Christian de Neuvillette.

I don't know how Theodorus thought this would turn out, but I was pretty sure there wouldn't be a happy ending.

I shook my head. "No. No, I see what you have in mind and the answer is no."

"I'll pay you," Theodorus said.

"Tell you what, you can pay me for my time coming out here and for almost being killed by Clovis's driving. Fifty bucks sound reasonable?" I walked over to the bookshelf and replaced the book in the approximate place I'd seen him take it from.

"I'll pay you twenty-five thousand dollars."

Shit.

I chose one of my angry voices. "What kind of parents let a fourteen-year-old kid have access to that kind of money?" Dramatists call that kind of line a deflection. I suppose everybody else calls it that, too.

"They don't," Theodorus said, sounding a little miffed, which I guessed meant he, a fourteen-year-old boy, was defending his parents. Interesting character note, that. "I've been saving my birthday card money."

Interesting character note *that*, too.

"You have some generous relatives," I said.

When he shrugged, the movement set up a wave in his flesh that traveled down his back and into his snail body. "It's not exactly the play," he said.

Twenty-five thousand dollars was right at the income I'd reported to the IRS the year before. It was also more than double what I'd made so far the year all this happened, and as I mentioned earlier, I didn't have any new gigs lined up. Whoever owned the performers' apartment in town was eventually going to kick me out, leaving me to ask my older brother, again, if I could crash in his spare room for the interim. I liked his kids. They liked me. His wife and I barely spoke.

"Not exactly the play," I said. "No, I don't see any épées anywhere."

"They used rapiers," Theodorus replied.

I wasn't entirely clear on the difference—the only swords I'd ever used were light, dulled, and designed to make a satisfying clashing noise when they were crossed in carefully choreographed combat. As I was in no position to argue the point, I took another tack. "Why do you need me? Why don't you just keep writing her letters?"

"There's a photo shoot," he said. "South of Broad."

South of Broad is the neighborhood in downtown Charleston with the horse-drawn carriages and the harbor view. I could see why some fashion brand would choose it for a photo shoot. "And she's coming to model for it," I said.

Theodorus smiled and nodded with enthusiasm. "She's going to fly over the harbor!"

"And she wants to meet you in person."

The smile disappeared and the enthusiasm evaporated. "That's right," he said sadly. Then he added, "I want to meet her in person, too. But I can't."

"You can't because you haven't told her about . . ." I trailed off. "Didn't I read somewhere that she's technically a joker, too? Because a joker is somebody the virus, what, changes physically? Not like the Four Aces, the people who—" I stopped. I'd almost said *people who look normal.*

"That's right," he said. "But it's different for her. Obviously."

"Theodorus," I said, kissing twenty-five large away, "I will not go and meet a famous supermodel who thinks she's in love with a—wait, have you even told her how old you really are?"

He looked embarrassed. "I'm a twenty-nine-year-old assistant professor at the College of Charleston. I specialize in Elizabethan poetry," he said. "I'm really good at tennis."

"That's pretty detailed," I said.

"It's, um, a lot more detailed than that."

"You have two choices," I said, having thought about it for a moment. "Continue the charade but come up with some reason you can't meet her while she's in town. Like you got called away on a family emergency."

"I'm an orphan and an only child."

"Of course you are. What happened to your parents?"

"They were lost at sea."

I sighed. "You didn't get that story from reading Elizabethan poetry. Hey, how do you pretend to be an expert on something like that, anyway?"

Theodorus gestured at the groaning bookshelves. "I became an expert on it."

The bookshelves made me remember something that I'd only half thought about. *L'œuvre complet d'Edmond Rostand.*

"Did you read *Cyrano* in French?" I asked.

"Yes," he said.

"Which you learned at a fancy private school?"

"No. I taught myself."

"You taught yourself French so you could read a hundred-year-old play in the original?"

"I taught myself French because it's the language of romance."

I shook my head, but then grasped at a straw. "Well, I don't speak French. So if Peregrine is used to reading letters in the language of romance, she'll find me out as soon as the waiter lights the candles at the dining experience of romance."

"Oh!" he said, in the same tone and with the same enthusiasm that had preceded him handing me the Rostand. He glided over to another bookshelf, this one filled with wooden boxes with labels on the front that I couldn't read from where I was standing. He pulled one out, rummaged around in it for a couple of seconds, then came back with something small and rectangular in his hands. It was trailing a cord.

"We'll use this!" he said, handing it over. It looked like a transistor radio to me.

"I have one of these," I said. "I listen to baseball games sometimes."

"It's not a radio. I mean, it's not *that* kind of radio. It's like a walkie-talkie. You can put it in your pocket and run the cord up behind your ear. The earpiece is really small, see? I'll be able to hear you and if she asks you to speak in French you can just mimic what I say. And other things, too. So, you won't have to memorize everything we've said to each other in the letters."

I picked up the cord, saw the earpiece at one end. It was black, and not, despite what Theodorus had said, particularly small. "She'll see this," I said. "How would I explain the fact that I'm apparently listening to a ball game during our date?" I couldn't believe I was humoring him this far. But pointing out problems in his plan was easier than just walking out and asking Mr. Bomar for a lift back into Charleston, which he probably wouldn't give me anyway.

Theodorus, as he was to demonstrate pretty much always over the long course of our friendship, was ready with an answer. "She'll think it's my hearing aid."

I balked. "Professor Witherspoon is hard of hearing?"

"Deaf in one ear," he said.

I knew I would regret the question, but I asked it anyway. "From childhood?"

"No," he said. "Because of the explosion."

I just looked at him.

"At the firebase. In Vietnam. I got a Purple Heart."

"Purple Heart."

"And a Bronze Star."

I pinched the bridge of my nose and closed my eyes. "You are a French-speaking professor of Elizabethan poetry and a decorated war hero whose parents were lost at sea," I said.

He nodded enthusiastically. "And I'm really good at tennis."

I was starting to wonder how many columns Peregrine had on her front porch. I asked, "Are you *sure* she doesn't know this is a scam?"

He looked taken aback, maybe even a little bit angry. Later, Theodorus would become quite well known for never losing his temper. But he was then, remember, only fourteen.

"It's not a scam. It's . . . it's a seduction."

The sadness that had come over me when I first entered the room had been unaccountable, at least in the moment. The sadness that overcame me now was quite clear in its source.

"I want you to think about this carefully," I said. "Why do you want to do this?"

He thought about it for a moment. Maybe a full minute, actually, because the silence seemed to stretch out forever. But I waited him out.

"Because she's beautiful and therefore to be wooed; she is a woman, therefore to be won."

Jesus.

I said, "*Henry the Sixth, Part One.* Act Five. Scene Three, I think. I guess your expertise in Elizabethan poetry extends to drama?"

"Not officially," he answered. "Not for our purposes."

"Look," I said. "I can't do this, and you *shouldn't* do it. You have to realize this plan will never work. What good does it even do you? You're obviously some kind of child prodigy genius and there has to be a part of you that knows this is a terrible idea. Why are you really doing this? Why did you bring me out here?"

He looked affronted again. "I brought you here because the *Charleston City Paper* said you were a mostly creditable Stage Manager."

Ouch. But I answered, "They said the kid who played George Gibbs was outstanding."

"He's too young."

"*You're* too young."

Theodorus drew a deep breath. Then he said, "What's the other choice?"

"What?"

"You said I have two choices, and one is to tell Peri that I have to leave town because of a family emergency."

Peri.

"You're a smart kid," I said. "I'm pretty sure you can guess what's behind door number two."

He nodded. "Me. Somebody nobody will ever love once they see him in person."

"You know your parents love you. Seems like your chauffeur and the cook love you, too, and that's saying something given that this whole setup is like something out of *Song of the South*."

"You know that's not what I mean," he said.

Yeah. I knew.

"You're handsome," he went on. "And famous."

I gave him a look, which he interpreted correctly.

"You're well known in the dinner theater world."

"That's better," I said.

"All I am is rich and lonely."

"This crazy plan won't change that," I said gently.

Theodorus went over to the desk, opened one drawer, changed gloves again. He picked up the last page on the right and studied it. Then he said, "This plan will let me dream for a little while longer."

This time it was me who stood silent for at least a minute. This time it was him who waited it out.

I guessed I was going to make twenty-five thousand dollars after all.

"Let me see that letter," I said.

The letter explained that she would be coming to town via train and wanted to meet for dinner. I checked the date. Two days ago. "She's going to be here *tomorrow*?" I asked and felt something like the panic of not fully knowing your lines the morning of a debut.

"The train is supposed to be here at two o'clock in the afternoon," said Theodorus. "It's usually late."

"Okay. Well, it is what it is," I said. "But I'm going to need a lot more to go on than reading all these letters and wearing an earpiece with you spouting French that I'll mangle when I try to say it."

I took the letter over to his desk and put it with the others. "Okay," I said. "This is going to mostly be improvisation, obviously. Frankly, that's never been my strong suit. But if that's what it has to be, then I'm going to need to know a few things. First and foremost, what's the secret?"

He looked confused. "That I'm not a professor?"

"Yes, I know that. I mean what's this in here about a secret the two of you have agreed to share in her letter?"

Theodorus said, "We're keeping our relationship a secret, so that the tabloid press doesn't follow me around or try to stake out my office at the college."

I shook my head. "Will you listen to yourself? You do not have an office at the college. You are not deaf in one ear, though you're obviously having trouble hearing what I've been trying to tell you. If your parents are lost at sea, then they got out on their boat in the hour since I've been here. Get a grip, boy! We need to make some decisions and I have got to have time to prepare for this role."

Theodorus nodded, then said, "She's in dry dock."

This conversation was not going well. What on earth did Peregrine being in dry dock mean? "I don't know what that means," I said.

"The boat. The *Cheerful Mermaid*. She's in dry dock. They're stripping and refurbishing the keel."

Okay. I *did* know what dry dock meant.

"Theodorus?"

"Yes?"

"Do you think me knowing what's up with your parents' yacht is going to be an important point in the various lies and misrepresentations I'm going to be trying out on a woman half again as old as you?"

Theodorus said, "Twice."

"I'll mention the boat twice?"

"She's twenty-seven. So, she's almost twice as old as I am."

Again, I closed my eyes and pinched my forehead. I didn't often get headaches, except on those rare mornings after I'd indulged in tequila.

"Okay," I said. "Okay, let's focus. How did all this start?"

He picked up the eight-by-ten glossy and looked down at it. He looked lost for a moment, but not in a bad way, necessarily.

Then he answered, holding up the picture. "It started when she sent me this."

It did not start when she sent him that.

It started when he sent her the first of many, many fan letters, all of which were carefully photocopied, filed in the aforementioned plastic sleeves, and locked up tight. He sent eleven before he received the glossy in reply.

I looked up from the file cabinet drawer. "You never considered that this might have been a little excessive?"

Theodorus had his answer ready. "It worked."

Good point.

I glanced at the poster hanging over the Xerox. It was the same image as the one in the photograph. A winged girl barely out of her teens, if she was even that, wearing a cheerleader's uniform in a style that had almost certainly never actually been worn by a real high school cheerleader, even in California, where Peregrine grew up. I mean she *was* a cheerleader in high school, wings and all, but this uniform had a V-neck so deep that there was danger of exposure not just up top, but also down below. So presumably this was a bespoke uniform. It probably wasn't made of polyester.

Pictures, letters, cards, and a lovesick teenage boy. A lovesick teenage boy whom I presumed had a plan.

"I presume you have a plan," I said.

I was already learning to read his expressions. He was hesitant. But then he said, "Sort of."

Sort of. That sounded about right.

Peregrine was something else.

I'm sure there are a few people, but probably just a few people in the entire world, who haven't seen her image, either in a still like the ones Theodorus carefully collected and studied, or in motion, on television. But those images, as good a job as they might do capturing her beauty, don't come close to capturing her raw charisma.

I've heard old-timers say that Cary Grant had charisma like that. I've heard Audrey Hepburn had it.

I once waited in a two-hour signing line to get a book of Annie Leibovitz photographs of Muhammad Ali. Leibovitz is famous and I suppose beloved as a photographer, but the reason the line was so long is that she was there with The Greatest. Ali, just sitting there, just cracking jokes and smiling, had that kind of charisma.

That was years later, though. Peregrine was the first person I ever met who was, in some way that was both ineffable and literal, *magnetic*. You couldn't take your eyes off her in person. You couldn't wait for her to speak, to smile, even to just, I don't know, *gesture*, which she did so effortlessly.

I saw her as soon as she entered the restaurant. So did everybody else inside. Hell, so did everybody else outside. Through the plate-glass windows, I saw cars actually stopping. A man walking down the sidewalk started to approach her, I guessed to ask for an autograph, but the woman on his arm held him back.

"Here she comes," I said softly.

"What's she wearing?" asked Theodorus, not softly at all, at least in my "hearing aid." He hadn't shown me how to adjust the volume.

The fancy spyware gadgets we were using had a limited range. Remember, this was the early eighties. He was in the back of a van parked in the alley behind the restaurant. This had been arranged by Mr. Bomar and had involved him peeling a few fifties off a roll he'd pulled from his pocket. I'd walked over from the nearby swank hotel Theodorus was putting me up in.

"Did you hear me? Check, check, one, two, three."

"I can hear you," I said. "But remember, from now on I won't be able to respond. Keep your suggestions to a minimum, please." We'd already been over this. His enthusiasm was getting the better of him, which would later be said of him by newscasters, captains of industry, and heads of state.

"What's she wearing?" This time he whispered.

"Shut up," I said, and stood, waved, and smiled. Time to be a college professor with a host of unlikely qualities.

She swept up, leaving a wave of gawking diners behind her and the maître d' trailing in her wake. He had a goofy grin on his face and was talking fast.

"We're so honored to have you here, Miss Peregrine. The chef is prepared to make you anything you'd like. Anything at all!"

She turned her head and smiled. "Just the stool," she said.

"Yes!" the man said. "Yes, of course! We didn't know which diner you'd be joining. I'll get it right away." He threw me a curious glance and I gave him a cool smile.

"Hello," she said, once he'd scurried off. We were both still standing. I was curious about the stool, but not so much that I didn't give her what I hoped was a subtle once-over. She was dressed more conservatively than in most of the many, many publicity stills and magazine covers Theodorus had shown me. An elegant gown in a deep-blue fabric I didn't recognize but assumed was expensive. Her wings moved when she held out her hand.

"Hello back," I said, and took her hand in my own.

"Say *enchanté*," said Theodorus. I ignored him.

"I don't really know what to say," I said. "I knew you'd look incredible, but it's . . . I don't know what to say. Finally meeting you in person . . ."

"Gives me a frisson of the utmost pleasure," said Theodorus.

". . . is amazing," I said.

She started to reply but the maître d' had returned carrying a plush stool. He'd been joined by a man in a smart suit, probably the manager or the owner, and a woman in a chef's outfit. We had a corner table, and it was getting a bit crowded.

I suddenly realized the purpose of the stool. She couldn't sit in one of the high-backed chairs because of her wings. I had a brief moment of panic wondering if this was something I was supposed to know.

Just in case, I covered. "We appreciate all the extra attention," I said. "But we'd prefer to have a quiet dinner if you all don't mind."

They were pros. They scraped and bowed right out of there, the maître d' taking the chair opposite mine with him as they went.

"What is she wearing?" came a whisper. I fought back a sigh.

"That dress really sets off your blue eyes," I said. "Who made it for you?" I knew from one of the articles that these days all of her clothes were gifted to her by famous designers. It's not like she could buy off the rack with the wings.

Another knockout smile. "Don't pretend you'd know if I told you," she said. "Are we going to sit down?"

"I'm too involved in my work to keep up with the names of all the fashion designers," Theodorus said. "She finds it refreshing."

"Please," I said. Once she'd perched on her stool, I took a seat. "I take it you called ahead to arrange for your seating arrangements."

She waved like it was nothing. "Well, I didn't call. That was Cindy."

"Cindy's her road assistant," came the voice in my ear. "She reads lots of romance novels."

"What's Cindy reading these days?" I asked.

"Oh, who can keep up?" said Peregrine. "Is this how we're going to do this? Ease into things with small talk?"

"What would you like to talk about?" I asked, smiling.

"Hmm, you didn't seem this shy in your letters." She smiled back. I was getting to like that smile very much.

"I guess it's because I'm more comfortable writing than talking."

"That's good!" said Theodorus. "Ask her if she read the last book I sent her."

"Speaking of books . . ." I raised an eyebrow.

"Ah yes," she said. "*Minor Poets of the Elizabethan Age.* Because the way to a girl's heart is through guys who were obscure even when they were famous." She laughed. It was like chimes. I realized I was starting to lose the plot.

"Tell her that's not true at all!" Theodorus sounded a bit like a petulant kid, on account of the fact, I guessed, that he could be a bit of a petulant kid.

"Next time I'll send you *Major Poets of the Elizabethan Age*," I said.

"That's stupid! That book would be five thousand pages long!"

I suddenly realized that my hand had unconsciously gone to my ear.

"You've sent me too many books already," said Peregrine. "Not that I don't appreciate them! It's just that it seems like the only time I have to read is when I'm flying from place to place, and I instantly fall asleep when I'm flying."

"What keeps you from crashing?" I asked.

She looked confused, shook her head in that way people do to tell you they don't know exactly what you're talking about.

I held my arms out, mimicked flapping wings.

"Oh!" she said. "Oh!" and laughed again. Then she blushed.

Definitely losing the plot.

"What's going on? What did she say?" asked Theodorus.

"Anyway," said Peregrine. "I read most of *The Faerie Queene*. It reminded me of *Huckleberry Finn*."

Now it was my turn to be confused. I hadn't read Edmund Spenser at that point, but when you hang out with Shakespearean actors you pick up all kinds of ancillary information about their favorite time period. I had, though, read the Twain in high school. I couldn't put the two together.

"What on earth is she talking about?" asked Theodorus. He sounded more mystified than I was.

"And now you're going to tell me why," I said.

Just then the waiter approached. He was cradling a bottle of wine in each arm. "The owner sends these compliments of the house," he said. "He thought you might want to try one of these vintages as you decide on your orders."

He hesitated for a moment, like he was trying to decide which of us to show the labels to. Then he set one of the bottles down next to Peregrine and one down next to me. Good waiter.

I perused the label for a moment, as if I read Italian. Wait, was I supposed to be able to read Italian?

"This looks excellent," said Peregrine.

The waiter nodded and made swift work of opening the bottle, pouring her a splash to approve, then, at her nod, filling the glasses that were already set out as part of the table service. He started to pick up my Italian bottle, but she held up a hand. "Leave it," she said. "My date's going to need it if I keep flummoxing him."

My laughter didn't sound anything like chimes, but it was genuine.

"What does she mean? How are you flummoxed?"

"Right. Huckleberry Finn and the Knights of Faerie. The little-known collaboration," I said.

"Hah," she said. "No, it's just the thing I remember most from Huck. I mean, other than the 'I'll go to hell then' line. It was when he was staying with the Grangerfords."

I nodded, trying to remember. "The family that said he could live with them." Then I twigged to it. "I remember! They had books and he read some of them. I didn't remember *which* books, is all."

"None of them were *The Faerie Queene*," said Theodorus. He sounded a little disappointed that Peregrine had apparently misremembered something.

"No, no," Peregrine said. "Huck didn't read *The Faerie Queene* there. Or anywhere else, I suppose. But he read *Pilgrim's Progress* and he gave the best review of it I've ever read of anything at all. He said, 'The statements were interesting, but tough.'"

This time we laughed together.

"I don't suppose fashion models have to worry about reviews," I said. I was growing increasingly comfortable with her, despite her charisma and her beauty and now, it turned out, her big old brain.

"Not in the way you'd think," she said. "Editors and photographers definitely have their favorites and aren't afraid to say so. Other models are the *real* critics, though."

"I can't imagine anyone criticizing you for your modeling," I said.

She shrugged that off. "What about you? Are there critics for the kinds of things you write?"

"Tell her peer review!" said Theodorus.

I shrugged too. "Peer review," I said. "Only my peers aren't nearly as beautiful as you. Or as interesting."

We kept trading smiles and it was her turn again. "I'm glad to hear it. I want to be the only fashion model in your life."

Wow.

"Wow," sighed Theodorus.

I must have looked stunned. "Take a drink of wine, Professor," she said.

I did. "My favorite reviews are of theatrical performances," I said. Why the hell did I say that?

"What are you talking about?" said Theodorus. "Stick to poetry! And tell her something else romantic!"

"Really? You've never told me that," said Peregrine. "In fact, I had kind of wondered about it. Being an expert on Elizabethan poetry seems like it would naturally lead to being an expert on Elizabethan drama, but you never wrote me about any plays."

"Tell her that there are significant and substantive differences," said Theodorus.

Before I tell you what I did next, I want you to remember that Theodorus and I were eventually to become great friends.

"Elizabethan drama isn't something I'm an expert on," I said, pulling out the earpiece. "It's something I love."

The early eighties were way before Charleston became a destination city for foodies. Actually, I'm not sure there *were* foodies in the early eighties, at least not the way there are now.

Anyway, dinner was memorable not because of the food (which was good; it just wasn't some fantastic fusion of West African and southern American cuisines or other world-class gastronomic fare like the city is famous for now) but because of the conversation, the laughter, the company.

Speaking of laughter, I should point out that Peregrine's laugh wasn't always delicate and discreet. More than once over the course of our meal together, she laughed from her diaphragm loud enough to cause the other diners to stop eating and look over with raised eyebrows. What am I even talking about? They were looking over with raised eyebrows pretty much constantly the entire two hours we spent drinking, eating, and talking.

I had told Theodorus that improvisation is not my strong suit, but I did myself proud that night. Having introduced the subject of plays and having learned that Peregrine could hold her own talking about them—at least about what was current in New York and in the tryouts and bus-and-truck shows—I hit on the strategy of telling stories about productions I had been part of but, with her, claimed to have witnessed or heard about.

So I told her about a time when I'd seen *Damn Yankees* and the deuce playing the devil could turn his face bright red and grow horns (one of my less successful performances; my singing voice is just barely passable enough for book numbers), and she told me about a show she saw at a festival of new plays that vaguely advertised itself as being about "the darkest days of the Wild Card" and then turned out to specifically be about the congressional hearings where Jack Braun ratted out his fellow aces and, this is the punch line, Jack Braun was in the audience.

I told her about a mixed-up costume quick change where I, playing Brick Pollitt, came on in Big Daddy's outfit and the guy playing Big Daddy came on as Brick and, this is true, we swapped roles and did each other's lines for the rest of the scene. "A bold and unexpected turn in an otherwise pedestrian production," said *The Sacramento Bee.* Only I didn't tell her one of the bold and unexpected actors was me, of course.

Toward the end of our time in the restaurant—at that point in really successful dates when both parties realize that it's time for whatever's going to happen next to happen—she said, "I can't believe we've been writing all this time and you never told me you know so much about plays. Especially plays written in this century!"

I took a risk. "Well, you never mentioned it to me, either. And I think it's good that there are still things for us to learn about each other, don't you?"

That smile. Man, that smile.

"Walk me back to my hotel?" she asked.

"Of course," I said.

I had a brief moment of panic that her hotel was the same hotel where I was being put up for the night. Then I realized that, as vague as he'd been on some of the details, that wasn't the kind of mistake Theodorus was likely to make.

It was surprisingly cool outside for Charleston for that time of year. Late summer was barely hanging on. We'd stretched dinner out long enough that there weren't very many people walking the streets. This was a relief, as I'm not sure what I would have done if a gang of fans had descended upon us.

As it was, we got some stares, and some smiles and waves, but nobody bothered us as we walked. Say what you will about how southerners can weaponize politeness, sometimes they really mean it.

About a block from the restaurant, she took my hand in hers.

About a block after that, I noticed the van following us along the street at, forgive me, a snail's pace.

At some point I had tucked the earpiece down under my collar. If Theodorus had said anything after that point, it hadn't been loud enough for me to hear him. I imagined he'd be full of questions about how the conversation with Peregrine had gone once I'd stopped listening to him.

We reached her hotel and there was that pause that happens

when you reach the hotel. She turned to me and took both of my hands in hers.

Theodorus's plan had been even hazier on this point than it had been on some of the other details.

"So," she said.

"So," I said.

"This has been pretty amazing," she said.

"It has."

"There's still a lot to talk about," she said. "And I really look forward to talking about whatever we come up with tomorrow night, don't you, Professor?"

I can't describe what I felt just then. Relief? Disappointment? Maybe even some shame? All of that, sure, and more.

I don't do Method. I didn't try to act from what I was feeling.

Instead, I kissed her. And she kissed me back. Wow, did she ever kiss me back.

When we parted, I said, "You kiss by the book."

"Isn't that Juliet's line?" she asked. "Shouldn't I say that?"

"I'd love it if you said that," I answered.

She reached up and, totally unexpectedly, ruffled my hair. "Have I told you that you're shorter than I expected you to be?"

This was getting into territory I hadn't been fully prepared for.

"Have I told you that you're funnier than I expected you to be?" I asked. Deflection? No. I meant it.

"That," she said, putting one hand on my chest and pushing a little, "is an even sexier line than Juliet's."

And that was the moment. I didn't need the eight-by-ten glossies or the spreads in the fashion magazines. Not even Hef's—not that his was a fashion magazine. I didn't need the interviews or the articles, I didn't need the correspondence, didn't need to know her assistant's reading habits or any of it. I didn't even need for her to be the most beautiful woman in the world.

I knew, in that moment, why Theodorus was in love. Because

even though I had doubted it, put it down to boyish infatuation and impossible fantasy, I knew *right then* how someone could fall in love with Peregrine.

"So," she said. "I don't know how late I'll have to work tomorrow. They never know with these outdoor shoots. Lots of waving light meters around and shouting at the sky."

I understood the impulse. I kind of felt like shouting at the sky myself.

"How about I just swing by here around four tomorrow afternoon and wait for you at the bar?" I asked.

"Excellent. Just don't drink too many piña coladas before I get here."

Piña coladas. Oh, Theodorus.

"I'll nurse them," I said.

She turned her face up, and I leaned in again.

Across the street, somebody leaned on a horn. I didn't need to look over to know it was a van.

"Good night, Peri," I said.

"Good night, Theodorus," she said. And was gone.

I crossed the street in front of the van. The headlights were on and I could only vaguely see Mr. Bomar through the windshield. When I rounded to the passenger-side door, I found that it was locked. I could see Mr. Bomar more clearly from that position, and he just kind of looked over at me.

I tried the door a couple of times, the way you do when you're letting the driver know you can't get in. Mr. Bomar obviously knew and obviously didn't give a damn.

But then the van kind of listed to one side, as if it was taking a curve and a heavy load had come unsettled.

This turned out to be a pretty accurate assessment of the following events. Well, maybe "unsettled" isn't quite a strong enough word for Theodorus's mood.

I just stood there and shrugged. Mr. Bomar looked back behind him, shrugged himself, then leaned over and unlocked the door. Just as I climbed in, it started to drizzle.

"Hey there, Clovis," I said.

Mr. Bomar just turned his head and looked straight forward.

I turned around to face the music and Theodorus was *right there*. His head and torso were stretched out of his shell to such an extent that his face was just a few inches from mine.

Over the years, he would come to master a range of expressions at least as broad and subtle as anyone's—any actor's even. But he hadn't been in that strange, mutable body for very long at that point, so I couldn't read his face. There was no mistaking what he said, though. "I trusted you," he said.

Which was not exactly what I expected. "What do you mean? I thought it went pretty well." I did not think that, from his point of view, it had gone well. I didn't think it *could* have gone well.

"Why did you stop listening to me?"

Acting and lying aren't the same thing at all. But that doesn't mean being an actor *prevents* you from being a liar.

"The machine stopped working," I said. "Maybe it was the batteries."

Theodorus retracted a little. "Clovis," he said.

I hadn't noticed the reel-to-reel sitting between the driver's and passenger seats. Mr. Bomar reached down and hit a button. The reels spun for a moment. He stopped the rewind, then punched PLAY.

"You kiss by the book," I heard myself say. Was my voice really that breathy?

"Just because you decided not to listen to me doesn't mean I stopped listening to you," said Theodorus.

"Theodorus," I lied, "I don't see what the problem is. You wanted me to pretend to be you—to be this version of you that you made up—so Peri could meet you in person. Or this other you . . . Hell, this is so mixed up you've got *me* confused. You want her to be in love with you, to stay in love with you. What did I do wrong?"

That stumped him. I knew he had to be upset, angry, confused. I knew that because, Method or no Method, I was myself upset, angry, and confused. One thing I wasn't, though, was a fourteen-year-old joker with a lot of money but very little experience with matters of the heart. "It was supposed to be just pretend," he said.

"You're only pretending to love her?" I asked.

"No. *You* were supposed to be just pretending."

I briefly entertained the idea that he had some kind of wild card mind-reading ability, but by this point I was committed. "Theodorus," I said. "We don't call it pretending, but for the sake of argument, yes, I *was* pretending." I was moving back into acting from bald-faced lying.

"She sounded . . ." He trailed off. If you've ever wondered what a kid whom fate has cruelly warped into an inhuman shape sounds like when he's choking back tears, well, he sounds just like any other kid choking back tears. "This was a terrible idea," he said.

I didn't have an answer for that. He was right.

It started raining a lot harder just then. The sound of it on the metal roof of the van was like a drum line, and the view through the windshield blurred. We sat there for what seemed like a very long time. Longer than you want a pause to go on in a play.

It was me who broke the silence. "What do you want me to do?" I asked.

Theodorus had withdrawn from where he'd been right behind me. In fact, he had retracted so far that his torso and arms had disappeared into his shell. His voice sounded shaky. "I don't want you to do this anymore," he said.

It seemed cruel to ask, but I had to know. "What about Peri? What about tomorrow?"

"I'll leave her a message. A family emergency, like you said."

But you're supposed to be all alone in the world, I thought. Oh, God.

"What do you want me to do now?" I asked.

"I want you to go away."

The rain hadn't let up, but I didn't bother asking Mr. Bomar for a ride back to my hotel.

The next morning, I was trying not to think about the events of the previous few days, and especially not the events of the night before. In order, I had considered and rejected the notions of contacting Theodorus, which I had no idea how to do, packing my bag and returning to the apartment where I'd been staying at the sufferance of the dinner theater management, which I wasn't sure would be allowed, and going to hang out at Peri's hotel and checking to see what time the bar started serving piña coladas.

I had rejected all of these ideas in turn because—it came to me like a punch in the stomach—I probably wouldn't be welcome any of those places.

So I was sitting in a chair in my fancy hotel room presumably being paid for by money from Theodorus's Christmas stocking or whatever, wondering when and even whether I was supposed to be checking out, and picking over the remains of my room service breakfast. The room came with a robe; I'd never stayed in a room that came with a robe.

I had just decided to call my agent on the assumption that I wouldn't have to foot the long-distance bill and was actually reaching for the phone when it rang. This took me aback for a second, but not nearly so much as the voice on the other end of the line when I answered, "Hello?"

"Mr. Fitzgerald," came the drawl. "This is Mr. Bomar."

"Oh," I said. "Oh, hey." I was trying to figure out what possible reason Mr. Bomar might have for calling me, then decided to hazard a guess. "Are you, um, are you calling about my fee?"

These days, with smartphones and all, you have the option of actually talking face-to-face over the phone. Back then, you more or less had to depend on the person you were speaking with to verbally express disdain. Mr. Bomar managed it with a slight sigh. I wondered if he'd ever acted. "No, Mr. Fitzgerald. My understanding is that there is an envelope waiting for you at your hotel's reception desk."

"Well, thanks. That's good. Because I have to tell you, Clovis, I just ate a thirty-dollar plate of scrambled eggs."

"That is of little interest to me, Mr. Fitzgerald."

"Right," I said. "Right. So, uh, what's up? How's your morning been?"

The pauses between sentences and words are as important a part of delivering lines on the stage as the dialogue itself. Those silences can communicate tension like almost nothing else. "My morning has been unfortunately eventful, Mr. Fitzgerald. It has been most unpleasant."

"I'm sorry to hear that, Mr. Bomar." You know? I really was.

"The unpleasantness shows no sign of abatement, Mr. Fitzgerald, because it has become necessary for me to insist that you come to my home."

Okay. Not what I was expecting.

"Well, like I said, I've already had breakfast, so . . ."

"Mr. Fitzgerald, I have arranged for a taxicab to pick you up in thirty minutes. You should be here within the hour."

This had gone on for about as long as I could take. "Why do you want me to come to your house, Mr. Bomar?"

This time the pause didn't feel tense. It didn't feel hopeful, it didn't feel cautious. It felt . . . worried. "Because Mr. Witherspoon used my address in his correspondence with Miss Peregrine."

"Okay. What's that supposed to tell me?"

"It's supposed to tell you, Mr. Fitzgerald, that this is where she came when she did not find Mr. Witherspoon in the offices of the English department at the College of Charleston."

Oh.

Oh, shit.

— — —

Mr. Bomar retired relatively young, so I actually only met him one other time after all this. I think it was around four years later, when I made my triumphant return to tread the boards of the Charleston Dinner Theater as Willy Loman. He actually came to the show with his wife and daughter.

Neither the wife nor the daughter was at home, though, when I knocked on the door of the suburban split-level ranch the taxi dropped me off at. No columns, if you were wondering.

Mr. Bomar opened the door, stepped aside, and pointed up a set of stairs. I guess he felt like he'd met his quota of talking to me for the day.

She was waiting in one of those dens that look like nobody ever sits in it. She was holding a coffee cup in both hands, her wings were folded behind her back, and it looked like she'd done some crying but was now past that part.

I stood in the doorway, as unsure of what to say as I've ever been in my life, before or since. She didn't look up at me, but she knew I was there. She said, "I don't shoot outdoors when it rains."

Of course. I didn't need her to line up the dominoes for me, not now that she'd knocked over the first one. The shoot was canceled, so she went to surprise her lover at work. Maybe give the under-grads a thrill and a reason to like the distinguished professor of Elizabethan poetry even more than they no doubt already did. But she couldn't find his name on the directory in the English depart-ment building, or maybe they didn't even have a directory, so she'd just gone straight to the secretary's office to ask for Professor Witherspoon's office number. Or it happened some other way. What was important was that all of the possibilities ended with her learning that nobody at his supposed place of employment had ever heard of a Professor Theodorus Witherspoon.

So what to do next? What to do when it turns out that your boy-friend isn't who he claimed to be?

Go to his house and confront him, of course.

Except it's not even his house.

Like I said, she didn't look up at me. Like I said, I didn't know what to say.

She did, though. "So, I know who I am," she said. "I'm an idiot. Now why don't you tell me who you are?"

"You're not an idiot," I said, like an idiot.

"You don't get to tell me what I am," she said, anger and sadness both in it.

"I'm sorry. I'm sorry, I don't know where to start. What has Mr. Bomar told you?"

She shot me a look. "Is that the man whose house we're in?"

I nodded. Clovis playing it close to the vest, as ever.

"Mr. Bomar has told me that he didn't have any cream and that he would have you here in forty-five minutes. Unless he was lying about the cream, he's told me one true thing then. Which is more than you can say, obviously, Professor Witherspoon. If that's your name."

This was going so badly. "No," I said. "No, I'm not him."

She set her coffee cup down on a side table, first carefully moving a coaster over to place it on. "You're not him," she said. "What's that supposed to mean? All those letters you sent, all the books and poems and cards. You obviously know all of that shit, so why did you pretend to be a professor of it? Why would I have cared?"

"I didn't—"

"Shut up!" she shouted. "Will you shut up?"

"No," I said. "No, you need to hear this. Listen, I did lie to you, I lied to you about everything, and I deserve whatever happens because of it and you deserve absolutely none of the hurt you're feeling. But the thing is, I'm not Theodorus Witherspoon."

Her wings moved then, fast, reflexive, like she was trying to take flight. A framed photograph hanging on the wall behind her was knocked awry—it was of a beach somewhere tropical. She ignored it. "You even lied about your name?"

"I don't know how to tell you this. No, I'm not Theodorus With-erspoon. But there really *is* a Theodorus. He's the one you've been writing all this time."

Confusion warred with the anger and sorrow on her face. "What the hell is all this?" she asked.

I tried to think of an answer, any answer that was true, that could come close to explaining this tangled-up situation. Finally, I asked her, "Do you know who Edmond Rostand was?"

Before she could answer, Mr. Bomar brushed past me into the room. He was dressed in his chauffeur's uniform and carrying a coat. "I brushed this dry for you, miss," he said. "And I've brought the car around."

Peri and I both looked at him, confused. "You already told me this isn't Theodorus's house," she said to him. "And you brought this . . . this man here to tell me he's not Theodorus. Who *are* you? Who are you *both*?"

Mr. Bomar held out her coat. "We are the accomplices," he said.

This time I sat in the front seat of the Duesenberg with Mr. Bomar. Once she had entered the back passenger area, Peregrine had reached over and slammed the door shut herself. Not that I had imagined she wanted me to sit next to her anyway. I could practically feel the ice of her gaze on the back of my neck and set-tled in for a silent and uncomfortable ride.

But, shocking me, Clovis Bomar began talking as soon as he pulled out of the driveway. "The Witherspoons have been a mon-eyed family in South Carolina since the late sixteen hundreds," he said. He took a hand off the steering wheel and waved vaguely in the direction of downtown. "Which is not unique among the wealthy and powerful of this city, of course. Their family history, like that of all their peers, is shameful."

Even if I had expected him to talk, this wasn't what I would have expected him to talk about.

"My faith, though, teaches the possibility of redemption. Now, I don't claim to know what redemption looks like for a family living in comfort so extensive that it is practically obscene. But I do know that there are families in this city who are wealthier than my employers, and whose characters test my belief in redemption far more than the Witherspoons. I've worked for some of them."

I noticed that he was driving much more carefully than he had on my previous ride out to the Witherspoon estate.

"But I am not the redeemer, of course. I am no judge. I am an observer."

We halted at a traffic light where we were apparently turning left. The turn signal of the old car was loud. *Click, click, click.*

"And it is my observation that Theodorus Witherspoon exhibits the potential to be a better person than his parents, who are better people than their parents were. Now, what does that mean?"

The traffic signal didn't have a left-turn arrow, so even after the light turned green, we sat there, waiting out oncoming traffic.

"It would take no great effort," Mr. Bomar continued, "for him to become a philanthropist of the sort who soothes his conscience and silences the ghosts of his ancestors through foundations and grants and charitable contributions. This is what his parents do, in fact. They have done, I suppose, good of some description. But they stay insulated from the people they believe they are saving."

In a bit of the old Clovis Bomar daredevil driving style, he sent the Duesenberg flying left across oncoming traffic in a gap I wouldn't have guessed the car would fit through. The driver of the car that almost hit us laid on the horn, but Mr. Bomar paid it no mind. Neither did I. I doubted Peregrine did, either.

I didn't turn to look at her during Mr. Bomar's oration. I wondered if she was listening. I found myself hoping she was.

"Young Mr. Witherspoon, though—Theodorus—has more than generosity in his heart. His magnanimity toward others is not self-serving. He does not seek redemption for himself, or even for others. He is . . . a dreamer. A dreamer of a sort that I have not encountered before."

The suburbs gave way to fields and forests.

"And what has happened to him will challenge his potential. His potential to do great good. His potential to redeem himself . . . himself, of course, being the only person he *can* redeem."

The ride was taking longer than I remembered from earlier in the week. I wondered if it was because Mr. Bomar was driving more sensibly or if it was because he was taking a more circuitous route, giving himself time to say his unexpected piece.

"Miss Peregrine, you are soon to learn some very painful things. More painful, even, than what you have already learned this morning. It may not be possible for you to forgive Theodorus for what he has done to you, just as it may not be possible for you to forgive me and this man sitting beside me. I do not ask your forgiveness, and even the apology I sincerely offer is tempered by the fact that my loyalty to Theodorus outweighs my shame at my role in this . . ." He trailed off.

"Farce," I offered.

"Tragedy," he said, then went on. "So, I understand if you will not honor, not even consider, my request of you."

There was silence from the back seat, but Mr. Bomar was a great one for silences. Finally, Peregrine said, "What is it? What's the request?"

"My request, miss," said Mr. Bomar, "is that you consider that what Theodorus has done, he has done from love."

Another long silence.

And then she said, "I know who Edmond Rostand was."

This time, the gates were open.

I still work, a little. The roles directors are willing to cast me in are limited, though, by my age and by the fact that my voice is raspy from projecting all those years. There are wireless micro-phones these days, of course, but the shows I'm in don't usually have that kind of budget, and even if they did, the venues are usu-ally small enough that they're not really called for.

So I'm semiretired, I suppose you could say. I saved up a little money over the years, though, and I get a check from Equity and a check from the Social Security Administration, and I more or less have an easy time of it. I never married, never had kids, never, as I've said, caught the big break.

I only watch television when somebody I know is on a show. I don't go to the movies because I don't like explosions or car chases. What I do these days is remember and read. The remembering has been well on display here. The reading, well, if I'm being generous with myself, I'd call it diverse, but more to the point it's diffuse. Disorganized and random. I read a lot of detective novels and a lot of biographies.

There's one book I return to again and again, though. A book that Theodorus sent Peri early in their correspondence, and that I first read—or tried to read; it's a challenge, or at least it's a chal-lenge for me—not long after I walked away from the Witherspoon estate and cadged a ride into the city off a guy who spent the trip talking to me about Jesus, which was kind of an interesting coinci-dence since I'd spent the trip out listening to Mr. Bomar talk about Jesus, in a more indirect and frankly more effective way.

Anyway, the book. Elizabethan poetry, of course. *The Faerie Queene* by Edmund Spenser. I won't relate the plot (plots) the way I did with *Cyrano de Bergerac* and I won't quote it at length. But I will quote it. Just one line. Book 4, Canto 6.

"For lovers' heaven must pass by sorrow's hell."

Theodorus Witherspoon and Peregrine were never lovers. But they sure put each other through hell. For Peregrine it was the revelation that the mysterious correspondent she'd fallen for was a kid, and a kid willing to lie to her and manipulate her for his own desperate reasons. For Theodorus it was the *fact* that he was a kid, that nothing romantic would ever come of it. Then there was my part in it, my role in his effort to live out vicariously, if only for a little while, if only for a day, the kind of relationship with Peri he wanted.

The last act started when Mr. Bomar called me to let me know she was at his house, waiting for a revelation she didn't really want and that he wasn't going to give her.

The last scene started when Peri and I made our way up the servants' stairs and down the plastic-lined hall to knock on the door of Theodorus's room. I'd already asked her if she wanted to know what he looked like or anything else about him before they finally met in person, but she demurred. For all her television experience since then, I don't think Peri could ever really be described as an actress. But she knew how to play out a scene, knew, somehow, that it was best if things happened the way they did, in fact, happen.

I knocked.

"Go away," came the voice from the other side of the door. "I'm not hungry."

"Hey," I said. "It's me."

He waited a minute. I don't know whether he was thinking about what to say or just trying to make me uncomfortable. Then he said, again, "Go away."

Then Peregrine said, "It's me, too."

In movies, people say, "Now wait just a minute!" In detective novels, the hero will pause a minute before saying something. These minutes aren't minutes, though. Minutes are sixty long seconds. What the writers of movies and novels mean, really, is that people wait for just a *moment*. And a moment is as long as you need it to be. Or want it to be.

Or want it *not* to be.

I think the wait from the time Peri spoke to the time Theodorus opened the door was actually a full minute, maybe even more. Measured in those long seconds, it dragged out. As a *moment*, though, it passed so quickly, it was so brief in the context of everything that had gone before. It was a pivot point, a measureless amount of time when everything hung in precarious balance.

I thought I'd done a pretty good job not blinking, either literally or metaphorically, the first time I'd seen my erstwhile director. But Peregrine put me to shame.

She took a look at him, nodded, then walked right past him to the Xerox machine where she stood looking up at the picture of herself as the Flying Cheerleader.

"I haven't seen this one in a while," she said. "I think they used the same tape to keep me in that outfit that you've used to hang this on the wall."

Theodorus flowed in a full turn so he was facing her. I stepped in and closed the door behind me. He still hadn't said anything. I noticed, though, that he was slowly doing the retracting thing, drawing the part of his body shaped like a normal human back into his shell.

"Don't," I said. "She deserves to hear what you have to say for yourself."

He turned his head, sharp, and glared at me. "What about what *you* have to say for *yourself*?"

Here's what I wanted to say. I wanted to say, *I'm an actor, I don't say anything for myself. I just recite what it says in the script.* But, and I've said this before, acting and lying aren't the same thing. So I took the coward's way out and kept my mouth shut.

"I don't want to hear from him, actually," Peri said. "And while I do want to hear what you have to say for yourself in general, Theodorus, first I have some specific questions."

Theodorus extended himself back out of his shell, just a little. He ponderously turned his head toward her, slower than I knew he could move. He nodded.

"How old are you?" she asked.

"Fourteen."

"Okay," she said. "Okay. How long ago did your card turn?"

He told her and I could tell she was doing some math in her head. "So you started writing to me before . . . before it happened?"

Another nod from Theodorus.

"What was the plan? At the beginning, I mean. I'm assuming you didn't concoct an entire persona and read all those books"— she gestured at the cases of textbooks and poetry and criticism— "before you wrote asking for an autograph."

"No." He sounded mournful. "That came later. When I read you like smart men."

"Well, you're certainly no slouch in the creativity department, I have to give you that," she said. "And you certainly convinced me of almost everything you told me in your letters."

If Theodorus had had any eyebrows, he would have raised one.

"They publish the names of people who win Bronze Stars in the paper, Theodorus. I have an assistant who mainly sits around reading Fern Michaels novels and is always glad for an excuse to go to the library on the clock."

Again, the slight drawing back into the shell. But he answered her, "Then why did you write me back? If you knew I made that up."

She lifted one side of her mouth. Half her glorious smile turned out not to be half as joyful at all. It was sad. "Because all of that stuff wasn't what interested me."

He said, "What did, then?"

"Oh, it was definitely the tennis," she said.

I couldn't help it. I barked out a laugh, then, horrified, put my hand over my mouth.

"I don't play tennis," Theodorus said, looking back and forth between us in confusion.

"I know that, you big dope," Peregrine said. And while he looked at her and blinked, I realized that she was surprising me again. I had intuited that she was kind, of course. But now here was a generosity of the heart that I had, frankly, never encountered.

Then she walked over to him. For the first time in my presence, she unfurled her wings. She held out her hands and said, "Here. Give me your hands."

Theodorus said, "Wait, I have to get gloves."

"No," she said firmly. "Give me your hands."

"It's . . . no, you don't understand. My skin . . ."

"I work in an industry where eighteen-year-old girls keep dermatologists on retainer," she said. "I'm used to skin that isn't perfect."

So he held out his hands.

"You," she said, "are not, cannot, and will not be romantically involved with me."

"I know," he said, ducking his head. "I know because—"

"No," she interrupted him. "No, you do *not* know the because. Or if you do, you haven't shown that you know it."

"I'm a freak," he said. "I'm a monster."

"You . . ." she said, dropping one of his hands, reaching up, and poking him in the chest, "are a fourteen-year-old boy. You are *not* a monster or a freak. Well, you have kind of a freakish ability to memorize thousands of lines of poetry, but that's not a bad thing."

When she lifted her hand, I saw a glistening drop of something fall to the floor. When she pressed her finger against his chest, it left an indentation.

"It's easier with the old poems," Theodorus said. "Because of the meter. You can kind of sing them inside your head."

"Okay then," she said. "That's interesting. But that's not what we have to figure out, you know? You're so smart, Theodorus. You're smart enough to know that a woman twice your age, even though she's a joker just like you, isn't in the cards."

"That's what I told him," I said.

"You shut up," she said.

"You're not a joker like me," said Theodorus.

"Why? Because I'm pretty and look like some people's idea of an angel?"

He nodded. So did I, in fact.

"That's bullshit," she said. "Do you think I *want* these wings? Did you know I've been to the clinic in New York and asked to cut them off? Did you know they *did*? But they grew back. They grew back in a day."

I was stunned.

"I know what it's like to want to be normal, Theodorus," she said. "But it can't happen for me. And it can't happen for you. But here's what you need to know about yourself. It was *never* going to happen for you, wild card or no wild card."

He looked confused. "Why not?" he asked.

"Because, you big dummy, you're a genius! You're a savant! You're growing up in a position to change the world, and I have absolutely no doubt that you will. I am declaring at this moment that you, Theodorus Witherspoon, will make the world a better place."

I'll never forget hearing her say that. I rarely talked to Theodorus about how we met, but I'm pretty sure that he never forgot it, either.

"But you're going to do it without me being your girlfriend," she added, and flashed the smile.

Theodorus giggled. Like an embarrassed kid.

Peregrine walked back over to the wall next to the Xerox. She reached up and unlatched a hook that I hadn't noticed before, and unfolded some shutters I hadn't noticed, either. I guessed she'd been in bedrooms in mansions more than me.

Light flooded into the room. She took a look at the windows.

"Do you mind," she asked, "if I take a little flight?"

What a gift, I thought. What a gift she was giving him.

"Yes!" said Theodorus. "I mean no! I mean, yes, fly, please!"

She opened the tall windows. "Do you have a way of getting outside?" she asked.

"Oh, I can glide right down the outside of the house. But then they have to spray off the brickwork."

"Give them a bonus, then," she said, and leapt.

You've probably only seen it on television. You've probably only seen her tightly furl her wings and dive through the air, spread them and catch a breeze, then fly in effortless, graceful loops, climbing and diving, on television.

You've seen nothing but a shadow play. You have not seen what Theodorus and I were so lucky to see that day.

Theodorus was pushing himself through the window, and I realized that I was soon to be left alone. I was sanguine about it. I knew an exit cue when I saw one.

I decided not to take the servants' stairs. I was kind of curious about the rest of the house and figured the worst the Witherspoons or any of their staff could do was kick me out, and out was where I was headed anyway.

The big central staircase struck me as a little tacky, actually. I reached the bottom and strode across the marble floor. Just as I reached the front door, someone called out from behind me.

An elegantly dressed woman with a teacup in her hand was standing beneath an archway, the entry to an enormous ballroom.

"I'm sorry, what did you say?" I asked.

"I said, and who might you be?" she answered.

"Oh! Sorry," I answered. "I'm the nominee for best supporting actor. Thank you for your consideration."

I saw her shadow racing along the pea gravel drive before I saw her. She gracefully landed right in front of me.

"Taking your leave?"

I took a bow. "Our revels now are ended," I said.

"You owe me something," she said.

I nodded. "Right, the truth. I will never be able to say how much I'm sorry for all this. How much I regret it."

"Do you really?" she asked.

"Am I really sorry?"

"Do you really regret it? All of it?"

Juliet's line came to me again. The way Peregrine laughed from her gut when something really struck her as funny. The way she was gentle with a lovestruck boy in a tragic situation.

"Of course," I said. "I should never have pretended to fall for you."

"Ah," she said. "Okay." Then she shot into the air.

I watched her go, my heart hollowing.

I sketched another bow.

I told you I was a good actor.

2010

In the Forests
of the Night

by Marko Kloos

The jet descended over a lush carpet of green that stretched from one end of the horizon to the other. Khan slid forward in his seat to get a better look out of the window, not caring for the moment that he probably looked like a tourist to the other people on Giovanni Galante's chartered private jet. He thought he'd had a concept of the rain forest in his head, but it turned out to be hopelessly myopic. To see this much wilderness, uninterrupted by the human clutter of towns or roads, was a little like coming face-to-face with the beating green heart of the planet itself.

This is what the whole world looked like before humans arrived and messed it up, Khan thought. The wildness of it all was breathtaking. Until now, he hadn't believed that his tiger half had come with a tiger's mind, but the sight of the jungle stirred something unfamiliar in his brain, a restless excitement at the thought of all the teeming life down there, a world full of prey for an apex predator.

They were already on final approach into the airport when he saw the first break in the jungle. They passed over a river that was a muddy brown ribbon snaking through the sea of trees, wider than twenty interstate highways. Once they were across, the signs of civilization began with a suddenness that was almost disorienting: roads and power lines, then buildings—multicolored metal roofs first by themselves, then in clusters and lines, right-angle geometry carved into the wilderness like gaping wounds.

"Welcome to Puerta de la Selva," Galante said from his seat across the aisle when the plane touched down on the runway. "The gateway to the rain forest."

In the seats behind Khan, Rafe and the third bodyguard, Jax, unbuckled their seatbelts even as the plane was still rolling down the runway, wheels thumping and engines whining under reverse thrust. Jax was as wide as Rafe was lean, smooth-shaven to Rafe's full beard, and almost as muscular as Khan. The bodyguard business was lousy with posers and braggarts, but these two new hires seemed to know their stuff, and Khan was glad that he wouldn't have to do all the heavy lifting on this trip.

The air that greeted him when the plane's door opened was surprisingly cool. He had expected oppressive heat and humidity, but when they climbed down the Learjet's ladder and onto the cracked concrete of the apron, it was maybe in the high seventies and a good bit less humid than Chicago had been.

"This isn't so bad," he said. "I thought it'd be hotter."

"Southern Hemisphere magic," Rafe said with a grin. "It's the middle of winter down here right now. I love coming here in August."

They walked into the terminal building, where the local police checked their passports and went through their bags with gloved hands. Khan noticed more than one wary look aimed in his direction, and the local cops seemed to be a bit more thorough with his bag than the others'. Finally, the police seemed satisfied, and Khan followed the others out of the terminal and onto the street.

"That wasn't so bad, either," Khan said to Galante when they were standing at the curb and waiting for their pickup. "Last time

I went abroad, they damn near gave me a full-body X-ray before they let me in."

"They don't care too much what we bring *in*," Galante said. "I pay them a pretty hefty landing fee to make sure of that. But you can bet your ass they'll go over everything with a microscope when we leave again."

Their ride was a large, upscale shuttle bus that looked wildly out of place amid the traffic of the city, where every other vehicle looked like it wouldn't have the slightest chance at passing a state inspection back home: old and well-used cars that had big dents and rust holes, rot inflicted on metal by a relentlessly wet and humid climate. The shuttle bus looked clean and new, and the inside was air-conditioned and stocked with bottled water and fresh fruit. A handful of other travelers had made their way onto the bus with Khan and the rest of Galante's entourage, and the four of them stood out in the group even more than the shuttle bus did on the road among the rolling junk heaps. There was a family of three, with a little boy of maybe six, who kept looking over at Khan and whispering in Spanish to his parents. Khan's mastery was limited, but he did understand *tigre* well enough. He thought about flashing his teeth at the kid and letting out a little purring growl for fun but decided against it.

The shuttle bus rumbled through the city on pothole-strewn streets. This was Khan's first time in South America, and he tried to take everything in from his window seat while sipping the complimentary bottled water. Everything felt just familiar enough— the brightly painted corrugated roofs, the throngs of people navigating the streets in overloaded cars or on well-used motorcycles that farted out blue exhaust—all the sights and sounds he knew from Central America. But there was just enough of a difference in the way everything looked that it made the place feel exotic and exciting.

They came to a stop at the riverfront ten minutes later. Khan looked around and failed to see anything that looked like a resort, only a boardwalk and a cluster of tourism-oriented shops.

"This is the place?" he asked.

Galante laughed. "No, this isn't it. You can't get there by road. It's a few miles down the river. The only way in or out. How do you feel about boats?"

"That greatly depends on the boat," Khan replied.

The boat was fine. It looked like something out of a fantasy movie with elves, an arched roof supported by intricately carved support struts, all light-colored wood and sleek lines. It came gliding up the river against the current from the north, cutting through the brown water with a foaming bow wave.

There was a small crowd waiting on the boardwalk near the dock. Khan scanned them out of habit to assess any potential threats. Some of the people here had arrived on the shuttle bus with him—the Spanish-speaking family with the little boy, a quartet of young men who were obvious rich kids out for a good time, and a few older couples in expensive attire. None of them raised Khan's concern level, but one of the people on the boardwalk stood out to him for reasons that had nothing to do with security.

Over by the far end of the boardwalk, a woman was looking out over the water at the approaching boat. She was wearing sunglasses and an elegant light-blue jumpsuit that left one of her shoulders bare. A matching pair of weekend bags stood by her feet. She wore her black hair in a braided updo that hinted at a lot of length. All in all, Khan thought that she was one of the most attractive women he had ever seen. He was wearing his own sunglasses, and he kept his head moving to make it look like he was checking out the sights around them like almost everyone else, but he couldn't help glancing over at the woman far more often than was necessary for a security assessment. In the sunlight, her skin looked like it had the same shade as his own, which made him guess she was of Indian or maybe Middle Eastern descent. Her jumpsuit looked expensive and tailored, and left no doubt that she was fit and very shapely.

The elvish boat pulled alongside the dock to tie up. A minute later, the crew had secured a gangway with a rope railing, and the group of resort guests began boarding.

Rafe and Jax were seasoned enough that Khan didn't have to tell them to board last, to make sure no potential attacker could choose to sit near them. When they stepped onto the boat at the back of the group, Khan saw that the woman he had spotted earlier was sitting near the back. The remaining seats were club-style, every two rows set up to face each other, and he sat down with Galante and the others, picking the side that let him watch the back of the boat. He glanced at the woman. If the tiger half of his face gave her any pause or surprise at all, she wasn't showing it. Her expression remained detached and relaxed behind her sunglasses.

Then they were on their way down the river. The engines of the boat were electric, so quiet that Khan could only hear the splashing of the screw at the back of the hull as the captain throttled up. "Odd spot for a resort," he said. "It must cost a fortune to keep the place supplied."

Rafe shrugged. "Ecotourism is all the rage right now. Sustainability and all that. And our friends charge plenty for the experience. It doesn't exactly cater to the budget traveler crowd."

Khan nodded. Every major criminal outfit had a way of turning illegal money into aboveboard profits. There was some admirable ingenuity in combining a socially responsible trend with a bulletproof way to launder dirty money, he thought.

They were almost in the middle of the river now, hundreds of yards from the shoreline, the dock half a mile behind the boat already. The water looked like coffee with a lot of cream, heavy with muddy sediment from the rain forest. Khan watched the wildlife nearby for a while, birds circling overhead and diving toward the water in quick dashes to snatch unseen fish. After a few minutes, he chanced another look toward the woman in the back of the boat's open-air cabin. To his surprise, he caught her gaze just as she turned quickly to avert her eyes, and he felt a heady little rush of excitement when he realized that she had been looking at *him*.

You're either a green assassin, or you like what you see, Khan thought. *I really hope for both our sakes that it's option B.*

The resort was nestled into the jungle on the shoreline where the Amazon made a long and lazy quarter-mile bend. Two dozen rustic cabanas stood in a wide semicircle amid the trees, surrounding a central lodge that was two floors tall and still managed to look like someone had put it together out of driftwood over the years, with a thickly thatched roof and wooden beams that had the appearance of centuries of age. Khan had learned enough about the expenses involved in making something new look convincingly old to know that this resort had cost a fortune to carve into the jungle, ten miles away from any roads or other infrastructure.

Their cabana was one of the units closest to the river. From the central lodge, walkways made of large tropical hardwood tree slices led to all the cabins like the spokes of a truncated wheel. Khan left Rafe and Jax with Galante at the lodge, which had a large restaurant and a swank-looking bar, then went ahead to the cabana by himself to do the initial security sweep. Once he was convinced that nobody had hidden any explosives or other unwelcome surprises, he went back to the lodge to fetch the others.

"What do you think?" Galante asked when they walked into the cabana Khan had just scoured for twenty minutes.

"It's as clean as can be," Khan said. "There's a lot we won't have to worry about without mobile networks out here."

"I mean *this*." Galante gestured at their surroundings. "Pretty fucking nice, isn't it?"

"It's posh," Khan admitted. From the outside, the cabanas looked basic and a little rough, but the luxury on the inside could hold its own against any high-end resort he'd ever visited: marble counters, polished hardwood floors, tasteful and obviously expensive furniture.

"Four bedrooms," Galante said. "I'm in the master suite. You three sort the rest out any way you want."

The three smaller bedrooms were all roughly the same size, so Khan picked the one closest to Galante, to have the shortest distance to the principal if something went down in the middle of the night. Rafe and Jax didn't seem to care much about their room assignments. Khan had them move into the bedrooms by the main entrance, where they would be the first line of alarm.

"We'll shout for you if anything goes down," Rafe said to Khan when they were all squared away.

Khan flashed a grin, and he saw with a little bit of satisfaction that Rafe jumped just a tiny bit at the sudden baring of the tiger teeth.

"If anything goes down, the odds are pretty good that I'll know it well before you," Khan said.

The resort had been pretty in the daylight already, but when the sun began to set, it transformed the place into something different altogether. The orange sky muted the vivid green of the jungle and gradually darkened it into blue and gray hues. The walkways from the cabanas to the lodge were lined with solar-powered lights, and as the sunlight faded, they came on one by one, glowing in the gathering darkness and outlining the paths with overlapping little pools of warm, golden light. And all around the resort, the jungle came alive with sounds, nocturnal animals stirring from their rest and beginning their own days.

With Galante hanging out at the lodge bar with Rafe and Jax by his side, there was nothing to do for Khan, who didn't feel like drinking and socializing tonight. Instead, he took a stroll across the property to reinforce the map he had been drawing in his head, then walked down to the river to look at the sunset.

The entire stretch of the resort's waterfront was a wide strip of manicured grass, interspersed with bushes and small trees, and some guests were mingling on the lawn to watch the sun setting beyond the jungle canopy. Khan was looking for a particular face, and after a few moments, he spotted it down by the water's edge.

The last few yards from the lawn to the river were a ledge of red clay, and the woman he had noticed earlier on the dock and the shuttle boat was walking on the clay with bare feet, taking slow and measured steps that told Khan she was savoring the experience. She was carrying white leather sandals in one hand, holding them by the heel straps. She had changed out of the light-blue jumpsuit she had worn on the ride here. Now she was wearing a sleeveless blouse and a summer skirt that ended just above her knees. As he was watching her, he felt an unusual pang of anxiety. He had never considered himself shy when it came to talking to women, not since his card had turned. The ones who were repulsed or scared by his tiger half usually made their distaste or fear unambiguous, and the ones who were intrigued by it seldom needed much encouragement to approach him. But right now he felt as insecure and awkward as he had been when he was still skinny and nerdy teenage Sammy Khanna, bottom entry on every girl's romantic wish list at his school.

For a moment, that new anxiety almost got the better of him, and he thought about turning around and going back to the lodge. But then she turned around to walk back the way she had come, and their eyes met before Khan could pretend to be looking somewhere else. She flashed a friendly smile at him, and he returned one out of reflex.

This isn't fucking middle school, he thought. *And I'm not shy little Sammy anymore.* He walked toward the river and nodded at the dark water behind the woman. "I have no idea what wildlife hides in there," he said. "But if they have alligators here, it's their hunting time right now."

"They do have alligators," she replied. "Black caimans. One of the biggest crocodilians on the planet."

She had a distinctly British accent that sounded incredibly attractive to Khan's ears.

"And you're not worried about ending up on the menu?"

She smiled again and shook her head. "Caimans are pretty rare these days. And I'd be a tough dinner to catch." She looked over her shoulder at the water. "Also, they have steel netting out right in front of the resort. It's bad business to let your guests get carried off by the local wildlife."

He laughed. "I suppose it is."

"Don't worry. I know this is a nature preserve, not a petting zoo."

They had been closing the distance between each other gradually as they were talking, and now Khan was standing right at the edge of the grass while she was on the edge of the clay, six feet away.

"You look like you wouldn't have anything to worry about out here," she said.

"I don't know," he replied. "A large alligator would be an interesting problem. But I'd hate to have to get into it with an endangered species."

She stepped onto the grass and put her sandals down, then slipped her feet into them. Somewhere in the darkness of the forest beyond the clearing, something rustled and splashed, and she looked that way, sudden alertness in her posture.

"Not a caiman," he said. "One of those water-pig things. I forgot what they call those."

She chuckled. "A tapir?"

"Hey, it's my first time in the jungle," he said. "Appearances notwithstanding."

"Can you see in the dark with that tiger eye?"

He nodded. "But not as well as you'd think. Just rough shapes and movement. My hearing is much better."

"So you could *hear* that it wasn't a caiman?"

"High center of gravity, walks on hooves, rustles the under-brush about this high up." He brought his hand to his waistline to demonstrate.

"You can hear all that exactly from a hundred yards away? I guess nobody ever gets to sneak up on you."

"Not usually."

"Quickly, and don't turn around. How many people are walking around on the grass behind you?"

He listened intently for a few seconds. "Seven. Two couples, three people by themselves."

She laughed brightly. "You were not just making that up. Impressive."

Khan had felt instant physical attraction to people before, but never like this. It was as if the specific combination of her appearance, smell, and voice had tripped a switch in his brain that had never been activated before, some sort of hormonal amplifier he hadn't known to be there.

She held out her hand.

"I'm Maryam."

It took him half a second to get over the case of sudden paralysis that had befallen him—an eternity in tiger reflex time. Then he shook her hand. Her grip was smooth and firm. "Samir," he said. As soon as the word was out of his mouth, he realized that he hadn't introduced himself by his proper first name in years.

"It's nice to meet you, Samir."

"You as well," he replied.

"Those blokes you came with on the boat," she said. "Friends of yours?"

His bodyguard sense kicked in again at the seemingly innocuous question and overrode the hormones, albeit with some effort. "Yeah," he said. "We're just taking a long weekend to get away from it all. Digital detox, and all that."

"This is definitely the place for that," Maryam said.

"What about you?" Khan asked.

She laughed. "You'll think it's kind of dumb."

"Try me."

"I made a bet with my sister. I was going to spend my holiday out at the oceanside resort in Lima. She saw an article on the reserve in *National Geographic* and said I should come here instead. She said there was no way I could go without a screen for an entire week and a half."

"No kidding," Khan said with a chuckle.

"I have a thousand quid riding on it."

"I don't think that's dumb at all," Khan said. "Even if I don't know exactly how much that is in dollars."

"I'd look it up, but it seems we don't have any network coverage out here," Maryam replied, and they both laughed.

By now, the setting sun was completely out of sight beyond the trees, and the lights from the lodge drew long shadows across the lawn. All around them, nocturnal creatures chirped and screeched in the jungle, thousands of voices in the warm evening air.

"I guess I should get this clay off my feet now before these sandals get stained permanently," Maryam said.

"Don't let me keep you," Khan replied. "I should go see what my friends are doing. But it was nice talking to you."

She looked at him for a moment as if in consideration. "I'm going to be frank with you. I didn't come here to pick anyone up. Or to get picked up by anyone. But maybe we can have a drink together sometime this weekend."

"I'm not here for that, either," Khan replied. "But I'd love to sit down with you for a drink. In a not-a-date sort of way."

"All right, then. It's a not-a-date. I am sure we will find each other."

She walked up the lawn toward the lodge, and Khan smiled as he watched her stride away.

I very much hope so, he thought.

The cartel people arrived the next afternoon on one of the little elvish boats. Khan accompanied Galante down to the dock to welcome them. It was a cloudy day, with a light breeze that rustled in the treetops, and the water of the river looked a bit choppier than yesterday, little foam crowns topping the ripples on the surface.

The cartel bossman was a stocky guy with curly black hair and a three-day beard shadow. He stepped onto the deck and greeted Galante with a hearty handshake. "Giovanni, amigo. Good to see you again." He looked over at Khan. "You brought a new face this time."

"This is Khan," Galante said. "He's been with me for a while, but he wasn't with me the last time I came here. Khan, this is Ernesto. We're going to be doing a lot of business with him in the future."

Ernesto nodded at Khan, who returned the gesture.

"Pleasure to meet you, jefe," Khan said.

Behind Ernesto, his two bodyguards appraised Khan from behind their sunglasses. They were mirror images of each other, obviously identical twins, dressed alike in every detail. Ernesto clearly didn't have any security concerns because he was already walking up the dock toward the lodge with Galante, strolling past Khan without an ounce of anxiety showing in his scent or his body language. His bodyguards followed, carrying weekend bags in each hand.

They had barely sat down at a table in the lodge restaurant when the waiter showed up with the first round, lowball glasses with a honey-colored drink in them that was topped by foam and dusted with nutmeg.

"Traditional welcome," Galante said to Khan and handed him a glass. "Ever had a *guaro*? Aguardiente. It's the national drink down here."

Khan had no idea what kind of liquor *guaro* was, but the drink smelled far less strong than he had expected, and when he took a sip, he was pleased to find that it was a tasty combination of anise and fruit. "*Está bien*," he said. Ernesto nodded his approval.

They finished their drinks, and another round came to the table. Khan tried to get the measure of Ernesto's bodyguard twins, who were named Antonio and Bernardino. They were jovial and chatty with Ernesto and Galante, but whenever Khan said something, they merely listened with polite interest and didn't engage, and he stopped trying after a while. When the group got ready to order dinner, three rounds of drinks later, he excused himself and left the table, detailing Rafe and Jax to watch Galante.

Outside, the sun was setting again. Khan walked the perimeter of the lodge to check for unusual sights or sounds. Then he went back to the cabana and did another thorough security sweep. Just like yesterday, there was nothing in the cabana that hadn't been brought in by them, and nothing was disturbed or out of place. It wasn't the first time he had been brought along by a client as security eye candy, but this place was such a low-threat environment that it felt like he was collecting money for nothing.

With zilch else to do, he walked around the lodge and down to the riverfront. To his disappointment, there was no familiar face watching the sunset from the dock tonight. He went to the edge of the dock and stood for a little while to watch the lengthening shadows on the water and listen to the noises of the animals in the jungle.

Maryam came around the corner of the lodge just as he was walking up the lawn again. Tonight she was wearing an emerald-green summer dress, one that sported a much shorter hem and a much lower neckline than the one she had worn the night before. Her hair was gathered at the back of her neck with a matching green ribbon. As she came closer, he could see that it was long enough to cascade all the way to her lower back. "Fancy bumping into you down here again," she said. "It seems we both have a thing for water."

"I like being near it," Khan said. "It relaxes me. But the sad truth is that I swim like a leaden duck."

She laughed and tucked a loose strand of hair behind her ear. "Is that because of the cat thing?"

He shook his head. "I was a really bad swimmer even before the cat thing happened."

"I apologize if that sounded like I was stereotyping your appearance," she said, and now it was his turn to laugh.

"It's a common assumption," he said. "I really take no offense."

"I'm glad." She looked a little flustered despite his reassurance.

"How has your day been?" he asked to get her mind off the subject.

"Quiet," she said. "It's a nice change from my usual pace, I must say. I took the canopy walkway tour this morning. It really is wild out there. I must have taken about five hundred pictures. How about you? How was your day?"

"Same," Khan said. "Minus the canopy tour in the morning. It feels weird to walk around all day without a device constantly going off in your pocket."

"I felt it buzz a few times anyway, but it was all just in my head," she said. "Phantom texts."

"I left mine on the plane. Wasn't thinking about pictures. Now I wish I had brought a proper camera. Remember those? A gadget that only did one thing?"

"My father has one that still uses film," Maryam said. "Remember *that*? I tried to teach him the whole digital thing, but he won't get in front of a computer. He's happy to stay in the twentieth century."

She looked back at the lodge, where the sounds of low voices and clinking dishes came through the mosquito screens on the open windows. "Do you have any plans this evening?" she asked.

"No, I don't," Khan replied without hesitation.

"I'm starving. Would you like to have dinner? We can do that not-a-date. I mean, while the opportunity presents itself. In case we don't run into each other again."

"I would love to have dinner with you," he said. "I mean, have dinner at the same table with you. In a completely un-date-like manner."

Maryam laughed. "All right, then. Let us have dinner in friendly proximity."

The lodge was a wide-open space where almost every table was visible from almost every other table. The only few spots that would have kept them out of sight of Galante and Ernesto's group were taken by other guests. When Maryam and Khan sat down together, he glanced over to Galante, who gave him a leering smile and a nod before returning his attention to the group.

"You're not having dinner with your mates tonight," Maryam observed.

"We're not really *mates*, to be honest," Khan replied. "We just travel together. They are doing a business retreat."

"And what are you doing while they are having their retreat?"

"I'm keeping an eye out. I'm in the security business. Personal protection."

"You're a *bodyguard*?"

He nodded. "What about you? What do you do for a living?"

"It's terribly boring," she said. "I work in international public relations."

"I don't think that's boring at all."

"Well, I've been on a few business retreats myself. I've been to international conferences. And I've traveled with a lot of company presidents. I rarely ever see a bodyguard with them. Especially not one like you. Your friends must be working in a much more interesting field than most people."

"They're in the import/export business," Khan said.

She smiled wryly. "Oh, I am quite sure they are."

The waiter arrived with the menus, which were appropriately eclectic for an eco-resort in the middle of the jungle. They spent some time perusing the options and talking about the entrées on offer. "*Piranha*," Maryam said. "I don't think I've ever had that."

"I can honestly say that I've never had that, either," Khan replied.

"Then let's try it," she said. "Let's get a little daring. I can get steak anywhere."

"I'm up for it," Khan said.

"Excellent." There was a twinkle in her eye when she said it.

"I did want to ask you about that tiger eye," she said. "If you really don't mind."

"I do not," he said. "What do you want to know?"

"What's it like?"

"My left one can see in the dark. But it's color-blind, and it's never in sync with the right one. It's like they are tuned to different wavelengths. I always see two pictures. I got headaches from that for years. Now my brain has learned to tune out one eye and just ignore the feed."

"How about that," Maryam said.

"In fact, the whole tiger side is a pain in the ass sometimes," he added. "Everything is asymmetrical, not just the eyesight. I get hotter more quickly on the left because of the fur. The left arm is stronger, so I can't max out weights at the gym without getting lopsided on the lift. And all my clothes need to be tailored to measure. And I mean *all* my clothes."

She laughed, and he was glad to hear the sound of it.

"That's not so bad," she said. "And I am sure it comes with perks."

"It does," he admitted. "But I am not going to lie. Sometimes I do wish I could trade those perks in just to be my old self again. My scrawny, symmetrical self."

Maryam smiled wistfully. "I would say that I know that feeling," she said. "But I'm sure I really don't, so I won't assume."

Khan returned the smile. From three feet away, she was beautiful, but from across the table, leaning toward him the way she did, with her gaze focused on his face, she was heart-stoppingly gorgeous. In the protection business, one of the oldest cautionary tales was that of the honey trap: the attractive person showing up in the principal's orbit who was seemingly tailored to the romantic tastes of the bodyguard. *Enchant, ensnare, distract.* But he had his instincts and his ability to smell stress and fear. He could tell that she was holding back on a lot of things, but there was no malice coming from her. He didn't know whether all the things she told him were the truth, but he knew that *she* believed they were true, that she hadn't manufactured them just to appeal to him.

I'm either extremely lucky, or she is extremely skilled and I am about to be the world's biggest dumbass, he thought.

For all its exotic flair, the piranha was just a fish, but at least it was a tasty and expertly prepared one. The wine was an exceptionally good pairing, and over the next two hours, they drank most of the bottle over dessert and post-dinner conversation. Khan noticed that Maryam could hold her liquor remarkably well for someone who was less than half his size. She was smart and funny and quick-witted, and he couldn't remember when he had last enjoyed talking to someone else this much.

Over at the table across the room where Galante and Ernesto were still holding court, the head count of their group had grown as the evening went on. The table for six had become a table for ten, expanded by another tabletop carried over and put into place by the lodge staff, and four women were sitting with Galante and his cartel friends. Under normal circumstances, Khan would have been right by Galante's side to make sure none of the new additions to the party had ill intent. But Galante had Rafe and Jax, and the women looked like they were not there entirely by fortunate happenstance, Khan had enjoyed a bottle of Colombian Chardonnay on top of a nice meal, and nobody seemed concerned about threat levels or close protection tonight.

If they are going to treat it like a party, then maybe I shouldn't feel bad about playing along, he decided.

They were long finished with their flan and almost at the bottom of the second bottle of wine when their waiter came over to the table. "Just to let you know, it is now nine o'clock and the kitchen is closed. They will turn up the music for the next two hours. The bar will be open until eleven if you wish to continue with your beverages."

"Thank you." Khan nodded at the waiter.

They looked at each other as the waiter walked off toward the kitchen.

"They will turn up the music," Maryam repeated. "Wonder how loud it will get in here."

They had the answer a few minutes later. The waitstaff moved half a dozen tables from the center of the restaurant and did some well-practiced reconfiguring, and the music from the speakers on the ceiling changed from classical background ambience to Latin dance tunes just a notch or two below nightclub-level volume.

Khan made a face. "I don't mind salsa at all. But this is a bit much."

"I agree," Maryam said. "This won't do at all. I don't want to have to shout for the rest of the evening." She put her napkin on the table in front of her and pushed her chair back. "What do you say we take the rest of this bottle of wine and then go for a walk outside where it's a little quieter?"

Khan looked across the room at the table where Galante and Ernesto were living it up with their entourage. The girls were now strategically distributed, each with a guy on either side, and they were all engaged in what looked like a local version of beer pong. Neither Galante nor Ernesto seemed at all concerned about being murdered. Between the two of them, they had four bodyguards at the same table. One more sitting nearby wouldn't make the slightest bit of difference. He resolved to come back in a bit to show presence again, but from the looks of it, this crew was going to stay here until closing time and probably well past. Nobody would miss him for a while yet.

Khan pushed back his own chair and got up. "I think that's a fantastic idea. Let's do it."

Outside and away from the lodge, Khan almost sighed with relief at the relative lack of noise.

"That must have hurt your ears," Maryam said.

"You have no idea," he replied. "It's like someone poking my eardrums with a shrimp fork."

"I'd say that I can imagine, but I know I probably can't."

"I have to hang out in nightclubs with clients. It's part of the job. But I have a special set of noise-canceling earbuds for that. Trouble is that I left them at home. Didn't think I was going to need them out here in the jungle."

The pathways from the lodge to the cabanas were lit up again with the solar-powered lamps, long chains of warm electric fires flickering in the darkness. The jungle was far from quiet, but all the chirping and screeching was music to his ears compared with the high-volume musical assault in the lodge. Khan didn't quite know whether it was caused by all this wilderness or the attractive company walking with him, but he felt like all his senses and emotions were amplified tonight.

"I want to show you the spot I found today while I was walking around," Maryam said. "It's rather neat."

"All right," Khan said. "Lead the way."

She walked around the lodge and down a torchlit path that didn't connect to any cabanas. Instead, it led to the nearby tree line, where it disappeared in the jungle. Khan saw the little pools of light from more electric torches glowing in the darkness amid the trees. He looked back at the lodge. *He's got Rafe and Jax and the twins,* he thought. *If something goes down, I'll hear it. I can be back there in fifteen seconds.*

If anyone had put this scenario in front of him as a theoretical exercise, he would have slapped the shit out of any protection team member who went along with it. She could be leading him away to clear the path to his principal, to make things a lot easier for a hit squad. But there was no sense of danger in the air. Maryam looked back over her shoulder to see if he was following, and there was a smile on her face and a twinkle in her eye that went to his head more than the wine they had just finished over dinner.

Fuck it, he thought. *If I die, it will be a sweet death. And if there's no danger, I'll end up kicking myself forever.*

He followed her down the path and into the forest. The torches marked the way as it was snaking through the underbrush. Even the managed jungle at the edge of the resort was so dense that he couldn't see the lodge or any of the cabanas anymore once they were a hundred feet beyond the tree line. The sounds fell away, too, until the thumping Latin beats from the lodge were muffled and indistinct.

At the end of the path, a hundred yards into the jungle, there was a little clearing. In the center was a cluster of small pools, arranged in a rough circle around a massive tree stump. There were shelves nearby with rows of folded towels, and a drying rack next to it. When Khan stepped closer, he saw that the tree stump was artificial but carefully crafted to look hundreds of years old just like the buildings at the resort. The pools were all carved out of the foot of the stump, but set at different heights, and the craftsmen had made privacy dividers between each pool that looked like gnarled roots. The water was obviously from an artificial source, so clear that it could only be filtered, and so warm that the surface was steaming a little in the humid night air.

"Nobody's here," Maryam said with a chuckle. "I figured the place would be full in the evening. But I guess nobody wants to walk off into the jungle at night." She looked at him and bit her lower lip. "What do you think? Want to get a little wet without the risk of turning into caiman dinner?"

He looked at the pools. The moonlight that had made it through little gaps in the jungle canopy around the clearing was painting silvery stripes across the surface of the water.

"I didn't bring a bathing suit," he said.

She smiled and shook her head. "*Bathing suit.* You Yanks and your puritan streak."

She reached up behind her neck and untied the ribbon that held her hair loosely together. Then she gathered it all up and used the ribbon to hold it in place in a quick updo. A moment later, she had slipped off her loafers and climbed out of her summer dress. Underneath, she was wearing a white bra and panties that seemed rather sheer to Khan even in the low light.

"There, that will do just fine," she proclaimed. She took a towel off the rack and walked around the artificial tree trunk until she found a pool that was at the right height for her liking. As she climbed in, she looked over her shoulder at him.

"Come on. Or are you shy about taking off your shirt?"

There were offers that were safe or even wise to refuse, but Khan quickly decided that this was not one of those. He unbuttoned his short-sleeved shirt and peeled it off his body, then kicked off his shoes. His khakis came down a moment later. Now he was down to his silk boxer shorts, but it still seemed like he was wearing about four times as much fabric on his body than she was.

The water of the pool was deeper than it looked from the outside. He stepped in and found that it reached a fair bit above his waist. His boxer shorts billowed up around him, the thin silk inadequate as makeshift swim trunk material. Maryam was a good deal shorter, and the water was all the way to her shoulders. The part of the pool closest to the central trunk had a sitting ledge, and she let herself float up onto it. Her underwear made no better swimwear than his own; her white bra was clearly not designed to remain opaque when wet, but it didn't seem to bother her at all.

Khan had never been shy about the appearance of his body since his card had turned, but he hardly ever found himself in a situation where he unexpectedly had to strip down in front of an attractive woman. He felt an unwelcome sense of self-awareness—something he hadn't experienced since gym day in middle school, when he'd had to bare his skinny and bony pubescent body to his classmates. But Maryam didn't show any indications that she was repulsed or turned off by the fact that the left half of his body was covered in orange and white fur with black stripes, that the left side of his face had three-inch canine teeth, or that rough white whiskers were jutting out from his upper lip. She just watched him with a little smile as he submerged himself slowly until he was in the water up to his shoulders.

"You're really built," she said when he had settled in on the ledge next to her. "Was that one of the cat perks?"

He nodded. "I was a hundred and ten pounds soaking wet before the cat event," he said. "Once I was through, I was more than twice that, and most of it muscle."

"I've never met someone like you."

"You mean a joker-ace?"

"They'd call you a knave where I live."

"Knave," he repeated. "Not sure I'd like that one any better. A lot of people back home are using 'jack' for that now. The younger ones."

"That's what *we* call a sailor. Clearly someone needs to standardize all this. It can get so confusing."

"Two countries, divided by a common language," Khan said, and she laughed.

"Samir," she said. "Indian?"

He nodded. "The old man came over from Punjab. And went right back there after I started to look like this. What about you?"

"I was born in Tehran. We left when I was two, when the Ayatollah took over. But I've been well and truly British ever since. Much to the dismay of my parents."

"I know that tune all too well," Khan said.

She lowered her voice a little for effect. "They'd be scandalized that I am in a hot tub with a strange man in my *underwear*. They think I'm way too modern to find a good husband. I suspect they are right. At least as far as their definition of 'good husband' is concerned."

"Well, they have nothing to fear, right? I mean, it's not like we're on a date or anything."

She smiled and shook her head. "Nope. Just some friendly proximity."

He hadn't really been aware that their faces had been gradually drifting closer to each other until she kissed him. It was a short, careful, exploratory sort of kiss, and the pleasant shock of it traveled through his nervous system like an electric surge.

"Close proximity," he murmured when she pulled back.

"Very close," she said. Then she leaned in to kiss him again. When he responded in kind, she scooted closer until her body was up against his, and he wrapped his arm around her to keep her from drifting away. This kiss lasted a lot longer than the first one. When their lips parted again, Khan felt his heart beating in his chest as if he had just run a sprint, even though he had barely moved a muscle in the last few minutes.

"That felt different," Maryam said. "In a pretty good way."

He nodded his agreement, unwilling to speak and risk sounding like a stammering imbecile. It felt like the temperature in the pool had increased by ten degrees. From the way his boxers had billowed out again in a way that had nothing to do with water movement, it was pretty clear that his body agreed with her assessment as well. Maryam put her hand on his chest, right on the demarcation line between skin and fur, and followed it down, tracing the line precisely. When she reached the waistband of his boxers, she didn't stop there.

"My," she said. "This *certainly* feels different."

Only the sound of approaching voices kept Khan from blowing multiple circuit breakers in his brain all at once at her touch. There were people coming up the walkway toward the moonlit pools, announcing their presence by softly talking and laughing in the darkness. Khan didn't know who they were, but right now he hated them more than he had ever hated anyone in his entire life.

She pulled her hand away and scooted back on the sitting ledge to create a little bit of space between them again, much to his regret. The voices came closer until they were right on the other side of the big tree stump behind them. They were talking in a language Khan didn't understand, maybe Portuguese, and the hushed giggles he heard made him think they had spotted the discarded clothes on the ground nearby.

"What are the blooming odds?" Maryam whispered. She pushed back a bit more until she slid off the seating ledge and stood in the deep part of the little pool once more. "Let's go," she said in a low voice. "Back to my cabana. Before I lose my nerve."

"I'm going to need just a minute," he replied.

She smiled and rolled her eyes slightly. "*Puritans.* I'm in Unit Five, last one on the right, by the water. Five minutes. Do *not* make me wait or there will be a nuclear explosion."

With that, she climbed out of the pool and picked up the towel she had left on the ground. She wrapped herself in it and walked off toward the spot where they had left their clothes.

"*Hey,*" he whispered after her. Maryam turned around, and he mimicked covering himself up to the neck. She walked out of sight, then returned with a fresh towel from the rack and tossed it in his direction. He caught it before it could land in the water in front of him.

Five minutes, she mouthed. Then she strode off, a smile on her face.

When he got to her cabana, she met him at the door, and he didn't make it five steps into the place before she wrapped herself around him and initiated a fast and furious Round One, which took place against the wall of the hallway. For Round Two, they migrated to the bedroom a little while later, and she turned down the heat to a slower boil, straddling him and controlling the rhythm and energy of their coupling. An indeterminate time later, he took the reins for a Round Three in the living room, causing the catastrophic structural collapse of a coffee table that had looked much sturdier than it turned out to be.

Round Four started under the shower in the bathroom and ended up back in the bedroom. However long Khan thought his dry spell had been, hers seemed to have been at least as long, because her willingness to keep ringing that bell appeared to have no limits in sight yet. Eventually, they disengaged from sheer physical exhaustion in the middle of Round Five, and they both stretched out on the bed underneath the labors of a ceiling fan that was utterly inadequate for dissipating the heat or evaporating their sweat.

"Now my parents would *definitely* be scandalized," Maryam murmured as they were lying next to each other, and they both chuckled.

"I thought you said you weren't looking to pick anyone up," Khan replied. He felt like he had just done a marathon with a hundredweight of bricks strapped to his back.

"Well," she said. "Something came up that made me change my mind."

The lights in the cabana turned off all at once, and the fan above the bed started to slow down. They watched the blades spin until they came to a stop, too drained to do anything else at the moment.

"Eleven o'clock," Khan said. "It's candles and torches from now until sunrise."

"Too bad. That fan was the only thing keeping me from combusting."

He closed his eyes and listened to the sounds of the animals and the splashing of the water on the riverbank a few dozen yards outside the bedroom window. He'd had no shortage of sexual encounters since he had become Khan—in the sorts of circles he moved as a bodyguard, there was always *someone* interested in an exotic fling—but nothing he had ever experienced had come even close to what had happened in the last hour or two.

"We could go back to the pools," he suggested without opening his eyes. "Or take a dip in the river. Take our chances with the caimans."

"My muscles are pudding right now," Maryam replied. "All of them. Let's take a bit of a breather first, shall we?"

"Let's," Khan agreed.

He listened to the world outside again. By now, he was in tune with the sounds of the jungle, and it was much easier to let his brain filter all the auditory input to find potential threats and dangers. But nothing out there was amiss as far as he could tell. The music from the central lodge had stopped, and there was a blissful silence coalescing as people left the restaurant bar and made their way to their cabanas for the night. The steady background mur-

muring of the nearby river was almost as good a soporific as the sexual release he'd just had. Together, they managed to make his limbs feel like they weighed five hundred pounds.

Next to him, Maryam's breaths had turned deep and regular. Khan gave himself permission to drift off as well, and he could feel the fog descending on his brain almost immediately.

Just a bit of a breather, he thought as he fell asleep.

When Khan woke up again, it was still dark outside and a light rain was falling.

He looked over toward the window and saw raindrops splashing against the mosquito screen and bouncing off the sill, darkening the wood of the bedroom floor underneath the open window with moisture. When he turned his head the other way, he saw that Maryam was gone.

He sat up and swung his feet over the edge of the bed. The tired achiness from earlier had disappeared again, wiped away by his rapid recovery factor while he was asleep. He got to his feet and walked over to the window to look outside. There was a light breeze driving the rain squall, and he welcomed the cool sensation of it on his face.

Khan walked out of the bedroom and through the other rooms of the cabana to look for Maryam. The hut was dark and quiet. All the windows were open for airflow, and the smell of moist soil was everywhere. He didn't know the exact time, but he could tell that it was well before first light. There were faint voices and laughter coming from the middle of the resort, where Galante and Ernesto were still socializing with their entourage in the lodge by candlelight.

Maryam was nowhere in the cabana. The place still faintly smelled like her, but his nose was not good enough to sniff out any clue to where she could have gone. His bodyguard sense was stirring again in the back of his brain and refusing to be quieted this time, as much as he wanted to suppress the notion that something wasn't quite right.

He found his clothes and put them on. Then he walked out of the cabana and stopped just outside to get his bearings without wooden walls all around him.

There was a new sound on the wind, very faint but noticeable in its out-of-placeness. It was a mechanical flapping, barely more than the idea of a whisper. He turned his head to let his ears pinpoint the source of the noise. Whatever was making that rhythmic flapping whisper was coming from the southwest, from upriver, the direction of the nearby city. He stood for a few moments to let the sound sink in, to let his brain dissect and analyze the pattern. When he realized what he was hearing, the surprise and nausea he felt almost lifted him off his feet.

I really am *the world's biggest dumbass,* he thought.

He took off running down the path toward the central lodge. The sodden ground splashed under his feet as he dashed for the lodge in the straightest possible line, ignoring the illuminated path of tree slices. The distant sound was louder now, close enough for him to hear it over the splashing of his shoes in the wet grass and the thumping of his heart in his own ears. Any remaining doubt in his mind about the possible source of the noise was gone from his mind. He knew what was coming toward them through the rainy night, and he knew what it meant because there was only one plausible reason *why* it was coming.

The helicopter appeared above the edge of the resort clearing, right by the riverside above Maryam's cabana, just as Khan leapt up the stairs of the lodge and wrenched the doors open. The staff had shuttered all the windows to keep out the wind and rain, and the inside was only dimly lit by some candles and oil lamps over by the bar and at the only occupied table in the room. Just as he had suspected, Galante and Ernesto were still up and drinking, along with their entire entourage. From the looks of it, they were far further in the bag than just a bottle of Peruvian white. When the door banged open, the twins whirled around in unison and stood up from their chairs, but one of them swayed and the other had to reach out to keep his brother on his feet.

We are so very fucked, Khan thought.

"Helicopter," he shouted at the group. "Coming in overhead from the city."

Ernesto cursed in Spanish. Rafe and Jax got to their feet as well, and they were only moderately steadier than Ernesto's twins. The women who were still with the entourage looked at each other in alarm.

"Fuckin' narcs," Galante said. He pushed back from the table but didn't make any move to rise like his bodyguards. Outside, the sound of the helicopter rotors was now drowning out all the other noises. Khan looked back through the open door and saw the dots from red and green laser beams dancing on the grass between the lodge and the edge of the jungle. Overhead, the helicopter pulled into a sharp nose-up flare and slowed to a halt in midair. With his tiger eye, Khan could see that the doors were open, and that someone was kicking ropes out of the chopper. They fell down, one on each side, and hung just above the ground, twitching and swaying in the downdraft from the rotors.

Khan pulled the doors shut and retreated into the restaurant. "We got a team fast-roping down," he said. "Are we fighting or running?"

"No fucking where to run," Rafe said. "And nothing to fight with."

"Let them come," Galante said. "If they're narcs, we can post bail by tomorrow afternoon. If they're some other cartel, we're fucked anyway."

Ernesto didn't seem to agree with Galante's assessment of the situation. He launched an angry diatribe in Spanish at Galante that went almost entirely over Khan's head except for "*tu puta madre*," which gave him the rough gist of it. Then he barked an order at his twin bodyguards, who squared off toward the door in the middle of the restaurant as if they were truly getting ready to take on whoever was about to come through.

Khan gave them space and went back toward Galante. "We don't want to be here if those lunkheads start fighting," he said. "I don't want to die in the middle of a crossfire. Kitchen. Back door. *Now*."

Outside, the helicopter revved its engines and climbed back into the sky, which told Khan that the strike team was on the ground and moving in. He pushed Jax aside and grabbed Galante by the arm to pull him out of his chair. He barely had his boss on his feet when the front door behind them burst open with the sound of splintering wood and groaning metal. Khan pulled Galante down onto the ground, then kicked the table over behind them, as inadequate as it would be as a ballistic shield. He knew the standard cop procedure, and he knew what was going to happen next, and there wasn't a damn thing he could do about it. He covered Galante with his body and cupped his own ears with his hands.

The flashbang grenade went off in the room by the door. Knowing it was about to go off didn't make it hurt any less even though he had his hands firmly on his ears. The explosion shook the room and killed his hearing instantly, replacing all the auditory richness of the nighttime environment with a shrill whistling sound that made his brain feel like it was getting bisected by a bandsaw at full speed.

When the initial pain had started to lift a little, Khan rolled over and peeked around the edge of the table he had tipped over. The restaurant was crisscrossed with aiming lasers and high-powered flashlight beams from half a dozen weapons. Two people in black uniform were lying off to one side, writhing in pain or at the edge of consciousness. Three more stood in the room just a few steps beyond the door. "*What the fuck?*" Khan said out loud. His voice sounded distant and muffled even to his own ears.

In the middle of the room, in the spot where Ernesto's bodyguard twins had squared off just a few moments earlier, a gigantic crocodilian took up most of the space between the overturned table and the door. It looked as black as the night in the beams of the weapon lights aimed at it, and it had two heads and a pair of thick tails. When it rose on its legs and raised its stance, Khan saw that it had six legs, three on each side.

Not a crocodilian, Khan thought. *An alligator. A two-headed fucking caiman. The motherfuckers are aces. Or one single ace together.*

The Antonio-Bernadino-caiman seemed to be in no mood to surrender. It whipped its heads around and let out a warning hiss that cut even through Khan's still-impaired hearing, and the insides of its mouths looked like something out of a capybara's nightmares, all teeth and black-streaked velum. Two of the cops opened fire with their submachine guns. From the effect it was having on the pissed-off two-headed caiman, it was no more effective than if they had thrown tennis balls. It lunged at one of the cops and snapped at him with two enormous jaws. The cop saved himself with a mighty leap backward, and the jaws snapping shut on thin air sounded like a double thunderclap in the confines of the restaurant. Another one of the cops tried to dash around the flank of the caiman, but one of the alligator tails whipped around and knocked him across the room and into a wall. Everyone except Khan was shouting—the cops, Ernesto, Galante, Jax, and even the usually cool and levelheaded Rafe. The women who had kept the cartel boys company were screaming as if someone had started a decibel contest.

Enough of that shit, Khan decided. He rolled over, grabbed Galante by the wrist, and made a low dash toward the bar and the kitchen beyond, dragging the other man with him.

They were three steps into the kitchen when the back door flew open and three black-clad narcs in body armor and face masks burst into the room, guns at the ready. Khan pushed Galante to the ground and launched himself at the nearest of the trio. He seized him by the front of his body armor and shoved him into one of the other cops with all the force he could muster. They both went down, yelling in distress and surprise. The third narc leapt to the side to avoid his colleagues and brought his gun up to aim it at Khan. Even with his reflexes and the quickness of his tiger arm, he barely got his hand on the suppressor at the end of the muzzle in time to deflect the weapon. It barked out a short burst of gunfire that hit a rack of pots and pans on the wall behind Khan. He seized the gun by the suppressor and ripped it out of the narc's hands, but it was attached to his body with a sling, and the man got jerked forward along with his weapon. Off balance, the cop stumbled and crashed into Galante, who was still prone on the floor where Khan had pushed him. Khan jumped forward and pulled the narc off Galante by the back of his vest. Then he threw him headfirst into the nearest dish rack, six feet away. The rack collapsed under the impact with a loud crash and buried the cop in a noisy avalanche of plates and bowls.

The other two narcs were scrambling to their feet behind Khan. They had almost made it when he reached them again. He cut their weapon slings with his claws, shredding the ballistic cloth on their vests in the hurried process, and ripped the guns away from them. Then he threw them through the open door and out into the darkness. One of the narcs backed away, hands raised in surrender. The other reached down for the pistol holstered on his thigh and closed his hand on the grip. Khan made a fist with his right hand and smashed it into the narc's helmet. The cop dropped to the ground so hard that his helmet bounced off the wooden floorboards of the kitchen. The other one still had his hands up, yelling something at Khan in Spanish that was beyond the scope of his high school language classes. It sounded genuine enough in its panicked fear, but he couldn't take chances and end up with a bullet in the back. He grabbed the narc and hurled him over to his unconscious colleague in the remnants of the dish rack, where he bounced off the edge of the nearby counter and joined the other cop in the pile of broken dishes.

Behind them in the restaurant, the caiman hissed again. It sounded even louder and angrier than before. Something crashed hard into something else, to the sound of suppressed gunfire and splintering wood.

Khan went over to Galante, who was still hunkered on the floor with his hands covering his head. "Time to get the fuck out of here," he said, and pulled Galante to his feet. "Let's go."

He rushed his boss out of the kitchen and through the back door, which was hanging askew in its frame and flew away into the darkness with one hard kick. They went out onto the wide strip of grass between the lodge and the nearest cabana. To their left, the river murmured in the darkness. To the right, on the lawn around the corner of the lodge, the fight between the huge two-headed, six-legged caiman and the drug cops had spilled out into the open. Khan crouched at the corner and watched the scene for a moment to gauge the situation. It was clear that the narcs hadn't brought nearly enough people or guns for this particular fight. The three or four remaining cops retreated from the caiman, guns blazing. The caiman was shockingly fast and nimble for something of its size. With its two heads and twin tails, it was hard to flank from any angle. The cops were trying to hold their ground, but it was clear to Khan that they were holding on to the short end of a nasty stick. Overhead, the chopper appeared again and hovered above the resort, adding the high-powered beam from its search-light to the general mayhem of the scene.

On his left, Khan saw movement out of the corner of his eye. Someone came out of the tree line near the path to the relaxation pools and made a straight line for the Antonio-Bernardino-caiman. For a moment, Khan's brain refused to process what he was see-ing. The woman who strode onto the grass in front of the lodge seemed to expand and stretch with every step, though she was still recognizably Maryam. She was barely out from between the trees when her summer dress was bursting at the seams with a dull crack that sounded like a suppressed gunshot. He watched in awe as she shrugged off the fabric shreds and strode forward with determination, seemingly growing a foot or two with every yard she covered. She was naked now except for some silky green fabric stretched across her loins and her long, flowing hair covering her breasts. When she was in front of the caiman, she was taller than the trees at the edge of the clearing, twenty feet at least, and her last few steps shook the ground perceptibly.

"Fuck *me*," Khan said, keenly aware of the fact that the woman who was now the height of a telephone pole had done just that to him not too long ago. *Is everyone a secret ace tonight?* he thought wildly.

Twenty-foot Maryam seized the gator by both heads as it lunged toward her and yanked it off the ground with a battle cry that rattled the wooden shutters on the windows of the lodge. They both crashed down onto the grass together, spraying sod and mud everywhere. It was a wrestling match of the titans. On the ground, Khan could see that the gator was not much shorter than Maryam was tall in her ace form. Under normal circumstances, he would have loved to stick around and see the results of the battle. But Galante, next to him, looked like his faculties had taken a temporary leave of absence, and Khan was reminded that he still had a job to do.

"That way," he said to Galante and yanked him to his feet.

They went down the grassy slope on the other side of the lodge, away from the battle that was unfolding. Khan had no intention of swimming to the other side of the river in the dark, but he knew that nobody was running the stupid little elf boats at night, either, and that the resort probably had someplace to park them for the night.

Behind them, Rafe and Jax came out of the kitchen side door. *"Wait up,"* Rafe yelled after Khan.

"Took you long enough," he shouted back.

They rushed to catch up with him, clearly shell-shocked but in better mental shape than their boss, who was only slowly gathering himself.

"I told you there was no place to run," Rafe said.

"I'm not *running* anywhere," Khan replied. "But they go in and out of here by boat. They have to keep those *somewhere*."

"Boathouse." Jax pointed to a structure at the far end of the dock, a low-slung wooden shack that jutted out partway over the water.

They rushed over to the boathouse, which was locked with a padlock that Khan wrenched off the door with a twist of his wrist. Inside, four of the wooden ferryboats were tied up on one side of the boathouse. On the other side, two rigid-hull inflatable boats were moored, and each of them had an outboard engine the size of a small refrigerator.

"Maybe the evening isn't totally going to shit after all," Khan said. "Look for keys. And I hope one of you knows how to drive a boat like that because I don't have a fucking clue."

Ten minutes later, they were a mile up the river, plowing upstream with one of the resort's inflatable motorboats, Rafe steering from the back with the tiller on the outboard motor.

"We're making one hell of a shiny wake," Rafe yelled against the noise from the motor, which was pushing them against the river current at full throttle. "If they come across us in that chopper, they'll spot us in no time."

"You stay on that fucking throttle. We need to get to the airport and get the hell out of here on the plane," Galante said. "Some of those narcs ate it. I got no mind to stay in this shithole for the next twenty years."

The trip downriver had taken almost an hour on the little elven boat, going with the current at sightseeing speed. The outboard motor on the inflatable was made of far sterner and more practical stuff, even if it wasn't as ecologically friendly as the electric elf boats. Fifteen minutes after they had left the resort's boathouse, the lights of the city river dock appeared in the darkness ahead. Rafe cut the throttle and maneuvered them to a tie-up spot.

"Unless you know how to fly that plane, we're going to need the pilot back," Khan said.

"No shit," Galante replied. He fished his phone out of his pocket and turned it on. "Oh, thank fucking God. There's a network." He dialed a number and held the phone to his ear. It took a while for the other party to pick up. "Steve," Galante finally said. "Get your ass to the airport right now and preflight the Lear. We are getting the fuck out of here."

Galante listened to Steve, who seemed to have some objections to the directive from his boss that Khan couldn't quite make out. Galante's expression darkened as he listened. "I don't give a shit if you have to fly that motherfucker in your underwear," he said. "Skip the flight plan. You can file it when we're airborne. And we can refuel in Panama along the way. Get that bird ready to taxi in fifteen, unless you want to find out how much weight you can lose on Colombian prison food." He ended the call and jammed his phone back into his pocket. "Go and find me a taxicab somewhere in this dump."

If there were any taxi drivers out there looking for business in the predawn darkness, they didn't seem eager to accept it from three obvious Yanquis, one of them a half tiger. The two cabs they tried to flag down drove past as if they didn't exist. It was a slow and arduous thirty-minute uphill walk from the riverside to the airport, which seemed an amazing distance to Khan considering the small size of the town. As they walked the empty streets, he expected a bunch of Colombian squad cars to show up any minute and surround them, for some free steel bracelets and a lengthy stay in a state-run hospitality facility. But if there were cops around, they were as unwilling to get entangled with them as the cabbies because they reached the airport without anyone stopping or accosting them along the way.

The grungy little airport terminal was empty. Outside, the Lear was standing on the apron, engines running and position lights blinking. They climbed up the airstair one by one and filed into the passenger compartment. Khan glanced at the pilot on the way past the cockpit to verify that the man had been able to put on pants before heading to the airport.

"What a fucked-up night," Rafe said. "I don't think that deal with Ernesto is going to happen."

"Fuck Ernesto," Galante replied. "And those fucking guys he brought. Coulda bought those narcs off if he hadn't let his boys off the leash." He dropped into a seat and glared at the open cockpit door. "Get this fucking thing rolling, Steve," Galante shouted at the pilot. "We're on the clock here. They figure out where we went, we're in a world of shit. That includes you, idiot."

Jax pulled up the airplane door and latched it, and he and Rafe took their own seats. Khan buckled in right away out of habit even before they started to taxi. It was a small airport, so it didn't take Steve long to roll along the single taxiway and line up with the runway. Khan allowed himself a relieved breath. In thirty seconds, they'd be up in the air, and nothing short of an air force intercept would get them back on the ground and into local custody.

While the plane was taxiing, Galante had gone to the Lear's bar nook and gotten four glasses and a bottle of bourbon. Now he offered one to Jax, Rafe, and Khan in turn. Jax and Rafe took theirs. Khan shook his head. "Suit yourself," Galante said, and dropped back in his seat. "I sure as hell need one after tonight."

The pilot goosed the engines, and the plane began its takeoff roll. Khan looked out of the window at the unexciting scenery outside, rusty airport perimeter fencing and a lot of darkness beyond. He listened to the increasing frequency of the tires going *thump-thump-thump* over the concrete segments of the runway as the plane picked up speed.

Then the pitch of the engines dropped again. The pilot put on the brakes so hard that Galante spilled his drink and almost slid out of his seat. "What the *fuck*, Steve," he yelled at the cockpit.

Through the open cockpit door, Khan saw something large approaching them from the far end of the runway, long dark hair and a lot of bare wet skin glistening in the beams of the plane's landing lights. Maryam came toward them at a quick trot, still twenty feet tall at least, blocking the runway with her bulk. The plane came to a shuddering stop.

"You have got to be shitting me," Galante said next to Khan. "The fuck did *she* get here so fast?" He looked around at his bodyguards and gestured toward the cockpit's windshield with his mostly empty glass. "Well? You gonna do your fucking jobs or what?"

Rafe barked a laugh. "What do you want us to do, boss? I left my bazooka at home."

Khan unbuckled his seatbelt and stood up. The other three looked at him as he straightened out as much as he could in the low cabin and flexed his tiger arm.

"I'll give it a shot. You guys stay put. She'll turn you into paste."

"She's three times your size," Rafe said.

"The bigger they are, the harder they fall," Khan said with a confidence he wasn't feeling right now. "I have good reflexes." He made his way to the aircraft door and opened it. "Back up and get ready to goose it," he told the pilot. "You get a clear shot down the runway, you get these guys the fuck out of here."

"See, there's a man who knows how to earn a paycheck," Galante said.

Khan suppressed his sudden desire to flip his boss the bird.

Then he took a breath and went down the airstair and onto the runway.

Let's see if I can keep her from turning me into paste, he thought.

Maryam was standing in the middle of the runway, a hundred yards from the plane, doubled over and breathing heavily. Seeing her in twenty-foot format gave Khan a feeling of cognitive dissonance. Just a few hours ago, he had been on top of her body, and she on top of his. She was the same woman in every detail, just many times her usual size—and judging by the fact that she had likely beaten the shit out of the Antonio-Bernardino-caiman, many times her usual strength as well. She watched him as he trotted toward her, obviously aware of the fact that the plane wasn't going to go anywhere as long as she stood where she did.

"Well, that turned out one hell of a date," he said when he was in conversational range.

She looked at him, and he thought he saw something like relief on her face. "It wasn't a date," she said. "Remember?"

"Yeah. Just friendly proximity."

She straightened up and started to walk toward him. He extended his claws. If she had kicked that double-headed caiman's two tails, there was no way he could take her in a straight-up fight, but there was no way he'd let her claim him without one.

"Put those away, Samir," she said. "I don't want to fight you."

"I go by *Khan,*" he replied. "You kept that whole ace thing from me."

"Well," she said. "That's part and parcel of the whole 'secret agent' job. I go by Jiniri. I'm an agent for the Silver Helix."

"International relations," he said.

"Well, it is, in a way."

"Jiniri," he repeated. "The Silver Helix is British. What are you doing here in Colombia?"

"Multinational drug interdiction task force," she said. "Twenty percent of the cocaine coming into Heathrow comes from Colombia. This was a joint operation. Lopping off the head of the snake. Two years of planning. They knew there were some aces in play, so they wanted me as backup." She looked at the Lear behind Khan. "We have their cartel friend. And they're not going anywhere. I know it's your job to protect them. But I will take them in and wait for the backup team to get here. I'm sorry."

"I can't let you do that," he said. "My boss is watching."

"You are really going to risk your life for that low-life slimeball?"

Khan shrugged. "I can't just collect a paycheck and then skip out on the job when the chips are down. That would be unprofessional."

Time was on her side, and they both knew it. If the narcs knew where she had gone, it wouldn't be long before they showed up in force. As much as he didn't want to test his abilities against hers, he had to take action now or accept defeat.

He charged at her, all senses alert for her countermove. It came in the form of a swipe from her right arm, but it seemed a little slow, as if she wanted to get him out of the way without hurting him too much. He dodged the swing and leapt past Jiniri, raking her thigh with his claws as he went. She let out a pained groan and turned to face him again. This time she swiped at him with her foot. She was much taller and stronger, but all that mass needed some time to get into motion, and his reflexes were excellent. He dashed underneath her leg and raked her other thigh, this time just above the knee, drawing blood again. He rolled away, narrowly avoiding another blow from her right hand. When he got up to face off again, he saw that his claws had given her two new tattoos, five parallel gashes on each leg that were oozing blood.

For the next round, he let her come to him. She moved more cautiously now, with shorter strides and less range to her swipes. There was still too much inertia in her kicks and swings, but he had to dodge every single one with plenty of margin because her reach was so much longer than his, and he found himself getting winded already even though they had been at it for less than a minute.

"It's like I am fighting with water," she said with what sounded like grudging respect. "That caiman was easier."

"I can do this all night," he said, trying to not sound out of breath.

Jiniri grimaced and put her right hand on one of the slashes he had inflicted. He briefly felt sorry when he saw the obvious pain on her face. "Damn, that's going to hurt like hell when I go back to regular-sized me," she said.

"I hope you heal faster—" he began. Then he jumped back when he realized she was trying to feint. He almost avoided the jab from her hand as it lashed out, but it still clipped his shoulder and the side of his head, and he flew backward for what felt like ten feet. He rolled back to his feet reflexively, his head ringing. Her follow-up was a kick that launched him into the air again. This time, it felt like he was airborne forever. When it finally came, the impact knocked all the remaining breath out of his lungs.

He rolled over and looked up to see her striding toward him with purpose. If their turn in the sheets earlier had made her feel soft enough toward him to moderate her first attack, he doubted she'd hold back now, not with him drawing blood and carving three-inch furrows into her flesh. He stood up slowly and settled into a low crouch to prepare for her next attack.

Behind her, the Lear's engines went to full throttle, and the jet leapt forward on the runway. Jiniri's head whipped around. Then she turned and started striding to intercept the jet on its takeoff roll. Khan dashed forward and leapt onto her back, using his claws for leverage as he went.

This time, she actually cried out in pain. Her hair, which fell down all the way to the small of her back, was as good as climbing ropes at her current size, but he had no doubt that it wasn't pleasant to have all three hundred pounds of him hanging off her scalp. He tried to wrap his arm around her neck, but it was like trying to hug the steel truss of a suspension bridge. She got to one knee and reached back with her right arm to pry him off her back. He let himself slide down her cascading hair to avoid her hand, then climbed back up on the left side of her. The Lear roared down the runway, picking up speed every second. Jiniri shouted out in frustration and reached for him, this time with both hands. He had to let go to avoid her grasp, and he dropped back down to the grass behind her. When she made for the runway once more, he jumped forward and raked his claws across one of her heels. She bellowed and went to one knee again.

He anticipated her swing as she whipped around, but her backhand caught him by surprise. For a moment, the world went *earth-sky-earth-sky* again. Then he was on his back on the grass next to the taxiway. He felt the vibrations of the ground as she ran off to catch the jet, but it roared past before she could reach it, a second or two too late.

Khan closed his eyes and listened to the sound of the Lear screaming into the night sky at full throttle. His chest felt like all the ribs on one side and most of the ones on the other were thoroughly broken. Even with his healing factor, it would hurt like hell for a good while.

When he opened his eyes again, Jiniri stood over him, one foot on each side of his body. If she wanted to squish him into the soil, he wouldn't be able to evade, not after the beating he had just received. "I hope that was worth the price," she said. "I should have seen that coming. I think I may suck at being a secret agent."

"You're a good secret agent," he said. "I absolutely believed that you really had the hots for me."

She looked at him as if in contemplation. Khan felt something like an electric surge, an energy that made the air taste like metal and smell like ozone. Then Jiniri started to shrink in front of his eyes, inch by inch and foot by foot. Ten seconds later, the woman standing astride him was Maryam again, back to her regular size, the way she had been when he had met her.

He still had his claws out. Her ace power was overwhelming, but her normal self seemed as fragile as anyone else her size. He knew that he would be able to beat her easily in her current state, that he could cut her to ribbons before she could go back to her giant size. But he also knew that she had made herself vulnerable again for a reason.

"*Ah. Ow,*" she said, and sat down hard on the grass next to him. The wounds on her legs looked so much bigger now than they had when she was twenty feet tall, and Khan felt a sharp pang of remorse. "That hurts a lot."

"I am sorry," he said. "You should have stayed the way you were."

"It'll pass," she replied. "I do heal. It's just not fun for the first few minutes. Damn, that's worse than a gunshot. It's like the world's worst razor cuts."

He sat up with a groan of his own, and they sat next to each other in silence for a little while.

"I do have the hots for you," Maryam said. "That was not a deception. I almost fucked up the mission because of that. The arrest team showed up thirty minutes ahead of schedule and I wasn't ready. Because my mind was somewhere else."

"I really, really want to believe that," Khan said. "Because it's a lot more pleasant than the idea that I got played."

She flashed a sad smile. "I didn't play you, Samir. *Khan.* I didn't *need* to play you. Your boss wasn't even the target. We were after the cartel."

He looked down at his tiger hand, which still had its claws extended, glossy black three-inch knives that could chop a side of beef in half with a single swipe. She was vulnerable now, but she had assumed that state to prove her sincerity, and he had no desire to hurt her again now that Galante was safely off the ground and on the way home. He retracted his claws slowly.

"Sometimes this job asks for a little too much," he said.

"Tell me about it," she replied. Then she leaned in and kissed him on the lips. "I'm glad you weren't there when the arrest team put the cuffs on everyone."

In the distance, he heard the whirring of helicopter blades, composite foils beating the air into submission in a distinctive mechanical fluttering pattern he could detect from miles away.

"Chopper on the way," he said. "Friends of yours?"

"The backup team," she said. "Colombian drug enforcement. And some SAS blokes."

"SAS," he said. "That will be one hell of an arrest attempt."

She shook her head. "I can't do anything about your boss. I was just too late to the punch, I guess. They'll be a little pissed off at the office back home. But we got the main target." She pointed at the darkness beyond the runway. "You know, Brazil is just a few miles to the east from here. And Peru is fifteen miles to the south. It's easy to cross that border away from official paperwork nonsense."

"That's good to know," he said.

By now the helicopter was close enough that she could hear it as well. She looked in the direction of the rotor noise, *whop-whop-whop* reverberating from the nearby hillsides in a foreboding echo.

"Get out of here," she said. "I really want to see you again someday. And that's no secret agent rubbish."

Khan shook his head with a smile. "It had better not be," he said.

She plopped back on the grass and closed her eyes. On her legs, the gashes he had inflicted were already starting to close. He was glad to see that her healing factor was at least as fast as his own. "For what it's worth, it really was one hell of a friendly proximity," she said. "Best one I've had in years."

"Same," he replied.

This time, he was the one leaning in for the kiss, and she responded to it eagerly. When their lips parted again, he felt contentment and regret, two conflicting emotions duking it out in his head, refusing to blend like oil layered on water. Whatever this was, it was not bound to happen again anytime soon, if ever.

"Goodbye, Samir," she said. "Take care of yourself."

"You, too, Maryam," he replied.

Khan got up with a low groan. Then he trotted off into the darkness on still-unsteady legs toward the sound of the nearby river, the smile still on his face.

2013

The Wounded Heart

by Melinda M. Snodgrass

"Honestly, I think most actresses make a *terrible* mistake trying to dress like the character when they go for an audition. First it's *quite* disrespectful to the costume designer, who has their *own* vision of how the character should look, so you've already put someone's back up when you come waltzing in wearing a Dior full-skirted dress complete with pumps and gloves and a pillbox hat."

It was such a specific and detailed description that Detective Francis Xavier Black—known to friends and enemies alike as Franny—could only assume that some rival for the part his girlfriend, Abigail Baker, had been seeking had done just that.

Still, the artless prattle that tumbled from her lips brought a small smile to his. "And honestly, most fifties styles were just *hideous*. Well, not the little-black-dress. That's classic and timeless and still quite chic. Coco Chanel really did understand elegance."

The cold February wind blowing through the glass and steel canyons of Manhattan set Franny's topcoat to flapping about his legs and Abigail shivered. He slipped an arm around her waist and pulled her close, wondering what Chanel would have made of Abby's tattooed arms, the pierced upper lip, and the black hair accentuated this week with streaks of bright red.

"I think the fact I just showed up in leggings, combat boots, and that oatmeal sweater showed them that I had *total* confidence in my acting abilities, and I didn't need to rely on that kind of . . ." Her nose wrinkled adorably as she searched for the right word. ". . . artifice."

They had taken the subway from Jokertown up to Columbus Circle to celebrate the fact that the rival in the full-skirted Dior dress had not actually succeeded in landing the part. Instead it had gone to Abby, which was why they were about to have a celebratory dinner at Per Se, one of New York's finest and hottest restaurants.

"And you were right. You got the part," he said, smiling down at her.

She wrapped her arms around his neck, stood on tiptoes, and gave him a head-spinning kiss. Franny sighed into the embrace, wondering anew how, after years of longing, he had finally begun a relationship with this charming, lovely, ditzy, exasperating woman. There was no measure by which he was as interesting as her previous lovers. He was just a nat, possessing none of the extraordinary powers the wild card virus had bestowed upon the fortunate.

But perhaps, he thought, that was the appeal. Abigail was an ace—though her power was probably more annoying than useful. She acted like a shortwave radio, picking up the powers of random aces and jacks around her, though only at partial strength. It had led to some notorious (and hilarious) disasters over the years. In Franny's arms, such catastrophes could not occur. He was the safe—*dull*, his treacherous mind amended—choice.

But also suddenly famous. Is that why she finally agreed to date you? It was a hateful little thought, and Franny pushed it firmly away.

"Of course I shall now have to forgo all of this for the performances," Abigail said, ruffling her hair, touching the piercing. "I think I can cover the tattoos with makeup should they want me in a short-sleeved dress," she added as they entered the lobby.

The moment they stepped out of the elevator onto the fourth floor of the Time Warner Center, the aroma of the food abruptly morphed into the scent of blood and corruption. Franny swallowed hard, forcing down the nausea. When he'd checked out the restaurant online, he had a feeling the nouvelle cuisine was going to send him back to Abby's apartment hungry. Now it seemed his treacherous mind didn't want him to eat at all. He assisted Abigail out of her ankle-length coat, shrugged out of his topcoat, and handed both garments to the coat check attendant.

Abby did look wonderful in her white wool dress and high-heeled boots. Franny was wearing a suit, but then, as an NYPD detective, he always wore a suit. There was only one way for a man to signal elegance and that was a tux, which most men only wore at their wedding. He slid a sideways glance at Abigail and wondered if she ever thought about weddings . . .

A maître d' who looked like she ought to be walking the runway at a fashion show escorted them to their table. Franny opened the menu and felt his wallet, along with his gut, cringe. A waiter popped up almost immediately to take their drink order. Abby ordered her usual glass of Chardonnay. Judging from the price, it was going to be better than the box wine she usually kept at the apartment. Franny asked for an Irish whiskey, neat.

She laid a slim hand over his, and he noticed her nails had been freshly done. The length made them look more like talons with their deep-red mirrored finish. He tore his gaze away. *Blood dripped from my fingertips after I pressed my hand to Jamal's neck, searching for a pulse I knew wouldn't be there, but I kept hoping . . .*

". . . like them?" Her voice seemed to be coming from a vast distance.

"Huh?"

"Do you like them? Or are they too . . . Vampirella?" She twiddled her fingers in the air. "Since I switched from blue to red for the hair, I thought this would work, but now I'm not at all sure."

His crushed skull had leaked red into the tight black curls.

"I mean, it will all have to go once we start rehearsals."

Their drinks arrived, and Franny downed his in one gulp. He then tipped the glass at the waiter, who cocked his head but took it away.

"Then I really do have to try and feel like a fifties housewife. How's your mum?" she asked in one of those blinding shifts of topic that always left him off balance. Piper Black had, in fact, been a stay-at-home wife and mother. What his mother didn't know, mustn't ever know, was that the money that enabled that life had been—

No, I don't need to go down that oft-trodden path yet again, either.

"Fine. I guess."

"I thought you were going to spend a few days with her up in Saratoga?"

"I just didn't have time. Work . . ." His voice trailed away.

It was a lie. What he couldn't face was sitting in a living room that was a shrine to the memory of police captain John F. X. Black. His father. The man he now knew to have been a murderous fraud. And he himself was too much of a coward to tell his mother the truth.

The waiter returned with his refill and he took a deep sip.

"I get it. I mean, it's just *exhausting* trying to keep them sorted. You think you've got them nicely settled with their own friends, bridge clubs and jumble sales to attend, and if you're *really* lucky a new boyfriend, and maybe *then* they will stop banging about in your life. But no, there they are again barging in with some absurd problem that could be solved *in an instant* if they would put even half a thought on it, but instead they have to call you and explain it all to you in *excruciating* detail, and when you tell them *exactly* how to handle it, they tell you you don't understand and then start in all over again. It's *maddening*."

Franny forced a smile. You couldn't be mad at her. It was who she was—maddeningly self-absorbed with the attention span of a hummingbird, but also adorable.

Then she surprised him by actually coming back around to him. "I have to say, as your resident expert on all things mothers, you are making a dreadful mistake. Best to just go up and let her fuss over you. I mean, you were hurt over there." Her eyes drifted from his shoulder to his torso, where he bore the scars from two bullet wounds. One scar was courtesy of a Kazakhstan mobster, the other a Kazakhstan cop. "Avoiding her is just going to make her cluck more."

"You make some good points." He toasted her with his drink and drained it. "I'll think about that." The waiter arrived to take their dinner orders. Apparently the man had figured out what Franny needed because he simply took away the empty highball glass and returned with the drink replenished. "I'd rather talk about your new part. Tell me more about it."

"Well, it's sort of an updated, avant-garde approach to *A Doll's House*, as reflected in a world of people with unnatural powers and abilities . . ."

As the evening went on, Franny had a feeling the minuscule portions so artfully arranged weren't doing much to soak up the amount of alcohol he'd been consuming—and honestly, he was just pushing most of the food around his plate. And indeed, when he needed to relieve himself and went to stand, he found the room swaying like a ferry in a heavy swell. He managed to reach the men's room without (he hoped) embarrassing himself, fumbled with his zipper, and finally got his cock out. He finished and shook off, but as he turned toward the sinks he tripped and barely caught himself on the edge of the basin. Raising his eyes to the mirror, he studied the dark shadows beneath his bloodshot eyes. Not getting a full night's sleep was clearly taking a toll.

Along with the booze, came an unpleasant reminder.

I need it to sleep.

Hasn't worked so far.

Shut up, he told the inner voice, and he headed back to the table. Before he reached it, a well-dressed man who looked to be in his late forties stood up and held out his hand.

"*Pardon.*" The word was said in the French way. "You are Francis Black, *mais oui?*"

"Uh . . . yeah?"

"I was one of the commanders of the Blue Helmets at Baikonur, at the Cosmodrome. I saw you there, before you and the aces took the truck into Talas. I know what you did." Franny couldn't control it. He flinched and rolled an eye toward their table. Abigail was watching, avidly, lips parted and eyes bright. "And I wanted to thank you. If you hadn't stopped the madness, I would not have returned home to my wife." He gestured toward the seated woman. "My children. I have taken care of your bill. It is the least I can do for saving me . . . and my troops." He pumped Franny's hand, then pulled him into a quick hug.

Franny almost tore himself away, ducked his head, and stumbled back to the table. There were only a few bites left of their shared dessert.

"You done? Can we get out of here?" Franny gritted.

Abigail looked over at the Frenchman's table. "We should thank him properly," she said quietly.

"Please! Let's just *go.*"

She hesitated, staring up into his face, then nodded. It felt like the stares of the other patrons were burning holes in his back as he fled the dining room.

"I thought you'd drowned in there," Abigail said as he emerged from the bathroom in her small apartment. "Though how one could possibly drown in a shower, I'm not entirely certain. I do sometimes miss a good soak, but the bathtubs in these apartments really are ridiculously small even if you are a relatively small person, and you are most certainly *not* a small person."

She wasn't wrong; he had stayed in the shower far longer than necessary, but it actually *had* been necessary to try to wash away the memory of both the day (a robbery gone bad with a shopkeeper dead and a teenager facing decades in prison) and the fatal reminder of Kazakhstan. He was also trying to boil the alcohol out of his system. He wasn't sure he had succeeded; the room seemed slightly off kilter.

Abigail was propped up against the headboard of the bed studying her script. The gauzy fabric of her nightgown allowed him an enticing glimpse of her breasts. He felt his own reaction nudge against the towel he had wrapped around his waist.

Abigail didn't miss it and gave him a suggestive smirk as she flung away the script.

"Come here, you." She tossed back the covers invitingly, revealing all of her body imperfectly veiled by the nightgown.

Franny obeyed, dropping the towel as he moved swiftly to join her, his gaze devouring every part of her from the multicolored hair, sparkling hazel eyes, and pierced upper lip to her red-painted toes. His cock twitched in anticipation of how that lip stud was going to feel raking along its length.

Bracing his hands on either side of her shoulders, he leaned down and kissed her, her tongue fencing with his. Then she pulled back and murmured against his lips, "That was really so nice of that gentleman. Now I don't feel so guilty about ordering that appetizer. I had thought about the foie gras, but they treat the geese so horribly that I resisted, but I suppose they don't treat the sturgeon all that well, either. I suppose there is no guilt-free food—well, maybe vegetables, but I really don't want to go completely vegan—but still it was nice of him to buy our dinners, and probably well deserved, from what he said."

Her fingertips stroked across the puckered scar on his shoulder and slid down to the other larger scar on his side. Franny stiffened. "Though I rather wish I knew what *exactly* it was that you did over there. The details are all rather vague, apart from people giving you credit. Well, you did tell me back in August that the world was ending . . . and then it didn't end and I gather you had something to do with that." She gave him a suggestive smile. "So I suppose I really ought to thank you *properly* for that." Her hand went to his now-flaccid cock.

"Oh." It was a mournful, disappointed sound and her gaze— questioning, concerned, and a bit guilty—met his strained stare.

"Sorry," Franny whispered.

He shifted to his side of the bed and pulled the covers up over his shoulders. Abigail snapped off the light and they lay in silence back-to-back.

The babies were impaled on a park fence. Blood and feces painted the metal uprights like a grotesque version of a barber pole's swirls, only in red and brown. Franny knew he should grieve, but instead he felt only horror and dread. And then all the little round heads lifted, and they *screamed* at him, their tongues writhing snakes and worms, blood dripping from the tips of pointed teeth.

Murderer!

The faces morphed into a single giant face filling the sky. Agent Jamal Norwood, one side of his head caved in, right eye dangling from its socket, and blood matting his dark hair, stared down at him. *"You killed me."*

Jamal's face shifted as if tentacles writhed beneath the skin and now it was an old woman crushing him beneath her accusing gaze as her body twisted and deformed and she screamed—

"You destroyed me."

The wizened body of an old man rested in his arms. Pleading

eyes gazed up at him. Franny threw him into a black void as the man cried—

"You abandoned me."

"Murderer! Murderer! Murderer!"

Whispering voices that increased in volume until the cacophony yanked him from sleep.

Franny shot bolt-upright in bed, shuddering with fear, a scream raw in his throat. Abby sat up, snapped on the lamp, and wearily clawed her hair out of her face. Her hand was cool on his shoulder.

"Another nightmare?" she asked, and while she tried to sound sympathetic, there was an edge to the words.

Franny glanced across her at the clock on the dresser. The green luminescent numbers told the tale—3:40 A.M.

"My rehearsals start tomorrow morning," she added.

"I'm sorry. I know you need your rest." He tried to smile but feared it was more of a grimace. "I'm not going to be able to get back to sleep. You rest; I'm going to head back to my own place."

He slid out of the bed, gave her a kiss, and, gathering up his clothes, went to dress in the bathroom where the light wouldn't disturb her. By the time he emerged, she was asleep, her gentle exhalations a soft whisper in the room.

Jokertown at a little past four in the morning was still a busy place. There were a few frat boys being chivvied out of Freakers so the staff could spend a few hours mopping spilled booze, food, and sweat off the tables where gawking tourists watched joker strippers perform before they opened again at 10 A.M.

A garbage truck was rolling down the street. The loud beeps, the growl of hydraulics as the cans were hoisted, tipped, and emptied, the shriek of metal on metal as the detritus was gulped into the body of the truck, formed the baseline of the urban symphony.

The noises added to his pounding hangover headache, and the sweet, sickening smell of rotting garbage had his stomach roiling.

Mr. Nieto was setting up his taco and burrito truck, getting ready for the morning rush of people coming off the swing shift: sanitation workers, healthcare workers, and, of course, cops. He gave a wave and Franny darted across the street to buy a coffee.

"No offense, *ese*, but you look like shit. Rough night?"

"I've had better. Hoping a cup of your coffee will help."

Money and coffee were exchanged. Nieto caught the sleeve of his overcoat. "Here, take a burrito—chorizo, eggs, and potatoes. Fix you right up."

The foil-wrapped burrito was warm in his hand, but the kindness was the real warmth when he felt so frozen inside. To Franny's utter embarrassment he found his eyes filling with tears. He turned his head away, hoping the older man hadn't noticed, muttered a thank-you, and walked away.

His hands were shaking as he tried to juggle both burrito and coffee in one hand and pull out his keys with the other. It was not a successful attempt and he spilled coffee onto his trousers. Muttering curses, he finally got the door to his studio apartment open.

It seemed a sad place, devoid of personality beyond the fact that a bachelor lived there. Flat-screen TV, a gaming console, recliner with a TV tray next to it, a pile of free weights stacked in the corner, a small dinette table with two chairs, and a bed. The only evidence of his personality was a bookcase filled with some of his law school texts, a few novels, and the games and music he'd purchased rather than downloaded to his Xbox and phone. Once the top of the case held photographs of the father he had never known. Those were gone now. All that was left was one picture of him and his mother on a family holiday in Maine, and his graduation photos—one from law school, the other from the police academy.

He finished the dregs of the coffee and ate the burrito, but his head was still pounding, and he felt like his eyes were too large for their sockets. He eyed the liquor bottles on the counter by the small fridge. Figured a little hair-of-the-dog wouldn't hurt. He then changed clothes and headed into work early. It was better than sitting alone in the apartment.

Franny's current partner, Mitch Moore, threw him a withering look when he arrived for their shift and found Franny already at his desk and working on reports. "Fuck you very much. Way to make me look bad," he grumbled as he slid into his chair.

"Nah, you manage that all on your own," Franny said. Mitch was currently a brilliant shade of green that matched his coffee mug. It was department policy that each pairing had to have one nat and one wild card—either joker or ace—so Franny had ended up with Mitch this time.

Moore was a deuce who might as well be a nat, since his power was so negligible. He could just change every part of him, as well as his clothes, to a different color—pink, blue, chartreuse. He couldn't even make it interesting by going plaid. Still, he was technically a wild card, so One Police Plaza was happy. Right now Franny's contemplation of how Mitch's blue eyes clashed horribly with the green skin and clothing was cut short when Officer Benjamin "Beastie" Bester came by and clapped Franny on the shoulder. Beastie looked like what would happen if some of Maurice Sendak's Wild Things decided to get frisky with an NBA star. He was seven feet tall, with fur, horns, fangs, and claws, but despite the ferocious appearance, he was the precinct's gentle giant.

"Hey, Franny, putting together a card came for Thursday night. Want in? We'd love to have ya." Admiration hung off every word.

Franny blinked up at the burly joker. Beastie had always been friendly, but then Franny had freed the kidnapped jokers from Baba Yaga's fight club, and the Highwayman had given the interview that named Franny as the other man, along with himself, who had literally saved the world, and Beastie's friendship had morphed into a deeply disturbing (at least to Franny) case of hero worship.

The whole saving-the-world thing might be a bit hard to get one's head around, but what was *very* real to the cops of the Jokertown precinct (dubbed by people outside the neighborhood as Fort Freak) were the missing citizens who were part of their daily lives. The people they'd sworn to preserve and protect. For the joker cops in particular, these were their schoolteachers, the shop owners from whom they bought a sandwich or a pack of cigarettes, their friends and neighbors, and, most crucially, a beloved priest. Many of whom had died in Baba Yaga's casino of horrors.

Overnight Franny had gone from being the entitled son of a former police captain, and a dude playing the nat savior to the benighted denizens of Jokertown, to everyone's hero. *Well, make that some people's hero,* he added as he glanced nervously around looking for Detective Tabby Driscoll. Tabby was an ace, and he had been loud in his complaints that it wasn't fucking fair that Franny, who had all the fucking privilege in the world, *also* got all the glory.

Still, Franny had discovered that fawning and hero worship were actually far more devastating than the constant hazing he'd been enduring.

"So, what do you say?" Beastie asked, looking anxious in the face of Franny's continued silence.

"Um . . ."

"Hey, Bester, maybe you could pull your puckered lips off Black's entitled nat ass and get me that file I wanted," Tabby sneered.

If Beastie's face hadn't been covered with fur, he would have been scarlet. Franny felt blood wash into his own cheeks, but he couldn't tell whether it was from embarrassment or fury. Beastie beat a hasty retreat. Mitch was trying to become one with his chair and in fact had turned the same dull gray as the fabric.

"Even by your low standards, that was a really shitty thing to do to Beastie. What the fuck is your problem?" Franny growled.

Driscoll leaned down, large, freckled hands gripping the arms of Franny's chair. He got so close Franny could smell what Tabby had eaten for breakfast on his breath. "My *problem* is that you're a walking poster child for fucking nat privilege. You make detective early, you go fucking rogue to goddamn Trashcanistan, and instead of getting fired, you're now the big fucking hero who saved . . ." He straightened and made air quotes around the final three words. "The fucking world." His expression indicated he didn't believe a word of it.

And he shouldn't. Everything about me is a lie.

Mercifully, Franny was saved from both responding and his spiraling self-recriminations when Mitch, who had taken a call, hung up the phone and said, "We gotta bounce."

Officer Miranda Michaelson, nicknamed Rikki, stood contemplating the woman's body floating in the bloodstained water of the bathtub. Someone—*most likely the missing husband,* her mind provided—had torn down the shower rod and jammed it through her body, cracking the porcelain of the tub. Rikki's partner, Bugeye Bronkowski, was unrolling the crime scene tape while techs snapped photos and took samples. It was crowded in the narrow bathroom, and it got worse when Detectives Black and Moore arrived.

Rikki watched Franny's blue eyes widen at seeing her, and quickly slide away. Shortly after he'd returned from that horror in Kazakhstan, they had experienced an intense, life-and-death situation, and it seemed like they were forming . . . *something.* Then that actress had flown through like an errant comet, swept Franny into her orbit, and he had totally ghosted Rikki. To be fair, it wasn't like they had actually *defined* their relationship, but it hurt nonetheless, and Franny certainly seemed embarrassed and guilty as hell as he kept looking anywhere but at her.

He also *looked* like hell. Normally he was a tall, handsome man with blue-black hair, deep-blue eyes, and a somewhat crooked smile, but today his skin was pasty white, and dark shadows hung beneath his eyes. She watched as he seemed to force himself to look at the woman's body. Rikki's eyes narrowed as his hands began to tremble, and she saw that the muscle in that square jaw was bunching as he clenched his teeth.

"So, what we got?" Mitch asked. Then held a hand to his forehead like a psychic reading an aura. "No, wait . . . let me guess. Not an intruder. Husband or boyfriend?"

"Husband; one Monty Tobin," Rikki answered. "Neighbors reported hearing them fighting last night. Apparently not an uncommon occurrence."

"So who found the body?" Mitch asked.

"College kid taking his dog out for a walk saw the front door was partially open. Stuck his head in and called. Nobody answered. He said it just felt weird, so he came inside," Bugeye answered.

"Bet he regrets *that* decision," Mitch grunted.

"He's pretty shook up," Rikki said. "Oh, and the kid says the husband is an ace, too. Basic strong guy. Worked at a local gym."

Rikki sneaked a look at Franny. It wasn't like him to be so silent, but he seemed lost in his own thoughts. *Or memories?* she wondered.

The ME, on his knees at the side of the tub, looked up and said, "Well, that would explain how he put a shower rod through not only the soft tissue, but her pelvic bone as well. Okay to take her now?" Mitch nodded. The doc stood up, gripped the shower rod in gloved hands, and grunted with effort as he pulled it out of the body with a grating shriek of metal on bone.

Franny let out a faint sound that was almost a whimper, spun on his heel, and left the bathroom.

"He okay?" Rikki asked Mitch softly. The detective just gave a helpless shrug.

Rikki started to slip past the crowd in pursuit, only to hear Bug-eye call after her, "Jesus, what is it with you dames and pretty boys? He dumped you *hard* and you're still mooning after him?"

Rikki flipped him off, left the bathroom, and went in search of Franny. She found him searching the couple's bedroom. From the rumpled sheets and blanket, he emerged with an iPad. It wasn't password-protected, because when he picked it up the screen sprang to life to reveal a tilted image. Franny turned up the volume on the iPad and they heard a toddler's wails.

"It's a nanny cam," he said tensely. "Kid must have grabbed the teddy bear that's hiding the camera."

For an instant the words didn't register, because she smelled alcohol on his breath and it was *eight thirty in the morning*. The next thing that registered was the desperate intensity in his voice and the frantic look in his eyes, as if this was his own child in danger.

"Let's see if we can find a photo. I'll get out an Amber Alert—"

"Wait," Franny said. He tilted the iPad to a new angle. "This looks like the material on the top of a roof." His eyes drifted toward the ceiling. "Maybe the husband didn't run that far."

"Hang on," Rikki began. "We may be dealing with a—"

He bolted out of the room.

"Shit!" Using her virus-enhanced speed, she shot after him and in two strides had caught and passed him. She placed a hand on his chest, holding him in place.

"This could be a hostage situation. We need to wait."

"Let's at least suss out the situation," Franny said, his tone pleading.

That did make some degree of sense. Rikki nodded and called in the request for a negotiator, then they left the apartment to find the stairs.

— — —

Dirty snow lumped in sad heaps against the parapets, and vapors from the vent pipes dotting the roof swayed and danced like a witch's gray locks. The wind off the river was icy cold, and they could now hear a child's hiccuping cries without the benefit of the iPad. The desperate, frightened, and mournful sound had Franny's chest clenching so hard his breath had gone short.

Franny and Rikki moved as silently and quickly as they could to take cover behind the looming bulk of the building's air-conditioning unit.

The whimpers resolved into a toddler's lisping cries of: "*Mommy, Mommy.*"

"Shut the fuck up!" came a bass growl. "Mommy ain't coming."

But more cops were. Franny could see the red and blue splashing against the wall of the apartment across the street.

The father had also spotted them, and an explosive *"fuck"* burst out. Franny heard a child scream in pain, then the crunch of footsteps on the gravel and tar-paper roofing.

"We can't wait for the negotiator," he said. Straightening, he walked out from around the unit, hands held up.

The man was short and skinny, and the bloodstained T-shirt clung to his narrow chest. He was gripping a little boy by his upper arm. The kid was maybe two, wearing only a diaper and a T-shirt, shivering, lips and toes blue with cold. He was clutching the teddy bear. As Franny watched, bruises bloomed across the tender skin and the child screamed again.

The children impaled on the fence posts, mouths stretched wide, screams filling my ears . . .

They were dead because of him. Because he had broken the wards that Baba Yaga had constructed to hold back the madness and death. He had helped to usher in the coming of a dark god.

For an instant Franny froze, then shook it off. He couldn't let it happen again. There could be no more dead children. "Hey, hey, easy," he said, his eyes flicking to the large kitchen knife the man held in his other hand. "Nobody has to get hurt here. I'm sure you had your reasons. Good reasons. Let's just talk about it."

"You aren't takin' my kid!"

"No, no, of course not." He edged closer. "Look, it's really cold up here. Your son . . . What's his name?"

"Ron."

"Short for Ronald?"

"Fuck off, pig, I know what you're doing." He jerked his head toward the screaming child. "Long as I got him, you aren't gonna shoot me."

"Nobody's getting shot. But if you want insurance, I'm a better bet." Franny pressed his hand against his chest even as he moved closer. "Your little boy is cold. Why don't you let my partner take him, and I'll stay with you? What do you say?"

Rikki wanted to pound her head against the metal casing of the air conditioner. What Franny had just suggested ran counter to every ounce of training they'd been given. You *never* swapped hostages. Rikki risked a quick look. Fortunately, the father was totally focused on Franny, who was continuing to move closer. She saw Franny's shoulders tense and she knew everything was about to go pear-shaped.

Franny leapt at the man, reaching for the hand that held the knife. It was madness, because from what the neighbor and the ME had said, the man was an ace and clearly stronger than a normal human. But Franny either didn't care or, in his impaired state, hadn't absorbed what they'd said.

Franny's hands closed around the man's wrist, knuckles going white with effort. The man yanked his arm away hard, shaking Franny loose with ease and slamming him into the parapet, where he lay stunned. Worse, the return swing of his arm sent the knife stabbing deep into the child's chest. Rikki gave a cry of horror as the child screamed—a raw visceral sound that Rikki hoped she never had to hear again.

Tobin released the toddler and stared, shocked, at what he'd done. His momentary distraction allowed her to kick into a run, snatching up the bleeding child. Using all her wild-card-enhanced speed, she raced down the stairs to find help.

Franny was disoriented enough that Rikki seemed to be just a blue blur. His head and back were throbbing from where he'd been slammed into the brick. He tried to stand but only made it to his knees—though that did give him a view over the parapet as the father, gripping windowsills and digging his fingers deep into the mortar between bricks, swung down the side of the building. Reaching the street, Tobin shoved a passing car so that it was sideways to the oncoming traffic, effectively keeping the police from pursuing.

Franny squeezed his eyes shut, his breath coming short and fast. When he opened them, he was staring at the blood pooling on the tar paper and gravel.

"So this is the hero. Stupid, stupid boy. You have no idea what you have done . . . " It was Baba Yaga's aged voice, each word edged with anger and tipped with an even more deadly sarcasm.

Franny gave a moan of despair and allowed himself to collapse back onto the roof.

Downstairs, Franny found that the second to Deputy Inspector Thomas Maseryk had arrived. Captain Harvey Kant was a joker of indeterminate age who seemed to have been at Fort Freak forever, but somehow managed to never retire. He had been promoted after the previous joker captain had been discovered taking kickbacks from Baba Yaga to turn a blind eye to the joker kidnappings. Kant was brown and scaly and looked like a dinosaur in a cheap polyester suit. His trademark cigar was thrust between his pointed teeth. There was no sign of Rikki or the child.

"Well, congratulations, Detective, we've gone from a simple domestic murder into nightmare PR clusterfuck," Kant said.

"The little boy, is he—"

"At the hospital."

Trying to ignore his pounding head, Franny straightened and forced his shoulders back. "I can explain, sir, and let me assure you that—"

"You're not going to explain *shit*. You're going to get your ass over to the clinic and get checked out for a concussion."

"How . . . ?"

Mitch cleared his throat. "You got a big bruise on your temple and forehead."

"Then you're gonna come back to the precinct and *then* you can explain to me why you thought you were a goddamn TV cop," Kant continued.

"Yes, sir," Franny mumbled.

Mitch clapped a hand on his shoulder. "Come on, buddy, let's get you sorted."

Kant looked up when Rikki stuck her head into his office. "What do you need, Officer?" Rikki stepped in and shut the door carefully behind her. "Oh, so this is gonna be one of *those* talks." He sighed and leaned back in his chair, causing the springs to squeak.

"Sir, I was on the roof with Detective Black—"

"So now you're gonna tell me he's a good cop, a dedicated officer, and the situation demanded—"

"No, sir, I'm going to tell you he's in trouble. And he needs to be put on administrative leave."

The captain leaned forward at that, and the membrane that

moved horizontally across his eyes began to nictate. "He had some time off after he got back from that mess in Kazakhstan. Went to counseling."

"Well, it wasn't enough. It didn't get to the root of the problem, and Captain Maseryk allowed him to come back too soon."

"So, what are you saying, that he's a glory hound? Looking to be a Big Damn Hero, trying to make up for the fact that Daddy *wasn't*?"

"That might be a small part of it, but . . ."

She closed her eyes briefly, remembering Franny's expression of horror and pity at the sight of the woman's body, and how he had withdrawn into what seemed to be a waking nightmare. And she had watched as *guilt* replaced all the other emotions that were playing across his face. Rikki drew in a deep breath, hating what she was going to say, what it would do to Franny, but knowing she had to do it.

"I think he was hoping the perp would kill him. Don't get me wrong, he was worried about the kid, didn't want the little boy to be hurt, but I saw the look on his face; he was a man looking to die." *And looking for punishment*, she added to herself, but she didn't say that aloud. She already felt guilty enough for what she was doing.

Kant nodded and waved her out of the office.

The curtains around the cubicle did nothing to block out the sounds of pain and worry from other patients in the emergency room at the Blythe van Renssaeler Memorial Clinic. Franny sat tensely on the edge of the bed, waiting to be examined.

A little nurse's aide, who had a circlet of long teeth growing out of her neck like a bizarre necklace, peeked around the curtain. "Excuse me, but aren't you that cop, the one that got back the jokers from Kazakhstan?"

Franny felt every muscle in his body tense, adding to the pain in his abused back and the pounding headache. He considered lying but couldn't form the words. He managed a stiff nod that was also half a headshake. The girl went on.

"Mr. Richardson, he lived in our building, and him and my mom were dating so we were so relieved . . ." The girl was continuing to talk, but her voice seemed distant.

Their names had been listed in his notebook. All the missing. All the lost. *All the dead.* Richardson was one of the lucky ones who didn't get dead. A teacher at the Jerusha Carter Childhood Development Institute, he was a joker with six insect-like legs and a human torso on top.

Franny had the sudden realization that the institute and the clinic in which he currently sat were both named in honor of wild cards—both women, and both aces who had died tragically. It seemed like tragedy was constant and inevitable. The memory of the blood on the roof returned, sharp and present. He could smell it. Or perhaps it was only blood from one of the injured that surrounded him.

". . . So I just wanted to thank—"

"Please . . . don't," Franny whispered. "Don't thank me."

He raised his eyes to meet the girl's, seeing the confusion, the hurt. The curtain was swept back to reveal Dr. Finn, a palomino centaur who was also the head of the clinic.

"I . . . I don't understand, why not—"

Franny's breath was going short. Finn interrupted. "Thanks, Gilly, but I need to examine Detective Black, so . . ." He jerked his head, indicating she should leave. After throwing one final confused glance at Franny, the girl hurried away. "Sorry about that."

"Apologize to her for me," Franny mumbled. He raised his eyes to meet Finn's. "Did they bring—"

"Yes, the boy is here. He's going to be okay. Now let's see what's going on with you."

– – –

The precinct was like a stirred ant hill when Franny returned. A BOLO had been issued for Tobin, and people were buzzing about how Rikki's speed had been the only thing that saved the kid. The looks from his co-workers felt like a lash against his skin as Franny hunched his shoulders, heading for his desk.

He didn't make it. Kant stepped out of his office and crooked a scaly finger at him. Mitch gave him a sympathetic look.

"Close the door," the captain ordered. Franny obeyed. "Sit down." He again obeyed. Kant sighed and rested his chin on his hand. "There have been some . . . concerns raised about this morning's events. I think it would be prudent for you to take some time off. Get some more counseling."

"I did. Right after I got back from . . . from . . . over there."

"I talked with Doc Engelberg. You bent the rules, signed yourself out of counseling early."

"I was fine. And I thought working would be more help," Franny said quietly.

"Well, you thought wrong. Frankly, you look like shit. So I'm not asking now. I'm ordering you to go back to therapy."

"How long will I be on leave?"

"That will depend on what the doc tells me."

Franny stood. "Yes, sir. May I go, sir?"

Kant waved a hand. "Yeah, fuck, go on." Franny made it to the door. "Kid, I've been here a long time. Seen more than a few cops eat their own gun. I don't want you to join that list."

"Thank you for your concern, sir. I'll try to avoid that."

As the door was closing behind him, Franny heard Kant mutter, "Too fucking polite to be a cop."

It was like a blow to the heart.

Mitch caught Franny as he was heading for the door. "You okay?"

"Yeah, captain ordered me to take some leave."

"Probably a good idea. You're moving like you're hurt."

Franny forced a smile that felt more like a grimace. "I've felt better. See you."

As luck would have it, he ran into Rikki on the stairs up to the front doors. She froze but with the air of a shy woodland animal on the verge of bolting. From the neck up, she looked like a very attractive woman with brown eyes, freckles, and brown hair in a perpetual ponytail. But if she smiled, you would see vestigial fangs, and he supposed that some people might consider the rest of her body grotesque. She had an extremely thin wasp waist, overly long legs, and a very large barrel chest. But he thought she was cute.

"I know what you did," Franny said, and Rikki tensed even more. He ran a hand across his face, felt the rasp of stubble against his palm. "Fuck, sorry, that came out wrong. I know *why* you did it. I understand, and you were right to report me. I nearly got that kid killed. If you hadn't been there . . ."

Her eyes were locked on his. "I didn't do it to hurt you. I'm worried about you. I was in the bullpen the day that crazy Steunenberg bitch opened the portal to Kazakhstan. Everybody was saying that you were the key and demanding that you go. You didn't hesitate; you went. And that time we were trapped in that creepy nightclub, you did it again. You were ready to kill yourself so me and Beastie and that Russian thug could go free."

He threw up a hand trying to stop her. "Don't. I'm not a hero." It was hard to force the words through a throat tight with unshed tears.

Rikki blinked hard. "No, I think you're a man who's trying to die. *And I don't understand why.*" She hesitated, then added quietly, "And I don't want that to happen. I don't know what went down over there. What you experienced." She gestured vaguely in the direction of the Atlantic and the distant Kazakhstan. "But I know what *we* went through, and . . . and discovering all that shit about your dad . . . That can't have been easy, so I'm . . . Well, if I can help, I'm . . . here."

He dug his hands into his pockets. Realized they were standing close enough that the white pennants of their breaths were mingling. He found himself remembering what it had been like when he had leaned down and kissed her. It hadn't been all that long ago, but it felt like a lifetime. Guilt twisted in his gut.

"I know. And I appreciate it." He stepped back and walked away. "I'm just not sure I'm worth it," he added, under his breath.

"Just not sure *I'm worth it."*

He clearly hadn't realized the wind had carried the whispered words to her. Rikki knew he was carrying guilt. A few months back they had worked together and ended up discovering that the father he had never known, but had been raised to idolize, had in fact been a vile man. And that had come on top of the hell of Kazakhstan. She just wished she had some idea of what he'd experienced over there.

Like the rest of the world, she had seen the nightmare images flash across her television screen—soldiers eating the bodies of the dead, a general shooting a journalist in the face. And it had gotten worse from there. Buildings transformed into towers of bleeding flesh. Then the people in and around the city of Talas began to *change,* to twist and deform. People tried to blame the wild card, but it wasn't the virus. It was something darker, more evil, and not of this world.

Of course, she thought with an ironic snort, *you could say that about the goddamn virus, too.*

Closer to home and in their own little sandbox, the precinct had discovered that one of their own captains, and a joker to boot, had been part of the plot that kidnapped jokers and forced them to fight to the death in Kazakhstan, for the amusement of the rich, bored, and idle.

Honestly, we probably all *need therapy,* Rikki thought.

She glanced down and realized there was blood staining the

cuffs and sleeves of her coat. She needed to call and check on the little boy, and make sure somebody had followed up with social services. Mom dead, dad in the wind; was there any family to take the child once he was out of the hospital? But maybe she'd get a clean uniform first.

Kant spotted her when she emerged from the locker room. "You good? Day's more than half over if you wanted to cut out early."

"I'm good, sir, but I'd like to follow up on finding next of kin for the boy rather than go back out on patrol, if that's okay."

"Carry on, Officer." He saluted her with his coffee mug and ambled back into his office.

Since Franny wasn't using it, she figured it would be okay if she settled at his desk to make her calls. A few hours later, she had determined that Judy Tobin had a sister in Idaho. She picked up the phone.

"If you're calling about Judy, we already know." The woman's voice held no grief; she just sounded put upon.

"Um, well, okay, but actually I was calling about your nephew—"

"Not our problem. *She's* the one who decided to go off to *New York.*" The way the woman stressed the words made them sound like swear words. "*And* marry one of them freaks. Kid's probably a freak, too. So, like I said, not our problem. I've got my own kids I've gotta protect."

The buzz of a disconnected line filled Rikki's ears while nausea filled her stomach.

She became aware of Mitch and Officer Bill Chen talking quietly nearby. "Not my problem," Bill was saying in an odd echo of the woman in Idaho. "He's *your* partner."

"Yeah, but he used to be *yours,* and the wife and I have Broadway tickets for tonight."

The only *he* the two men had in common was Francis Black. Rikki went to join them. "What's up?"

"The new owner of Squisher's called. Franny's been in there all afternoon. He's drunk off his ass and disturbing the nat clientele who want the 'Jokertown experience.'" Mitch's tone indicated the quotes around the final two words.

Rikki knew what that meant. Nats came to Jokertown to feel a little bit wicked, like they were risking danger, but they didn't want to actually *be* in danger. Franny was clearly disturbing that balance.

"I'll go get him," she found herself saying.

The place definitely smelled less aquatic now that Squisher had been gathered to his maker. The new nat owner had left the huge tank where Squisher had once resided in place, and had kept the name, but it no longer felt like Jokertown with the track lighting and modern furniture. There was a gaggle of nat college-aged girls grouped around a table in the corner. Only one other table was occupied, by a pair of twenty-something nat men. Rikki figured they'd end up at Freakers before the night was out, watching joker women strip for their amusement.

Franny was slumped on one of the stainless-steel and crystal barstools. He leaned heavily on one arm while with his other hand he clutched a highball glass that he was trying and failing to raise to his lips. His cheeks and jawline were shadowed with dark stubble, tie loosened, collar open. The nat owner stood glaring in the doorway of the back office, arms folded defiantly across his chest while the cute, and also nat, female bartender pretended to be interested in what Franny was saying . . . or, more accurately, slurring. Unfortunately, what he was saying came through loud and clear as Rikki headed over to him.

". . . girlfriend is amazing . . . really cute . . . did I mention she's an actress? Really good one. English, love that accent. I get to hear it a lot. She's got different-colored hair . . . and tats . . . and piercings. She's very . . ." He gestured with the glass, sloshing whiskey over his hand while he searched for a word. "Avant garde. But sometimes I miss my old girlfriend. Well, I'm not sure if she *was* my girlfriend. I think she *could* have been. Abby's great, but Rikki can stay . . . *focused*, you know what I mean? Did I mention Abby is an actress?"

"Several times." The bartender sighed.

"She talks a lot. Makes it kind of easy because then I don't have to, because I might say the bad stuff out loud . . . about the dead people . . ." His shoulders hunched and his head dropped as he whispered, "I don't want to kill anyone again."

Rikki watched the girl's eyes widen and she retreated, stepping back from the bar. "He's a cop. It's okay," Rikki said, moving to Franny's side.

His words had shaken her. Rikki knew that in the course of his duties at Fort Freak he'd never killed anyone. What had happened in Kazakhstan? Who had he killed? Or was he talking about that FBI agent, or Father Squid, or any of the other jokers who had lost their lives over there? Would she ever know? Did she need to know? Did she *want* to know?

And since when had she been his *old girlfriend*? Let alone one that he missed?

She got an arm around his waist and hauled him off the barstool. "Come on, Detective, let's get you home."

Franny was weaving and staggering as they started to climb the stairs to street level. Rikki tightened her grip to help steady him. Once on the sidewalk, Franny looked around, disoriented. "It's dark," he declared.

"That's 'cause it's night." She tugged to get him moving.

"It wasn't night went I went in."

She glanced up at him. "Have you eaten anything today?"

"Of course . . . Maybe? I think?" He shook his head and gave her a sweet if befuddled smile. "I don't remember."

They were taking up a lot of the sidewalk, which earned them glares from their fellow New Yorkers, but Rikki had a feeling that if she released his waist Franny would not remain upright. In fact, as she looked at him, he was starting to look a little green around the gills.

"Are you going to puke?"

"Uh-uh." But as she watched, he heaved and clapped a hand to his mouth. She quickly shoved him over a city trash can while he vomited up an afternoon's worth of booze.

"Oh, Francis Xavier," she breathed. "What's Abby's address?"

He was vaguely aware of the two women talking, but it seemed muffled, as if coming through several layers of cotton wadding.

"... *hasn't eaten* ..."

"... *never cook* ... *restaurants every third step* ... *New York, you know* ... *carry away* ... *not a thing in the place* ..."

"... *drinking all afternoon* ... *hurt* ..."

He wasn't sure how it got resolved, but it must have gotten resolved because he heard the front door of the apartment open and then close as he leaned back on the sofa, a hand over his eyes. It felt like a troop of troll drummers had taken up residence inside his skull, and his stomach was a yawning, aching pit.

"Well, you're quite the mess."

He peered through his fingers at Abby. "Sorry. She shouldn't have brought me here."

"She said you were hurt. I'm not seeing blood, which rather worries me. When your clothing comes off, am I going to be treated to an unpleasant surprise? If so, I'd rather like to be prepared for whatever I'm going to see before I *actually* have to see it. As you may have gleaned by now, I'm not exactly the Florence Nightingale type. I'd be rubbish at winding bandages or knitting bandages or whatever it was they did back then, so ... What happened?"

"I don't want to talk about it," he muttered.

"Yes." She paused then added, "And that's rather the problem, isn't it?"

The sharp edge on the words, and the fact the bald statement had not been followed by a long discursive discussion of Christ-knew-what, had his full attention. Franny pulled his hand away from his eyes and looked up at her. She was standing in front of him, arms akimbo, mouth tight, and a frown between her brows, but her eyes told a different story. They were glistening a bit and the expression they held was a complex mix of worry, confusion, and helpless nervousness that verged on fear.

His own emotions were far less complicated. All he felt was self-loathing—for causing a child to be hurt and allowing a killer to escape; for making it necessary for a fellow officer and a woman he respected and admired to feel forced to report him; for causing his girlfriend to have that haunted, vulnerable look; for Jamal, for Father Squid, for . . .

He choked out a sob, then covered his mouth with a hand, holding back any further sounds of grief. Abby's stiff demeanor crumbled, and she fell against him, wrapping her arms tightly around his shoulders.

"Oh, you dear, dear man. I'm so sorry. I didn't mean . . . Really, it's fine . . . no need to say a word. Let's just get you into bed. Things will seem better in the morning. They always do . . . Well, that's what they say at any rate. I'm not sure why that is. Maybe there is something to that thing about light and depression."

Once again, the avalanche of words acted as a bandage to his lacerated soul. Papering over the wounds, covering them up. Allowing them both to step back from the emotional precipice.

She led him into the bedroom and helped him out of his coat and shirt. Clucked over the dark bruises across his back, stroked the bruises on his face. He insisted on a shower; he reeked of sweat and booze and hospital. It took two brushings and mouthwash before the taste of vomit was finally out of his mouth.

Abby insisted on rubbing arnica cream onto the bruises, and she located the pain pills Dr. Finn had prescribed and had Franny swallow a couple before getting him tucked into bed.

He clasped her hand as she started to stand up from the edge of the bed. "Thank you. I don't deserve you."

"Oh, nonsense." She cocked her head to the side like an inquisitive bird. It was adorable. "Well, actually, I should probably say yes, shouldn't I?"

"You totally should."

A shudder ran through his body as a sudden chill set his teeth chattering. Abigail pulled up the covers and tucked them under his chin, kissed the tip of his nose. "Let those pills do their magic. I'll be in in a bit. Need to run lines before tomorrow."

He managed to nod.

When Rikki arrived at her parents' apartment, they were in the small kitchen and moving around each other with the ease of long practice. June was pulling a roast out of the oven while Nick finished mashing the potatoes. His forked tongue was showing a bit as he concentrated on the task.

"Oh, Rikki, honey, would you get out the water glasses?" June called.

Rikki stepped over her mother's six green tentacled legs and began filling glasses with ice and water from the fridge.

They were soon settled at the dining room table. Given June's joker physiology, she perched on a hassock. Nick began carving and handing out plates.

"Saw on the news about that kid. Terrible thing," her father said.

"It's a blessing you have your powers," June said. "When Mrs. Galloway came into the store today, she said that little boy would have died if it hadn't been for you."

"And how would Mrs. Galloway know that?" Rikki asked as she speared some green beans.

"Her son is a nurse at the clinic."

"Ah."

"News also said that young man you were seeing got hurt, too." Their eyes were on her. "We weren't seeing each other." Franny's face, guilt-ridden and exhausted, rose in her memory. "And he . . . Look, could we just *not* talk about this?"

Everyone fell silent apart from the clink of silverware on china. Then her mother, in a tone so casual it was awkward, said, "Oh, I ran into Martha Walenski at the bus stop. Did you know Rudy has moved back to Jokertown?"

"No."

"Wasn't he the boy you went to prom with?"

Rikki dropped her fork onto the plate with a clatter. "You know damn good and well we did, and no, you and Martha are not going to try to set us up."

"Miranda, please don't take that tone with your mother." Her father's lizard-like eyes had gone from doting to stern.

"Honey, your dad and I aren't getting any younger. We'd like the chance to dance at your wedding," June said.

"I'm playing the field," Rikki said lightly, trying to ease the tension as she resumed eating.

"Really? I'm not sure you're even showing up for practice," her mother said, half under her breath.

On top of the day she'd just had, Rikki was not having it. Her knuckles whitened as she clenched the fork in her first. "Stop pretending this is about dating. You and Dad made your choice. Please respect mine." Her tone was harsher than she intended, but her decision to *never* have children was an endless circular debate that she had endured for far too many years with her parents. Her father pointedly changed the subject.

After what felt like hours, the awkward meal came to an end.

Rikki helped her mom with the dishes and made her farewells. As she walked to the building's elevator, she found herself thinking about the dynamics of parents, children, and the crushing burden of meeting those parental expectations.

Her parents desperately wanted grandchildren, but years ago Rikki had made the decision she would never get pregnant and run the risks her parents had willingly accepted. June and Nick were both jokers, which meant that the odds of them producing a healthy, viable child were fantastically small, and indeed it had taken them three tries before Rikki was born. She was their miracle baby. But Rikki was a cynic where miracles were concerned, and she was not willing to risk the odds—not when there were plenty of children, like today's little boy, in need of a stable, loving home. When the time came, Rikki would adopt, and her parents would have their grandchild.

Once again, her thoughts returned to Franny. He had been raised to follow in his father's footsteps—a man who had been held up to him as a paragon, a hero to be emulated—only to discover John F. X. Black had been none of those things. He had been a crook, a murderer—and had even joined forces with an evil and powerful ace who had spread death and destruction across New York City.

"It was all a lie. My entire life is based on a lie!"

That's what Franny had said to her after their harrowing experience in that nightclub of the damned. But Captain John F. X. Black's picture still hung in the precinct among the other captains of Fort Freak, because the brass didn't really want to admit that the story around him was a myth. As the police commissioner had said when Franny tried to get it removed, *"It was almost forty years ago, Black. Nobody gives a shit."*

But Franny did. And it was eating at him, destroying him from the inside out.

— — —

A massive figure loomed over him. It was armored with the bodies of the dead. Jamal Norwood, right eye hanging grotesquely on his cheek, was attached to the monster's chest. The massive joker El Monstro hung off one leg, his shoulders spattered with blood and brains from the bullet Franny had put through his skull. The rest were faceless, like the people he'd gunned down as they'd made their mad raid into the city of Talas to kidnap a dark god.

He stood fighting to keep his balance in the back of a speeding truck, in his arms a wizened old man. Evil stared out of the sunken eye sockets, waiting to devour him, filling his thoughts with the pain he would soon endure. The pain this man would inflict. A slow blink and suddenly the person looking up at him was not the monster, just a sick, dying old man begging for mercy. Franny gave a heave and the body arced away from him, exploded on the slate-gray ground. Abandoned in hell to die alone. And the god had *seen* him . . .

"*The same mercy shall be shown to you. I'm coming for you. Hear me . . . remember me . . . fear me.*"

Once again Franny woke screaming.

Abby jerked upright, the sheet and blanket falling to her waist. She grabbed them up again and clutched them against her chest like a child holding a favorite toy. Franny snapped on the bedside lamp, needing to see that the dead were not in the room.

The look in Abby's eyes was frightened, grieving, and also showed a woman at her wit's end.

He reached out for her, but she warded him off with an up-raised hand. "I . . . I just can't. I can't do this. Not tonight. Maybe . . ." She jumped out of bed, grabbed her clothes, and began to dress, her movements jerky and uncoordinated.

Franny heard the front door close. Drawing his knees up to his chest he rested his forehead on them. For her sake, he knew what he needed to do.

— — —

It was almost midnight when Rikki finally admitted that her mind was not going to let her sleep. A hot toddy sounded like just the thing. She made her way to the kitchen only to discover she was out of both honey and lemons. She stared into the cabinet wondering if a bowl of cereal would do and decided it very much would not.

Both Freakers and Squisher's would still be open at this hour, which meant her choices were nats or strippers. Well, the strippers were jokers, and Charlie, the late-night bartender, was generous with his pours for the cops of Fort Freak.

The weather was absolutely shitty, a freezing rain that turned to sleet just as she reached the entrance situated between the legs of a giant neon woman with six breasts and a come-hither smile. Given the weather, it was no wonder the place was pretty dead. Rikki surveyed the handful of customers.

She spotted a few of the Jokertown regulars, older men who mostly stared down into their drinks. The dancer currently performing seemed to sense she wasn't going to earn much in tips, so she wasn't putting in a lot of effort.

There was one other person not looking at the stage—a person she had just seen a few hours before. A glass of white wine sat in front of Abigail. Rikki gave a mental sigh. *Not my problem*, she thought firmly, and slipped over to the bar.

"Seems to be that kind of night," Charlie remarked. He jerked his head toward Abigail. "Lot of unquiet spirits. So, what's got yours all in an uproar? By the way, good job with that kid."

Rikki gave a humorless laugh and pressed a hand to her forehead. "God, this place is like the quintessential small town. Everybody is all up in everybody else's business. It's a wonder there are any secrets that are safe."

"Oh, there's still plenty of secrets," came a voice from the far end of the bar. Rikki and Charlie glanced over at the portly, middle-aged man whose hairline seemed to be heading for the back of his neck. He laid a couple of hundreds on the bar and walked out.

"Was that . . . ?" Rikki began.

"Croyd? Yeah, maybe," Charlie said.

"How like the man." Rikki gave an involuntary jump. Somehow she had missed Abigail leaving her table and sliding onto the barstool next to her. "Honestly *any* man, to not even *notice* I was sitting *right over there*." The English accent was firmly in place, but the words were very, very, very slurred.

You have got to be kidding. Why me? Rikki offered up to an uncaring universe. The uncaring universe didn't respond.

"I mean it's not like Croyd and I didn't spend a *significant* amount of time together. We had *adventures*." Abigail paused, took a deep sip of her wine. "I miss adventures," she added mournfully, then an expression of horror so extreme it was almost comical crossed her face. "Actually, *no,* no I don't. I don't want any more adventures. I don't like adventures. I mean, it would be all right if the adventures were like in the movies. You finish, and everyone walks away with a quip and a swagger . . . But real adventures . . . they aren't like that, are they?"

She looked at Rikki with desperation in her hazel eyes. "No," Rikki said quietly. "They aren't. They have consequences. And it's always the civilians that have to pick up the pieces."

"Exactly! Civilians. People with *ordinary* problems. Like where to have lunch. Or should you buy that purple blouse even though you know it makes your skin look positively yellow. Or when you break off your engagement three weeks before the wedding. I mean everyone's in an uproar, but no one comes out of it all cut and bruised and with *nightmares.* I mean the *nightmare* would have been going through with it and finding yourself living in Sheffield and pregnant and miserable . . ." Rikki felt her eyebrows climbing toward her hairline.

"Everyone does ultimately live in their own little worlds. My world is the theater with an occasional foray into film. My world is quite nice so I'm very happy to discuss it—well, when it isn't horribly disappointing and almost soul crushing. And the rejections are so frightfully *personal*. *You're too short, you're too tall, your breasts are too* . . . well, they're never right— But other worlds make people become very . . . closed off.

"I mean, I understand if their world isn't particularly *nice*. And maybe they think you wouldn't be interested . . . or they don't want to burden you with the . . . well . . . ugliness in their world. But it does make it rather difficult to sympathize, much less understand when he . . . they *won't talk*. 'Language is the blood of the soul,' as someone once said." She wrinkled her nose, frowning down into her glass. "I actually think it might have been one of you Americans, though it does sound rather un-American. You're all much more . . . goal-directed, I suppose. Reflection—much less self-reflection—isn't the first thing that comes to mind. But if talking shows you a person's soul and then they refuse to talk and all you get is silence when you're trying to be there for them, then it does rather suggest he—they—don't have . . . a soul. Except nobody could be in *that much pain* if they didn't have a soul. I can off-load my pain into a character. Very convenient."

She gulped down more wine. Her hand closed conclusively on the stem. Staring straight ahead at the display of bottles behind the bar, she added, "You're in his world. I was always just a fantasy for him. Then he became the storybook hero . . . another fantasy, but neither of us are who we *actually* are."

Rikki heard again the heartfelt grief in Franny's voice. "*It was all a lie. My entire life is based on a lie!*"

Abigail slid off the barstool and stood swaying. She groped in her purse for money, tossed it onto the bar, and turned to leave, but instead she ended up spinning around very, very quickly several times and crashing into a nearby table.

"Oh bloody hell!" she yelped, rubbing at her hip where she had slammed into the table. "Who's the bloody ace?"

Rikki watched as Abby left Freakers walking very, very slowly, like a woman who had discovered the floor had been carpeted with eggshells and oil.

"Do you have any fucking idea what that was about?" Charlie asked.

Rikki nodded slowly. "I think . . . she was asking me for help."

Franny leaned on the edge of the bathroom sink in his apartment, nursing a hangover headache. The cold water washing down four aspirin hit his empty stomach, which gave a lurch. He gripped the edge of the sink and willed himself not to vomit. He had left Abigail's apartment last night before she returned. She didn't need his drunk, hungover ass in her space.

He vaguely remembered Rikki's arm around his waist, but not much else until the nightmare that had sent Abby fleeing from her own apartment. He hoped he hadn't done or said anything too embarrassing to Rikki. Of course, it wasn't really going to make any difference. He'd already established that he was a lousy choice as a potential boyfriend, and professionally he was a reckless cop who nearly got a kid killed. His phone buzzed with an incoming text.

Rehearsal canceled this afternoon. Lunch? My treat. Did you sleep? We should talk. Actually rather need to talk. Can you talk? I mean are you up to talking? Of course I know you know how to talk. Stellar.

Franny stared at the wall of words and hoped that *Stellar* meant the restaurant at the top of the Empire State Building, and wasn't some Briticism of which he was, as yet, unaware.

Another buzz. **PS. 2:30. Meet you out front.**

Another buzz. **PPS. Or the lobby.**

And another. **PPPS. Not the lobby. Too crowded. Tourists.**

Franny waited, anticipating another Abigail message, but she seemed to have run down. It was one thirty. He'd just have time for a shower and a shave.

– – –

Per her instructions, Franny was waiting out front of the Empire State Building. He spotted Abigail among the crowd on the sidewalk across the street. He also spotted something out of the corner of his eye that seemed somehow . . . off . . . but when he looked more closely, the person was no longer in view. The WALK sign was well into its inexorable countdown just as Abby reached the curb. Instead of waiting she started to run, except it was a *run*. Franny's breath caught in his throat as she almost bowled over a businessman. There was a large clot of people on the sidewalk, and Franny realized that she was not going to be able to slow down before she careened into them like a bowling ball into a line of pins.

Franny pushed off the wall where he had been leaning so she slammed against his chest instead. His arms closed around her. "Whoa, what was that?" Franny asked as he caught his breath.

"Sorry, sorry. While I was out and about last night I must have been near an ace." She pushed back her hair that had become tousled by her headlong run. "I mean, honestly, sometimes I wish they could wear like a little cat bell or something so I could have a bit of a warning before I discover I'm suddenly invisible—which would be a disaster onstage or on camera—or likely to burst into flames or . . . or God knows what."

"Speed is Rikki's power," Franny said quietly as he gazed down at her.

She avoided his eyes and began to tug him toward the entrance. "Well, we might have run across each other last night. Quite by accident, I assure you. And really, the Chardonnay at Freakers is perfectly dreadful. I suppose since they are selling mostly to tourists, they assume it doesn't matter, it's not like there will be a lot of repeat customers, but you'd think they'd keep something better for us locals."

They entered the building with a clot of tourists no doubt hoping to catch the sunset from the observation deck. He once again had the sense of someone in the crowd that seemed familiar and froze. People flowed past them and Abby looked up, a frown between her brows.

"What?"

He shook it off. "Apparently nothing. Occupational hazard."

"It must be *exhausting* to have to always be so hyper-alert," Abigail said as they waited for the dedicated elevator to the restaurant. "Do policemen ever relax? On vacation? Taking a drive? At the movies? Well, I suppose not, since Americans have this dreadful tendency to go on shooting sprees."

The elevator arrived and they stepped in. Since it was after the lunch rush but before dinner, and they were going directly to the restaurant on the top floor, they ended up alone in the car. Franny rested his shoulders against the wall, watching as Abigail fell silent and began to fiddle with the hem of her jacket.

"Abby," he said gently. "It's okay. I know why you wanted to talk. What you want to say, and I understand and agree with your decision. You don't even need to say it."

Those big hazel eyes, brimming with misery, were raised to his. "I feel like I'm abandoning you right when you most need . . . someone . . . something . . ." She made a vague gesture.

He gathered her hands in his. "It's not your job to fix me or save me or even love me. And I shouldn't have made you into some sort of dream-come-true. You deserved to be more than a fantasy."

"Oh, Franny, I'm sorry."

"Don't apologize. Let's have a nice . . ." He glanced down at his watch. "I guess it's still sort of lunch?"

She gave a somewhat watery laugh, stepped back, and quickly wiped her eyes. "Probably more like tea."

"Well, I hope they've got something more substantial than those little fingers sandwiches. I'm pretty hungry," he said as they stepped out into Stellar.

The space had once housed Aces High, where the wild card

elite—those lucky enough to have drawn an ace (or jokers with powers and bodies that weren't *too* disturbing)—had partied. Now it was just another expensive New York City eatery.

They were escorted to their table and retreated behind the large ornate menus that both of them were clearly using as shields. Franny wondered if he should just quietly excuse himself. Abigail had had her say, they had officially broken up, and really the prices were shocking.

There was a loud bang from overhead and they both jumped.

"What the hell?" Abby yelped.

Franny set aside the menu and felt his racing heart finally beginning to slow. "They're doing some work on the antennas on the roof. I read something about it in the *Times*."

"I thought there was a dirigible mooring mast on top," Abigail said.

He chuckled. "Not anymore, since dirigibles haven't been a thing for, oh, I don't know, sixty years or so. In fact, no dirigible ever actually moored here. It was just a publicity stunt, so the builder could claim this was the tallest building in the world."

The look of outrage on Abby's face was adorable, and he felt both regret and guilt. *You can't fucking keep her just because you're so fucked up and broken and useless.* He closed his aching eyes, but oddly the image that rose up before him was Rikki.

There was a shout of alarm from the front of the restaurant, followed by a crash. Franny jumped to his feet to see that the maître d's stand had fallen, and the host was struggling as a familiar figure held him by the throat.

It was Monty Tobin. He was still wearing the bloodstained T-shirt, but he'd added an elegant topcoat that Franny could only assume he'd taken off someone he'd mugged. Franny also realized it was Tobin he'd seen earlier, moving through the crowds.

Tobin threw the maître d' into a nearby table with the air of a man tossing aside a tissue. One of the busboys, a big guy, charged

Tobin. The ace's arm drew back and he punched the man hard. Franny heard the busboy's jaw break. Tobin turned to Franny, his expression twisted with fury and desperation.

There were whimpers of fear from the few diners who remained. The rest of the waitstaff were frozen in place. Franny really wished he hadn't left his service pistol in his locker at the precinct, but Kant's final words to him had made an impression.

"Abby," he said out of the corner of his mouth, "use your speed. Get these people out of here."

"Out? Where to?"

"Kitchen, bathrooms, anyplace. He's here for me."

"I'll come back for you."

"Don't! Get the civilians clear."

He heard the maddened clack of her heels on the marble floor, then Tobin was on him, his hand locked around the back of his neck, a steel vise that had the bones in Franny's neck creaking.

"You fucking pig, you made me hurt my kid!" His breath was hot and fetid in Franny's face. "You're gonna pay." Though Franny was a solid six feet, Tobin flung him effortlessly over his shoulder and bashed through the balcony doors.

The sound of sirens rose up to meet them.

Rikki had gone into work still mulling over her encounter with Abigail, still completely conflicted over what to do about Francis Xavier Black. Fortunately, she didn't have to make a decision until her shift ended, so she had continued to look for solutions for the little Tobin boy, and had located a great-aunt who lived in Temecula, California, who had been horrified to learn of her great-niece's death and was happy to take custody of the child.

Rikki had been sharing the good news with Bugeye when the call had come in: Tobin had been spotted in Midtown. It was technically well out of their jurisdiction, but Tobin was an ace and supposedly the cops of Fort Freak were best prepared to deal with a wild card, so Midtown had screamed for help.

As she and Bugeye were driving north, the 911 calls from Stellar started coming in and getting dispatched to the in-car computer. Among the names was one Rikki recognized—Abigail Baker— who reported that the man had taken a hostage, a police officer . . .

She eyed the traffic moving like an advancing glacier that lay between their car and the Empire State. Throwing open the door she called to Bugeye as she jumped out, "I'll meet you there," and took off running between the cars crawling up Fifth Avenue.

The *Times* had been right about the roof antennas. Unfortunately for Tobin, there were struts supporting the cocoon and platform that had been built around the antennas to keep any falling rivets, tools, or other materials from striking pedestrians down below. Tobin grabbed one, wrapped his legs around the thick metal cable, and shimmied up until he could kick a hole through the heavy canvas and lurch onto the workmen's platform.

A couple of the hard hats started toward them, but Franny bellowed, "Stay back! Get out of here!" One of the largest workmen hefted a heavy wrench and gave Tobin a calculating look. "Don't! He's an ace." That penetrated, and the handful of workers who could fit in this small space retreated down the submarine hatch that gave access to the roof.

Tobin allowed Franny to slip from his shoulder, but kept a painful grip on the back of his neck. "So, what's the plan, Tobin?" Franny panted. "You gonna throw me off?"

"I'm not going to prison for killing that bitch. I'll die first!"

"What about Ronald?"

"His fucking name isn't *Ronald*. It's *Ronan*, and you fucking killed him!" Tobin screamed, his spittle hitting Franny in the face.

Franny was about to reassure him that the boy was okay, recovering at the clinic, but the words died in his throat. To do that would send the man to the clinic, endangering both staff and patients.

Better that it ended here.

Rikki hated that she was forced to ride the elevator, but running up eighty-six flights would have even her arriving tired and out of breath, and she was pretty sure she would need all her speed and skills once she got there. The elevator deposited her at the restaurant. A couple of building security guards were already there. Rikki took a quick glance around, noting the shattered glass doors and the broken host stand.

Abigail was there, talking with one of the guards, but broke off when she spotted Rikki and raced over to her. Rikki had to grab her by the arm to bring her to a stop.

"He grabbed Franny. He took him . . . up! I should have done something. I have your power, but I didn't do anything. I should have come back, grabbed him, run away, saved him . . ."

Rikki put a hand on the other woman's shoulder. "It's okay. You did the right thing. You're not trained for this."

Rikki hurried to one of the guards. "Is there a way up to the roof?"

"Yeah, I'll show you."

She had to shoulder past the large roughnecks milling at the base of the ladder. They registered her uniform and one of them called, "That guy is fuckin' nuts, Officer. You want help?"

"Thanks, but how about I call if I need you?" she suggested as she started climbing.

She emerged from the hatch to see Franny and Tobin at the edge of the platform near a hole in the side of the cocoon. She heard Franny say, "You want to do it? Great, let's *do* it. Got nothing to live for now, amirite?" The wind was whipping and whining around them, the torn edges of the canvas snapping like a whip.

Franny had a manic grin as he grabbed Tobin around the shoulders and threw his weight against him. Tobin swayed precariously. The bleak look in Franny's eyes sent a jolt of fear into the pit of Rikki's stomach.

"Franny! *Francis Xavier Black!* Don't you dare!" Startled, his head jerked toward her. "What, you can save other people, but don't have the fucking courage to save yourself?" Her throat felt tight.

She saw Tobin's muscles tense, his eyes sliding to the edge of the platform. Desperate, she yelled, "*I'm* the one who took your kid. After *you* stabbed him because you are a total fuckup. No wonder she wanted to leave you." It was a total stab in the dark, but the barb seemed to hit home.

Tobin's face went brick red. He began to turn toward Rikki. His hand was pressed against Franny's chest ready to shove him aside—a shove that very well might send him off the roof. Rikki's own muscles bunched ready to run, hoping to grab Franny before he plunged twelve hundred feet to his death.

She bought you time, you spineless fuck. Do something! He's about to go for her. Hurt her.

Franny's eyes flicked desperately, and he spotted the scaffold just overhead. Peeking off the edge was the end of a heavy metal beam. Ropes ran down from the sides of the scaffold to a pulley near his left foot. Knowing he had only seconds before Tobin would attack Rikki, Franny lashed out with his foot and hit the handle. The rope went zipping and whining through the pulley wheel, and one side of the scaffold dropped with a jerk and a crash. A beam came sliding down, and one side of the flange clipped the top of Tobin's head.

He stumbled backward and started to pitch off the edge. Franny threw himself onto the hard metal of the roof and grabbed desperately at Tobin's ankle with both hands. Felt himself slipping inexorably toward the lip as the man's weight pulled him forward.

Then Rikki was there, wrapping the scaffolding rope around Franny's hips and running backward, pulling them both to safety. Catching his breath, Franny quickly pulled the syringe provided to all law enforcement and injected the powerful sedative into Tobin's neck. Rikki pulled handcuffs from her belt. By the time Bugeye and Bill Chen boiled up through the hatch, Tobin was unconscious and restrained.

Franny and Rikki sat on the steps leading up to Jetboy's Tomb. One of the spotlights that illuminated the statue had burned out, so only his profile was visible. The mournful cry of a ferry horn was carried across the water. A pair of teens, hands tightly clasped, came hurrying into the square around the tomb, spotted Rikki's uniform, and beat a hasty retreat.

"Underage drinking or were they going to share a joint?" Franny asked.

"Probably booze; nobody cares about pot anymore," Rikki replied.

Franny took a bite of his burrito from Mr. Nieto's truck and chased it with the soda they'd bought at Antoine's Corner Store. Rikki's mom had given them a cat-who-caught-the-canary look when they walked in. Rikki responded by rolling her eyes and Franny felt his face going red with embarrassment as he recalled the last conversation he'd had with Abby . . .

It had taken hours to question all the witnesses, and Franny'd had only a brief moment to talk with Abigail. He had started to thank her for protecting the diners and staff, but she stopped him, pressing her fingers to his lips. She then jerked her chin toward Rikki, who was busy taking down witness statements.

"She's in your world. You're in hers. Do not fuck this up."

He gave a snort. Rikki now cocked her head, looked up at him inquiringly. "What?"

"Just thinking about Abby." He took a deep breath, wondering why emotional honesty always had to be this hard. "She told me not to fuck this"—he gestured between them—"up." He then added, "Like I did before. Assuming there ever was anything . . . And let me state for the record, whether we had anything or not . . . I'm sorry. I was an ass."

"You kinda were, but in the interest of full disclosure . . . My mom sent me almost the same identical text after we left the store."

"We seem to have a lot of yentas in our life," Franny said.

Rikki shoved him with her shoulder. "What would you know from yentas? You're a good Catholic boy." Rikki paused, staring down at her half-eaten burrito, then added, "So, what do you think . . ."

"I think I'd like that. Very much . . ."

She raised her eyes to his. "I hear a but."

She had on her cop face, but he saw through it. "Not because of *you*. It's *me*. I want to actually be the man you think I am before that happens. You shouldn't have to deal with my shit until I get my shit sorted out. I'm going to start seeing Dr. Engelberg again, and—"

"That's all great, but why is it only *you* who gets to set the timeline and the rules?" He gaped at her. "Being in a relationship means you're there for *all of it*—the good and the bad, the highs and the lows."

He studied her face. How the shadows highlighted her cheekbones, how the breeze off the ocean fluttered the tendrils of hair that had escaped from her ponytail, how she just lived with such calm authority, comfortable in her own skin, secure in the knowledge of who she was. How, because of her help, she had given him the chance to find out who he might be, free from the looming shadow of his father.

"Did you know you're very wise?" He gave her a sideways smile.

He slipped an arm around her wasp waist and she shifted until they were snuggled close together. He sobered and gave her a serious look.

"Rikki, what if, at the end, I decide I don't want to do *this* anymore?" He gestured at the badge clipped on his belt.

"That's okay. You don't love people because of their careers. You love them because of who they are."

He bent and gently brushed his lips across hers.

"Shall we get out of the cold?" she suggested.

"And the dark," he added.

As they walked away, her hand cradled in his, Franny realized that for the first time in a long time, he believed that might just be possible.

2019

Echoes from a Canyon Wall

by Bradley Denton

I peered past my reflection in the bus window, my blue-tinted specs pushed up to my forehead, trying to catch a glimpse of the Grand Canyon in the fading light. I was having no luck.

"Bloody stupid trees," I muttered.

The lady in the seat behind me pressed her face between my headrest and the window. She spoke into my ear. "They're ponderosa pines," she said. Her breath was warm on my cheek, and I caught a whiff of peppermint. "Some spruce and fir, too, I think."

I managed to respond with a small grunt. I knew I should turn to look at her, for the sake of politeness. But what if she flinched at a close-up of me? My eyes are such a pale gray that they're almost silver, with a few odd flecks of green. They look luminous and bizarre against my wheatish skin. So does my spiky hair, so blond it's almost white.

Or so I've been told. That's why I prefer to meet new people when I'm wearing my specs. But if I flipped them down now, it would seem rude, wouldn't it?

On the other hand, if I turned to her barefaced, whether or not my appearance startled her, she would see my pupils widen. And she would know I was, um, interested. Which I doubted would be appreciated. Not in response to chitchat about pine trees.

But I was already smitten. I had taken a sharp breath the moment she'd boarded the bus in Flagstaff.

The lady was small, slender, Asian. Elegant in demeanor, though she was dressed for a May trip to the canyon: Hiking boots, almost as substantial as my Doc Martens. Tan cargo pants and an olive T-shirt with a moon-and-stars silkscreen design. Dark-blue hoodie over one arm, for the chilly evenings. She was lush without being posh. Mid- to late twenties. So, five to ten years older than me.

She had lovely skin a bit lighter than mine, and intricate green-and-purple tattoos on her arms and neck. Vines and orchids. Strong cheekbones, a small upturned nose, and large, dark eyes. Not-quite-straight, near-black hair with streaks of chestnut down to her jawline. One soft wave angled over her right eyebrow.

She was a work of art containing works of art, and I had wanted to crane my neck to keep watching her as she'd walked by. But of course I hadn't. And then I'd felt her slide into the seat behind mine. At which my pulse had quickened.

I know. I was projecting unreasonable desires onto an innocent stranger. But I had been gobsmacked.

Now, with her face between my headrest and the window, she gave a small "Hah!" in response to my grunt. "What's the matter, don't you like trees?"

Oh, splendid, she was teasing me, straightaway. And my stupid eighteen-year-old brain said, *All right, mate, you're in a proper relationship now.*

Well, I did know a bit more about her than at first sight. I knew her breath was warm, with a hint of peppermint. And I knew she had what I would call a middle-American accent. She might be from Ohio or California. Or any point in between.

Maybe that wasn't much information. Nevertheless, I was certain I wouldn't mind kissing her.

With some discomfort, I remembered my most recent FaceTime call with my Big Sis, Michelle. I'd mentioned a girl the other Who roadies and I had met at the hotel breakfast buffet the day after the Albuquerque show, and I'd made an almost-joke about how it had broken my heart to hit the road again. Because I thought I might be in love.

Michelle had laughed. "Of course you are, Freddie," she'd said. "But don't worry. You'll fall in love with a girl in Las Vegas, too. And then in Phoenix."

Well, I'd showed her. I had not fallen in love in Phoenix. I'd waited until arriving at the North Rim . . . for the family vacation Michelle was paying for.

But this new love match was already hitting me harder than the one in Albuquerque. Or even the one in Vegas.

The kid is off the bus. I'm outside the Grand Canyon Lodge. Leaning against the wall, smoking a cigarette.

What do you care?

If you were worried about my health, you wouldn't have recruited me for SCARE. Besides, cigarettes can come in handy in our line of work. They did when I was interrogating illegals for Immigration and Customs. That little orange glow can be a powerful motivator.

So don't worry about me and the cancer sticks. I sweat neurotoxin from my fingertips, remember? If I eat a piece of fried chicken, I might swallow enough to paralyze a rhino. But I just keep eating. A little smoke ain't gonna hurt me.

Too many people at the moment, all of 'em from the bus coming to check in. I'll wait until he's alone, and full dark. He'll be in one of the deluxe cabins, you said? Yeah, I got one of the little ones, back up the road a way. But that was for my cover. I don't plan to spend any time there.

I'll take him in his cabin. They're duplexes, two units per building. So he'll be alone, since his sister and niece won't be here to occupy the other unit. I'll get him after he's asleep.

No one'll hear, no one'll see. And the kid won't have time to cut loose with one of those fifty-megaton yells. Scratch him on the neck while he sleeps, he'll be paralyzed before he can wake up. Put him over my shoulder, lug him to the van. Parking lot's close. It's just the trees that make everything look isolated. He weighs, what, a hundred forty? No problem. If anyone sees us, I tell 'em he's drunk. They don't buy it, they'll be makin' dirt angels.

I'll buzz you as we blow out of here, and you can have the plane meet us at that old airstrip fifteen miles north. We'll be on our way to New Mexico by two, three A.M. Land at your snazzy underground Containment Center by sunup.

At least, that's how it'll work as long as nobody screws with me. Michelle Pond is stuck at LaGuardia, right? The Amazing Bubbles is grounded?

Whaddaya mean, "Don't worry, Morpho Girl ain't coming, either"? What was she gonna do, flap me to death with her butterfly wings?

Pond, though, is another matter. Don't know if I could score on that big ol' broad before she hit me with one of those cannonballs she throws. Even if I could, she might be immune to my venom.

I mean, hasn't someone tried somethin' like that by now? Whaddaya do with a broad who just gets bigger and stronger when you hit her or shoot her? Well, how about you poison her, genius? Unless that don't work, either. Got me?

So keep Michelle away from here, just for tonight, and that's all I need.

Jeez, that kid is ugly as a pig on stilts. His hair ain't like that naturally, is it? With that Bollywood skin?

Wait a minute.

He's with a chick.

I'm telling you, he's with a chick. They're getting stuff from the baggage wells together. She's all smiley and she just touched his arm.

You said he'd be alone. You said he was coming here to meet up with Pond and her joker brat.

Christ on a cracker. This ain't some ace what's-their-faces sent to protect him, is it? Carnifucks, Midnight Asswipe, whatever you call them?

Or is this just some random nat? He get himself a girlfriend?

I'll pretend I'm texting, zap you a photo.

Damn. They're inside. Lemme finish my cigarette, then saunter in and get a shot.

I can give you a rough description now: She's short, petite, looks Korean or Vietnamese. Maybe mid-twenties. Has floral tattoos on her arms and neck. Baggy T-shirt and some cargo pants that don't do her ass any favors.

So, Asian chick, marginally hot, and tattoos. Is there some ace you know of looks like that? Knives shoot out her eyes or hornets fly out her nose? Mustard gas from her hoo-hah?

I'm asking, is she somebody I gotta worry about?

I'll get you that photo. Hold on to your dick.

Gotta say, I am not loving this subvocal comm thing. Don't mind talkin' in my throat, but your whiny voice in my jaw is startin' to get on my nerves.

There, cigarette's done. Heading inside. No, I just don't like surprises, that's all. I'll deal.

Hey, I used to roll with all kinds of crap when I was with ICE. That's how I got my name, you know?

Not "Ronnie Dwight." That's my Christian name. I mean my he's-a-bad-mothafuckah name.

See, I noticed the detainees started whispering the same thing every time I went to the bullpen to take one of 'em to the box. Like they were calling me a name, being derogatory.

I don't know Spanish, so I just grabbed one of 'em who spoke some English and made her tell me. She didn't wanna. But she did.

That's right. "El Alacrán." Yeah, with that funky accent mark. I'm a scorpion, baby.

But they'd been saying it like they'd step on me if they had a chance. Like a bug.

So I got me some of them long acrylic fingernails and I filed one to a point. Glued it to the nail on my index finger. After that, whenever I came to get me a greaseball, I'd point at the chosen one and say, "Your ass belongs to El Alacrán." It scared the piss out of 'em.

If it didn't, I'd slash one of 'em and smear a little venom into the scratch. Once that hombre or señorita was on the floor, the others would start behaving themselves.

Okay, they're in line at registration. And there's your photo.

Find out who she is. If she and the kid split up, cool. If they don't, I need to know if she'll be a problem.

Yeah, I got enough venom for both of 'em.

Ain't ever a shortage. Ask any of those illegals I just told you about. The ones you can still ask.

You speak Spanish?

So here I was, pulling up to the Grand Canyon Lodge on the North Rim while chatting up an eighteen-year-old roadie for the Who.

I didn't mean for it to happen.

Michelle will never believe that. She'll think I did it to punish her for breaking my heart. For telling me Joey had needed her. And she had needed Joey.

Not that cruel, calculated revenge had never crossed my mind. Doesn't it cross the mind of anyone who feels betrayed by someone they've loved?

But even if I would have done that to Michelle, I wouldn't have risked my relationship with Adesina. The girl is my goddaughter, and I'm her Auntie Ink.

I wouldn't have hurt Freddie, either.

At least, not until I found out I might have to.

Before it started, all I knew was that Carnifex and the Midnight Angel had left SCARE. But I didn't know why. In my current job with the Committee on Extraordinary Interventions—which is under the United Nations, after all—I've been looking at the rest of the world so much that, for a long time, I didn't grasp what was happening here at home. Back when I'd worked for the Special Committee for Ace Resources and Endeavors—another "committee," but in fact a major US government agency—it had been a well-intentioned if sometimes heavy-handed bureau to regulate aces and protect the public. Apparently, that mission began to change when President Towers got his hands on it. Or maybe even before that.

Because things never go bad all at once, do they? We're all in a big pot of water, and the people in charge can turn the heat up so slowly that we don't realize we're being boiled alive until it's too late.

Then the Midnight Angel showed up at my apartment one evening in street clothes. Which was a surprise, since she and I weren't friends. We had met, but it had been related to our jobs. And on all the occasions I had seen her, she had been in her black leather work clothes. So I would have expected a phone call, at least, before she rang my doorbell.

But I let her in anyway. You don't say no to a soldier of God who can summon a flaming sword. Besides, the fact that she had come to my home, incognito, was my first clue that something was wrong. Once inside, she produced a gizmo and swept my apartment for bugs. That was my second clue.

Then she told me that she and Carnifex needed allies who could keep their mouths shut. After some research (which I assumed meant "spying on you"), they had decided I would be sympathetic to their mission. And would be trustworthy.

"I think we're right about that," the Angel had said. "But if not . . . I've prayed on it, and the Lord has told me to do what I must. Especially if we're about to be betrayed to SCARE."

So their departure from SCARE had been about more than a minor disagreement.

Also, I had better watch my p's and q's.

The Midnight Angel explained that the Special Committee for Ace Resources and Endeavors was being transformed into a federal police force beholden only to President Towers, and that its new purpose would be to neutralize political enemies. To that end, SCARE was recruiting or forcing certain aces to become weapons against anyone who threatened the ruling party.

I was horrified. But I didn't know what she and Carnifex thought I could do about it. I was a Committee factotum, nothing more. It's not like my little deuce power would be much use against a secret police force of aces. Sure, I could bring what they were telling me to the Committee's attention—but so could they.

As it turned out, they didn't want to tell the Committee at all, for fear of open conflict between the UN-sanctioned Committee and the Towers-loyal SCARE. It's best to avoid situations that could lead to, say, a war between the United States and the rest of the world.

Instead, Billy Ray and the Angel were fighting a covert action, thwarting SCARE's recruitment and planning however they could.

At the moment, they were busy with anti-SCARE operations in both New York and DC, as were the few other aces they had on their team. So they needed someone—me—to go west. Not as any kind of fighter, but as a set of eyes. As, well, a snoop.

"You have a lot of vacation time," the Midnight Angel said. Which meant they'd been going through my personnel records. "And the Committee can get by without you for a few weeks."

I supposed that was true. "What kind of snooping are we talking about?"

For the first time since showing up at my door, the Midnight Angel gave a slight smile. "Do you like classic rock?"

So, yeah, I'd followed the Who and its crew through the last five cities of their US tour, changing my appearance at each concert and hotel on the off chance anyone might look at me twice. That's easy enough to do with different clothes, tinting my hair, and changing my tattoos. Which I can do at will. Any colors, any patterns, anywhere on my body. And I can rearrange my facial shadings better than any makeup artist.

So I was able to snoop on Freddie "Amplifier" Fullerton throughout the Southwest, make note of who spoke with him and when, and watch to see if anyone else seemed to be following him. And I reported on everything via encrypted text messages to Carnifex and the Midnight Angel.

You see, Billy Ray had an informant who'd been providing him with the names of aces SCARE was thinking of "acquiring." And after one of Freddie's amplified shouts had flattened a mob of drug-enraged rioters in New York's Jokertown in December, his name had gone to the top of the list.

Inflict some physical harm on him, and he would immediately shout with a force far greater than the force of whatever had hurt him. He could produce the sonic equivalent of a hand grenade if you slapped him . . . or of a bunker-buster bomb if you shot him. Then, after recovering, he'd be ready to do it all over again. Whether he wanted to or not.

So you could, for example, flatten every person in a protest march without deploying any goons in black body armor. You'd get all of the skull-cracking with none of the bad optics. Heck, the news cameras might not even see what had really happened. And if they did . . . Well, just blame it on the kid with the big voice.

But by the time I followed Freddie to the North Rim, I was starting to think he might be in the clear. I hadn't spotted anyone who seemed SCARE-like in Denver, Reno, Albuquerque, Las Vegas, or even in Phoenix, the last show of the tour. And aside from his crewmates, I hadn't seen Freddie interact with anyone except for two young women in Albuquerque and Las Vegas.

The poor kid hadn't done too well.

I guess the third time was the charm.

In Albuquerque, I had a text from Adesina. I hadn't told her where I was, so she probably thought I was still at work at the Committee offices in Manhattan.

Auntie Ink! So cool! Mom and I are going to the Grand Canyon to meet Uncle Freddie on May 18. I've only seen it in pictures. Wish you could come. Because Grand Canyon!

Also you should meet Uncle Freddie sometime. You would like him.

Yes. Well.

I shared that info with Carnifex and the Midnight Angel, and Billy Ray answered:

We know. Source believes SCARE may prevent Amazing Bubbles from departing NYC, providing opportunity to acquire F at Canyon.

No airline seats available Phoenix to Flagstaff. F will travel by bus.

Avoid scrutiny. Rent car, drive to Flagstaff. Board bus there. Will send itinerary.

Stay close to F. Your presence may discourage SCARE. Do not identify self or inform F of situation. Could contact Bubbles, who could cause incident.

If Bubbles detained NYC, assume SCARE at N Rim. Then M Angel will arrive ASAP to extract. Keep phone GPS-enabled.

If SCARE attempts to acquire F before M Angel arrives, trigger shout to defend. AMN.

AMN meant "Any Means Necessary."

It was a sickening sensation, knowing I could have a legitimate reason to hurt Freddie Fullerton.

Because I was jealous of him. In a deeper, uglier way than I had ever been jealous of anyone else.

Sure, Adesina called me her Auntie Ink. But Freddie really *was* her Uncle Freddie. He was Michelle's long-lost half brother, the son of her father and one of her old modeling chums, the brother she had never known she'd had, and—to hear Adesina tell it—the brother she'd always wanted.

So in December, after the riot, Freddie had been able to walk right in, and Michelle had accepted and loved him. He hadn't needed to make any effort at all.

At least, not like the effort *I* had made.

But in light of the SCARE situation, I would have to get over that. Or at least ignore it. As Rick says to Ilsa in *Casablanca*, the problems of three little people don't amount to a hill of beans in this crazy world.

Which is kind of hilarious, since the Amazing Bubbles is not one of the "little people," in any sense.

But I am. And I would try to do something for this crazy world anyway.

Looking back, I know I should have confided in Freddie at the outset, despite what Carnifex had said. When we met on the bus, I should have told him right then that I knew his sister and his niece. I should have told him the real reason I was there.

But that evening and that night, I didn't even tell him my real name. I started to, then cut myself off before uttering the *t* in Juliet. So he thought I was Julie. And I didn't give him a last name at all.

I didn't think Adesina had shown him a photo of me, because he gave no sign of recognition. But then, I had also lightened my hair, altered my tattoos, and shaded my eyes, cheeks, lips, and chin. I didn't look like any photo he could have seen.

In other words, I wasn't myself. I wasn't the Juliet Summers who only slept with women. I wasn't the Juliet Summers who had loved the Amazing Bubbles.

I wasn't even Morpho Girl's "Auntie Ink."

That night, I was Julie.

And Julie turned out to be someone else altogether.

Got an ID *on her yet?*

"Not on any list of known aces." But that don't mean she ain't one, does it?

What the hell is "Occam's razor"? She got razor blades for toenails or something?

Keep looking. You oughta be able to find her somewhere, even if she's a nat and a civilian.

Goddammit. She might have made me.

I'm heading back outside. I'll get eyes on the kid again when he goes to his cabin.

Here's hoping the woman is just a rando and not somebody the Bobbsey Twins sent.

Whaddaya mean, who are the Bobbsey Twins? Read a book, dumbass.

I helped Julie get her bags into the Grand Canyon Lodge, and then we queued up with the other escapees from the bus. The big, vaulted lobby was all rough wood and limestone, just what you'd expect. All of it lit by a golden glow from lamps suspended by long, almost invisible cables.

"Do you know if your sister and niece are here yet?" Julie asked, glancing around. I had told her I was meeting Michelle and Adesina, but so far I hadn't told her they were the Amazing Bubbles and Morpho Girl. I supposed she would recognize Big Sis, at least, as soon as she saw them.

I was looking forward to being with them, but not in a hurry. After all, once they appeared, that might be the end of my time with Julie. I had some guilt at that thought. But then I remembered Big Sis's remark about how often I was likely to fall in love. So she, at least, would understand.

Outside of our check-in queue, only a few strangers occupied the lobby. A family of four leaving the dining room. A couple of lads about my age sitting on a rustic cowhide couch, deep in whispered conversation. A tanned middle-aged bloke slouched in a chair that matched the couch, staring at the screen of his phone. That was it.

Maybe Big Sis and Adesina were already in our "Deluxe Western" cabin. Michelle had sent me photos. Each building contained two units, with two queen beds in each unit. A doorway between the beds led to a bathroom and storage area, and a connecting door next to the bathroom led to the other unit. One unit in our cabin would be for Michelle and Adesina, and the other for me. So not only would I have a holiday with my two favorite people, but I'd have some privacy, too. Which was something I never had on the road, since I was always sharing a room with one of the other roadies.

I took my phone from my jean pocket to see if I could get a signal. I had to hold it over my head and turn it back and forth, but then it buzzed furiously.

There were four texts. Three were from Big Sis:

Freddie our flight is delayed two hours. Something mechanical. Might not get in until late.

Flight now delayed three more hours. We get to Flagstaff in middle of night. Will be at GC Lodge in morning.

Flight canceled. Soonest we can depart will be tomorrow afternoon, which puts us in Flagstaff tomorrow night and North Rim Monday morning. Have fun until we show up. PS. Let me know when you get this.

The fourth text was from Adesina:

Uncle F this sucks.

"Aw, bollocks," I said.

Julie looked at me quizzically. "Are you British? You haven't sounded like it before now. But 'bollocks' is a pretty British word."

I nodded. "That's what it says on my passport."

"It says 'bollocks'?"

More teasing. If she wanted to fend me off, this wasn't the way to do it. "No, that I'm British, Miss Wit. But my mum spent years in the States before she went back to London and had me. So I started off sounding like her, then like a mixture of her and my schoolmates, and then like, I don't know, maybe Neil Young. I've been told my accent sounds midway between Brighton and Minneapolis, via the North Pole."

Julie gave me a delicate smirk. "Ah, that explains why you pronounced 'bollocks' like a Zamboni driver in Saskatoon."

"You're so sweet," I said, with what I hoped was charming mock sarcasm.

She still had that little smirk. "I do what I can."

I wanted to kiss her even more.

I tapped my phone. "My sister and niece can't be here until Monday morning. Their flight was canceled."

Julie's smirk vanished. "Oh! Oh, no." She sounded dismayed to a degree that startled me.

The queue moved a bit, and I shifted my backpack and scooted Julie's bags ahead of us. "Well, Big Sis says it's a mechanical problem. And it's better to be late than to crash." Although a crash would just make Michelle extra big and powerful. And if Adesina could get out before impact—well, Morpho Girl can fly. Still, best for the rest of the passengers not to take off with a defective scozzwozzle or whatever.

Julie glanced to her left, then bumped into me. "Sorry," she said. Her voice had changed. She was almost mumbling.

For a weird moment, I thought I saw one of the vine tattoos on her neck curl a bit tighter. "Would you like to sit down?" I asked. "We can always check in later."

She smiled, but it wasn't convincing. "I'm okay," she said. "Low blood sugar, I think."

I could relate. But as I looked across the lobby toward the lodge dining room, its lights went out, and the hostess put a chain across the entrance. It was 9:30 P.M.

"Looks like we're out of luck," I said. "Maybe there are vending machines."

Julie shook her head. "I have snacks. Once we get checked in, I'll be happy to share." She looked to the right. "But at the moment, I need to find a ladies' room. Would you mind watching my bags?"

She headed off, taking her phone from her cargo pants as she disappeared into a hallway.

I'll do anything you want, I thought.

I was feeling even more guilty now, because I was actually glad that Big Sis and Adesina wouldn't be arriving for another day and a half. I was so glad, in fact, that I wanted to shout.

But that would be a bad idea, since I might blow the roof off the lodge.

I had never given that kind of shout from anything but pain, so I wasn't even sure it was possible, otherwise. Still, I thought I should be careful. Because I had the strangest sense of impending joy.

And who knew what that would do to me?

None of your *intel says he has a girlfriend. But he just now took her to his cabin.*

And I'm telling you, that kid is not smooth enough to pick up a woman on a bus. Or a train, a plane, or whorehouse.

Which means she's picked up him.

Woman like her, picking up a dork like that?

So keep looking. Get a driver's license, a police record, Facebook page, something with a name and some history. Hell, there's gotta be a credit card tied to her bus ticket and lodge reservation.

Meantime, I'll stay in the trees and watch.

What's the soonest the Pond woman could show up?

Monday morning. You sure?

In that case, I can hold off. I could try to put the chick down and snatch him right now, but I'd rather be sure it's gonna be easy. Guess I'll make like the pope and shit in the woods tonight.

– – –

I went to Freddie's cabin with him. He was in number 309, attached to number 306—which was empty, since Michelle and my godchild were stuck in New York.

Unit 306/309 was right on the canyon rim, just a few dozen yards from the lodge's east terrace. Leave it to Michelle to wrangle the best. Even Billy Ray hadn't managed to get me a cabin that good. I was booked into 312, four buildings north.

Freddie had offered to walk me to 312. We could have our snack there, he'd said, and he would go to his cabin right after.

But I needed to stick with him, because I had spotted someone in the lodge who had made me nervous. If anyone I had seen might be a SCARE agent, it was him. Lean, tall, leathery. Brand-new black baseball cap with a blood-red Arizona Diamondbacks logo. A fringe of dark, gray-peppered hair between the cap and his ears. Long sideburns. Narrow, ice-blue eyes. And a khaki shirt and blue jeans, both also brand new.

Once I spotted him, I excused myself and scooted off toward the ladies' room. I held my phone down at my side, shot some photos behind me, and got lucky. In the restroom, I sent a pic of my suspect to Billy Ray and the Angel.

The Angel replied within thirty seconds. **Don't recognize. But could be someone new.**

That wasn't much help. **So what do I do?** I asked.

She did not try to assuage my fears. **Stay close to F. As noted, will arrive to extract when possible.**

I was not reassured. **I am not reassured**, I said.

There was a pause of twenty seconds.

Trigger shout if needed, she wrote then. **As discussed.**

I sent her a smiley face with X's for eyes.

So, after we collected our cabin keys, I asked Freddie if we could have our snack at his place instead of mine. My excuse was that my cabin was back in the trees and would have no canyon view. And since there was a full moon tonight, the view from 309 might be amazing.

The cabin was limestone and pine, just like the lodge itself. Once inside, we each took a turn in the bathroom, then started a fire in the gas fireplace in the corner of the main room. I put my smaller suitcase on one of the beds and dug out cheese, salami, trail mix, grapes, and bottles of water.

Then, since it was in the mid-forties outside, I put on my hoodie, Freddie put on a gray canvas jacket, and we took our feast to a little porch that looked out over the Grand Canyon. Or, to be accurate, over the Transept, a secondary canyon that links up to the Bright Angel Creek tributary, which links up to the Colorado River and the Grand Canyon itself. They're all part of the same vast sculpture. If sculpture could be carved by the hand of God, or someone similar.

The moonlight shining over all of it, even with scattered clouds, was . . . impressive, I suppose, since "magical" and "transcendent" seem even more trite than "carved by the hand of God." But if you've never been there, don't judge. You don't know how much capacity you have for clichés until you've been dropped smack in the middle of where the clichés were born.

But all of that hit me in the first few seconds. Then I was looking away at flatter ground to see if the sinewy, lanky man from the lodge was approaching. I saw no one, but that meant nothing. He could be crawling up through the scrub just down from where we sat.

Or maybe that dude hadn't been SCARE at all. Maybe he had just been alone in the lodge waiting for friends or family to arrive, as Freddie was waiting for Michelle and Adesina.

Which was what Freddie started off talking about, out there on that little porch while we ate grapes and cheese and gazed at moonlight on canyon walls. Michelle and Adesina. Which caused me no more anguish than an ax to my forehead.

He asked about me, too . . . but I told him the bare minimum. Born in Korea, never knew my birth parents, adopted by Americans and raised in California. Now tell me what it's like to be a roadie for the Who.

"I feel like I've been doing nothing but talking about myself," Freddie said. His breath came out as a puff of crystallized smoke. "And trust me, being a roadie isn't all that fascinating, although I do like it."

"Well, it gives you a chance to see the world," I said, gesturing at the magnificence before us. "For example."

He took off his tinted spectacles and slipped them into a jacket pocket. Then he looked out over the canyon.

"This is thanks to my sister," he said. "Otherwise, I wouldn't have seen any more of Arizona than the concert venue and the hotel in Phoenix." He turned back toward me. "Thanks for not freaking out just now. I mean, when I told you who she is." He let out another crystallized breath. "I'm still trying to reconcile the Michelle I'm getting to know with the Amazing Bubbles that everyone has heard of. If you know what I mean."

I knew better than he could guess. In fact, I knew of at least two other Michelles that weren't anything like the ones he knew. "What about your niece?" I asked.

Freddie grinned. "She's the most what-you-see-is-what-you-get person you'll ever meet. I mean, my Big Sis and the Amazing Bubbles are different people, because they have to be. But Adesina and Morpho Girl are one and the same. I've watched her fly people to safety from a fire, play Mr. Entwistle's bass lines from *Tommy* lick for lick, and argue with her mum over whether chicken salad should have walnuts. And she has the same attitude in all three situations. She's always—who she is."

I couldn't help grinning at that, myself. He was right. That was Adesina.

"Goodness, Freddie," I said. "You sound like the proudest uncle on Earth." Which didn't surprise me. After all, that was how I had always felt about being Auntie Ink.

He nodded. "Brother, too. But you know, I didn't earn it. I just showed up and got this fantastic family."

I had a pang. It was as if he'd read my mind.

My phone buzzed. I had to check it, because it was going to be something from Carnifex or the Midnight Angel.

"Sorry," I said, pulling out the phone. "I'm an admin at a security firm, and they keep pestering me." Which almost wasn't a lie.

I held the phone so Freddie couldn't see the screen. There was a text from Billy Ray.

No ID on your photo yet. But if civilian, could ID quickly. Avoid.

M Angel en route soon as possible. May require 18–24 hours. Shelter in place.

I put away my phone and shivered. I was sure a hundred pairs of eyes were watching us from the darkened trees.

"Everything okay?" Freddie asked.

"Just getting chilly." I stood. "Could we go inside?"

I didn't think he'd object. And he didn't. I knew what he was hoping for. But I was going to disappoint him. And I was going to disappoint Billy Ray, too. I didn't think I could string Freddie along and keep him in the dark for another twenty-four hours.

So I was going to tell him the whole story. I was going to tell him that the Towers administration wanted to turn him into an anti-dissident bomb. He deserved to know. And maybe then we'd have a better chance of staying safe until the cavalry arrived. Otherwise, if SCARE jumped us before I could aim an Amplifier shout, what would I do? Tattoo myself to resemble a werewolf? All five foot one of me?

We went inside. The fire we had started was flickering on the walls, the ceiling timbers, the beds.

There were large windows on the west and east walls, beside each of the beds. I went to the one on the west, which looked out over the Transept, and closed the curtains.

"Do me a favor," I said, heading across the room. "Lock the door."

Freddie set our dinner leftovers on a small table and gave me a look.

Those eyes. In the firelight, the green flecks in his silvery irises caught the light like bits of jade. They were the same shade of green as Michelle's eyes.

I looked away from him as I closed the curtains over the east window. "Listen," I said. I dropped my voice, afraid someone might be just outside. "I need to tell you—"

I turned back toward him, and he was right there. His hands went to my face. They were chilly from our time on the porch.

Then his mouth was over mine, and it wasn't chilly at all.

I did nothing for maybe five seconds. Then I put my hands on his chest, meaning to push him away.

Instead, my fingers clenched his jacket.

He was kissing me like the first time Michelle had kissed me. A kiss that didn't hold anything back. A kiss that meant what it said.

In that instant, I wasn't there anymore. I wasn't in a limestone cabin on the North Rim with a boy I barely knew. Instead, I was somewhere I had wanted to be for a long time.

I didn't break the kiss. Freddie did.

His hands slid down to my shoulders.

"More?" he asked. He was so close that I felt his voice as much as heard it.

My fingers were still knotted in his jacket, and I pulled him back to me. When we came up for air, I said one word. Whispered it. Or maybe just breathed it.

"Shit," I said.

She's not coming out.

I saw her get a key, so she has a cabin, too. But she's staying with him.

Getting closer to see if I can hear anything. Don't like it out of the trees, though. Full moon. Porch lights beside the cabin doors. Gotta stay in the shadows.

I can hear the kid and the woman now. Yeah, they're screwing.

But even when I get right next to the wall, they're pretty quiet. Nobody's yellin' Oh, Jesus God! *or nothin'. You'd think the kid, at least, would be louder. Given what he's supposed to be capable of.*

My wife used to yell Oh, Jesus God! *if you must know. Toward the end, I think that was the only thing she liked about me. It was for damn sure the only thing I liked about her.*

It used to wake up our boy. He'd run in bawling that he'd heard a monster. I swear, he knew he was cockblocking me.

I can slip into the empty unit without them hearing me. Then jimmy the connecting door and come up on them from the bathroom. Slash them both before they know I'm there.

Paralyze 'em in mid-pump. Speaking of cockblocks.

Then I peel them apart, wrap the kid in a blanket like a sausage, and haul ass. Leave the woman drooling.

Moving around to the door to 306 now.

It wasn't as if it was my first time. Or second, or third.

Okay, it was my fourth.

But it was different.

It was different in the way the view from the rim of the Grand Canyon is different from the view from the top of the Empire State Building. They're both pretty great, but only one of them gives you a sense of what eternity must be like. Only one of them makes you feel that if you were to shout into the depths, your voice would reverberate forever.

That was what being with Julie was like.

The bed was beside us as we kissed, but I don't remember falling into it. And I only remember two things about getting undressed.

I got my arm stuck in my jacket. Julie had to help me, and she only laughed a little.

And once my shirt was off, Julie traced the tattoo on my chest, the Fender Deluxe Reverb amp, with her finger.

Then the bedspread and blankets were on the floor, and so were our clothes. We lay on our sides. Both her legs were wrapped around my left one, pulling me close. I was holding her so that her upper arms were pinned to her sides.

For the longest time we stayed like that, both trapped.

When we finally released each other, I moved down, kissing her throat, shoulders, breasts, belly. The tattooed vines on her shoulders and neck seemed to twist and writhe in the firelight, and they followed me. But I didn't stop to wonder at that, even as the vines began to interlock across Julie's hips, and buds sprouted among the curves and tangles.

I closed my eyes then, and the taste of her was everything. She was every fruit on every tree on the bank of every river, all the way to the sea.

I stayed that way until she began to shudder. Then I opened my eyes and saw all those buds on all those vines burst all at once. All across her skin, all up her hips and ribs and breasts, all the way to her throat and chin and mouth. Purple and scarlet orchids overwhelmed the twisting green vines, everywhere, their petals trembling.

It wasn't the firelight playing tricks. It was Julie, blooming. Her tattoos had a will of their own, and they grew wild.

I understood her then. I understood her better than I had ever understood anyone else. Because I knew what it was like to have a gift that could overwhelm you in an instant. I knew what it was like to be at the mercy of your own power.

She made a sound. It wasn't a moan, or a scream, or any of those other things people say happen. It was more like a chord from a distant choir. Or a wave crashing on the other side of the world.

The orchids exploded and spun into pinwheels. Purples and scarlets merged with blues and golds, pulsing and whirling.

It was like being at the center of the galaxy as all of its stars were being born.

Then, even after the bursts and whirlpools subsided and came apart, the colors remained. They rippled in gossamer sheets like the northern lights.

I pulled away, got up, found my backpack on the other bed, and unzipped its inner "just-in-case" pocket. I took out one of the foil coins, pulled it open, and went back to Julie.

The northern lights still shimmered, but Julie wasn't moving. One hand was on her belly, the other at her chin. Her fingertips brushed her lower lip. Her face, like the rest of her, was tattooed with slowly rippling sheets of color.

I put on the condom. "Is this all right?"

Her colors froze. I didn't know what that meant.

But I didn't have time to ask.

"If we go slow," she said.

Her colors rippled again, and she reached for me.

Whaddaya mean, "Hold"? *I just got into 306. Hang on, lemme go outside again.*

Okay, I'm in the brush. You finally got an ID?

Her file is classified? *She works for the* Committee?

Fuck me. She's an ace for the United Nations?

Whaddaya mean, "That's unclear"? Is she a member of the Committee or not?

Stop saying "That's unclear," you skidmark.

Just tell me what you got.

"Juliet Summers. Korean American, age twenty-eight. Employed by the Committee. Has been seen with various Committee aces in hot zones.

"Her role appears to be administrative. She is also known to

have been a production assistant on Season One of American Hero."

"*Production assistant*"? *Okay, if she were an ace, she woulda been a contestant, wouldn't she?*

"**Often displays varying tattoos. Seems able to alter these patterns at will. Nicknamed 'Ink.'**

"**Identification has been hampered by apparent facial alterations. Body tattoos are radically different from any file image, but no two images have been the same in this regard.**"

That's it? She can change her tattoos? Big dang whoop.

Unless . . .

Listen, if she can change her skin's pigmentation, can she change other things about it, too? Like how tough it is?

I'm saying, if I scratch her, will I break the surface? Will I paralyze her or just piss her off?

And then could she, like, grow spikes or something? Put her head down and gore me in the nutsack?

Hell yes, I'm serious.

Am I dealing with a chick who has a cute ability to accessorize, or am I dealing with a rhinoceros?

Yeah, you get back to me, dingleberry.

At first, it was almost like being with Michelle.

His mouth tasted almost like hers. His neck tasted almost like hers.

And when he slid down and kissed me, and made my tattoos move on their own—

That was a lot like Michelle, too. Not exactly the same. But so close.

And when that part was over, I knew, in my marrow, what a bad idea this was.

But then, when he asked for more, I gave it.

It was different. But it was nice. He got ahead of me, but slowed down when I asked. I don't think that had been a problem for him before. Or maybe no one had said anything.

My tattoos were under my control again. So I gave Freddie lots of pretty patterns and colors, making them as wild as I could.

Because I wanted to make him happy. At least for a little while. Maybe that wasn't the right way to feel, or the right thing to do. But it was what I wanted.

And right or wrong, the one thing I'm glad about, out of everything that happened, is this:

I did.

I made him happy.

You woke me. *What time is it?*

Seven fifteen A.M. *Still sorta dark outside.*

A light just came on in 309. They're still there.

Yes, I was asleep. Long about two thirty A.M. *I got tired of squatting in the cold. So I decided to check out 308 and 310, which have a view to 309. Neither unit was occupied, so I let myself into 308 and started a fire. Found half a ham sandwich in the mini fridge and ate it. Was dry and stale. Then I watched.*

By four A.M. *it was clear neither of them was coming out, so I decided to get some shut-eye. You don't want me rummy-dummy when I need to make a move, do you?*

It's not my fault this chick showed up. Maybe you should have had a contingency for something like that.

I know. Random events occur during every operation.

But this doesn't feel random. If she works for the Committee, then she's likely acquainted with former SCARE leadership, if only in passing.

Say what, now?

"Rumored to have had a sexual relationship with Michelle Pond"?

And now she's doing the kid brother?

Jeez, and people call me *sick.*

This could be good news, though. Maybe her being here has nothing to do with us, or with the Bobbsey Twins. Maybe Summers is just part of the family vacation.

Perverted family, sure. But aren't they all?

I just need to know whether she can mess with me. You got that answer yet?

As far as you can determine, she's able to change her tattoo patterns, but that's it. Otherwise, she's got plain old human skin. All right, then.

Sun's coming up. And they just came out. Kid looks like a puppy that found a stack of Milk-Bones with a side of gravy.

She looks, I dunno. Can't tell if she's happy, sad, hungry, or bored. Asians are inscrutable, man.

Whaddaya mean, that's racist? Jesus, I'm probably gonna kill her. Do I really need to be politically correct?

They're heading for the lodge, no doubt aiming for a hot breakfast. And I hear other people up and around now, too. So it's gonna be a while before I can make a move.

Best to wait for nightfall, anyway.

I'll assume you're right, and that the chick can't do anything more than change her tattoos. Even so, I'll use enough venom to put her into respiratory arrest. Why take chances?

The kid, I'll just paralyze. It'll wear off in a couple of days.

For now, I think I'll get me some of that hot breakfast, too.

After I go to the can. That ham sandwich ain't sittin' too well.

Breakfast in the lodge on Sunday morning was fantastic. Pancakes, blueberries, and American bacon. Plus the occasional eye roll from Julie when, I guess, I happened to gaze at her a little too intently.

Afterward, we hiked south to Bright Angel Point. It's an easy half-mile paved trail, but it ascends two hundred feet. So the pine trees around the lodge give way to scrubby pinyons and junipers that seem to grow right out of the limestone. It's like flying from the Earth to the moon in a few hundred yards.

The moon itself was hanging off to our right, over the Transept. To our left was the deep, rocky plunge of Roaring Springs Canyon. I was behind Julie, and I had the sense that I was following her up that narrow ridge into the sky.

Her tattoos had reverted to the appearance they'd had when I'd first seen her, on the bus. Hiking behind her, though, all I could see of them were the vines on the back of her neck. And then only when her hair bounced out of the way. It was as if they were trying to hide, but couldn't quite manage. They were green and growing, and they had to be seen.

I couldn't help thinking of how I had already seen them grow and bloom. And I was hoping I would see that again.

But ever since we had left the cabin, Julie had seemed different. Still funny, nice, and apparently glad to be with me. But not like she had been the night before.

I knew it was stupid to expect otherwise, especially since other people were coming past us down the trail. And we had just met the evening before, so it wasn't like we were boyfriend and girlfriend.

Although I had already started thinking about that.

It was almost 9 A.M. when we reached the point. At that moment, we had it to ourselves. The sun was on our left, and straight south of us, the peaks, spires, and walls of Bright Angel Canyon glowed with layer upon layer of pinks and golds. Beyond them, to the southwest, more walls and peaks stretched away toward the South Rim, melting into a distant haze.

I took out my phone and snapped some shots. Then I checked for messages, but the phone hadn't had a signal all night or morning. I'd thought I might pick up a bar or two when we'd gone to breakfast, but no luck.

Julie looked out over the view for a few minutes. "Well," she said at last, gazing into rocky chasms of infinity. "That's better than a poke in the eye."

It was. And since we were alone now, and there was a guardrail, I leaned in for something else I hoped would be better than a poke in the eye.

Julie flinched away and looked back down the trail.

About twenty yards from us was a tall, wiry man in a black cap and sunglasses. He was taking a cellphone photo of the view to the east and didn't seem to notice us. I recognized him as the tanned bloke I had seen in the lodge the night before. "Do you know him?" I asked Julie.

She gave her head a shake. Then she looked out over the canyon again, but her forehead was creased.

I leaned in again, but not for a kiss. "What's wrong?"

Instead of answering, she said, "Any more texts from your sister?"

I still had my phone in my hand. "No. Still no bars. But they can't be here before tomorrow morning, so there's probably nothing more I need to know right now, anyway."

Julie turned away from the view and took my hand. "Let's see if we can sign up for a mule ride."

I wasn't sure how I felt about that. I was glad Julie still wanted to hang out with me, but I had hoped we might spend more time together in the cabin. My selfish thought was that I could do "touristy" things when Michelle and Adesina were there . . . but that I had only one more day to be alone with Julie.

I wondered if she would stick around once my family had arrived. I hoped so. I knew Adesina would like her. And given how amused Big Sis had been at my not-quite-romantic encounters on the road, I was rather looking forward to introducing her to someone who was not so not-quite.

Julie and I started back down the trail, and the man in the cap and sunglasses came up to take our place at the point. He gave us a slight nod and a thin smile, as one does.

Julie's hand tightened on mine.

I wondered if that meant anything close to what I wanted it to mean.

I am not *getting on a fucking mule.*

Animals don't like me. And the feeling is mutual. So I'll hike, thank you very much.

Better to keep my distance, anyway. Summers gave me the stink-eye at Bright Angel Point. Or maybe she just has resting bitch face.

Oh, sorry. Was that sexist?

I'll be sure to call her Ms. Summers as I put her down.

You know, I could probably just wait for them to return. The mule ride takes them to the Supai Tunnel, whatever that is, and then brings them back up. What are they gonna do, jump off and run into the canyon to get away from me? They don't even know who I am.

Yes, I'm sure. Women give me the stink-eye all the time. In grocery stores, in elevators, at the ATM machine. I don't know what their problem is.

Can you hear me?

Of course. I'm going down into the canyon, so reception has fuzzed out. On my end, anyway.

Getting warmer as I descend. Working up a sweat. Stepped in mule shit twice already. Sun's bright, right overhead. But it'll be down near the lip of the canyon by the time we head back up.

"We." Tail anyone for a day or two, and you start thinking you're in some kinda relationship. Even if you wind up killing one of them and dragging the other to a hole in the ground.

Hey, we're going into a hole in the ground right now. Ironic, eh?

Hello?

I was tired of your voice anyway.

I'm staying fifty yards behind the last mule. Summers and Fullerton are on Mules Six and Seven of twelve. I can't see them all the time, because of the switchbacks and brush.

There are other hikers, too, which is good. I've even let a few pass me. But I don't think Summers would notice me anyway. She's been talking to Fullerton and pointing at stuff.

Yeah, here we are, beautiful, towering walls of rock. Sharp blue sky, couple of lazy white clouds that look like they were painted there. Cloud shadows swimming far below.

Like I said, it's a hole in the ground.

I had been riding behind Freddie all the way down the North Kaibab Trail, but my mule nudged past his as we came into a flat, rocky space below the Supai Tunnel. The mules all knew what to do here, and each had a preferred spot along the iron-pipe railing at the edge of the clearing. Our trail guide dismounted, tied his own mule to the rail, and then tied the others one by one, having each rider dismount in turn.

My mule was named Ike, and I gave him a pat on the neck as I dismounted. He ignored it. I had the feeling Ike was not big on bonding with his riders. We were just loads to carry.

The day had become sunny and warm, more so as we'd gone farther into the canyon. I was wearing cheap sunglasses I'd bought at the lodge gift shop, and I had tied my hoodie around my waist about halfway down the trail. I was wearing a cranberry-colored ribbed tank top, and there was a V of perspiration below my collarbone. Freddie gave it an obvious look as our guide tied his mule.

I took my phone from my cargo pants. I had checked it a few minutes earlier, but there had been no signal. There wasn't one now, either. So I had no idea if Billy Ray or the Angel had been trying to get in touch.

I also had no idea how close the Midnight Angel was, or even if she was on her way. And now I realized that if I wasn't getting a signal, she couldn't home in on my GPS, either. But I'd had a signal at the lodge and had sent a text telling her that Freddie and I were taking the mule ride. So at least she would know which trail we were on.

That might be important. On one of the trail's switchbacks, I had looked up and spotted the rangy dude in the ball cap. He was hiking a short distance behind our mule train.

After dismounting, Freddie patted his mule as I had patted mine, but his turned and nuzzled his arm. He had tucked his jacket into a rawhide loop tied to his saddle horn, and he was bare-armed in a new black Who T-shirt. His mule got in a good lick, then lowered its head and snuffled his faded black jeans.

"What's his name?" I asked Freddie as we started up the short hike to the tunnel. "My guy is Ike, but he doesn't like me as much as yours likes you."

Freddie gave a chuckle. "It's a 'she,' and I think she likes me because I'm salty. Her name is Clementine."

"Clementine, of course," I said. "That explains the tune I heard you humming. How is it that a lad from London knows an old American song like that, anyway?"

He shrugged. "I know a lot of old American songs, especially if they were in old American films. And the first film I ever saw about Wyatt Earp's shootout at the OK Corral was *My Darling Clementine.* Henry Fonda, Victor Mature. Twentieth Century Fox, 1946. Watched it on the telly when I was nine or ten, I think."

I had known he was a classic-rock geek, but not that he was a classic-film geek, too. "And here you are in Arizona at last," I said.

Behind his blue-tinted spectacles, his eyes widened. "On a mule named Clementine!" Then he frowned. "But the film was shot in Monument Valley, which is over a hundred miles northeast of here. And the real Tombstone is all the way down by the Mexican border."

I had to laugh. He had gotten so freaking serious about his film trivia all of a sudden. It was adorable.

He looked sheepish. "Too big a nerd?" he asked.

"No," I said. "Just right."

We stepped into the Supai Tunnel. It was a narrow passage about fifteen yards long. Eight feet wide, ten feet high. It had been blasted through a wall of solid rock back in the twenties. The temperature seemed to drop twenty degrees as we came into it.

Freddie stopped and looked behind us. More people from our group were starting up to the tunnel, but they were still down close to the mules. The people who had gotten here before us had already gone through to the other side.

I knew what he was thinking. "Freddie," I said, and he kissed me.

I kissed him back. *What the hell, Juliet?*

Then he pressed me against the tunnel's rough wall and kissed me harder.

I glanced down the trail. And I thought I saw the lanky dude with the ball cap coming into the flat space with the mules.

I pushed Freddie away.

He looked confused. "I'm . . . sorry?"

I pulled him toward the far end of the tunnel. "There are things you don't know," I said.

We came out to an incredible view of towering cliffs and a tree-lined abyss that plunged to the center of the Earth.

Freddie didn't seem to notice.

"Like what?" he asked.

I took my phone from my pocket again. Still no signal.

Some of the people who had already come through were heading back toward us now. This was the turnaround point of the mule trip, and once we had all gone through the tunnel, taken in the view, and had a bathroom break in the outhouses, we would ride back to the trailhead. By the time we returned to the lodge, it would be almost sundown.

If Freddie and I were lucky, the Midnight Angel would be there waiting for us. Otherwise, we might have a rocky night.

I reached up, put my hand on Freddie's neck, and pulled him down to kiss his cheek. Just his cheek.

"I'll tell you when we get back," I said.

He didn't say anything. He just nodded, once. Then he looked out over that tremendous view. But he still wasn't seeing it. His face was motionless. It was the face of someone who had heard bad news before and knew when more was coming.

After a minute, we went back through the Supai Tunnel and down to the mules. I didn't see the rangy dude anywhere.

But he was there. I was sure of it.

Caught Summers giving me the stink-eye again. It was from a distance, but it was definitely aimed at me. So I slipped off the trail into the brush. Squatted and waited for the mule train to pass by on its way back up.

Heard a rattle before the first mule reached me. Looked down and there was a diamondback coiled beside my right boot. Maybe a four-footer. Tail buzzing, head up, neck cocked.

Couldn't move away without revealing myself. So I extended my right index finger with the long, sharpened nail.

Here, snakey. Here, snakey snake.

Dumbfuck went for it. Nail caught him in the roof of his mouth, fangs on either side of my finger. He was stuck.

I unfolded my middle finger and let my venom drip over his snout, into his mouth, and into his wound.

Then I shook my hand, and snakey snake dropped and writhed in the coarse dirt for a few seconds.

Summers and the kid passed by. See you soon, assholes.

When all the mules were well up the trail, I stood and stretched. Made my knees and shoulders pop.

I picked up snakey snake, put his tail in my mouth, and bit off the rattle. Then I chucked him far out over the big hole in the ground. Snakey snake spun like a slow helicopter blade and vanished down among distant scrub.

I took the rattle from my mouth, spat out a little blood, and stepped *back onto the trail. I rattled my new toy as I started upward, watching the dry brown segments flop back and forth.*

So I had some fun on my hike after all.

I liked my mule, Clementine, and I enjoyed the trip to the Supai Tunnel more than I'd thought I would. In fact, I liked it a lot, right up until just after I kissed Julie.

Then I knew something was wrong. Bad wrong.

It would have been awful enough if she had decided that the night before had been a big mistake.

But the way she said, "I'll tell you when we get back," I knew it was worse. Girls had told me "I've had enough of this" before, but they hadn't kissed my cheek when they'd said it.

So the two-hour ride back up seemed to flash by in about five minutes. That's the way time works. When there's something wonderful ahead, an hour might as well be a thousand years. And when there's something bad, it just can't wait. Clementine zipped up to the rim like a falcon.

On the ascent, Julie rode ahead of me. She glanced back a few times. Once she even smiled. One of those sad smiles someone gives you when something shitty is waiting around the next switchback. But it was still a smile, and her sunglasses had slipped down so I could see her eyes. There were no tattoos on her face now.

I hadn't taken any photos of her and didn't think I would. So whatever happened next, I would have to trust my memory of what she had been like.

They say your memory lies. But I didn't think that would be true for my memories of Julie. Even if it was . . . well, what does it matter if a memory of joy is a lie?

I was on automatic pilot throughout the climb to the trailhead and the shuttle ride back to the lodge. The sun was low, already touching the rim of the Transept, and turning the western sky a dusky pink by the time we disembarked. The air was cooling, and I had put my jacket on. Julie's hoodie was still around her waist.

"We should get dinner," she said, taking off her sunglasses. She looked at our fellow passengers as they filed into the lodge. "And we should stay with people."

I assumed she thought if we went back to the cabin, I would try to pick up where we had left off that morning. But I knew she didn't want that, so I wouldn't have. "I understand," I said.

"You really don't. But I'll try to change that."

I followed her into the lodge and into the dining room. I had the sensation of walking off a cliff.

My phone began buzzing in my hip pocket as we were seated next to a west window, away from most of the other diners. Outside, the Transept displayed a mix of reddish light and shadows across its massive walls. But I couldn't appreciate the view. I checked my phone and found messages from Big Sis, all sent within the previous two hours.

Freddie we still can't get a flight.

I have a bad feeling. Need to ask some friends if they know anything.

Do me a favor. Stick close to other people. Groups. Don't go hiking alone.

Let me know you're okay.

I typed out **I'm fine** and tried to zap it. But the indicator said PENDING instead of SENT, and I knew my signal had faded yet again. I put the phone away.

"Messages?" Julie asked.

I nodded. "My sister. She's worried about me. I think it's because she can't get a flight, and it's stressing her out."

Julie's lips pressed together and she brought out her own phone. "Yeah," she said, looking at the screen. "Michelle's sent me a note, too."

I stared. Julie's face had changed. Her cheeks were more rounded, her chin less sharp. She looked up from her phone. When she spoke, her voice was low. "That's the first thing I need to tell you. I know your sister. Adesina, too."

It was as if she had told me she was a frog in human form.

"How?" I asked. "I mean—how?" I heard my voice as if it were ten feet away, speaking from a box stuffed with cotton.

"Michelle and I have known each other since she was on the first season of *American Hero,*" Julie said. "I was a production assistant, doing my part to keep the 'reality' in 'reality show.' But now I work for the Committee."

"She," I said. I tried to swallow. "She hasn't mentioned you. She's never mentioned a Julie."

"My name is actually Juliet." She was looking at me as if forcing herself to maintain eye contact. "Juliet Summers. And I'm not surprised if Michelle has never mentioned me." She let out a breath. "We still work together as necessary, but we aren't as close . . . as we used to be."

At that moment, a waiter brought us water and menus. Julie—no, Juliet—waved away the menus and ordered two veggie burgers. Which would have been fine, if I had felt like eating.

Then, as the waiter left, the part of my brain that should have been making connections all along finally began to work.

Her name was Juliet. She worked for the Committee. She had tattoos she could change at will. She had known my Big Sis since the *American Hero* days.

Since before Big Sis had adopted Adesina.

They had once been close.

"But Michelle is right to be worried now," Juliet said, "because—"

"Auntie Ink," I said. My voice was even farther away now. "You're the one Adesina calls Auntie Ink. It's because of your tattoos, isn't it?"

Now Juliet closed her eyes. "Yes. Adesina is my goddaughter."

You can't trust memory. Memory lies. That's what they say. I wished it were true.

Because now I remembered one of the texts Adesina had sent me. It had been in late December, just after I had said goodbye to her and Michelle in New York and had gone back on the road.

I can't wait for you to come back so we can shop for my new amp, Adesina had written. We've almost got Mom sold on it. Oh, and I want to see if we can have lunch with my Auntie Ink. You'll love her, because she's awesome. But she and Mom had a "thing" a few years ago, and some stuff that's "none of my business" happened. They don't talk much now. But she's still my auntie, and you're my uncle, so you should know each other. And sooner or later she and Mom will get over themselves, and we can all do things together.

". . . So the people who sent me didn't want to tell the Committee, and especially not Michelle, because she's had a hair trigger ever since a mission in Kazakhstan. Not that it's her fault. Just imagine demons from another dimension invading your brain and forcing you to commit atrocities, and then imagine trying to suppress those impulses afterward—while also trying to forgive yourself. Don't get me wrong, she's done an amazing job recovering. But at some level she's still like a bomb that might or might not go off. She even attacked *you* during the Roosevelt Park riot because she thought you were going to hurt Adesina."

I wasn't processing what Julie—no, Juliet—was saying very well. "But I *wanted* her to attack me," I said. "That was the only way I could shout loud enough to stop the riot."

She and Mom had a "thing" a few years ago . . .

"I know," Juliet said. "But if she were to do something like that now, to protect you, it could lead to violence with a US government agency called SCARE. Because SCARE is looking for aces they can use as weapons . . ."

Some stuff that's "none of my business" happened . . .

"Aces like you, Freddie."

But she's still my auntie, and you're my uncle . . .

I stood up and pushed my chair away.

"I don't want a veggie burger," I said.

Then I left the dining doom. I heard "Auntie Ink" calling after me and I started to run.

I wound up outside in the falling night, in the trees. I thought I was northwest of the lodge, but I wasn't sure. I found a narrow path going down, and then limestone steps that went down farther.

The steps took me to a wider, flatter path, and I followed it north. Sometimes it was illuminated by the rising moon, and sometimes there were too many trees. Sometimes the earth to my left dropped away into the Transept, its distant walls glowing, and sometimes I was running through a darkened forest.

It was stupid. It was childish.

But I had waited my whole life to meet my Big Sis. And now I was going to lose her. As well as the niece who had flown me out of a burning theater when she had just been a kid at a Who concert, and I had just been a roadie she had seen collapse. Brave Adesina with the beautiful wings.

I had only had them for five months. Only since the fire at the Bowery Ballroom, and the madness of the riot that followed.

Somehow, that madness had produced a miracle: my family.

But now they were gone, because of what I had done. And with whom.

Julie was gone, too.

Because there had never been a Julie at all.

I would have to stop running sooner or later. Sooner or later, the trail would end. Or maybe it would just turn and drop into the Transept.

Might as well see which it was.

This is gonna work out fine.

They were in the dining hall in the lodge. I was watching from outside, from the west terrace. They were next to one of those wide, tall windows.

Then the kid got up and he ran out. Summers tried to follow, but he was faster.

I was pissed at first because I'd lost sight of him. So I started around to the main entrance, but before I could get there, he popped out in front of me, still running, and headed toward the Transept Trail. Into the trees and down.

No idea why. But who cares? Sun going down, temperature dropping, and most other tourists getting dinner or heading to their cabins. Hardly anyone on the trail. And no lights, except the moon.

So I took off after him. Glanced back as I started down, and saw Summers coming out. She was looking around like she had no idea where he'd gone.

I got down to the trail, spotted him twenty or thirty yards ahead. He was wearing a gray jacket that might as well have been a beacon. I followed him north along the rim of the Transept, the trail taking us in and out of the trees.

Half a mile in, two old farts came puffing along in the opposite direction. One was grumbling to the other about being out after dark. Those were the only other people.

Just before that, I heard Summers calling "Freddie! Freddie!" far behind me. Only twice, then nothing. My bet is she went back to Cabin 309 to look for him there.

After a mile, the kid slowed to a walk. I dropped back so he wouldn't spot me.

Then he left the trail, heading into the trees to the left, toward the Transept.

That's where I am now. In those trees, watching him. About ten yards away.

He's taken off his jacket and is sitting on it with his back against a tree. The tree is at the edge of a rocky clearing that looks out over the canyon. There's a gentle slope from there for maybe forty feet before it starts getting steep.

Great view from where the kid is sitting, if you like that sort of thing.

Gigantic moonlit rock walls in the distance, rising over an enormous dark chasm.

Majestic as all fuck.

But I don't think the kid is digging it. His head is down. I don't know if he's asleep or if he's just being a pouty little bitch.

Either works for me. His arms are exposed.

Head check behind me and to either side. Nothing but trees, air, and canyon. Some distant noises from up the slope to the east, toward the campground and highway. Two or three hundred yards away, at least, with lots of trees in between.

I'll come up behind him. Slash him on his right arm.

I don't think he'll be able to yell. If he does, I'll be behind him, so he'll just blast the trees on the other side of the clearing.

Then I'll help my drunk young friend to the parking lot.

Moving in, slow and silent.

Will let you know when he's down.

. . .

. . .

Hold up. His phone is buzzing.

. . .

He ignored it. Or is asleep.

Ten feet.

. . .

Goddammit, Summers is here, yelling.

*He's turning, gotta slash **now**—*

SHIT!

Outside the lodge, I called Freddie's name. There was no answer.

Maybe he had gone back to the cabin, so I started in that direction. Then stopped. That was the last place he would go. He would never want to see it again.

Up the highway? No, that led to the North Kaibab Trailhead, and he would never want to see that again, either.

To the northwest, then, toward the Transept Trail. I ran around the corner of the lodge—and caught a glimpse of a tall, lanky figure in a baseball cap heading down the slope. Moving fast.

I had been right. That leathery man was SCARE. And now he was taking his chance to get to Freddie without anyone else around. I took off after him at a run. I was away from the lights of the lodge now, but there was moonlight.

When I found the stairs down to the trail, I paused for a moment to take my phone from my pocket and tap a text to the Midnight Angel:

Need you -now-.

I hit SEND but returned the phone to my pocket without looking to see whether the message had gone out. It almost didn't matter. Either she would find us in time or she wouldn't.

When I reached the trail, the lanky figure was vanishing into a cluster of trees thirty yards ahead. So I followed at a jog, hoping to keep him at a short distance for now. If he caught up to Freddie, I would have to do something. But I was trying not to think too hard about what that would be. If I did, I might not do it.

The dirt-and-gravel trail was flat, following the rim of the Transept. Two elderly men passed me, walking in the opposite direction. One of them was accusing the other of trying to starve him to death. It sounded like a nice problem to have.

The moonlight came and went as the trail slipped in and out of the trees, sometimes swerving close to the rim of the canyon and then swinging out again. The Transept in the moonlight was gorgeous, but I couldn't appreciate it. All I could think was that Freddie or I might fall into it.

Or, more likely, be thrown.

Ahead of me, the shadowy figure in the ball cap came in and out of view. But whenever I could see the trail beyond him, I caught no glimpse of Freddie.

Then, perhaps a mile and a half from where the trail had begun, the lanky man was gone. There were trees on either side of me, but no canopy, and the moon brightened a long stretch of the trail ahead. I saw nothing and no one.

I stopped and held my breath, listening for footsteps, for voices, for anything. I heard crickets. I heard a breeze in the trees. I heard my own pulse in my neck. Nothing else.

So I took out my phone again. There was one bar. I hoped Freddie had at least one, too.

I sent another text:

Freddie, where are you?

And held my breath again.

Farther ahead, off to the left, toward the Transept, I heard a faint buzz.

I cut into the trees and angled for that sound. I changed the tattoos on my arms and face to dark, dappled camouflage.

Maybe I could get to him before the lanky man could. Maybe we could run back to the lodge together.

Maybe he wouldn't hate me. Maybe Michelle would be my friend again, and Adesina would still want me to be her Auntie Ink. Maybe monkeys would fly out of my ass and start marching in a monkey parade.

I couldn't hear his phone buzzing anymore, so I began to shout. "Freddie! Freddie, tell me where you are!"

And then I was in a clearing covered in rocks, twigs, and pine needles. The Transept yawned ahead, its distant walls glowing the color of rust.

Thirty feet away, at the left edge of the clearing, Freddie sat with his back against a tree trunk. Moonlight shone from his spectacles and his spiky hair. He didn't look toward me. His head was down.

At first I didn't see the other man. But then his hand came around Freddie's tree like a leathery claw.

"*FREDDIE!*" I screamed.

Freddie raised his head and began to turn toward me.

As the claw raked down his arm.

He hadn't turned all the way. That was what saved both me and his attacker.

Freddie's mouth opened and—

It was as if a barrel of dynamite had gone off. The lanky man, caught by the edge of the shock wave, was thrown back into the darkness. Twenty feet ahead of Freddie, the clearing exploded as if hit by a meteor, and dirt and rocks leapt into the air. Trees on the far side of the clearing snapped, their tops flying off into the night.

Then the edge of the shock wave reached me, and I was tossed backward. My ears almost burst.

I hit the ground and slid into a pine trunk with a force that knocked out my breath and sent a stabbing pain through my ribs and chest. Dirt, twigs, pine needles, and rocks began to fall. All I could do was cover my head until it was over.

When it stopped, I managed to roll away from the tree and get to my hands and knees. My ears throbbed, and my ribs, chest, and gut burned. But my head, arms, and legs seemed intact. I was covered in dirt, and I started coughing.

Freddie's cry echoed through the Transept, to Bright Angel Point and beyond. It was a shout of shock and pain, transformed into rolling thunder.

I made it up to my feet but almost fell again as more fire shot through me. I guessed I had two or three broken ribs.

"Freddie," I wheezed, wiping dirt from my eyes.

He was in the clearing, crawling toward me, using his left arm to pull himself. His right arm and both of his legs were limp, dragging in the dirt. His spectacles were gone, and his silvery eyes stared up at me as he dragged himself through chunks of rock and broken tree limbs.

I tried to rush to him, but another hot stab shot through me, and it knocked me down. So we crawled to each other.

When I reached him, he collapsed, his body twisting so that he looked out into the Transept. I knelt behind him, my knees against his spine, looking outward with him as a cloud of dust settled around us. The dust seemed to make the canyon walls glow with even more intensity.

"Pretty," Freddie said. His voice was a rasp.

I tried to lean down to him, but another stab of fire stopped me.

"I can't feel my arms and legs," he said.

A long, deep scratch, caked with blood and dirt, curved down Freddie's upper right arm. I put my hand over it and it was like touching marble.

"That man was with SCARE," I said. I looked into the trees where he had disappeared. "He wanted to take you somewhere they could make you do things for them. He must have drugged you. But we can fix it. People are coming to help us fix it."

I reached for my phone, and yet another stab went through me. And when I managed to get to my pocket, I found that my phone was gone. It had popped out when I had hit the tree.

"I'm sorry I ran away," Freddie said.

I squeezed his arm. He didn't feel it. "I don't blame you. I'd run from me, too."

Freddie turned his eyes up toward me.

"I wasn't running from *you*," he said.

I didn't understand.

"I love my Big Sis," he said. "And I love Adesina. But—"

Someone coughed. I looked up and saw the leathery, lanky man emerge from the trees. He was limping and his cap was gone. He was bald on top, and a fringe of dirty hair stuck out over his ears like a hideous clown wig. He was twenty-five feet away.

My camouflage did me no good now, out in the clearing in the moonlight, kneeling over the Amplifier.

"Skank," the man said in a voice like hillbilly Death. "You're a real pain in my shitter, you know that?" He limped toward us, silhouetted against the Transept.

"—but Juliet," Freddie whispered.

I looked down at him, and he gazed straight up at me.

"I love you more," he said.

Then he turned his head away, toward hillbilly Death, toward the canyon.

A chunk of limestone the size of a toaster lay to my left. I twisted to pick it up, straining not to pass out.

It was about twenty pounds. I lifted it high over Freddie's head. "I'm sorry," I said. I hoped he heard it.

I brought the rock down hard, and Freddie's shout blasted away from us, cutting a trench that threw more dirt and rocks into the air. It pushed Freddie back against me, knocking me over, sending the chunk of limestone flying.

And it blew the lanky, leathery man out and away like a scrap of paper, high over the depths of the Transept.

I struggled back to my knees as the dirt and rocks began to fall again. The lanky man was still soaring up and away, dwindling and flailing in the moonlight.

He seemed to hang at the top of his arc for the longest time, shining weirdly, his arms and legs gyrating ever so slowly.

And then he dropped. And dropped. And dropped.

Until a bright, burning light streaked down from the darkness, swooped beneath him, and lifted him up again.

That light came toward us then, and as it drew near, it separated into a pair of fiery wings . . . and a flaming sword held in the right hand of a tall, sable-haired, pale-skinned woman dressed in black leather. In her left hand, she held hillbilly Death upside down by one ankle.

The Midnight Angel touched down ten feet from me and Freddie, dropped the man to the dirt, and kicked him onto his back as her wings vanished. She swung her sword so that its tip burned half an inch from his nose.

"Don't you move," the Midnight Angel said. She spoke in the voice of a southern belle who would serve you a mint julep just before she gutted you.

Echoes from a Canyon Wall 241

As if the flaming sword weren't eloquent enough. The man glared up at her, but he remained still.

She looked at me. "I got here as soon as I could."

I knew it was true. And we both knew it hadn't been soon enough.

I looked down at Freddie. He was curled into a fetal position. Like a young boy, asleep.

Out in the Grand Canyon, his second cry of pain was still echoing. It seemed to go on forever, reverberating through all the peaks and chasms, all the cliffs and spires, all the way down the Colorado River, all the way to the sea.

This was your *fault.*

You said it would be easy. You sent me alone.

Sure, I could have stung the Midnight Angel the moment she grabbed me. She would have fallen to her death, and bang, one less problem for you.

Of course, I would have been a grease spot at the bottom of the Transept, too. But I reckon that would have been a price you were willing to pay.

Oh, I could have tried something afterward? Sure, why not? If I'm gonna get fucked, why not with a sword of fire?

Which reminds me. You can go fuck yourself with a rusty crowbar. Wrap it in some barbed wire first, so it's ribbed for your pleasure.

You still want me on the team or not?

That's right, she let me go. What were she and Billy Ray gonna do, lock me up in a secret dungeon? Secret dungeons are your bag, man. But Carnifex doesn't seem to have made plans for POWs.

I have no idea why the Midnight Angel didn't just kill me. Maybe the thought of you and me having this conversation amused her.

I'm in the van, miles away from the North Rim. But I ain't telling you where. I've already ripped out the van's GPS, and once we're done talk-

ing, I'm taking a chisel to my back tooth. Then you can't track me that way, either.

You don't think I will?

Listen here, ol' buddy. I think I got me a fracture in my left arm, and it feels like my right rotator cuff is ripped. Not to mention a twisted ankle, plus a groin pull from being yanked around upside down by one leg. And there's a noise in my head like a goddamn Chinese gong. It has put me in a mood.

You want me to come back to New Mexico?

Well, I want my completion bonus. All of it. I see that money in my account in the next fifteen minutes, or the tooth with the comm is gone, and so am I.

You want El Alacrán to keep playing for SCARE, then pay up.

Okay, good. No, that's fine. No hard feelings. I appreciate the bonus. Muchas grassy-ass.

What the hell? No, I ain't gonna change my name to "Diamondback" for you. Because I got a whole different kind of venom than a rattlesnake, that's why.

Besides, rattlesnakes are pussies.

I'll bring you the proof.

This time, I didn't dream.

I had been hit hard enough during the riot in December to be knocked unconscious for days. But even in those depths, I had dreamed.

Now I had nothing. I was in an ocean of ink, alone, without even a nightmare.

And with that thought, I knew I was awake again.

Ink.

Auntie Ink.

Julie.

Juliet.

I heard her voice now, like a feather brushing my ear.

"His finger moved," she said.

A deeper female voice replied. "I hope so. This is his last day in Flagstaff. He's on a plane to New York tonight whether he's awake or not."

The thunk of a door opening, and a whoosh of air.

"I'll get the nurse," Juliet said.

The thunk of a door closing.

I smelled alcohol, plastic, and all the other odors that were among the reasons I hated hospitals. Ever since I had wound up in one when my card had turned, three years before. After which I had vowed never to see Mum again, for fear she would hit me again and make me shout so loud I might kill her.

I opened my eyes and found that the head of my bed was raised so I was almost sitting up. It took me a few minutes to focus, but when the fuzziness coalesced, I saw a dark-haired woman with penetrating eyes and alabaster skin standing to my left. She was dressed in something black and skintight.

"Praise the Lord," she said. It was the sort of thing almost everyone I knew would have said with some irony. But not this lady. She was as serious as a hammer.

I tried to speak and sort of managed. "So," I croaked. "I'm not in hell?"

She gave me the smallest hint of a smile. "Not yet. Do you remember me?"

When I tried to shake my head, I regretted it. It was as if my skull were held together by weak strands of mozzarella.

She sat down in a vinyl-upholstered chair beside my bed. "I'm the person who has stood watch for the past three days so no one would drag you off to an oubliette in New Mexico."

Which made no sense. But I could tell from the lady's tone that she felt a little put out. So I said, "Thank you." Then, after thinking a moment, "Guardian angel."

One of her eyebrows rose. "Close. It's the Midnight Angel. And you're welcome. But I have things to attend to, so I'll be leaving as soon as my replacement arrives. It's been a pleasure to meet you, Mr. Fullerton, but I hope we don't meet again. Would you like to know how you can help that be the case?"

I had a feeling she was going to tell me regardless. And it hurt to talk, so I didn't. But I blinked.

"You can help," she said, "by returning to the UK and staying out of North America until we have a new administration in the US. Until then, our government will only see you as a commodity or a problem. And in either case, you'll wind up in that oubliette. Do you understand?"

I blinked twice.

The Midnight Angel stood up. "Two blinks usually means 'no,'" she said. "But whether you understand or not, stay on the other side of the Atlantic. And the Pacific, too."

The door opened then, and a man in blue scrubs came into the room. The Midnight Angel moved out of his way, and he did various nurse-type things such as shining a light in my eyes, checking my blood pressure, examining the bandage on my right arm, making me tell him how many fingers he was holding up, and touching the soles of my feet while asking if I felt it. Then he gave a nod and stepped away.

"Doctor will want to have a look," the nurse said, opening the door again. "But I think he's all right. No sign of concussion, and all the toxin seems to have been flushed."

Julie—no, Juliet—came in then. She was wearing a sleeveless violet pullover and dark-gray slacks. And the tattoos on her arms and neck were different now. They were all roses, from the top of her throat down to her wrists. Lavender, blue, and black roses, with thin, thorned stems crossing one another.

She thanked the nurse as he left, then she stood just inside the closing door, looking at me.

A black rose in the center of her throat turned scarlet, then black again.

A buzzing sound came from the Midnight Angel, and she produced a phone from I don't know where. "Mr. Fullerton," she said, glancing at the screen, "your escort to New York, and from there to London, has arrived. So I'll take my leave." She went to the door, opened it, and nodded to Juliet. "Thank you, Ink." Then she looked back at me. "And God bless you." The door clicked shut behind her.

I tried to look at Juliet without staring.

"That lady is a trip," I rasped. "Shouldn't she have left a silver bullet or something?"

Juliet smiled. "No, it'd be a flaming sword. There's a whole shtick." She stepped closer, moving stiffly. "I guess some of those old American movies you watched as a kid must have starred the Lone Ranger. Silver bullets and all that."

I couldn't help smiling back. "Actually, it was an old American televised serial. Clayton Moore and Jay Silverheels. And their horses, Silver and Scout. ABC Television, 1949 to 1957." My voice was getting stronger. "For a long time, I was obsessed with the idea of being a western hero. Wyatt Earp, or the Lone Ranger, or Tonto. It seemed quite the romantic lifestyle, watching it from that little flat. Riding a horse over the rugged plains, saving the endangered, aiding the imperiled, helping the helpless. All that rubbish."

Juliet was beside me now. She touched my cheek and it made me shudder. "Well, now you've ridden a mule, at least," she said.

"And it was lovely." My voice started to fail again.

"Yes," she said. "We'll always have Ike and Clementine."

I tried to reach for her hand, but I couldn't seem to raise mine from the bed.

She stepped farther back. "I wrote you a letter," she said. "It's in your backpack, with your clothes in the closet over there." She gestured across the room and winced. "Everything's been laundered. It all got so dirty up there on the North Rim."

I was worried about her. "You made a face. Are you hurt?"

"Just a few cracked ribs," she said. "I'll be fine."

Then she put a hand over her eyes, and the blue and lavender roses on her wrist crept onto it. Their stems slipped onto her fingers, and the thorns drew tiny drops of blood. "I wrote you a letter," she repeated. "How quaint is that? But I didn't have your email address."

Juliet lowered her hand, and now her face was covered in lavender, blue, and black roses, too. "I have Michelle's and Adesina's, though."

I drew in a deep breath, and it hurt.

"I didn't write the same things to them that I wrote to you," she said. "Or the same thing to Adesina that I wrote to Michelle. But they needed to know."

I tried to reach for her again, and this time my hand rose. But she was too far away.

The handle on the door clicked.

Juliet turned toward it. "It would be worse for you," she said softly, "if I loved you, too."

The door opened and my Big Sis, the Amazing Bubbles, stepped into the room.

She was wearing her usual black leggings and oversized, loose top. This one was jade green, matching her eyes. Her hair was down, like silver waterfalls on either side of her face. She was heavy enough at the moment that she looked dangerous. She could knock down the entire hospital, if she chose.

Michelle and Juliet stood there, each looking at the other, saying nothing.

Big Sis had no expression.

All I could see of Juliet's face was her right profile. But the roses there had turned black.

After a minute or more, Big Sis came farther into the room. Juliet stepped forward and caught the door. "Goodbye, Freddie," she said.

As the door closed, I looked at Big Sis. She was watching me, but she still had no expression. And she still said nothing.

I closed my eyes. That was it, then.

I had thought the worst moment of my life was behind me. I had thought that when Mum had hit me in the face, and I had shouted my first terrible shout and flung her across the room, nothing could be worse.

Then, when I had found my sister and my niece, and they had accepted me, I had thought nothing could be better. But then I had met Julie. Juliet. Ink.

Now Michelle and Adesina would never see me the same way again. They would never see me without seeing me with Auntie Ink, betraying my sister, blindsiding my niece.

The Amazing Bubbles was here to be my escort. My safe passage. That was all.

I lay there for the longest time, my eyes clamped shut, my fists clenching the stiff hospital sheets.

The chair beside my bed creaked.

A moment, a minute, or an hour later, Michelle spoke. Her voice was so soft I could hardly make out the words:

"She's a really good kisser, isn't she?"

I couldn't open my eyes. But I gave a scarce, shallow nod.

And felt my sister's hand close over mine.

2020
The Long Goodbye

by Walton Simons

En Route to Chicago, 2020

The private jet was a rental. Jerry had more
than enough money to own one, but he only occasionally left New
York City, so it seemed like a needless frivolity. Normally when he
traveled for non-business reasons he wore his Jerry Strauss face,
but this time he was William Creighton. It seemed appropriate.
The wild card had given him the ability to shapeshift. It was quite
useful in his line of work as a detective.

He slowly swirled the cold drink glass in his right hand, clinking the melting ice gently against the sides. After a deep breath he
took another sip—a whiskey sour, not usually his drink, but this
was an unusual moment. He moved his finger across the surface
of his tablet, hesitating above the PLAY button of a YouTube video.
The title was "Unknown Woman Dancing," but the woman wasn't
unknown to him. It was Irina. He'd been standing behind the camera when the film was shot. Over a hundred years ago.

He started the video.

She moved across the frame from left to right with perfect fluidity, her arms gracefully extending and selling each move her body made. Her legs rushed underneath her and brought her to a moment of taut stillness. Then she smiled, like she knew something special that no one else would ever know. Jerry took a deep breath.

After the YouTube countdown, another video started. Two men and one woman were seated in chairs, having just watched the film of Irina dancing.

The taller and older of the two men, his back braced perfectly against his chair, said, "This brief clip is believed to be of one of the stars of the legendary Fortune Films Studio, the lost kingdom of Atlantis in the history of film. It was located in Chicago, during the early teens of the twentieth century."

The woman, who wore her dark hair in a bob, tilted her head before speaking. "What little is known comes from newspaper articles and notices of the day, and from a few diaries. Although no features or short films from the studio exist, its work was considered groundbreaking for its era."

"Yes," said the other man, raising a finger. "Supposedly the company used editing techniques and camera movements that were unheard of at the time."

"You'd better believe it," Jerry said softly. "We had an entire century-plus of films to steal from. And we stole from the best."

"Yet Essanay and Selig Polyscope Company are the studios remembered as the pioneers of the Chicago film industry." The tall man's back had gotten straighter, if that was possible. "And Essanay did bring Charles Chaplin to Chicago, where he filmed a series of classic shorts."

Jerry muted the video. "Essanay; give me a fucking break. I'll give even money they were spying on us to see how we were doing it. And Chaplin went back to California after a few months."

He went back to the video of Irina and played it through a few more times. He remembered the soft noises her feet had made on the floor and the swishing of her costume. Mostly he remembered

the smile, because she'd been smiling at him. He didn't recall for
certain, but he was sure he'd been smiling back. Those were the
days.

Chicago, 1913

A well-built man in suspendered pants and a rolled-up denim
work shirt was unloading ice from a People's Pure Ice wagon
when Jerry drove up in his red Pierce-Arrow 66. The car backfired
as he stopped in front of the two-story brown brick house, mo-
mentarily startling the man who was hefting the ice from the back
of the truck with a large pair of tongs.

Jerry slipped out of the vehicle and opened the front gate. "If
you'll bring it into the kitchen, we have a large pan for it there," he
said. He was exhausted from his excursion with John Fortune. The
man nodded.

Jerry unlocked the door and made way for the ice man to enter.
He indicated the kitchen to the right and set a large aluminum pan
on the heavy oak table. "Here is fine." The man dropped the ice
into the pan with a thud and wiped his hands on his pants. Jerry
gave him a quarter, which was a generous tip. After fishing an ice
pick out of one of the table drawers, he set it in the pan and carried
it slowly up the stairs. His shoulders and back ached from the digging and reburying he'd done with John Fortune.

Jerry straightened his shoulders when he reached the top of the
stairs and elbowed the bedroom door open. Irina looked up and
smiled, folding the latest issue of *Cosmopolitan* closed and setting it
on the ornate bedside table. She was wearing one of his white
button-down shirts and not much else. "You boys get it done?"

"Yeah, but it took a while. Enough loot for a pharaoh." He set
the ice on a table in front of the fan and turned it on to blow cool
air on Irina. He indicated the ice pick. "Make yourself useful while
I take a shower."

He struggled out of his damp clothes, dumping them heavily

into the hamper, and pulled the circular curtain closed. Reaching behind it, he turned the shower handle. The pipes vibrated and shuddered as the water passed through them. Jerry stepped into the tub and into the curtained wall of soothing water. He bowed his head and stepped forward, letting the spray rush over the back of his neck and his shoulders. His muscles started to relax and he took several deep breaths. He now had more respect for the poor men who had to dig graves for a living, at least pre-backhoe.

He stayed in the shower until the hot water was almost gone. After toweling off and donning a robe, Jerry made his way back to the bedroom. Irina had made two whiskey sours, with plenty of ice. One was already in her hand. Jerry picked up the unattended glass and took a sip. He'd gotten fond of the taste over the past few years, but this one needed stiffening. He opened the bottle of Old Forester and poured in a finger or so.

"Thirsty man," Irina said. "I assume Mr. Johnson is now in his final resting place—well, until you dig him up in 2017 or so."

"Yes, indeed." The headstone said TOR JOHNSON, the appearance Jerry had assumed at the poker game in 2017. It was a high-stakes affair. Jerry had been a bodyguard, John Fortune was a player, and Irina was a bartender/hostess. The game had gone sideways, and things were on the verge of getting dangerously ugly. Somehow, the Sleeper, also a bodyguard, had dislocated them in time—although to the best of his knowledge they all wound up in Chicago, and naked to boot. No doubt that looked better on Irina than on Jerry in his Tor Johnson guise, or even John Fortune. Irina and one of the other players, Pug, had ended up in Chicago a few years earlier than the time Jerry and John Fortune arrived. Croyd had already encountered Irina and Pug, but because she saved his life, he'd allowed her to remain in the past. Pug had apparently been whisked back to the present. In any case, Tor Johnson's casket was now full of things that were inexpensive in 1913, but would be worth plenty in 2017.

"So now that you've taken care of your future, assuming this all works out, are you ready to focus on the present?" Irina sipped at her drink.

Jerry sat on the bed next to her. "If by focusing on the present you mean lying down and knocking back a couple of these bad boys, then yes. Any chance I can have you massage these aching muscles?"

"I might be inclined to fetch the liniment and give you a decent rubdown if you direct a bit of attention to me." She patted a place on the bed next to her.

"My goodness, ma'am," he said, "I will surely miss you."

Irina sighed. "I thought you were still trying to convince me to let the Sleeper bring me back with you."

Jerry took another large swallow. "Is that still an option, or are you just playing with me?"

"I'll never tell." She batted her eyelashes dramatically, then shrugged. "Everything is still an option, until Croyd shows up." She looked directly into his eyes. "There are pluses and minuses to both sides. You have to understand how awful things were for me back in the future."

Jerry figured it was time to back off. She'd come with him, or she wouldn't. He decided to change the subject. "How about some music?"

"Sure. Then get over here."

"What do you want to hear?"

"Surprise me."

"I'll surprise both of us." He fished a disk out without looking and pulled off the brown paper cover. He placed it carefully on the turntable, cranked it up to speed, and placed the needle at the edge. After some hissing and popping, Al Jolson began singing "You Made Me Love You."

"Lovely," she said.

Jerry sat on the edge of the bed and took the drink from her hand. He took a sip and gave it back.

"Don't get comfortable. You'll just have to put on another record in a few minutes."

"Miss your iPad?"

"Yes. Along with plenty of other things. You know what I don't miss?"

"What's that?"

"Shaving," she said, parting the shirt.

Jerry eased his head between her legs and traced a line with his tongue along her inner thigh. This was the right way to end a hard day's work.

Jerry entered the private office at Fortune Films and tossed his hat onto the rack, à la James Bond. "What's the rumpus?" he said to John Fortune, who was seated behind his own desk. It was his customary greeting, stolen from *Miller's Crossing*.

The office was well furnished, with two dark-wood desks side by side, a comfortable couch, several file cabinets, and colorful posters from their films. *Frankenstein* was Jerry's personal favorite. The artist had perfectly captured his/the monster's face. Jerry had strayed far from what Jack Pierce would create for the Universal classic. He felt a little bad that they hadn't paid the Shelley estate, but any potential lawsuits would vaporize with Fortune Films and the nitrate film stock they were making their pictures with. That was the Sleeper's part in the story. Jerry felt he might show up any day.

"Can't complain. You look all-in. Gravedigging, or a late night with Irina?"

"Both. You must be tired, too. That was a lot of shovel work."

"Totally bushed," John Fortune said. He didn't look up from his work. As usual his work suit, blue today, was perfectly pressed. "Still, there's plenty that needs to be kept up with to keep our operation running."

Jerry and John Fortune had complementary skills when it came to the studio. Fortune was the organizing aspect of their partnership. He was always on top of how to make the best use of their money to benefit the studio and its owners. Jerry supplied the passion and filmic know-how, not to mention his ability to change his appearance. The public attributed that to his being a magician with makeup, when in fact it was his wild card ability. Of course, only he, John Fortune, and Irina knew that. This was 1913. The wild card wouldn't happen for another thirty-plus years.

"You know, John, you've got a real knack for direction." Jerry was sincere. His partner had a good, if reluctant, eye for framing a shot. Initially, Jerry had been behind the camera for scenes he wasn't performing in. Now he was more and more comfortable with John Fortune in charge of the shot.

"Thanks," Fortune said, placing a stack of papers in one of the many folders on his desk. "If I had less of this to deal with, I might take it up full-time."

Jerry eased his aching body into his slat-backed rolling chair, which creaked acknowledgment under his weight. "Take a gander at this, partner. I've been working on my Cyrano face."

Jerry took a breath and concentrated. His nose lengthened considerably, and his forehead took on a sloping, backswept appearance.

"Imagine me with a mustache," he said, winking.

"And a wig," John Fortune added. "But don't get too far ahead of yourself. We have to finish *Song of Solomon* first."

"It's a good thing there's no production code at this point. None of Irina's costumes would pass a censor."

Someone knocked at their office door. Jerry returned his face to standard Creighton. "Come in."

Helen Guentzel poked her head around the slightly open door. "May I come in, gentlemen?"

"Of course, Helen," Jerry replied. "I'll bet you've got something to show me."

Helen took several quick steps to Jerry's desk. She was wearing an artist's smock over her gray work dress. She wore thick glasses and had quick, masterful hands. Her aging fingers were smeared with charcoal, the medium she preferred using for her sketches. Helen carefully spread several of them across Jerry's desk, taking a moment for a sidewise glance to check his reaction. She'd been the head of the art department since they founded the studio, and her work rarely disappointed.

"These are top-quality, Helen. You've outdone yourself." He pored admiringly over them. They were varying sketches of some tortured, grotesque person. "Wonderfully expressive. This is some of your best work." He turned to John Fortune. "You should take a few minutes to appreciate these."

Fortune rolled his chair over to Jerry's desk and nodded. "Striking, Helen. Who are these sketches of?"

"Erik," she said. "From the story *Phantom of the Opera*. A recent work by a French gentleman, I believe. You might not be familiar with it."

"Actually, I am." Fortune smiled. "That makes these all the more impressive."

Helen tilted her head forward modestly. Compliments from John Fortune were harder to come by than those from his more enthusiastic partner. "You are too kind, sir."

"I'd like to hold on to these, Helen," Jerry said, "give them the thorough attention they deserve. Thank you."

"Of course, Mr. Creighton." Helen knew her presence was no longer required and left the room, shutting the door firmly behind her.

"We're doing *Phantom of the Opera*?" Fortune gave Jerry a bemused look.

"I doubt we'll have time. The production slate is pretty full, and the Sleeper could show up anytime. But I want to keep her busy, maybe give her a bonus. World War One is right around the bend and that was a rough time for a lot of Germans here in the U S of A." Jerry turned back to the sketches.

"You've got a point. And no Social Security until FDR. I hope she does okay." Fortune exhaled. "I hope everybody who works here does okay."

Jerry's mind was already elsewhere. He picked up one of the sketches and held it up for Fortune to see. "Doesn't this look a lot like Mr. Dutton from the poker game?" Charles Dutton was a wealthy skull-faced joker who'd been cleaning up at the table until the Sleeper blew up time around all—or at least some—of them.

"Close enough for jazz," Fortune said, after a quick glance. "Are you taking this as a sign that Croyd is going to take us back to the future really soon now?"

"Might as well. Can't dance," Jerry added with a smile. It was an homage to his partner Jay Ackroyd at the detective agency in future time. Jerry missed him. "It has to happen, and soon, or we might change the course of history. At least, that's how time travel works in the movies."

"I guess so. Now let me get some work done, so we'll have enough capital to finance the studio while we're waiting for Godot." Fortune went back to his ruled ledger.

"Okay, I need to grab some java before going to 'makeup.' " He made air quotes with his fingers. "We're shooting a tricky scene this afternoon."

He exited the office and strolled through the area of the studio where artists and construction crews assembled the necessities for making movie magic. On his left were wardrobe, the prop department, an editing room, a small area for pre-production art, and another one for large furnishings. Looking to his right he saw the work space for the heavier equipment: large painted backdrops, lighting, and tracks and dollies for the setups where the camera needed to move. All of them had to be moved to the set as needed. They'd hired several burly types to fill that bill.

Jerry had never been able to pin down the feeling he had for his studio family. He liked most of them and appreciated them all for doing their jobs well, but it was hard to forge any kind of deep emotional relationship with them. He wanted them to do well in life and hoped they would all be successful, whether they stayed in the movie industry or not. But it was hard not to see them as ghosts, in a way. When he made it back to his real time, they would all be dead. The only real emotional anchors he had were Irina and John. They made his life more substantial, less like a dream. The work helped, too. Sometimes he still felt like he was playing life with Monopoly money.

A man carrying an oversized floral arrangement caught Jerry's eye. He was young and short, and he wore an ill-fitting cap. "Excuse me," Jerry said. "You look like you could use some help getting to where you need to go."

"Yes, thank you." He pulled a piece of paper from his shirt pocket and unfolded it. "I need to find a Miss Irina. Does she work here?"

"Yes, she's likely in her dressing area. I can show you, or if you're in a hurry I can take them to her myself." Jerry smiled.

The deliveryman shook his head. "No, sir. I'm supposed to take this directly to her. I'd appreciate you showing me, though."

Jerry guided him through the maze of work areas, taking considerable satisfaction from the open-mouthed stares this impromptu studio walk-through elicited from the young man. "I tell you, sir," he said, "this place is . . ." He didn't finish the sentence.

"Yes, it is." Jerry decided to throw in a little Bogart. "The stuff that dreams are made of. Follow me."

The deliveryman continued to take in the wonders of the studio from behind the massive bouquet. A few minutes later they arrived at the door to Irina's dressing room. Jerry rapped his knuckle on the door. No answer, which didn't exactly surprise him. They'd had a late night and she wasn't on call until much later. He opened the door, stuck his head in, and flipped on the light.

Jerry motioned for the young man to follow him in. "You can put them here, right next to the makeup table."

He thanked the young man and slipped him a tip, and then lingered for a moment in the room. He searched the floral arrangement for a card, but didn't find one. Irina had a secret admirer, or perhaps just a discreet one. Jerry looked further, not sure what he might find. There was another floral arrangement behind her dressing screen. He looked it over. Also no card and the flowers were still fresh, so they'd arrived pretty recently.

Somebody's getting fresh with my girl, he thought. Jerry was aggravated. He didn't need Irina to have another reason to stay in 1913. Then again, it had been a long time since he'd given her flowers.

Chicago, 1911

The coverlet of the massive four-poster bed was strewn with red rose petals. Jerry and Irina were naked except for the few petals sticking to their flesh. Jerry had chosen Palmer House for the night, out of both sentiment and its luxurious setting. The furniture was elegant and polished, there was a chandelier twinkling overhead, and the glassware was of the finest crystal.

"This is quite extravagant, Mr. Creighton," Irina said, plucking a petal from her cheek.

"For some reason, I thought you deserved it." His skin tingled from the exertions of the past hour. It felt good and he was nowhere near played out. Jerry hadn't told her who he really was yet. Not that he didn't trust her, but he tried to keep his Creighton and Strauss identities—and lives—separate.

"Well, I do enjoy maximum spoilage." Irina slipped into twenty-first-century speak more often than Jerry, but they both still did it.

"I should order us some champagne. That was an oversight."

"No, no, no!" Irina said, sitting upright in the bed. "I want to make us some drinks. I've got a talent for it."

Jerry remembered she'd been tending bar at the poker game, among her other duties. "As well as dancing and romancing, but I doubt they'll send up the fixings for whatever cocktail you have in mind."

"Why not?" Irina was part petulant, part confused, and entirely adorable.

"It's getting late, you know," he said. "The bar may be closed, or this might be something they just don't do."

"I'm going to make us some whiskey sours," she said. "They're easy but I make the best one you'll ever pour over your lips. All I need is whiskey, lemon juice, and simple syrup. I'm going to get what I need even if I have to dance naked on the table."

"I think there may be an easier way." Jerry started getting dressed. "You noticed the manager when we walked in?"

"Barely. My mind was elsewhere."

Jerry transformed his face to mirror the manager's looks. "Convincing?"

Irina's eyes widened a bit, but she recovered quickly. "Well, we need to get you back into your tux. A bit of a shame; you'll just have to take it off once you come back." She paused for a moment. "You really can look like anyone?"

Jerry shrugged into his tux jacket. "Anyone I've seen who made enough of an impression for me to remember. Help me with the tie, will you?" Once fully dressed, Jerry checked himself out in the mirror. "One officious hotel manager, coming up." He kissed Irina on the cheek and opened the door. "Keep the bed warm."

"Before you go, can you look like Robert Pattinson?"

Jerry shook his head. "The *Twilight* guy? He didn't make much of an impression on me."

"Figures," she said with disappointment. "How about Keanu Reeves?"

"That I can do." He quickly shifted his look to match that of the actor.

"Wow, nice. Now say 'you killed my dog' in Russian."

"Russian is not exactly a second language for me." He took a second to recall a line from *The Great Escape*. "*Ya vas lyublyu*." According to Charles Bronson, it meant "I love you."

Irina furrowed her brow. "What does that mean?"

Jerry reshaped his face to duplicate that of the hotel manager. "It means I'm headed downstairs."

He was pulling off his tie when he returned fifteen minutes later. "What mademoiselle wants, mademoiselle gets."

"Where's my liquor and mixers?"

"You can't expect the manager to deliver it himself. That would look out of place." Jerry glanced at his gold watch. "I'll give them ten minutes tops."

"Okay, get out of your clothes."

"Maybe I should keep them on until your stuff is delivered." Jerry did go as far as taking off his jacket and hanging it over the back of a mahogany chair.

"No, no. Take them off. I'll throw on something and take care of the help." She gave him a wink.

Jerry reluctantly complied. Not that he wasn't used to being naked in front of her, but he'd have to hide out in the bathroom when the hotel staff arrived with the goodies.

When he'd shed every stitch of clothing, Irina said, "Now make yourself look like me."

Jerry was taken aback. He'd never had a request like this one before. "Really?"

"Yes, hurry."

Jerry did as she requested. Because of his larger body mass he was taller, but otherwise a duplicate of Irina. He turned slowly around, so that she could get a gander. "Satisfied?"

"Damn," she said. "I still look really fine."

Jerry laughed. "No shit. Don't you have a full-length mirror?"

"Yes, but I'm not crazy about mirrors. They're so unforgiving."
She took another long look and smiled approvingly. "I mean, I'm
not a college girl anymore."

"Women tend to lose their looks much more slowly than they
imagine. Most women, anyway. Can I change back now?"

There was a sharp, staccato rapping at the door. Irina threw on
an almost floor-length, beautifully crocheted shawl and walked
over to the door. "Get behind me."

Jerry had no idea what she had in mind, but he wasn't all that
bothered having someone see him in Irina's body.

Irina opened the door and motioned in a middle-aged man in a
hotel uniform. He carried a silver tray containing the requested
items.

"The lemon juice is freshly squeezed," he said, taking little notice of the nearly identical women, naked, who stood only a few
feet away. "Will there be anything else?"

"We'll let you know," Jerry said in Irina's voice.

Irina dashed across the room for her purse and pulled out some
cash for a tip.

The man nodded respectfully when it was handed to him.
"Thank you so much," he said, and left.

"Wow," Irina said. "He didn't even blink. I expected some kind
of double take, as it were. That dude must have seen it all in his
time."

"It's Chicago." He was amused by her playfulness, even though
it hadn't worked out as she planned.

She hand-waved her disappointment away and moved to the
drink fixings. "Prepare for a new level in alcoholic entertainment."

Jerry laughed and got into bed. "That's a pretty high bar for
me." He took a moment and weighed the words he was about to
say. "You know, you should come by the studio and let us do a
screen test of you."

"Really." Intent on her mixing, Irina kept her back to him. "Do
you want me around to keep an eye on me?"

Jerry returned to his original form, plumped up a feather pillow, and set it behind his head. "I'm wounded. What I'm really hoping is to exploit your beauty and talent to further my own career as a filmmaker. I am a director, after all. Show me some respect."

"Okay," she said, walking over to the bed with a drink in either hand. "As long as that's it."

"You have my word as a movie mogul."

Irina handed Jerry one of the glasses and slid in beside him. It was cool against his fingertips. He took a mouthful and savored it. "Verdict?"

"Damn good." He took another swallow. "If your screen test doesn't work out, the company will keep you on as bartender."

"That's very generous of you. Are you sure you can afford me, in either capacity?" She took a large shot of the whiskey sour. "I am very good."

"I'm sure we can find the cash somewhere."

After an hour or so, the bedcovers were knotted up and kicked entirely from the bed. Jerry had his eyes closed. His breathing was ragged.

Irina licked her lips, took a drink, and smiled. "Even better after something salty. So you want to tell me how you went from being naked and penniless to a producer/director?" She waited a moment for an answer. "You don't have to talk about it if you don't want to."

Jerry shook his head. "We're not obscenely rich, but we're not hurting, either. Just be aware it's not an entirely flattering story."

"I guess none of us covered ourselves in glory at the start," Irina said. "Or the new beginning, or whatever you want to call what happened to us."

"Yeah." Jerry knocked back two large swallows of whiskey sour. "The short answer is: I stole. I stole clothes, food, money, or whatever I needed to survive. My power helped a lot. I just didn't know what it was like to be dirt-poor. You see, I was born to wealth. I never had to worry about where my next meal was coming from, or a roof over my head, or clothes to wear. It was always available. I'll never forget what it's like to be really hungry. What a miserable feeling. Some people, the poor ones, I went back and tried to find to repay them, but I couldn't remember their faces. I just blotted it all out. Or my memory is going."

"I'm not judging," Irina said. "You know that. Not with my history. Just so you know, I wasn't a prostitute. But there was no way I could put myself through college on what I made. So I sometimes fucked guys for money. It wasn't a career choice. Life is expensive."

"That's okay. The first great love of my life was one of Fortunato's 'geishas.' She was a heroin addict and a lesbian." Jerry shook his head and indicated to Irina that his glass was empty. "It was a really healthy relationship."

"Fortunato, the ace from back in the day?" Irina took the glass and refilled it.

"The same. One of the most powerful aces around. Some kind of magic. He also happened to be John Fortune's father, but that's another story. In any case, he's dead now. John has had one hell of a life."

"Yeah, I read about it in my wild card history class. I feel sort of mundane in the company of you two."

"I wouldn't worry about that." Jerry took a moment to refocus on his past. "In any case, early on I couldn't be picky about who I took advantage of. As my circumstances, and clothing, improved I was able to move in a different circle, with the upper-crust set. I didn't feel so bad stealing from them. They had money to spare. Next year I'm planning on making a killing by betting any rich takers that *Titanic* won't make it to New York."

Irina made a face. "Making money off the dead."

"Yeah, it sounds bad, but it's not like I can save them. And even if I could, I probably shouldn't. Changing the course of time and all that. Can I trust you with something very few people know?" Jerry wasn't sure why he was going to say this, but it felt right.

"Probably. If you didn't, like, murder someone." Irina looked puzzled.

"My name isn't really Creighton. That's just the one I use for my private detective and bodyguard work." He paused, giving himself one last chance to back out. "My real name is Jerry Strauss."

Irina took another sip. "Okay. Thanks for telling me. I guess this is important information back in 2017. Are you telling me this because the Sleeper has agreed to leave me here?"

"No." Irina had told him the story about her and Pug and their encounter with Croyd and John Nighthawk. Nighthawk was another ace. "It just seemed like I was divulging personal secrets and that's my biggest one."

"So what are you going to do if the Sleeper doesn't show up before movies evolve away from nitrate film?" Irina plucked a single rose petal from her belly. "That's the deal, right? None of your work survives, so you don't change history?"

Jerry shrugged. "That's the basic concept. Not sure what happens if Croyd and Nighthawk don't show, but I think they will."

"Maybe. Croyd's a peculiar guy."

Jerry looked straight at Irina. "So before you drain every last bit of fluid from my body, can I count on you to do a screen test?"

"I'll give it my best shot," she said.

Irina was seated in a straight-backed chair wearing a blue silk georgette dress. He'd instructed makeup to emphasize her facial features but not attempt to define them, and they'd done the job to a T. Her dark hair streamed over her shoulders and down her back.

Jerry took his place beside Fred Lessley, the cameraman. "Don't be nervous, Irina."

"I'm not nervous, but these lights are quite hot. Could you provide me with a fan?" She looked around hopefully. After a few moments, a young man appeared and handed her a teal fan. Irina shook it open and began to fan her face. The fan didn't match perfectly color-wise, but this was black-and-white, so it didn't really matter.

"She looks great, boss," Lessley said.

"Okay, what I want you to do is start by giving us a profile, then look into the camera as if you know something I . . . well, the audience . . . doesn't."

"That shouldn't be too hard." She paused. "I'll just keep the fan in my lap."

"That's fine," Jerry said. "And we're rolling." Lessley's capable hands turned the crank in a practiced motion.

"Okay, cut." Jerry thought a moment, trying to come up with interesting directions for her. "Are you ready to go again, Irina?

"Action. All right, you look up slowly. You don't expect to see anything. You look higher, still higher. Now you're amazed, you can't believe it. You want to scream, Irina, but your throat is paralyzed. Maybe if you didn't see it. Throw your arms over your face and scream. Scream for your life."

Irina did exactly as directed, emoting with conviction until Jerry told her to scream, at which point she let out a little yelp. She turned to Jerry. "It's not like anyone can hear me. That should be enough."

"Right," Jerry replied. "Fred"—he turned to the cameraman—"you know that special film in the vault? The new stuff, not nitrate? Go get that."

Fred walked away purposefully, each step as measured as his hand on the camera had been.

Irina walked over and gently rapped the fan on his forehead. "Do you really think I've never seen the original *King Kong*? I'm not a cinema philistine."

"Sorry, I just love that scene." Jerry also loved that a woman her age had seen *Kong*. "I want to take a short break to change the film in the camera, but I'd like to get some footage of you dancing. There's a costume in the dressing room."

"Back soon," she said.

Irina was ready before Lessley had the camera loaded. She filled the time by dancing in the small stage area. She was wearing ballet shoes, a dark leotard top, and a matching short frilled skirt. A black ribbon held her bound hair. Irina wasn't a trained ballet dancer, but she moved with grace, precision, and confidence.

Lessley made last-minute adjustments to the camera and made sure it was moving freely along the lateral axis of the tripod.

Jerry walked over to Irina. "I know you can be very sexy, but there's no need for that. Just show the camera how you move."

"Don't worry," she whispered. "Absolutely no twerking."

Jerry took his place behind his cameraman. "Action."

Irina was controlled and powerful as she moved. She sold every arm and leg extension, rolled her shoulder ever so slightly. And at the finish, she smiled. Damn, what a smile.

"You get that, Fred?"

"Yep, kept her nicely in frame. Want to do it again?"

"No, that looked fine to me." He winked at Irina. "When this is processed and printed, I want it brought straight to me. Her screen test, too."

Lessley nodded.

Jerry walked over and kissed her hand. "That was really good."

"So from that you can tell if I have star quality?" She headed for her dressing room, her slippers moving almost soundlessly over the floor.

"Well, from this we can tell if you're worth taking a chance on. I'm guessing yes, but we'll see. The camera never lies."

Jerry motioned John Fortune into the editing room as his partner was passing by.

"I just got Irina's screen test and wanted you to have a look at it." He rolled his chair over to make room.

Fortune took a seat in the chair beside Jerry. "Does it really matter what I think?"

"Of course. I can't be objective about her, so I'm relying on you to give an unvarnished opinion."

"Then that's what you'll get." Fortune twirled his finger so Jerry would set the small reel of film spinning. "Let's see if the camera likes her."

It only took a minute or so for the screen test to play through. "Well?" Jerry asked.

"Let me see it again."

Jerry did as John requested. They sat silently together in the flickering light, watching Irina.

Fortune nodded. "She's got a quality, that's for certain. I suppose I can find the money to put her on contract."

"Thanks. I know she'll be delighted. It's a step up from dancing, and I need a permanent leading lady. I can't get by on my faces forever."

"The public seems to like you," Fortune said. "Maybe they'll take to her as well. She is much prettier than you, that's for sure."

"That she is." Jerry smiled, thinking of the time he'd spend with her later. "You know what's a damn shame?"

"That the Sleeper is going to leave her here when he whisks us back to the present? You two do make a good couple."

Jerry was silent for several heartbeats. "Maybe I can convince her to come with us."

"Maybe, but she hated who she was in 2017."

Jerry sighed and shook his head. "Okay, change of subject. You know what frustrates me? So many of the projects—books—that I would love to try to adapt to film haven't even been written yet. You know I love detective stories. The great detective authors—Dashiell Hammett, Raymond Chandler, S. S. Van Dine—haven't created those works yet. Drives me crazy."

"We did Sherlock Holmes."

Jerry nodded. "True, but after release I was afraid Conan Doyle would sue, or give me a thrashing. Oh well, we have plenty of projects to keep us occupied." He ran Irina's footage through the editor again. "Can you imagine the two of us as Nick and Nora?"

John Fortune laughed. "You're no William Powell."

Jerry laughed, too. "Go ahead. Crush my dreams."

"Where's Irina's dancing footage?"

"Oh," Jerry said. "I put that in the vault. I can go get it if you like."

"No, that's okay." John Fortune scratched his head. "We have a vault?"

"Well, the safe. I call it a vault."

John Fortune laughed. "We're not Disney."

"Even Disney isn't Disney yet." Jerry clapped his partner on the shoulder. "Let's get a bottle and celebrate. Our future, until the Sleeper shows up, is looking bright."

Chicago, 1913

The party at the studio had been planned for over a month. Jerry had been in charge of most of the arrangements, which included plentiful food and drink for all attendees and a small orchestra. Most important, Jerry had overseen the guest list. Thomas Ince, D. W. Griffith, and Mack Sennett, along with many of their technicians and players, were arriving by train from Hollywood. Chaplin had begged off. Jerry was fine with that, given Chaplin's penchant for womanizing. They had invited Edison and Frederick Armitage from New York. Edison had declined, of course. It was impractical to invite filmmakers from the Continent; the French in particular were influential at the time. He'd even asked George K. Spoor from Essanay, although Jerry was convinced they'd been spying on Fortune Films for some time. He assumed several Essanay stars—including Broncho Billy Anderson, Ben Turpin, and Francis X. Bushman—would be there as well. Fortune Films had made sure each of its employees received a handwritten invitation from both partners. It was likely to be a lively evening.

Jerry finished tying his bow tie. He'd done it enough times that he'd become serviceable at it. After putting on his Capezio black jazz oxfords, he pulled on his white gloves and checked himself in the mirror. He was pleased enough to head for the door. Irina met him there and gave him the once-over. She pinned a yellow boutonnière to his lapel and nodded approvingly.

"Not bad at all. You look every inch the movie mogul." Irina did a slow turn for Jerry. She was wearing a nearly floor-length red satin dress. The neckline was low enough to draw second looks, but not revealing enough to be scandalous. What was sure to be unacceptable was the slit in the left side of the dress that rose to her knee. She was wearing Narcisse Noir, a perfume guaranteed to lower Jerry's IQ by at least double digits.

"Wow," Jerry said. "I need some adjectives or something."

"I had the slit tailored in. Just in case I wanted to dance something other than waltzes." She pulled it to the side to reveal her lower leg.

"I'm sure you'll have plenty of takers in the dance department, but save a few for me."

She smiled. "You know I will."

Jerry and John Fortune stood shoulder-to-shoulder at the studio entrance, welcoming the seemingly endless stream of guests. Irina had affixed a boutonnière to John Fortune's suit as well. The arrival of the guests from California turned an already lively affair positively boisterous. Most of the crowd had migrated into the central area where the food and drink were being served. The lighting was electric, but there were also candelabras on the tables where guests could seat themselves.

"Let's join them," Jerry said. "We didn't throw this shindig to be doormen."

"True enough," Fortune said. "Isn't this a misstep if we're trying to keep our historical footprint as small as possible?"

"Maybe, but my vanity and curiosity demanded it. This is the dawn of American cinema. It's the only chance to meet some true pioneers, even if they aren't as good as we are." Jerry clapped his partner on the shoulder. "Besides, it's just a party. What could possibly go wrong?"

"Nothing, I'm sure," Fortune said, picking up a glass of champagne and nodding in Irina's direction. She was surrounded by a group of interested partygoers, almost all of them male.

"Can I borrow your face for just a few minutes?" Jerry asked. "I want to see exactly what's going on over there."

Fortune gave him a stern look. "No. Just no. You and Irina have been great together, but lately you've been coming off the rails. This is a great opportunity for you to avoid doing something stupid. I suggest you take it."

"Sage advice." Jerry started wandering indirectly toward Irina and friends. Francis X. Bushman said something Jerry couldn't make out. Irina laughed. His unshakable conviction that the Sleeper could show up any day now was making him unstable. His partner was right, and yet he had a hard time being cool about this.

He decided the direct approach was best and was making straight for her when a man grasped him by the elbow.

"Am I correct in assuming I'm speaking to Mr. Creighton?" The man at Jerry's elbow was a couple of inches shorter and appeared several years older than Jerry. He was quite dapper in his tuxedo.

Jerry nodded. "Yes. And who may you be?"

"My name is Henry Charles, sir. I'm pleased to make your acquaintance." He extended his hand.

Jerry smiled weakly and shook the man's hand. "Good to meet you, sir. Did you travel here from California?"

"Excellent guess. I work for Mr. Griffith, designing and rendering backdrops and such. One of your films, that is your and Mr. Fortune's, appeared to have a painted element that was clearly not a backdrop. Would you mind sharing how you managed such an effect?"

Jerry was loath to give up the technique, even though they hadn't been the first to use it. Still, Mr. Charles was a guest. "Matte painting. Large paintings rendered on glass that are seamlessly combined with the live-action film element."

"I thought it must be something of that nature. Would it be too much of an imposition to ask if I might see one or two of them?"

"I don't think..." Jerry paused and pondered a moment. "Well, I suppose a peek wouldn't harm anything, since you're a fellow artist."

Mr. Charles beamed.

"Follow me, please." Jerry took his guest on a particularly circuitous route to the room where the glass paintings were stored. He opened the door and turned on the light. "We keep each painting in a metal frame with casters to allow for easy movement." He rolled one of the paintings out. It was a medieval castle on a bleak hill against a darkened sky.

"Beautiful," Mr. Charles said.

"As one of the hosts, I need to return to the party. But you can feel free to examine them if you promise to be careful. Don't touch the glass. It readily takes fingerprints."

"You're very generous."

"Not at all," Jerry said. "I'll trust you can find your way back when you're done."

Jerry changed his face to that of Mr. Charles and walked briskly back to the main party area. Irina was surrounded by men, but so were several other female guests. There were also knots of tuxedoed men, no doubt talking business.

After casting a sidelong glance at Irina, Jerry sauntered over to the food table. The chicken, roast beef, spaghetti, and vegetables had been significantly picked over. There was still plenty of champagne, though. Jerry picked up a glass, took a cool sip, and headed in Irina's direction.

"Yes, ma'am, bodybuilding was an important part of my regimen. I heartily recommend it to all young men." Francis X. Bushman was noted for his amazing physique.

"Indeed," Irina said. "Then again, if more young men did as you suggest, you might have more competition as a leading man."

Bushman smiled. "Bodybuilding can only do so much. Other things"—he turned his profile to her—"are the work of nature and can't be duplicated."

You might be surprised, Francis, Jerry thought.

Jerry noticed John Fortune carrying on a conversation with Ben Turpin, who looked unremarkable without his trademark crossed eyes, but his partner was also keeping tabs on Irina. Jerry knew John Fortune wasn't the type to try anything, so he must be keeping a protective eye on Irina. Not that she really needed it.

John Fortune glanced over at Jerry/Mr. Charles, then paused and looked back. He frowned and patted his boutonnière with his finger.

Jerry knew pulling it off right there was a bad idea. Suddenly, he saw Irina turning toward him, did an about-face, and took a quick step in the opposite direction. Unfortunately, at just that moment, a man bent over to pick something up from the floor. Jerry's momentum caused him to flip over the man's back and land on his ass with a thud.

Ben Turpin laughed. "Now, that was a piece of work. You should be in slapstick."

Jerry scrambled up off the floor. "It's okay. I'm fine." In fact, he felt a significant twinge in his lower back. Despite that, he made a beeline for the nearest restroom. Fortunately, it was unoccupied. Jerry turned on the light, darted in, and assumed his Creighton appearance. He massaged his back as best he could and then sat down on a chair in the corner. He tried to imagine a way things could have gone worse. Short of killing himself or someone else, Jerry couldn't think of a thing.

Irina opened the door and shut it hard behind her. He could tell by her face she was understandably angry, but was relieved she wasn't furious.

"Why are you such a fucking idiot? You go to all the trouble and expense to throw an industry gala and then outdo yourself in the stupidity department."

Jerry sighed. "I think I come from a long line of idiots." It wasn't true; his family had been at the smart end of the spectrum for generations. "Sorry I messed things up."

"What does it say about me that my relationship with you is the most normal one I've had?"

Jerry almost opened his mouth to speak, then realized a smart man would say nothing. He pretended in that moment to be smart.

"Are you hurt?" Her expression softened a bit.

"My back's a little jacked up." He touched it and winced. "A couple of drinks now and some ice later and I'll be fine."

Irina removed her shoes. "I know something that will take the pain away. At least for a bit." She carefully hiked up her party dress and straddled him. "I'm not going to do all the work."

Jerry fumbled with the buttons of his tuxedo pants and pulled them open. Irina lowered herself onto him. He breathed in her perfumed scent and ran his fingers through her hair.

A few minutes later Jerry's back still hurt, but he didn't really care. Irina was looking into the mirror and touching up her makeup. "I'm going to rejoin the party and mingle," she said. "I might dance or flirt with one of those gentlemen, but I won't be bringing them in here. Fine with you?"

"I'm good," Jerry replied.

"Now pull yourself together and go enjoy these people. You brought them all here to satisfy your curiosity and your ego." Irina sat in his lap and donned her shoes. "The rest of you I've already taken care of."

He bloody well planned to do exactly that.

It had taken the better part of a day to clean up the stage area where the party had taken place, and when it was done the partners had decided to give everyone the rest of the day off. They were expected back the next morning ready to go.

Jerry had alternated hot and cold compresses on his back and was nearly pain-free. He was walking past the stage area where the workers were setting up for a particularly complex shot when he saw someone carrying another large bouquet of flowers. It wasn't the same man who'd delivered the last batch. Jerry had to get to wardrobe and couldn't take time to head him off, so he went over to one of the men assembling the stage.

"Art, you see that fellow with the flowers?"

"Yeah, I do, sir," Art said.

"Well, find out where those flowers came from and who is sending them if you can." He pulled a twenty-dollar bill out of his wallet and pressed it into Art's rough hand. "I'll find someone to fill in for you here."

"Whatever you say, sir."

Jerry couldn't give the matter much more thought. They had rehearsed the shot he wanted a few times without actually rolling film, and although there had been a couple of minor glitches, it had come off. He walked over to wardrobe where the dresser with his costume was waiting. Getting into costume was an important process; it helped him get into character. The fabric was scratchy but otherwise quite comfortable, although it rustled when Jerry walked. Not that anyone would be able to tell in a silent movie. His boots were cumbersome and it had taken a while for Irina to teach him to dance in them, even the few steps that were necessary for the shot he had in mind.

Next he went to his makeup room to apply some greasepaint and powder, but not too much or it would destroy the naturalistic look of his appearance. For *Song of Solomon* he was an Arabian scoundrel, hopelessly in love with a princess. He liked putting on the dashing, handsome face. So much more becoming than William Creighton.

The complex shot he had planned was for a dream sequence, which was Jerry's idea, where Jerry, the courageous hero, dances with the princess, Irina. The crew had laid an outward spiral of rails slightly underneath the dance floor. Over the rails in sections several feet long and equally as wide were hinged pieces of the dance floor that fit seamlessly into the whole. The camera was seated on a cart that was pulled slowly along the rails during the shot. As the camera cart moved forward, the crew lifted the hinged pieces of the flooring up to allow Lessley and his camera to move forward, and then dropped the floor sections back into place so that the rails were never visible. The shot began at Jerry's and Irina's feet and then panned up as they began to dance. When the camera approached the end of the spiral, Irina stopped dancing and turned away. If everything went as planned, it would be a showstopper. Irina had choreographed the moves, which were exotic and passionate. The greatest burden was on Lessley to pan the camera smoothly while maintaining his cranking speed. Jerry had no doubts he could do it.

Irina was already on set when he arrived. She looked ravishing. Her costume was revealing, to say the least. Jerry would need to keep his mind on his performance first and foremost.

"You look lovely," Jerry said. "Please try to cover for me if I drop a step or two."

Irina smiled. "I'm the one who needs a bit of covering, and you've got too much invested in this one to muck it up yourself."

"Your lips to the cinema gods' ears."

John Fortune was on the set, totally comfortable in the role of director.

Jerry and Irina took their places in front of the camera. Lessley raised a hand, indicating he was ready.

"And, action." Fortune said.

Jerry looked at Irina as they started to move together, but imagined the camera making its graceful arc around them as they danced. He heard the planks being raised and lowered and the cranking noise of the camera.

"Cut." Fortune walked over and clapped them both on the back. "That was excellent." He turned to Lessley. "Did we get it?"

"Yes, we did, sir."

"I'd like to do another take," Jerry said. "Just to be sure."

"You're the director." Fortune looked back at the crew. "Get back into place, everyone."

Jerry took Irina's hand and put his arm around her.

"Action."

This time he wasn't thinking as a filmmaker. Jerry was dancing with the woman he loved. Moving with her, looking into her eyes, being a part of her. He smiled unconsciously.

"Cut."

"That was definitely better," she said, kissing him passionately on the mouth.

"Yes, it was."

Jerry heard something above him snap and the hiss of a cable cutting the air. Out of the corner of his eye he saw something moving in their direction.

"Look out!"

Jerry didn't know who shouted, but the massive light fixture was swinging directly toward Irina. He grabbed her and pushed as hard as he could. For a moment he thought he'd made it. Then he felt something slam into his lower leg and he was spinning through the air. Jerry's shoulders caught the brunt of the impact, but his head hit the floor hard. Fade to black.

— — —

Jerry's nose was stinging when he came to. He took several deep breaths and opened his eyes. He was lying on the couch in Irina's dressing room, a pillow under his head. John Fortune was sitting in a chair next to him, a vial of smelling salts in his hand.

"Still with us?" Fortune asked.

"I think so." Jerry's ears were ringing. He felt the left side of his head. There was a lump rising there. His right lower calf and ankle hurt like hell. "Is Irina okay?"

"She's fine. Worried to death about you, of course. Everybody is." John Fortune took a deep breath. "She's gone to see if Dr. Sullivan will come take a look at you. I'm guessing he won't say no." Dr. Sullivan had made several calls to the studio when someone was injured or having a medical issue. He seemed fascinated, or maybe amused, with all the goings-on related to making movies.

"We got the shot, didn't we?" Jerry was so discombobulated he couldn't remember.

"Yes, we did. Twice, actually, since you insisted on a second take. Good choice, too. That second go-round was a barn burner."

Jerry smiled despite the pain. "Have it printed up by tomorrow morning. I really want to give it a look."

"We have to make sure you're okay before you make plans to do anything."

Jerry tried to sit up. John Fortune put a hand on Jerry's chest to hold him in place. "Other than this lump on my head, I think I'm okay," he protested.

"Let's give the doc the final say."

There was a knock on the door. Irina opened it and ushered Dr. Sullivan into the room, medical bag in hand. She gave Jerry a concerned look.

Dr. Sullivan motioned John Fortune out of the chair and sat down. First he took Jerry's pulse, then checked his respiration. After that he examined the lump on his head and took a long look at Jerry's eyes.

"Much pain, young man?"

"A fair amount. I would think some aspirin might do the trick."
He managed a brittle smile.

"You should be a doctor, then." He examined Jerry's arms and
torso to see if there were any injuries to his upper body. "When I
was growing up we didn't have movies, just the stage. I always
had an itch for it, but my parents said you couldn't make an honest
living pretending to be someone else."

Jerry winced at that.

"Did that hurt?" Dr. Sullivan asked.

"No. I was just thinking of something else." He pointed to his
feet. "I think my ankle is hurt. You might want to check there."

"I'm working my way down, young sir," he said, prodding Jerry's hips. "We'll get to your ankle soon enough."

Soon enough didn't take long. Dr. Sullivan's probing of Jerry's
right ankle caused it to sing with pain, but the doctor was still able
to articulate it fully.

"We're going to stand you up very slowly and see if you can put
weight on your leg," the doctor said. "I think it should be safe."

He and John Fortune lifted Jerry up, with a slight assist from
Irina, and stood him on his feet.

"See if you can put weight on that ankle."

Jerry took a tentative step. It hurt, but was manageable. "I think
I'll be fine."

"I see you still want to be a doctor, but I agree. If the ankle gives
you trouble you can use a cane until it improves." He picked up
his bag. "Also, there's no indication of a concussion, but someone
should spend the night with you, keep you awake. If you start
having issues, go straight to the hospital."

Jerry reached for his wallet and realized he was still in costume,
as was Irina. He sat on the couch.

"I'll take care of him, Doctor," Irina said.

"You're a most fortunate man, Mr. Creighton." He headed for
the door. John Fortune went with him.

Once they were alone, Irina sat in the chair and gently caressed Jerry's face. "Oh, your poor head."

"I'll be fine. You'll just have to figure out a way to keep me awake." Jerry tried to wink, but the skin on his forehead had tightened and it didn't really work.

"You could have been killed," Irina said. She was shaking slightly.

"Well, you could have, too," Jerry said. "I saw what was happening. You didn't. You'd have done the same for me."

"I know. I just, the idea that someone would risk their life to save mine." She looked on the verge of tears.

Jerry gave her as much of a hug as he could manage from the couch. "We're both pretty shaken up. For the record, there's nobody's life I'd rather save."

"I owe you."

"Not really, but if you feel obligated, you can name your firstborn after me." He started shedding his costume. "Let's get out of these. Then maybe John can help you get me home."

As if on cue, John Fortune poked his head back into the room.

"Can you help Irina get me to the car?"

"Certainly," John Fortune said. He and Irina helped Jerry up and supported him from either side as he limped outside.

As they moved into the main area, Jerry blinked. Every employee of Fortune Films was standing there, looking on with concern.

Jerry smiled and gave a thumbs-up. "I'm okay. I'll be back before you know it. Thanks for taking the time to . . . let me know you care."

They responded with a soft clapping, meant more as encouragement and solidarity than applause. A couple of them patted Jerry on the back as they moved slowly toward the exit. He hadn't realized they actually cared about him. Jerry could impersonate people, but for all his gifts, sometimes he couldn't read them at all.

Even if Irina came with him, when the Sleeper took him back to the future, it was going to be hard to leave Fortune Films behind.

Jerry had been away from the studio for three days. The absence from his work hurt more than his head, back, and ankle combined. Irina had stayed home the first day, tending to his every need. He enjoyed it, to be sure, but he persuaded her to go back to work. They could film around him for a few days, but if both leads were out, the project ground to a standstill.

When he did make it back to work, everyone he met greeted him with a smile and a sincere "Welcome back, Mr. Creighton." It felt good, even though he wasn't entirely sure he deserved it.

His first port of call was the editing room. Jerry wanted to see how the scene they'd shot before his accident had turned out. John Fortune met him there and they watched both takes several times.

"The crew did a great job," Jerry said, "especially Lessley. That second take really does work. I'm completely satisfied."

"Glad to hear it," John Fortune said.

There was a rap at the door. It was Art. "Excuse me, but you inquired about something the other day, Mr. Creighton. I got the information you requested. Well, some of it." He handed Jerry a slip of paper.

"Yes, of course." Jerry took the paper and tucked it into his pocket. "Thank you, Art." He'd half forgotten about Irina's secret admirer and almost felt foolish worrying about it. Still, no point in leaving something half done.

"Anything important?" John Fortune asked.

"Probably not, but I may as well take care of it. I'll be back shortly."

The paper had an address and a business name: *Empire Florist*.

Jerry didn't want to drive; in fact, Irina had been behind the wheel this morning coming into work, so he ordered a cab. Less than half an hour later, the cabbie deposited him at Empire Florist.

A hanging bell over the door tinkled welcome when Jerry entered. A variety of floral scents filled Jerry's nose. The sensation was pleasurably intense. There was a tall, thin man behind the register. He was cutting the stems of flowers in a precise and yet practiced manner. Doubtless he'd done it thousands of times.

"Welcome, sir," he said.

"Empire Florist is an interesting name for your business. Empire calls to mind New York," Jerry said.

"Yes, I'm a proud New Yorker myself. I want my business to reflect that, even in Chicago."

"I've spent some time in New York," Jerry replied, removing his hat. Of course, most of that time was decades from now. "An employee of mine visited your establishment recently, looking for some information about a customer."

The man looked up and nodded. "Yes. I remember. I also recall he went away disappointed."

"Indeed. I've come to see if I might persuade you. I understand your reticence, but I thought perhaps we might come to an accommodation." He patted his wallet.

"I sell flowers, sir. Flowers make people happy. Look around." He opened his arms. "Doesn't being inside here make you happy? The smell, the beauty? You want information, which is something I don't trade in. Flowers always make people happy. Knowledge is a riskier thing. So I must say no."

"Perhaps if I explained the situation in its entirety, you might understand my position more clearly." Jerry realized why Art had come back empty-handed. This fellow was one tough nut to crack.

"I know your situation. Some other gentleman is trying to turn your lady friend's head by sending her flowers." He lifted a single rose and smelled it, then smiled. "This is a smart thing to do. All's fair in love and war."

"I would say that depends on your viewpoint. I'm the aggrieved party."

The florist came out from behind the counter and put his arm around Jerry's shoulder. "See here, sir, this is your woman. You have the advantage. To win with her all you have to do is match the favor he is bestowing on her. You needn't outdo him."

Jerry thought it over for a second. "So I just need to buy her flowers, too?"

The florist clapped him on the back. "I would have felt better if you'd come to that conclusion without my help. It makes it seem like I'm trying to hustle you."

Jerry nodded. "Maybe you are, but it's still a great idea. Not sure why I didn't think of it." He held his hands as far apart as possible. "I want the biggest, most beautiful arrangement you have. How long will it take you to get it ready?"

The florist contemplated a moment. "We're low on roses, but I'll work around it. Say, tomorrow afternoon."

"Have them delivered to this address." Jerry handed him a Fortune Films business card. "For Irina Adamczyk."

The florist jotted Irina's name on the card, making sure to have Jerry spell it out in full. "You're a very wise man. I can personally guarantee you she'll cry when she gets these."

Jerry felt relieved, almost happy. Why hadn't he thought of sending flowers?

The cab ride back to the studio had a few too many bounces and his head was aching when he arrived at the office. John Fortune was, predictably, behind his desk focused on the ledger in front of him.

After fishing a couple of aspirin tablets out of his desk, Jerry washed them down with a glass of water and seated himself. He hoped the aspirin would kick in quickly.

"Are you up to shooting another scene?"

"Sure," Jerry said, "I need to get back to work." Besides, in the upcoming scene he and Irina had a major kiss.

After finishing the scene, he returned to his dressing room. There was a knock on the door and Lessley came in. "Mr. Fortune wants to see you in your office."

Jerry stripped off his Arabian knights costume and got into his work clothes, then headed for the office.

They were there. Croyd and John Nighthawk.

"I think I saw Irina," Croyd said. "Not surprised she hooked up with you two. She froze when she saw us, then backed away. Like she was thinking about something, then got scared. Anyway, she's not on our agenda. You two are."

It was the moment he knew had to happen at some point. Jerry was torn, wanting to go back to 2017 but hating to lose Irina. It was her decision, though. Fate was directing this scene, and all he could do was read his lines.

John Fortune was far less disturbed by the turn of events than Jerry. The conversation was brief, but to Jerry it seemed to take forever. Every moment he hoped Irina would enter the room, saying she'd changed her mind, asking to return with him.

But she didn't come. The moment passed. Then they were gone.

One thing Jerry felt certain of. The florist was right. Irina would cry when she got the flowers.

Chicago, 2020

Fortune Films had disappeared more than a century ago, but by some miracle Empire Florist had stood the test of time, still operating out of the same location. Jerry sat in the back seat of the limo, pleasantly buzzed from the whiskey sours. How many had he drunk? Maybe not enough. He was nervous, like he was on a first date.

The interior of Empire Florist looked nothing like it had over a century before, but it smelled the same. A young woman smiled at him when he entered.

"How can we help you, sir?"

"You have an order for Mr. Creighton, I believe. A rather large arrangement."

"Yes, of course." She walked around the register and looked

into the back of the store where the flowers became bouquets. "It's probably going to take a few minutes. You can take a seat if you like." She pointed to a chair.

Jerry sat with his thoughts. When the Sleeper brought him back, he'd resolved to think of his Fortune Films adventure as something of a fantasy, a piece of his life that he lived that was separate from reality. It was too hard to deal with the loss, so for years he put his feelings and memories away and concentrated on getting back to his life. It wasn't hard to do; business was brisk at the Ackroyd/Creighton detective agency. He was busy and happy to be distracted. But the video of Irina had been like cold water in his face.

"What do you do, Mr. Creighton?" the young woman asked, trying to make small talk.

"Well, I've done a lot of things in my time, but right now I'm thinking about writing a book." It was true. Jerry was committed to making it happen.

"What's it about?"

Jerry smiled. "The title is *The Lost History of Fortune Films*." Why not write about it? It's not like he could do any damage to the timeline now.

She looked puzzled. "I don't think I've ever heard of Fortune Films." Then she nodded. "I guess that's why it's lost."

"Yes. But if I can find a publisher, you'll have a chance to learn all about it."

Jerry felt he had enough influence and money to make it happen. If not, there was always self-publishing. He felt he owed it to everyone who had worked at the studio. It was the least he could do for them. He couldn't include everything he knew about Irina, or John Fortune, or himself. He'd keep their personal history during the studio days hazy.

Of course, despite the research he was going to put together, some would regard it as fiction. But the story would be there. That was what mattered. He needed to do it now. His memory wasn't what it used to be.

A middle-aged man with thinning hair and glasses perched precariously on his nose walked out with an armful of flowers. "Mr. Creighton, here's your order."

Jerry took the flowers. The man opened the door so he could exit without a struggle.

"Come again."

Jerry would be doing that. From now on he was planning regular trips to Chicago to visit Irina, to make up for lost time. The intoxicating scent of the flowers kept his mind occupied on the way to the cemetery. Jerry had been in touch with the caretakers and they'd furnished him with a GPS location for her grave.

It was a short walk to Irina's final resting place. He had some idea of what had happened to her after Fortune Films. She moved to Hollywood; Jerry had confirmed she'd maintained a residence there for two years, but had never landed a starring role. After that she'd returned to Chicago and made her living as a dance instructor. She must have enjoyed that. Irina was such a wonderful dancer. She'd gotten married in Chicago to a Vance Carson and together they had a son, but her husband had died. Jerry couldn't find an obit on him and wasn't sure what happened. Their son was killed in the Solomon Islands during World War II, and Irina died a few years later of sepsis.

Jerry looked at the grave next to Irina's. The headstone read RIP JERRY CARSON, BELOVED SON OF VANCE AND IRINA CARSON, WHO DIED IN SERVICE TO HIS COUNTRY.

Irina had done as he asked. It had been a frivolous request at the time, but now it meant more than he could express. Jerry hoped she'd had a happy life, to the extent anyone does, and that she'd known he loved her. She must have known.

Jerry tried to get a handle on his feelings, looking down on her grave. He was sad that she was gone and that they hadn't had more time together. It was what she had wanted, though. Mostly, he felt gratitude, something Jerry wasn't very familiar with. He was grateful the Sleeper had dislodged them all in time, grateful for Fortune Films and everyone who had helped make it a place where he could realize his filmmaking dreams, and grateful for a partner like John Fortune. But mostly he was grateful for Irina, who helped make the best time of his life everything he could have wanted.

He swept away the leaves covering her grave and carefully set the vase of flowers onto the earth.

"I love you, Irina," he said. Then he walked slowly back to the limo.

On the plane to New York he'd need several more whiskey sours, not to make him forget but to help him remember. He wanted to remember it. Irina most of all.

2021

What's Your Sign?

by Gwenda Bond and Peter Newman

CHAPTER 1

Stuart

Colin's Nissan Micra had to be at least fifteen years old. Which was funny because he drove like a fifteen-year-old with a stolen car—too fast and with a cavalier approach to road safety. It screeched to a stop in front of me and the door swung open. A flagpole protruded from the back seat, partially obscuring his grin.

"Are you ready, Stuart?" he asked. "It's going to be a big day."

"I guess?"

Colin looked at me the way my mum did when I was being miserable. "Come on, now. Where's your positivity?"

I picked up the folders littering the passenger seat and attempted to get in. It's hard to be positive while inserting yourself into a space that's too small for you. There was no point in saying so to my boss, though. As far as he was concerned, being upbeat was mandatory.

"Sorry," I said. "Of course I'm up for it. Totally up for it . . . Can you tell me what's going on? The email just said 'major charity event.'"

"Love to," he replied, pulling away a few seconds before my

seatbelt clicked into place. As he talked I tried to get comfortable, but that was easier said than done. The seats had been pushed forward to pack all the banners, T-shirts, collection buckets, ribbons, and other Reachers paraphernalia. My knees were jammed tight against the front of the dashboard, and my hair spikes brushed the roof unless I tilted my head at an uncomfortable angle. For the record, I'm not that tall. Colin just drives a really small car.

"Your work has got us some media attention so we're moving fast to take advantage. The press will be there, along with some guest speakers and a few celebrities."

"What kind?"

"Mostly national. BBC, ITV, a fair few of the papers, along with Sky News and a couple of others."

"I meant what kind of celebrities?"

"Oh! A bit of a mixed bag. We've got Stella Sumner doing readings for auction. She's a TV fortune teller from the States. There's Karl Beck from that sci-fi show with the space vampire." Colin pulled a face. "The one my husband is *crazy* for. He's going to be signing photos for people. But what you'll really be interested in is . . ." He paused dramatically.

"Is what?"

"The Silver Helix are sending some."

I turned to look at him fast enough to bang my head. "Seriously?"

"Thought that would get your attention."

I've always loved the Helix. Aces who work for queen and country. Well, king and country these days. Redcoat is my absolute favorite. I have the official guide to Redcoat's lineage at home. Limited edition. It covers all of them, from Henry Astor who first took on the mantle in the fifties, to Jason McCracken who wears the coat today. It's by far the most expensive thing I own. The pages are edged in just the right shade of red.

Like I said, Redcoat's my favorite, but I follow all of them as best I can: Stonemaiden, Pygmalion, Jiniri, Enigma, Archimedes, even the new ones like Payback. Especially the new ones. They're the future. To say that I was excited at the idea of meeting one was a massive understatement.

"Is Redcoat coming? Please tell me Redcoat is coming!"

"They couldn't confirm who they'd send, but I have it from the royal offices that someone will be coming. Pretty exciting, eh?"

I just nodded, dumbstruck. I was going to meet one of my heroes.

"And," Colin continued, "there's the main event."

"What's that?"

"You, of course!"

"Me?" My heart began to sink. There was a good chance I'd have to do something embarrassing in front of the Silver Helix. "What do I have to do?"

"Nothing. We're going to auction off your name."

"What?"

"You're the hero of the Barnet Blaze now and we need to work on your branding. That means you need a proper name. I had the idea of getting the public to pick one so we can raise some money at the same time."

"Oh, God, no."

"If *we* don't pick one, the press are going to stick with Do-Gooder, and you don't want that, do you?"

Colin took my stunned silence as agreement. He did that a lot. The truth was, I didn't want to be called Do-Gooder, but that didn't mean that I wanted someone else to choose my name for me. "What if I don't like it?"

"It'll be fine," he replied, weaving the car back and forth through traffic hard enough to knock my head against the window. "Trust me."

Twenty minutes later we pulled up outside my parents' house. I hadn't moved out long ago, but it already felt odd coming back. Growing up, I'd never thought of it as small. It'd just been home. Now, though, I was seeing it with fresh eyes. There were damp patches on the outer wall, and the gutters were busted. Green paint cracked and peeled off the front door, showing hints of pale-yellow origins. The place was old and in need of the kind of work neither of my folks could afford. I stepped onto the short path that led past the little rectangle of garden. My dad's rosebush was being bullied into a corner by the nettles. It bothered me that it wasn't being looked after.

I pulled out my key and wrestled with the lock until it let me in. "Hello?" I called. "It's me."

Kelly was already waiting at the bottom of the stairs, shoes on and ready to go. I raised a hand in greeting, already feeling better for seeing her, and she beamed. Kelly's had my back ever since she was a little girl, and that makes a big difference to me. Literally. I'm an ace that gets my power from other people believing in me, and Kelly's my first and biggest fan. Around her, I'm stronger, faster, just all-around better. I feel different inside, too. More confident. More like me. My senses immediately sharpened and I became aware of the perfume Kelly had liberally doused herself with, and the underlying smell of damp in the walls. Upstairs, I could hear Dad having an afternoon nap, and Mum biting her nails in the kitchen.

"Hi, Mum," I called through the door.

Her voice floated over from the other side. "Hi, love. Sorry, I can't come out. I'm on hold with the bank." Then it rose to a hard shout. "Kelly! Hurry up. You're brother's here! Don't keep him waiting." Then soft again. "I don't know what's going on in that girl's head sometimes, I really don't. I told her to— Oh, sorry, hello, can you hear me? Yes, this is Mrs. Hill . . ."

Her voice trailed off as she moved farther from the door.

Kelly has brown eyes like mine. She rolled them at me.

I gave her a weak smile. Things have never been good between her and Mum and Dad. I don't really understand why. "Ready to go?"

She hopped from the stairs like an excited little girl. Kelly's sixteen but she looks at least two years younger, which she hates. I totally get it. I was a late bloomer, too.

I'm not really sure how we managed to fit Kelly into the car, but we did. The next few hours flew by helping set up for the fair, which was being held in the main hall of Barnet House, one of the biggest schools in the area. Ordinarily, Reachers would have used a much grander location, but Colin had gone with it because I'd saved a busload of their pupils during the fire and it was good publicity. The venue was also being given to us for free, which helped. The hall was big, if a little musty. The stairs up to the stage creaked as Colin took me up there.

"The lighting's limited, so when you come out, be sure to stand forward."

"Sure. Is there anything you want me to do before my event?"

"Talk to people, tell them about what we do and how important it is. Casually of course. And remember, the more you smile and engage with the public, the better they feel—and the better they feel, the more likely they are to donate."

"Got it."

As soon as the doors opened, people flooded in. Any doubts I had soon vanished. At least a few of them recognized me, and more than that, they believed in me. I felt my power grow that little bit stronger. There's a point where I start to be able to do things well beyond the realm of a normal person and I was edging into that now. I noted a few of the crowd were wearing bandages under their clothes. Probably survivors of the fire. That was quickly confirmed when I went over to see how they were doing. One of them asked to shake my hand and, before I knew it, a circle of cameras had sprung up around us, microphones bobbing overhead like scorpion's tails.

I'm trained to handle disasters rather than the media. Something about the pressure to say something catchy for the cameras tends to lock me up.

"Graham McHugh, ITV," said one of the journalists. "We understand you've just got back from assisting relief efforts in Mexico."

"That's right."

"Can we expect to see more of you in the UK now?"

"I go wherever I'm needed. Reachers is an international organization."

That question was easy to handle. I'd been briefed on what to say. The ones that followed were less orthodox and they came thick and fast. I fumbled my way through the answers.

"Why did you choose such a colorful look?"

"To be visible to my team and the people who need me."

"How does your ace work?"

"No idea. I'm just glad it does."

"Are you single?"

I went about as red as the dye in my hair. "Uhh, yes."

"What are your views on joker terrorism?"

"It's wrong, obviously, and I . . ." Had gone completely blank. This was still a very contentious topic that Reachers, with its joker outreach program, was bang in the middle of. Luckily, at this point Colin appeared with a microphone and took over, quickly shifting the topic back onto the survivors of the fire. Kelly was with him, holding a bucket. That man never misses a trick.

As soon as I was done shaking hands and wishing everyone a speedy recovery, I retreated from the cameras and went over to the main Reachers booth. There was a large cardboard version of me dressed as I was now: blue jeans, white T-shirt with the Reachers logo, red boots, fingerless red gloves, and a customized fireman's jacket sprayed blue with gold plates on the shoulders. It's weird looking at a life-sized version of yourself at the best of times, let alone when it's posed with a cheesy grin and pointing to itself

with both thumbs. I turned my attention to the big sign next to it
that said:

NAME OUR HERO! £10 to suggest a name for the list. Speak
to us here or pay using the Reachers app.

I looked down the list of suggested names so far and wasn't
exactly thrilled with what I saw:

- *First Responder.* Okay, I suppose.
- *Disaster Man.* No.
- *Do-Gooder.* I'd expected that one at least. Still no.
- *Stuart the Hedgehog.* Bad as it was, this was not the worst op-
  tion here. That dubious honor went to:
- *Hero McHeroface.*

I stared at the list for a while, a growing sense of panic in my
gut. This would not do. I threw a tenner into the bucket and added
Blue Guardian to the list. Sure, it was the name I came up with
when I was twelve, but it was still better than all the other options.

Kelly was frowning at me.

"What is it?"

"I don't think you should suggest names."

I waved a note in front of her. "You want to suggest one for me?
A good one?"

"No." She took my hand and started to drag me across the hall.
"I've got a better idea. Let's go and find out if you're getting a
name you like."

"How are we going to do that?"

"We'll get Stella to read your future."

"Stella? Is she a friend of yours?"

"No, but I watch her on TV all the time. She's really good. She'll
know how the vote's going to go."

"I don't think that's how fortune tellers work."

"Come on, Stu. Please." She put on her begging face. The unfairly cute one. "It'll be fun."

Under her big-eyed stare I cracked pretty fast.

So we went and joined the queue. A gaudy-looking tent had been set up on the stage, the roof rolled back and the flaps open so that the audience could see what went on. People stared at me as we waited. Some more openly than others. I did my best to acknowledge them with a smile. A crowd had gathered around the tent, a really big one, along with a couple of cameras. There was another reading already in progress and you didn't need enhanced hearing to know that something was wrong. But you did need enhanced hearing to catch what they were saying, and to detect the tone of strained politeness.

"There's no need to be like that, my dear," said a man. He sounded well spoken, older. There was something familiar about him. "I was just paying you a compliment."

"I think we're done here," replied a woman's voice. It was no-nonsense. American. And pretty annoyed.

"But you haven't finished my reading!"

"Next."

The man's voice turned into a whispered hiss. "Do you know how much money I've had to raise in order to have this?"

"Next!" she repeated, loud enough that everyone around, including the journalists, would hear it.

The scrape of a chair being pushed back was like a shrill cry. Then people were parting to make way for the man. He wore an expensive shirt and silver cuff links with a flamboyant waistcoat and cravat. His double chin was more prominent than in the pictures I kept, but there was no mistaking him. Two spots of red burned on his cheeks while the rest of his face had gone very pale.

"Hey," said Kelly. "Isn't that Pygmalion?"

She was right. It was Pygmalion of the Silver Helix. Close enough for me to reach out and touch. This was a moment I'd been waiting years for. I had so many questions for the man and so many things I wanted to say. And not a single one of them managed to get from my brain to my mouth. It was awful. I just stood on the stairs to the stage staring up at him with my mouth open, like some spiky-haired idiot.

"Excuse me," he said gruffly.

I jumped back out of his way. "Sorry."

And then he was gone, striding off into the distance while I lambasted myself for making such a terrible first impression.

"Next," repeated the fortune teller.

It occurred to me that at some point the people between me and the tent had moved aside. Probably to allow for Pygmalion's exit, but also, Stella didn't seem to be in the best of moods. Maybe this wasn't such a good idea after all.

I felt Kelly's hands on my back. "Go on."

She gave me a push. Enough to make me take a step forward. As no one else was moving, it caught everyone's attention. A few people cheered and I found myself taking the last few steps onto the stage where Stella sat. I don't know what I expected her to look like exactly. Maybe one of the old women that does the horoscopes in the papers, with heavy makeup and a shawl. Or some other circus stereotype. I couldn't have been more wrong.

She had film-star hair, with the kind of blond curls that I didn't think people could pull off in real life. Despite that, she was casually dressed in jeans and a black T-shirt. It wasn't massively different to what I was wearing, except that her T-shirt probably cost twice what mine did, and on Stella, it just looked cool. There were bright tattoos on her arms, all symbols. It took me a moment before I realized they were signs of the zodiac. I don't know much about star signs, but Kelly's birthday is in May and I knew the horned circle on the fortune teller's forearm was Taurus.

Stella quirked an eyebrow at me and I realized that I'd been staring.

"Sorry," I said, feeling like a giant twat.

"Are you here for a reading?"

Was I? A big part of me wanted to go and bury my head in the sand somewhere before I embarrassed myself further. But I found myself nodding. It was too late to back out now.

"What's your name?" she asked as I approached.

"Stuart."

"Nice to meet you, Stuart. I'm Stella." She glanced at something on her phone. "Hmm. I don't have your name down here."

"Oh." I stopped as it dawned on me that I *was* being a massive twat. Pygmalion had mentioned raising money for his reading. Of course he had! This was a charity event but Stella wasn't doing readings for free. Everyone who came up onstage would have paid for the privilege. I was trapped. I couldn't afford to buy the slot myself and I couldn't afford to back out, not with half the country watching.

Stella looked at me long enough for me to wish I was dead several times, and then she turned to the cameras. "If you'd like to hear my reading for Stuart, donate now, using the Reachers app."

With Kelly and the crowd behind me, my eyes could easily see the progress bar on Stella's phone as the tiny numbers began to climb, turning from red, to amber, to green before my eyes.

We hit the minimum target in less than a minute.

"Huh," said Stella. "Looks like they do."

I mouthed a silent *thank you* to the cameras as I took my seat and gave them a thumbs-up. The chair was set quite far back from the table, enough that my knees weren't under it.

She glanced up at me. "You mind coming a little closer?"

It's strange. I only pulled that chair in a few feet but it changed the atmosphere instantly. The growing crowd and the cameras were still there, just less present. I became aware of entering Stella's space. Of her proximity. The scent of her perfume tickling my nose. I worried that I might be staring again but if she was annoyed, she gave no sign. In fact, I couldn't read anything from her at all, which was quite intimidating.

"You ever done this before, Stuart?"

"Uh, no. First time."

She nodded, unsurprised. "I'm going to need some things from you before we can start. When were you born?"

"Fifteenth of April."

She started making notes. "What year?"

"Two thousand."

"Okay." Another note. "You know the exact time of your birth?"

"Sorry, no." She frowned, just a little, and I suddenly found myself wishing I did know. "I could call my mum and ask her if you like?"

"No, that's okay. Where were you born?"

"Barnet Hospital."

"This is your hometown?"

"That's right."

"Interesting. Give me a minute and I'll be right with you."

I sat back in my chair and watched her work. I don't know if it's because of my wild card or just the way I am, but I'm always aware of other people around me. Where they are, what they're doing, how they're feeling. And it struck me just then how totally absorbed she was in her task. As if the rest of us weren't there. It was mesmerizing. She was so . . . contained. So at ease. She was filling out a chart that looked like a giant circle divided into wedges, like sections of a clock, with thick circles at certain points where the lines crossed. It would have been easy for me to read what she was writing, but that felt wrong somehow, so instead I watched her hand as it moved across the chart. The way she held her pen. The quick, decisive marks she made.

It came to me that I was looking for clues about her. That I wanted to know more about Stella Sumner. Maybe more than I should. The thought brought a little heat to my cheeks.

And that was the exact moment she looked up at me. "Ready?"

I looked into her eyes and realized that, no, I was in no way prepared for her or any of this. I nodded anyway, put on my best smile. "Absolutely."

Stella

I was so jet-lagged I could go from a featured celeb at this bonkers UK charity event to an extra in a *Night of the Living Dead* movie at any moment. My mother had insisted I take a red-eye "across the pond" from Nashville (through Chicago), which would've been great if I could manage to sleep on airplanes.

Truth was, being *in* the sky disconcerted the hell out of me. I liked having it high overhead, knowing precisely which constellations and stars were above me even when I couldn't see them.

So when I landed at Heathrow and my chirpy, mid-twenties, go-getter new publicist Vickie-short-for-Victoria presented me with a packed itinerary for today, I wanted to weep. I'd envisioned ignoring my seasoned traveler mother's advice and sleeping all day in a nice, comfortable hotel bed with the blackout curtains drawn. I'd throw a video up on my *Oh, My Stars!* YouTube channel, then explore the city by night, for my own reasons.

But it wasn't to be. Instead, here I was, using every ounce of energy I had left to focus enough to produce these star charts. At least it was for a good cause.

Vickie had positioned herself right behind the handsome young ace man across from me—Stuart—and was nodding enthusiastically at me. Her tidy row of black bangs didn't so much as lift in the effort.

"Ready?" I asked him.

Stuart had big puppy energy, exuding likability and decency. Things that my analysis supported. He'd stumbled onto the right gig. I wondered what his ability was.

He said "Absolutely" and gave me what could only be described as a dazzling smile. I leaned in a bit despite myself. The unpleasant cravat-wearing older ace who'd kept trying to performatively flirt instead of focus on the reading had tried my patience. He'd kept prodding about whether love was in the cards for him, all but batting his eyes at me. When I'd honestly answered that I didn't think it was, his reaction had been an over-the-top flounce. I had seen the panic in Vickie's eyes, read the equivalent of a silent *Oh, no, so* this *is why no one likes her as much as her mum in the States* thought bubble. This was my UK charm offensive. Taking over Mom's astrological empire so she could "retire" (yeah, right) wasn't going smoothly at home. She had made me the new face of the business in the efforts of attracting a younger, revitalized fan base, but she was still very much operating behind the scenes. Which was why I was now here to build my brand. The very thought made me want to vomit.

I smiled back at him.

There we were, two strangers smiling at each other a little too long. The click of a phone photo being taken by someone watching us reminded me this was a performance.

"Here we go," I said, louder. "Your hometown hero, Stuart here, is an Aries, of course. And something tells me he's too sensible to believe in all this astrology business."

The crowd laughed.

"But also too polite to say so," I added.

Stuart's expression turned adorably sheepish. He shrugged.

"It's okay," I said conspiratorially. "I don't know how much I believe it, either. Let's see how I did."

"You don't believe in it?" Stuart asked with what seemed to be sincere curiosity.

My turn to shrug. "I believe the stars are a tool and our reactions to what these ancient systems show us can be extremely telling. They can help us be who we are meant to be."

My mother believed in it all completely. She said my opinions made me modern, and I used her same methods for creating both daily horoscopes and personalized readings like this. But to her true believers, my slight skepticism made me a . . . well, less-than-stellar substitute for her.

I could see Stuart struggling for the right response, so I threw him a line. "But it doesn't matter what we think, just whether the predictions are helpful. I believe you'll agree there are stranger things in this world than our character being predicted by the stars?"

The crowd loved Stuart's nod.

"But you really don't believe in all this?" he asked, worried, like I was ruining my entire career. It was sweet and probably not wrong. He added, "What about the tattoos, then?"

"These are in memory of the person who taught me all the constellations." Fans knew the reason for my zodiac sleeves but never brought it up. And I never talked about Dad publicly. It felt too much like revealing a secret about myself—and yet I'd done just that.

Stuart reached a hand across the table to touch my arm. "I'm sorry."

More camera clicks. Vigorous whispering. Someone would be videoing this whole thing. *Right, back to business.* "It's fine; you couldn't know. Now let's talk about you."

Stuart gathered himself back into his seat, folding his hands in front of him. "Do your worst."

"You, sir, are a hero," I said.

"The uniform gave me away." But he said it with a smile.

"Yes, but also your stars. And not everyone who wears a uniform is a true hero." I paused, consulting the lines of his chart. "You take the initiative. You're a natural leader, although a bit shy. Which is unusual for an Aries, but probably a good thing. It makes you easy to be around and trust." I looked up to find him listening with rapt attention. "You're genuinely committed to making the world better. If you see a situation where you can help, you don't hesitate to jump in. You feed off positive energy. What's your power?" My own curiosity had finally gotten the best of me.

A man from the crowd chimed in. "He's a proper super—he saved our kids from the fire!"

A smattering of applause broke out and I scanned the crowd until I found the man. He stood beside a young boy with traces of healed burn scars on his cheeks. He nodded enthusiastically along with his dad.

Stuart raised a hand to wave away the applause, but it clearly pleased him. Until someone called out, "Hero McHeroface!" I caught the flicker of a frown at that.

A girl close to the edge of the stage said, "What will his hero name be?"

She had the same jawline and forehead shape as Stuart. "Your sister?" I asked.

"Kelly," he agreed. "She brought me over here."

I grinned. "What's your question, Kelly?"

She put her elbows on the edge of the stage. "Stuart's getting a hero name here tonight by popular vote. What'll it be?"

None of the conversation before had told me what he could actually *do*, but pressing for more details would not be part of my job or this reading. Still curious, I gave his sister the bad news.

"I'm afraid this doesn't work like that. I couldn't say—but hopefully it's *not* Hero McHeroface." Kelly looked disappointed I didn't provide an answer, and Stuart like he wanted to shout his agreement to please not give him a silly name. I moved on. "Family is crucial to you—you'd do anything for them and—"

"Who cares? Tell us about his love life!" a woman from the crowd put in.

"He'd have to have one," Kelly said over her shoulder with a laugh.

Stuart's cheeks flushed bright red.

The woman said, "That means he's single. What about you, Stella Sumner?"

Vickie the publicist decided to answer for me. "She's single, too!"

Obviously, I would have to kill her later. Or at least have a word with her about how much I valued my privacy.

"What do you say, Stuart?" someone else called out.

There wasn't usually this much crowd participation in even

charity readings, and this train had gone way off the tracks. I needed to get control over the situation. I was eight years older than Stuart—too much older for this kind of speculation. Not to mention, people with secrets like mine couldn't afford to get too close to anyone. There were good reasons I stayed single.

"Please," I said with a note of *knock it off,* "I need to concentrate." I squinted down at the star chart as if determining Stuart's fate in love. The restless crowd had settled a little by the time I turned my attention back to Stuart. His cheeks were still pink. "Venus rules love and relationships, and an Aries like Stuart brings an innocent charm to relationships. He has a childlike quality."

There, no one would suggest anything more after I basically called him childish.

Stuart had gone solemn. It wasn't a look I could've pictured on him.

"Here," I said as gently as I could and pushed the chart toward him across the table. "I don't have time to go into everything, but this is yours to keep. Can everyone give Stuart a round of applause for being such a good sport?"

The crowd complied, and there were a few more stray camera clicks.

Our hands touched as Stuart took the paper with its zodiac diagrams from me and our eyes met for a long moment. The degree to which I *felt* the brief connection—like a strong shot of espresso injected directly into my veins—was strange. And unwelcome.

Except, after Stuart took the chart and rejoined the crowd, stopping beside his sister and then signing an autograph for someone, I realized I should've thanked him. Suddenly, I was wide awake.

"Who's next?" I asked and Vickie-the-way-too-helpful steered the next victim toward the table.

Chapter 2

Stuart

I spent a good ten minutes on autopilot after the reading. People came and talked to me. Kelly definitely talked to me, too. She was teasing me, I think. It's hard to say because I wasn't taking in a word anyone was saying.

I was thinking about Stella.

The memory of her hand touching mine made my fingers tingle. Had she liked me or was she just being professional? Probably a big part of her job was putting people at ease. I doubted she gave that kind of attention to everyone. She certainly hadn't to Pygmalion. That meant she liked me more than Pygmalion! A little smile crept onto my face. The assistant had said Stella was single. I was single and she was single. Maybe that meant that we could . . . Then I remembered Kelly saying I had no love life in front of the cameras and my ego died a second death. And then I remembered Stella talking about love on my chart. She'd said I was childlike. Innocent. Which was sweet, but the polar opposite of sexy. Why not just say virginal and be done with it? She probably didn't even see me as a grown man.

That little smile faded away.

I clearly had no chance with her.

Luckily for me, there were other anxieties to take my mind off things. The day raced by in a flurry of handshakes and smiles and small talk. Sometimes Kelly would rescue me when I struggled; sometimes Colin would move me on. Before I knew it, I was making my way onto the main stage again. It was time to find out the results of the auction and what people would call me for the rest of my life.

Colin was on the mic, talking to the packed room. "I'm pleased to tell you that the secret bidding to name our hero has ended and we will be bringing you the results shortly. Before I get to that, however, let's take a moment to reflect on the incredible work

Reachers has done to help the most isolated members of our community. All thanks to your kindness . . ."

He went on for some time as I stood next to him. Like the crowd, I was a captive audience. What he was saying was important but I'm ashamed to say I wasn't really listening because I was too busy begging the universe to have mercy on me. I'm not particularly superstitious or religious, but I silently offered all manner of things to any interested gods in return for a good result.

"I'm pleased to announce," Colin began, snapping my attention back to the present, "that we have a special guest to bring you the results. Please give a warm welcome to one of our nation's true heroes. An esteemed member of the Silver Helix. The one and only . . . Pygmalion!"

I joined in the applause just as enthusiastically as everyone else. The man that took the stage was very different to the one I'd seen leaving Stella's tent earlier that day. He seemed to bask in the attention, and his smile gleamed under the lights. I could see a gold envelope in his hands. My future was contained within it.

The fact that my new name was going to be presented by a member of the Silver Helix did make me feel better. So long as it was good. Please let it be good.

Pygmalion gave me a firm handshake and then took over from Colin on the mic. "I imagine you'd all like me to get on with it." I nodded without thinking and a few of the crowd chuckled good-naturedly. "Very well." He opened the envelope and took out a piece of paper. There was the slightest pause, and his brows rose in surprise. "Well, that *is* memorable!" Pygmalion quipped.

My heart, which was thudding uproariously at this point, began to sink.

Pygmalion cleared his throat. "And the winning name is: Hero McHeroface!"

There was laughter and applause. I felt sick but did my best to smile. Hero McHeroface was the worst of all worlds! How had I allowed myself to get into this ridiculous situation? What had I been thinking? No. Wait. This was Colin's fault. He had done this to me. I wondered how lenient the judges would be after I killed him.

When the crowd settled again, Pygmalion handed me the envelope to keep as a souvenir. As he did so he leaned in and whispered, "Chin up, man. Best act pleased even if you're not. It's for a good cause."

I straightened up immediately, shamed by his words. Reachers saved lives, often getting to people who would otherwise be overlooked or abandoned. So what if I had a silly name? The money it raised would help to make the world better. For the rest of the day, I remembered how damn lucky I was, and tried to do my job.

To my surprise Pygmalion hung around afterward. He came over to me as I was helping pack things away. "I'll be on my way soon. But it was nice to meet you, Hero McHeroface."

I winced. "Still getting used to that."

"You know, things have changed a lot since I took up service. We had to concern ourselves with the press, of course, but not the constant scrutiny. Less cameras. Less pandering to crowds. No social media at all. Much more fun, if I'm honest. Still challenging, of course. It took me a long time to get used to the attention."

"How did you do it?"

"Practice, dear boy. Lots of practice. A bit of public speaking at university helped, too." He looked at me for a moment and then gave a kindly smile. "I could give you a few tips if you like."

"Really? That would be amazing. Thank you."

"Not at all. This business is difficult enough. The least we can do is help each other, and I wouldn't want to see such a promising young man led astray." He wagged a finger. "Unsavory journalists and high-profile Americans are best avoided in my opinion."

I looked down. "You mean Stella."

"Indeed I do. Beneath Ms. Sumner's delightful exterior lies the cold, dead heart of an American businesswoman."

"You think so?"

"I saw your little exchange. I thought she played it beautifully. A little bit of teasing, a little hint of romance, just enough to titillate the crowd. All for show, of course." He gave me a conspiratorial look. "Mark my words, she's doing it for the ratings."

"No, she's not like that," I replied, not wanting to believe it.

"Oh, yes. That's why she ended my reading early. She tried to tempt me with her feminine wiles. Practically offered herself up on a plate, and then turned on me as if I was the one being indecent."

"But you're Pygmalion. Why would she turn on you?"

"For the controversy. Because controversy attracts attention and that's far more valuable to the likes of her than our feelings."

"I hadn't even considered that."

He put an arm around me. "Ah, to be young and innocent again. Don't you worry, my boy. I'll keep an eye on you from now on."

Stella

The school gym housing the event had cleared out slowly over the course of the evening. I never had made it over to vote for Stuart's handle. The interest his reading generated had kept me busy for the rest of the night.

"I'll just get us a car to take to your flat for tonight," Vickie said.

"No," I said, and when I saw how stricken she looked I decided to give her a break. "It's not so far from here. I'd rather walk. Wind down a bit."

I always stayed in apartments when I traveled. I claimed it was for better concentration, that the energy of a place with too many people like a hotel could disrupt my ability to work. The excuse was complete bullshit, but having a job like astrology meant you could get away with a lot of that before anyone batted an eyelash. Really, I preferred private entrances and exits.

"If you're sure?" she asked. Then she spotted a smiling man in a slightly wrinkled suit and waved him over. "Hi, Colin—you didn't get a chance to meet Stella earlier, did you? Stella, this is Colin—he runs Reachers, the charity the fundraiser is for."

"It runs me ragged, she means," Colin said. "But I love the work we do. Thanks for being here—we appreciate the help."

I spotted Stuart's spiky hair, so he was still here, too. He was deep in conversation with the creep I'd read before him, name something ridiculous and over the top. No way I planned to talk to that guy again.

"It's been a pleasure," I said. "How did you do tonight?"

"So much better than expected!"

I couldn't resist asking. "And what did Stuart's name turn out to be?"

"You know Stuart?" Colin asked.

"She gave him a reading," Vickie put in. "Big hit with the crowd."

"Ah, that explains how much we raised on naming chances." Colin frowned. "I don't think he likes the winner."

Oh, no. "Hero McHeroface, hm?"

Colin nodded. "But we can shorten it to Hero most of the time."

"That fits," I said. Vickie and Colin were watching me. "With his profile," I clarified.

"I can call him over." Colin scanned through the gym and the cleanup crew. Stuart had started pitching in with the cleanup, and the older ace had vanished.

"No need," I said quickly. "I'm dead on my feet after flying in this morning."

"Of course, thanks again," Colin said, and hustled away with a small wave.

"I'll see you tomorrow," I told Vickie firmly and made my escape.

The early-summer evening air outside felt a little like slipping into a bath. Barnet was a relatively small town, and my rented flat should be only a fifteen-minute walk away. The streets were quiet and I relaxed, no longer on the clock.

I took a breath and a pause, then found my phone and texted my mother that I'd arrived safely *and* stayed up all day. Even though it'd be late night there, she texted back immediately: **Are you having fun?**

My mother, so concerned that I didn't have enough of it. This scheme to send me over here had been hers, and I'd only agreed because the level of disappointment with me as her heir back home stung more than I wanted to admit. It wasn't so easy to step into the shoes of a woman who'd started with nothing and then made herself into the Dear Abby of horoscopes. Celeste of *Oh, My Stars* was a legend. Meanwhile, her daughter was a goth emo hipster ditz tattooed maniac of a replacement, depending upon which comments section you were reading.

I knew my predictions were solid, and I did have my supporters. They were, as hoped, younger, and left adoring messages on YouTube and also mean comments about paywalls that meant they couldn't read the full column on news sites. Luckily, the video content was all free (well, ad-supported free).

The traffic suggested an opening to grow the audience over here, where Mom had never made as big a splash. And so here I was. But was I having fun?

Not yet, maybe tomorrow, I said.

My phone rang a few seconds later and I answered. "You're going to drive me to gray hair," my mother said.

"So you've been telling me for the last decade, but your stylist would never let it happen."

"Touché," she said. "You really didn't have fun? You usually like doing star charts—when Vickie asked, I said that would be a good one."

"You were involved in my itinerary." Of course she was. I might now be the face of the business, but Mom wasn't ready to let go of everything yet. And to tell the truth, I didn't want her to. "The people were nice."

I leaned back against the wall of the building.

"Good," she said. "You have some breathing room over there, my little stargazer. Try to appreciate it."

"Noted."

"I know you probably didn't take the pill I put in your bag and sleep on the way over, so go. Get some rest."

"Love you, busybody who knows everything," I said.

"Love you, too, honey."

I hung up and the tiredness from earlier washed over me in a wave. Time to get some shut-eye, and not just because my mom told me to. My boots made a comforting, solid sound on the pavement as I crossed the street and started up the sidewalk.

I didn't notice at first when a second set of sounds joined me. Not until that unmistakable sensation hit—it's one every woman who's ever walked through a city alone at night knows.

The feeling of being watched.

And, after I discerned the other set of footsteps, of possibly being followed. I didn't get paranoid as a rule, but I wasn't from here and the fact that the streets were otherwise deserted—and now weren't, based on the heavy steps behind me—made me err on the side of caution. I dug around in my bag, pausing under a streetlight to glance behind me in a way that would be less than obvious.

Shadows partly concealed the man, and I hoped distorted the size of him. He was large and broad-shouldered; his own shadow included the silhouette of an overcoat that definitely wouldn't be needed for a few more months. He'd stopped when I did.

I decided to lose him. There was no reason to take a chance.

So I took a second to memorize the map on my phone screen of how to get to my flat, and then stashed it and walked ahead at a speed carefully the same as before. The footsteps stayed behind me.

There was a pub on the corner ahead, light spilling from the windows. *Perfect.*

I slipped in through the door, into a night that felt completely different. Small groups of friends dotted the room, laughing and drinking pints. Threading through the tables, I went straight to the bathroom, not checking to see if he followed me in. Because it wouldn't matter. I latched the door lock and put my purse in the trash first. Then I removed my clothes and added them, and covered the whole mess with paper towels from the dispenser by the sink.

I unlocked the door and envisioned the night sky above me, past the ceiling, past the roof, up and up, a vast darkness pricked with starlight. I conjured those stars in my mind, picturing the shape of a crab limned between them by invisible lines. And I summoned the form of it into my own skin.

I folded in on myself, shrinking down smaller and smaller, my back curving as it grew a small, hard shell. I didn't become a crab. Cancer was a zodiac form that allowed me to become most any small shelled creature that the constellation had ever been used to symbolize. I went with ancient Egypt's favorite form of the sign.

And so when I left the bathroom, it was to skitter under the door as a scarab beetle, dodging through feet and chair legs until I got back outside through the briefly opened front door.

Once again, the street seemed deserted. There was no sign of the shadow man. Still, I didn't slow down until I made it to my rented apartment and transformed back. I grew and grew until there I was, naked and bone-tired. I pressed in the memorized code to the door.

Inside the clean, chic studio space, I felt more like myself. I could've gone back to get my stuff, but it wasn't worth the energy. I traveled with a small baggie of extra phones and duplicate SIM cards for this reason. Airport security occasionally questioned it, and I pled absentmindedness that caused me to lose phones at a rapid rate—more eagerly accepted bullshit. There was never anything in my bag that couldn't be easily replaced, just in case I needed to transform.

I'm convinced part of the reason my mom became such a, well, star, is because of her marriage to my dad. There was something too delicious for people about the astrologist and the astronomer, famous opposites who attracted each other and everyone around them in the clear glow of their love. Dad's work took us all over the world, which I didn't appreciate as a surly teenager who longed for the great clichés of friends and normal life TV promised me like a birthright.

My card turned on the absolute worst day of my—and Mom's— life. Dad was working at Mauna Loa for the summer, on some big secret project, and I'd spent most of the time there ignoring gross come-ons from tourist boys and their fathers. Dad usually phoned when he realized he'd work late to say good night, so we weren't worried when it crept past sunset and he hadn't called. Not until the knock on the door.

Mom had collapsed at the news of Dad's death, a freak accident at the observatory, malfunctioning equipment, a fall, and they were so very sorry. I ran out the back door of our rented cottage and into the night to look at the stars. Dad had taught me the constellations, Mom the symbolic meanings. These were the stars we all loved together. My birth sign, Leo, was there above me—and blinding, incomprehensible physical pain seared through me and left me in a new body. I became a lioness. A confused and angry and heartbroken lioness, and in that form I kept running all night. I woke hidden near a lava field, naked, covered in dirt, and with a secret to keep from my mother. It would've been too much to put on her on the heels of Dad's loss. And she was so out of it that I managed to. Then just like the running that night, I kept on. I kept my secret from everyone, which wasn't so easy during the early years, when I had little control over what sign of the zodiac I turned into when. But I'd done it. No one knew about my ace power.

Sometimes I wondered what it would be like to tell her, tell any-

one, but I'd kept it secret for so long now . . . I couldn't imagine
anyone finding out. If I had it my way, no one ever would. Mom
would feel betrayed I hadn't trusted her sooner, which I couldn't
take. Anyone else—who would it be? There were some parts of
yourself it was safer to hold close—even if secrets sometimes made
for lonely nights.

I pulled on an oversized fresh T-shirt to sleep in and powered
up a new phone, popping in the SIM. My mom hadn't texted anything more, but I had several notifications from my social media
accounts. I crawled under the covers of the giant bed, clicked
through, and found a photo of me sitting across from Stuart. The
lights from above were far more flattering than I'd have guessed,
to both of us.

The shot had been taken when I'd given him his star chart.
Touching hands, for all the world, we looked like we were on a
date—and not just any date. A good one.

The comments were mostly non-haters of mine and a user
named Kellytastic I suspected was Stuart's sister. At least for once
they weren't complaining about how I was no substitute for Mom.
They were too busy speculating about our chemistry. Cute.

I doubted I'd ever see him again.

CHAPTER 3
Stuart

It was a few months before I saw her again. Just like before, I had
a lot of other things on my mind and had pretty much forgotten
that first encounter. Stella had become something of a dream to
me. Half remembered and slightly unreal. Pygmalion's words had
cast her in a new light but I couldn't stop myself feeling wistful
whenever her name came up. And it did come up. After my reading people had asked me on social media if we were dating and

when I said no, they replied *Why not?* The picture of us, the one where we were touching hands, popped up on my feed every few weeks with a new hilarious comment and, according to Kelly, we were still being shipped online.

It was September, and Colin and I were at the Troubadour Theatre in Wembley Park, tucked away in one of the dressing rooms. A lot of people far more famous than me had used this space before. It was humbling, and I was nervous when Colin came to get me. And miffed. Perhaps even annoyed. I'm not great at being on my own. Not only am I powerless, my thoughts tend to go to the worst places. Colin's faith was like a shot of sugar, raising me from the depths.

His appraisal was as quick as it was positive. "Looking good, Hero. You ready to go?"

Technically, I was, but I didn't move from my seat.

He stood by the door with that infuriating smile on his face. "Too late to be getting cold feet now. Come on. It'll be fun. Who knows, maybe this will be the start of something beautiful."

My glare bounced off him like a bullet from Redcoat's chest. The problem with Colin is that he genuinely believes in me and the charity, and he believes that things will all work out for the best, even when the evidence says otherwise. It was like the man's superpower. Despite myself, I felt a little better now that he'd arrived, and with Colin resistance is futile, so I put all of my misgivings into one loud sigh before following him. The walk to the stage was long enough for me to gear myself up and then get nervous all over again.

Last time, Reachers had auctioned off my hero name. This time they were going to auction off the rest of me. For a date. Dating is awkward at the best of times, but this was taking it to a whole new level. I imagined all of the worst kinds of winners: a Britain First fanatic, almost anyone from my old secondary school, or someone foul like Katie Hopkins or, ugh, Piers Morgan! And the worst of it was, I'd be honor-bound to give the winner the best date possible. Would Colin expect us to kiss for the cameras? Oh, God, he probably would.

I told myself that Britain First members wouldn't want anything to do with Reachers and that people who'd gone to my secondary school couldn't afford a winning bid. But that opened up another can of worry. Would anyone bid for me at all? If they didn't, I'd suffer social death live on national television. If they did, the higher the bid, the more I'd be expected to perform.

We were stopped at the side of the stage, and someone came and applied some makeup to my cheeks and forehead while someone else asked me to thread a microphone through my T-shirt. A few quick technical checks and we were on our way. "Don't forget to smile," said Colin as he and I ascended the stairs. I was glad to be in uniform when we stepped out onto the stage. I wear safety boots when I'm doing emergency work and they give me a little bit of extra height. Between that and my hair, I look quite a bit taller than my natural five foot ten. The blue fireman's jacket has metal plates on the shoulders and broadens me considerably. I didn't used to be this vain, honestly, but the sudden media attention had underscored all my physical shortcomings.

There was another, more important angle to all of this, though. My powers seemed to draw their strength from the belief and confidence of others. Kelly always had faith in me, as did my parents, a few friends, and people like Colin. They enabled me to become my best self. But I couldn't take Kelly with me into dangerous situations, and without her around, I was just an ordinary guy in brightly colored clothes. The more people knew about me and saw me as a hero, the more they trusted me on sight, the more useful I could be. Colin's plan wasn't just to raise money for Reachers, but to raise the public awareness of me and enable my ace.

The stage lights were dazzling. Beyond them, I could just make out rows and rows of red-backed seats. The Troubadour held up to about two thousand people and, by the sounds of things, it was pretty full. A wave of applause washed over us, and with it, a new-found sense of strength. Anxiety settled into mild worry. My breath came that bit easier. Senses sharpened, muscles grew stronger. I could feel that I had a few fans in the crowd, real ones. The wave I gave them was genuine.

"Good evening, ladies and gentleman," said Colin. "I think we all know why we're here tonight." He gave an exaggerated eyebrow wiggle that got a filthy laugh from the audience. "This is your chance to date an ace. All expenses paid, no matter how long the night goes! And he's a fine-looking specimen, wouldn't you agree?"

There were a few cheers and the odd wolf whistle.

"Why don't you give them a twirl, Hero? Let them see what the fuss is about."

Because I'd rather die? I didn't say. I just stapled that smile to my face, opened my arms, and turned for the crowd. Unbelievably, I saw people standing up with their phones to take pictures. It was surreal. Colin kept up the patter throughout.

"If you want to come face-to-face with McHeroface, you need to act now! Remember that all money bid tonight is going directly to Reachers, which means that whatever happens, you're all winners in our eyes."

Behind us was a large projector screen that showed alternating images of me, a candlelit table for two, and a countdown clock. I did my best not to look at it. Instead, my eyes roamed the crowd. Many of the people here would also be bidding. For every person I saw that seemed okay, there were three or four that really didn't. A group of particularly rowdy women sat in one of the boxes. A hen party. Loud in the way only drunk people can be. One of them wore a cheap tiara and was blowing kisses in my direction.

Colin had noticed them, too. He got me to wave at them, and they all laughed hysterically and waved back as a spotlight picked them out. "A special good evening to Tiffany and her angels, who've clubbed together to ensure she enjoys the last days of sin-

gle life as much as possible! If you'd like to support Tiffany's bid
to date our Hero, the number to call is on your screen now. Or you
can use the Reachers app."

Tiffany leaned over the edge of the box to scream: "I love you,
Heroface!"

I decided in that moment that I'd date anyone Colin threw at
me, so long as it wasn't Tiffany.

"But what's this?" said Colin. "I'm just getting word that we've
got another special guest in the audience." The spotlight began to
race among the rows of seats, dancing over faces too fast for most
people to follow. But I could follow it, and I could see the direction
it was going, so I was already grinning by the time the light had
settled on her face.

"Stella," I whispered. There was a mix of surprise and excitement in my voice; amplified as it broadcast through the speakers.
My face went tomato red to hear it. The microphone! I'd forgotten
I was wearing a microphone. I cleared my throat and tried to
deepen my voice. "Hi, Stella."

She looked as surprised as I was and mouthed back a hello.

"Can we get a mic over there?" asked Colin. "I'm sure we'd all
like to hear what she's got to say."

Stella

Here we were in the spotlight together again—although this was
way more public than the reading I'd given Stuart. That was a
smallish local charity event. This was a televised big deal.

The cameras on us now were the real kind. Beside me, Vickie
fidgeted as if she might jump out of her skin if I misbehaved. It'd
been her who'd talked me into showing up for this charity event
for Reachers and who'd talked me into a fancier half-sheer version
of my regular T-shirt ensemble; I'd refused to budge on the jeans
and boots. That and remembering how cozy she and emcee Colin

had been at the first event made me wonder how much of this moment had been cooked up by the two of them.

The speed with which the runner with the microphone appeared at the end of our row and started shimmying in toward me all but confirmed my theory.

Stuart's surprise was real, though—just like mine. And I couldn't leave him hanging, which he clearly half expected. His nerves radiated even through his winsome good-natured indulgence of the spectacle, and I suspected I wasn't the only one who'd noticed the slight stiffening of his posture at the wild bachelorette party's attention. I hadn't managed to save him from Hero McHeroface. The least I could do was save him from humiliation and a horrible fate now.

I'd never admit it, but I'd kept an eye on the news related to Reachers, worrying when I read about them being sent to some far-flung locale to rescue people that I might see Hero McHeroface had been injured. Certainly, I'd never mentioned anything about it to Vickie. *But* she did like to show me the notifications when the fans who wouldn't let it go brought up our photos from that first night in England. Her charm offensive was going well, but she'd told me earlier in the week she was determined to take me to the "next level."

"I know this was you," I said under my breath. She put a hand to her chest like, *Me?* I gave her a look.

The mic holder finally made their way past the other people and arrived at my seat. Vickie grabbed my arm and urged me to my feet, trapping herself awkwardly beside the smiling volunteer. Better than she deserved, the chirpy (okay, fine, also good at her job) schemer. I smiled back at the volunteer, then at Stuart. Who, to be honest, I could barely see any more with the spotlight shining down on me.

"Hi there, Stuart," I said, and paused for effect. "Fancy meeting you here."

The crowd loved it to the tune of squeals and laughs and applause. I lifted my hand to shade my eyes so I could catch his reaction.

He laughed, too, but the nerves weren't quite gone. "What are
the odds?" he asked.

Good job. We grinned at each other across the way-too-crowded
room.

Vickie lifted her hand to shield her words from the mic and
whispered, "Ask him out!"

There was a tense silence, and I didn't know what would be
worse. I could not say anything else and see what happened or . . .
"Stuart," I said, "do you think I should bid on you?"

That the words had come out of my mouth were as much of a
shock to me as . . . anything I'd ever said. I was far too old for him,
not only in years but attitude. Vickie practically bounced up and
down next to me. She had her hands clasped under her chin like a
little girl.

"It wouldn't hurt my feelings," Stuart said with a hint of shy-
ness that made me understand why Vickie might behave this way.
He was adorable. If—again—too young for me.

Colin spoke into the mic then. "It feels like maybe we have a
date here that's meant to be—what do you think out there? Use the
number on the screen below now or hit the app if you want to see
our own Hero and Stella Sumner out on the town together."

I sat down and waited with active tension as the time to choose
Stuart's fate elapsed. He joked with Colin onstage like before. But
his posture was looser. He seemed full of confidence, but not in the
irritating way. The bachelorettes shouted my name, "Stella!" and
gave me giant thumbs-downs and shouted for people to vote for
Tiffany instead.

I shrugged and said, "It's for a great cause, everyone, vote your
consciences!" as loudly as I could make myself.

My cheeks were burning at the unscheduled performance I'd
been asked to give.

"Three—two—one—" I held my breath when Colin raised his hand and counted the end of the clock as it ran out. "And that's an end to bidding for our own Hero—let's see who the lucky lady will be . . ." Colin paused. "Got any plans for the weekend, Stuart?" he asked, playing at casual.

Stuart narrowed his eyes at the other man, who was absolutely enjoying himself. I wanted to punch him, too. The waiting was excruciating, even though I told myself I didn't care about the outcome. This was a ridiculous situation. I just wanted it to resolve.

Uh-huh, my little stargazer: I could hear my mother. At least she wasn't here and wouldn't see the video of this all the way back home. I'd never hear the end of it.

"Nervous?" Colin asked Stuart along with a raise of his eyebrows.

"A bit, yes," Stuart said.

"How about you, Tiffany?" The spotlight found her and she shrieked.

The bachelorettes had won, then. They were hometown favorites, I guessed, and I got ready to plaster a huge, gracious smile on.

"But wait a second. How about you, Stella?" Colin asked, the spotlight swiping back around to me. "Are you nervous? Or do you already know how this is going to turn out?"

Vickie poked me in the ribs with her elbow. Which really should have been my move. "I'm just happy to be here supporting such a great charity."

"Well, we're grateful to hear that—but of course the public has chosen to send *you* on a date with our eligible Hero here. We wish you the very best time!"

The crowd dissolved into applause and I felt way more victorious than I had any right to—very Sally Field, "You like me! You really like me!"—when the obvious answer was they liked Stuart. It was impossible not to.

"Congratulations, you'll make a lovely couple," a woman with enormous earrings leaned forward from the row behind us to tell me.

Vickie gave me another cheeky nudge as Colin moved on and some of Tiffany's bachelorette party made that we're-watching-you motion between their eyes and me. *Don't worry, girls, I'm out of it after that.*

"All in a day's work?" I asked Vickie.

"Oh, come on, it'll be fun," she said, batting her mink lash extensions.

"Will it?" I asked.

She shrugged.

What was this obsession with fun? It probably meant she'd been put up to this by my mother. I could envision the conversation between them now, with Vickie mentioning the cute hero I'd met that first night and how people loved us together and and and . . .

We hung in until the end of the hour and I figured we'd leave and *if* we went on this date for real the arrangements would be handled via phone calls and texts. But Vickie steered me toward the backstage area. "We should say hello and figure out next steps for you and Stuart."

Vickie had the demeanor of a pushover but was really the exact opposite. She could get you to do almost anything. Case in point, this entire evening. "Fine," I said.

"Do you want to touch up your lipstick?" she asked.

Too far, Vickie. "No, thanks," I chirped back at her. She made a face.

We reached the wings and a security guard said, "No one allowed back here, miss," but Vickie was already shouting, "Colin!"

He made his way over with a huge grin. "That went better than we could've imagined," he said. "Thanks for playing along," he said to me.

Stuart walked over, a little hesitant, just in time to hear that. I swear it hit him like a physical blow.

"Hah," I said, "you should thank Stuart for playing along. I had no idea. I was just here to support Reachers."

"They did this?" he asked and looked between Colin and Vickie. But I noticed his shoulders relaxed at the news I wasn't in on it.

"Yes. I'm afraid we've been managed by our publicity handlers," I said. "Sorry about that."

"You said yourself it's a great cause," Vickie said.

"You don't need to apologize," Stuart said. "Without you, I might be, ah, looking forward to an evening out with someone else out there."

The Tiffany brigade, I'm sure we were both thinking. "True. Now you're stuck with me."

"Speaking of that," Vickie interrupted, "when shall we schedule your big date? I'm thinking this could be a great opportunity to raise even more money . . ." Vickie and Colin launched into a conversation about us that Stuart and I were obviously completely unnecessary for.

"Did you think the hero line would be like this?" I asked, taking a step closer.

He considered. "I thought there would be less bidding on me."

"Really?" I asked. "How's your sister—what was it, Kelly?"

A real smile then. "She's doing pretty well." It faded. "I worry about her sometimes."

"Why?"

A click and a flash cut into what felt like an actual conversation, and a nice one. Of course, it was third wheel Vickie snapping us with her digital camera.

"We'll talk soon, I'm sure," I said, regretting not finding out the answer about his sister.

But the last thing I needed was to encourage Vickie's fixation on this. Particularly if my mother *was* involved. Which I'd be getting to the bottom of as soon as I got back to my apartment here in London.

"Bye, Stuart," I added.

"See you soon, Stella." I had the feeling he watched us as we walked out of backstage. I would have to be careful not to stomp on the puppy's heart. Maybe we could be friends.

Stuart

"See?" said Colin as he drove me home. "That wasn't so bad."

"No. But it could have been." I thought about Tiffany and her "angels." Ugh. Too close.

"You need to have more faith in me, Hero."

"Maybe if you told me what you were up to beforehand instead of springing it on me, I would!"

"I couldn't tell you about Stella because it had to feel spontaneous. You're not exactly the best actor in the world."

"Thanks," I replied with all the sarcasm I could muster.

"No, I mean that in a good way. People respond to you because you're genuine. They can see how much you like her and they're all for it."

"What do you mean?"

"Oh, come on. You practically glow every time you see her."

"I don't!"

"Yes you do. It's adorable."

I was glad that it was dark and Colin was looking at the road so he couldn't see me blushing. "I hardly know her."

"That's what the date is for."

I turned toward the window to hide my grin. "Yeah."

"Like I said. Adorable."

"Shut up."

Colin just laughed.

For the rest of the journey my thoughts drifted through imagined dates with Stella. Nothing very coherent. Just us sitting at a restaurant together, her smiling at me. Me smiling at her. I was just imagining what it might be like if we got close when a nasty thought occurred to me: The word *date* was awfully vague in the context of a Reachers event.

"Colin?"

"Yes?"

"What is this date going to be exactly?"

I got a sidelong glance. "That's up to you, Hero."

"Colin! Don't mess me about. What's the plan?"

He sighed. "There's no grand plan. You're going to have dinner together and—"

I cut him off. "Where?"

"The Ivy."

"What's that like?"

"It's in Covent Garden, near the West End. Lots of famous people eat there. It's the perfect place for a celebrity couple to have a first date."

I frowned. It did sound nice. Maybe a little too nice. What was I going to wear? It occurred to me that she'd only ever seen me in the clothes I wore when I represented Reachers. This time I'd be in my own clothes. Stella had style. I didn't. She was going to realize that the moment she saw me. Shit. I reimagined us meeting for this date. Her looking fabulous and me looking . . . like me. She wasn't smiling in this version.

"We're going to cover the food and drink," Colin continued, "so you can be as generous as you like."

"How private is it going to be?"

There was a pause, long enough for me to know I wouldn't like the answer. "Nothing too invasive. Just a quick interview with each of you beforehand."

"That's it?"

"And another one afterward, where we see how it went."

"Oh, God."

"But the date itself is totally private . . . apart from a photographer, who will be taking discreet, tasteful pictures for our website."

"What if it goes badly?"

"It won't. Trust me. The worst that happens is you get a free meal in good company. Stella needs this to work as much as we do."

And there it was. Pygmalion's warning came back to me then. Stella had an angle here, just like Colin did. For them, it was about seizing an opportunity to get publicity and to raise money. What was it for me? I wondered. An obligation as part of my job? A fun distraction? An actual date with an actual woman that might go somewhere? I knew what I wanted it to be, but I didn't know about Stella. I had the feeling she was much better at acting than I was.

CHAPTER 4

Stella

Date night found me standing in front of my closet contemplating breaking my de facto dress code and pulling out an actual dress— the lone one I'd packed, on the off chance I had to meet the king or something. I had officially entered bizarro world. My mother, of course, sensed this disturbance in the Force—to mix universes— and called at just that moment. I couldn't lie. I was grateful for the distraction.

"Yes, Mom," I said, putting her on speaker.

"Please, is that any way to greet your darling mother?"

"My darling mother who engineered this date in the first place?" I asked and sat down in the cushy leather chair in the corner of my London apartment. I'd been here for a few weeks, and so it had developed the air of a tornado having been through. I'm what could charitably be described as a slob.

Discarded T-shirts littered the floor and a notebook sprawled open with notes for tomorrow's column on the bed. I hadn't transformed in at least a month and the stars overhead at night made me itchy in my skin. But London felt dangerous in that respect—so many surveillance cameras.

"I simply told Vickie she was a PR genius," she said. "Which she obviously is."

"Mom."

"When's the last time you went on a date?"

It's not like I was a virgin. But relationships? Not my thing. I liked Stuart. Anyone who could get a name like Hero McHeroface from the crowd and go on being an actual hero was obviously a better-than-decent person. Which certainly would not describe my previous type, who was perfectly okay with a one-to-three-night stand and then see ya.

"What if he takes this seriously, Mom?" I collapsed on the bed next to the notebook. "Did you think about that? He seems like an actual nice guy."

She went quiet for a second. "Oh," she said. "You're worried about him. This is so interesting. Can you tell me when he was born?"

"*Mom*. I read him the night we met, so you don't need to. And no, I'm not worried about him for that reason. I'm worried about him because he seems like a sweet kid."

"Kid? He's twenty."

"Too young for me."

"He could learn a lot from a *slightly* older woman. And maybe you could learn how to have fun."

I sighed. A heavy, we've-been-through-this sigh. "You're the romantic. Not me."

"It's the most disappointing thing, sweetie," she said. "You'll get over it eventually. All cynics are just romantics who haven't met the right person."

I mouthed the last words along with her. This was not a new conversation. So I tried to distract her with something that always, *always* worked. "How are the numbers looking?"

I listened as she sat down at her desk and clicked her computer to life. I could picture every step of it. Her office was a brightly colored mix of charts, product samples for our online store, and stacks of spreadsheets. I missed her.

"Who cares?" she said, figuring out what I was up to before she started rattling off statistics and ad revenues. "I just want you to be happy."

She meant it, I knew that. "I'm not not-happy."

"That's not good enough for our daughter."

Tears pricked at the back of my eyes, threatening to ruin the makeup I'd spent a full ten minutes on. It got me every time. The casual *our*. Her refusal to even consider moving on from Dad. There was probably nothing healthy about it, and yet my kind, hippie-vibes, approachable mother shut down anyone who suggested she would ever love another man with a firm, "That's not up for discussion."

"I miss him, too."

"Every day," Mom said.

"I meant right this second, because he'd tell you to back off and that no one is good enough for his baby girl."

My mom snorted. I'd successfully lightened the mood. "I think he'd have gotten over that after you were an adult. You better go get dressed. Wear something nice."

She hung up before I could protest. She did that sometimes. The ninja.

And she was right. Traitor Vickie would be here any minute.

I put on my usual T-shirt and jeans purely out of stubbornness, but when the buzzer signaled my publicist's arrival I added a necklace with all five of the birthstones attributable to Leo—peridot, onyx, ruby, carnelian, and amber—arranged on delicate silver as if they were planets. And a leather jacket.

Vickie eyed me and said, "The Ivy's posh. Are you sure you don't want to dress up a bit?"

"This is my signature look," I told her. "So no."

She must have sensed she wouldn't win this one, and I'd just make us late arguing. She herded me into the back of a waiting car, ordered the driver to "Drive on," and started to talk a mile a minute. "I've already been by the restaurant and checked out the lighting and the camera setup for the interview outside. All you have to do is five minutes of a joint interview with Stuart, promoting Reachers, plugging your brand, and making googly eyes at each other."

"Leading people on, you mean." Possibly leading Stuart on, which I wasn't comfortable with at all. "Can we have a minute before the interview? In private?"

Vickie examined me, as if trying to decide whether I would go rogue. It was tempting. But mostly I wanted to make sure that no one got hurt by this publicity game.

"I'm nervous, too, you know," she said.

"Oh, are you going on a fake date engineered by your publicist and your mother?"

Vickie blinked. "No. I set it up and I have an unpredictable client. This is for the best. People like the two of you together. What's so wrong with making people happy?"

"Why is everyone obsessed with happiness?"

"It makes the world go 'round?" the driver put in. He had a swirl of silver hair and a lively voice.

"That's love," I corrected.

"What's the difference?" he countered.

Hah. He should meet my mother.

Vickie leaned forward. "You won't repeat anything you've heard on this drive, will you? We'd appreciate your discretion?"

He tapped the brakes, then went on. "It is part of my code to never repeat people's secrets. I've been driving for twenty years and I'd never . . ."

I settled back to let Vickie clean up this mess of her own making.

Stuart

Kelly answered the door and looked me up and down.

"Aren't you going to let me in?" I asked.

"You haven't spiked your hair."

It was true. I'd been trying to decide how to wear it in the days leading up to my date with Stella. As Hero McHeroface I always appeared with my hair spiked up and dyed. I'm still trying to figure out which color mix is best, but I tend to go with Redcoat red and varying amounts of gold. Kelly gets me to add glitter sometimes but I prefer not to. That stuff goes everywhere. This date had come about because of Reachers but I was the one going on it so I'd decided to go as myself. It felt like the right decision until I saw Kelly's face.

"Should I spike it?"

She shrugged.

"Kelly, seriously. Should I spike it?"

"It looks okay down, I guess."

I should have spiked it. What had I been thinking? No. It was okay. I could still fix this. I dashed past Kelly and upstairs to the bathroom. I faintly heard the sound of my mum's hello drifting up after me. The tap dripped like a ticking clock as I foraged in the cupboard. They should have fixed that by now. At the back was an almost empty pot of gel from when I lived here. Mum had kept all of my old toiletries in a little plastic bag in case I popped over to visit. I blew a kiss in her general direction and got to work.

Once my hair was done I went into Mum and Dad's bedroom. The Ivy was posh, and I didn't have anything suitable to wear except my interview suit. Which was okay, but the ties I had were way too formal for a date. My original plan was to buy something new but Dad was adamant that I borrow his stuff instead and, against my better judgment, I'd agreed to come here to get ready. He'd laid out a number of ties on the bed, along with several shirts. There was a red shirt with black rose edging that was cool but hard to pull off, and a charcoal-gray shirt that seemed safer. As I tried to pick between the two, I heard his slow footsteps on the landing.

"Wear the red one," he said. "It goes with your hair."

"Dad, did you ever actually wear this?"

"When I was dating your mother."

"Did she like it?"

He gave me a smile that briefly took away the years. "I don't recall any complaints. Actually, the tie that goes with the other shirt will work with that one. Try them together."

I did and he looked pleased until he saw the knot I'd tied.

"You should use a full Windsor. It sits better."

"I don't know how."

"Come here then, I'll do it."

For a few moments I was sixteen again and Dad was doing my tie, and I was still hiding my ace and he was still hiding his illness, and I felt looked after. My throat was a little tight when I thanked him.

"How much do you like this girl?"

"Stella's not a girl, Dad. She's a grown woman with her own show."

He chuckled. "Well, in that case, you better have these." From the pocket of his dressing gown he produced a small box. I took it and opened it to find a set of silver cuff links in the shape of dice. "They're my lucky set," he told me as I fastened them in place. "Never let me down."

"What does that even mean?"

"You'll find out," he said, and I immediately wished the earth would swallow me up.

"It's just a date."

"Sure it is. Talking about dates, shouldn't you be on your way by now?"

I looked at my watch and realized, to my horror, that he was right. "Bye, Dad," I said as I fled the room. "Bye, Mum," I called as I ran down the hall. Kelly opened the front door for me.

"Oh," she said as I passed her, "you've spiked your hair. I thought you were wearing it down."

I glared at her over my shoulder.

"Good luck!" she added, closing the door.

By the time I arrived at the Ivy, everyone else was already there. Colin was giving instructions to the cameraman, and I could see Stella chatting with her PR woman. Or, more accurately, I could see her listening to her PR woman, who was talking through her smile at about a hundred miles an hour.

My heart lifted and sank when I saw my date. She was wearing jeans and a T-shirt, but the jewelry was exquisite. Stella had somehow managed to look casual and fancy at the same time, the way that Hollywood stars do. More to the point, I was overdressed in comparison. Shit. I knew I shouldn't have spiked my hair.

"There he is!" said Colin, with obvious delight. "Ready to start?"

"One sec," Stella replied and, to my surprise, headed straight toward me. I suddenly realized I had no idea how to greet her. A handshake was too formal. Maybe we should hug? Or I could kiss her on the cheek? Was that too forward? If I just said hello that could come across as cold, and I didn't want to insult her. What did Americans do? And why hadn't I thought about this until now?

She quickly crossed the space between us and it struck me that, my hair aside, we were about the same height. Unlike my work boots, my smart shoes were flat, bringing me down an inch since last time. Her first impression would be that I'm shorter than she'd thought. Great.

"Hey, Stuart."

"Hi."

I thought she was going to stop, but she kept going until she was definitely in my personal space. She opened her arms for a hug. Just a hug, I wondered, or a hug and kiss? I had no idea what

I should do! Fleetingly I wished Kelly were here for support. If she were powering my ace, I'd be able to react faster. And I'd be more confident. Next to Stella I felt incredibly mundane. But, mundane or not, she hugged me.

I hugged her back.

It was . . . How can I put this? We fitted. I could feel her warmth through my shirt, and she hugged me close so our bodies pressed together. I'd expected something quicker, more for show, but this felt natural. She held me for a long moment and I held her. It seemed right. Maybe this was going to be the start of something beautiful. I felt her breath on my ear as she whispered:

"Look, we both know this isn't real, but that doesn't mean we can't have fun, right?"

My mouth moved before my brain could react. "Right."

"Thanks, Stuart. That is such a relief. It's all pretty weird, but at least we're in it together."

I didn't say anything, I was still in shock. She stepped back from the hug and I felt the air turn colder on my chest.

"So." She held out a hand. "You ready, partner?"

I nodded and took it.

We walked to the door of the Ivy where Colin and the cameraman were waiting. They were already filming. Of course they were. I felt a thousand things all at once, most of them bad. I should have been relieved. There was nothing to worry about now. We could pretend for an evening and then get back to our lives. I wasn't relieved, though. I was upset. Pygmalion was right; this was all about ratings and money. I'd wanted it to be something more. I'm such an idiot.

Stella nudged me in the ribs and I belatedly realized that Colin had asked me something.

"Sorry," I said.

"That's okay, Hero. We can see your mind is on other things." His smirk sent the blood to my cheeks. "I was just asking if we could interview you individually but it's clear you're already inseparable. What do you think, Stella? Are the stars looking favorable for you both tonight?"

She glanced up at the overcast sky. "I don't know about the stars, but Stuart looks great."

Colin laughed loudly. "That sounds like a yes from Stella. What about you, Stuart, excited for the future?"

It took me a moment to find my voice. "I can hardly believe this is happening. It's like . . ." *someone has plucked out my heart and started tearing it into pieces* "a dream come true."

Stella

We'd finished the awkward interview, so at least we'd be on our own. Well, almost. Until later.

Colin and Vickie were talking to the videographer, no doubt congratulating themselves in the process. Both were beaming. Stuart and I drifted closer to the restaurant entrance.

The Ivy definitely lived up to Vickie's description as "posh." We were in the theater district and the restaurant was in a building that wrapped around a corner in a dramatic V with the front announcing its name and a moon-and-stars motif on the glass, which was probably why they'd picked it for our date. Patterned glass on the rest of the windows blocked the view inside. The dramatic angles reminded me of a miniature version of the Flatiron in New York, where Mom's book publisher was based.

"Should we wait here for any last marching orders?" Stuart asked, pausing on the sidewalk.

"We could ditch them," I suggested. Then, still feeling bad at how casual I'd played the evening with my jeans, I said, "But then you'd have worn that fabulous outfit for nothing. My mom told me to dress up, and that's why I didn't."

Stuart smiled. "She's a meddler then?"

"You have no idea."

"My dad made me retie this tie," he countered. "Kelly insisted I get ready at their place."

I remembered our abbreviated conversation the other night. "You were saying you worry about her?"

"Her moods, yeah." Stuart started to lean against the wall and stopped himself. He wasn't used to being dressed up, I could tell. Not like this anyway. The uniform made him more comfortable, this suit less so. "She's always been my biggest supporter, though. I don't think I'd be where I am without her."

I considered. "Well, that's true," I said.

Stuart gave me a confused look.

"She dragged you to my table, I mean. That first night."

"She did that," he said. "But that's not what I mean. She believes in me. It makes me stronger. My ace works that way—it draws from people's positive feelings toward me."

I hadn't even considered the fact I might be able to learn from Stuart what someone else's ace was like—how it felt—without sharing that I had one, too. "Interesting. How do you mean?"

"I can sense how people are feeling. If the people around me believe in me, it makes me strong. The more, the better."

"And if they don't?" I asked.

"Then I'm normal. I'm still figuring everything out."

I wanted to ask a thousand more questions, and number one was if he could tell how I felt about him. I liked him, and I didn't want *that* giving him the wrong idea.

Vickie and Colin interrupted us then, and she said, "Great job so far. Ready to nosh?"

"Yes, thanks," Stuart said, and put his hand at the small of my back to guide me forward. It was nice, strong and steadying, like we were a team.

The doorman swung open the outer door to admit us, and Vickie came in and explained who we were to the maître d'. The space was lovely, all dark wood and classic flourishes and elegant table settings and a packed central bar. The head waiter whisked us to a table in view of most of the restaurant.

"They don't usually allow photos inside," Vickie said, "so this is a big deal for them, too."

The videographer trailed us, having exchanged his video camera for one with a long lens, and took a couple of experimental snaps.

I couldn't help wondering how they prevented people from taking photos in the era of smartphones, but was comforted that we might not end up with unapproved pictures splashed all over Twitter this time. That must have been part of why Vickie chose this place, hoping to control the images. I had to admit that was smart.

The waiter pulled out my green leather chair and then slid it under me. Stuart had already taken his own seat across from me.

"Smile," the photographer said, and the people at the tables nearby looked over curiously. They were British, though, so they also pretended not to be interested at the same time. It was an intriguing feat, lots of fake-scanning of the room.

I smiled. So did Stuart.

The flash blinded us. Vickie bustled the photographer back out with a hopeful wave to me that I barely took in through the remaining dots from the flare.

I blinked as my vision cleared. Stuart had perked up, and he did look a bit puffed up in the chair. The interest from the tables around us?

"At last, we're alone," I said. "I don't know about you, but I feel like we just ran a marathon. And I'm starving."

I spoke too soon. Colin rushed past the maître d' and came to Stuart's side. He passed him a credit card. Smooth.

Stuart transferred it to his suit pocket, and Colin beat a hasty retreat.

"Is this unusual for Reachers?" I asked with a shake of my head.

"Do we seem that amateur hour?" Stuart asked, bristling a little.

I'd hurt his feelings. "No, no, that's not what I mean. I've read up on the organization. You guys are doing great things."

"You have?" Stuart asked, as if he was surprised.

No way I was admitting I sometimes looked for his name. I'd found a few articles about his first hero appearances. "Did you always want to be a hero, Hero?" I asked.

His smile was shy. "You know the Silver Helix?"

"I believe I met one—Pantaloon, was it?" I knew that wasn't his name, but I'd intensely disliked the man. Throwing a fit and taking off. At a *charity event*. No, I didn't like him at all.

Stuart laughed with an uneasy edge. "Pygmalion. He's been very kind to me."

"Glad to hear it." Maybe he was only a weird entitled creep to women. A lot of men could be described that way in my experience. Stuart would learn in his own time that it didn't speak well of them.

"I've always followed them—not specifically Pyg, but some of the others."

"Your hair." You couldn't do homework on the heroes of Reachers without absorbing a few things about the rest of the British heroes.

"Yes, it's inspired by Redcoat." He picked up his water glass and there was a clatter as he raised it to take a drink and some splattered out. His lap must be nearly soaked. He looked so mortified, and also as if he'd just realized this was not a conversation for a date, even a fake one. I wanted to tell him not to worry. I pretended not to notice the spill.

"It suits you," I said.

The waiter interrupted, bringing menus and reciting a litany of specials. Knowing he must be uncomfortable, I asked if we could order right away and we did.

Stuart got up quickly. "I'll be right back."

I'd expected as much. I waved over the waiter as soon as he disappeared to the powder room.

"Change out his napkin, and please put the bill on this." I slid the waiter a credit card. There was no reason for a charity to pay for this evening. We were to raise their available money, not spend it.

Stuart

In the sanctuary of the Ivy's toilets, I looked in the mirror and asked myself what I was doing. The idiot opposite had no more idea than I did. It would have been easier if Stella was horrible. But she wasn't. She was nice. She was *reasonable*. It's very difficult to be angry with someone who is reasonable, especially if you like them.

Pretending to be on a date felt a lot like actually being on a date. I was certainly just as embarrassed to have spilled water down my trousers as I would have been on an actual date. I stepped back so I could survey the damage. It was significant: a dark stain in just the right place to suggest that I'd wet myself. How very sexy.

I looked for some hand dryers, wondering if I could use them on my trousers. There weren't any. The Ivy was too classy for such things. However, next to the marble sinks were disposable towels for hand drying. I grabbed a handful and retreated into one of the cubicles. Standing there, in a toilet, on a fake date, with paper towels pressed to my crotch, I wondered how my life had reached this point. It was tempting to just make my excuses and leave. When I stepped out of the cubicle, however, the man in the mirror gave me a look. He knew the truth. The truth was I didn't want to leave. I wanted to spend more time with her, even though it hurt to do so. Did that make me naïve? Desperate? An idiot? Probably all three, but I already knew I was going to go back in, smile, and indulge the fantasy for as long as I could. Don't judge me.

The stain was, frankly, not much changed by my efforts. Perhaps it was paler than before, but it still looked like I'd had an accident. Hopefully, if I strung the meal out long enough, it'd be gone by the time we had to go and be filmed again. If it wasn't, I was going to have to jump out of a window or something.

I was aware I'd been gone awhile and hurried back to our table. By skirting the outside of the restaurant, I was able to minimize the amount of time my lower half would be in her field of vision. Luckily, she seemed absorbed by a bouquet of flowers that definitely hadn't been there when I'd left, and I was able to sit down without getting her attention.

The flowers were expensive looking. Two dozen roses, mostly red, with a small circle of lavender ones in the center. They were tied with a colorful bow, and must have been delivered while I was away. Did Colin arrange this without telling me? For a moment, I considered pretending I knew about them, but the expression on Stella's face warned me against that. She was frowning deeply as she read the accompanying note.

"Looks like you have an admirer," I said.

She glanced up at me, but barely met my eye, and started looking around the restaurant.

"Everything okay?"

"Not really," she replied, passing the card that had come with the flowers over to me. It was creamy white, with little red ribbons drawn around the edges. Flowery black writing spelled out a simple message:

I see you, my love. I am coming for you.

Now I was frowning. Even Colin was smoother than that. "Sounds a bit sinister."

She took my hand and leaned closer to me, drawing me in. I leaned forward, too, trying to ignore the way my traitorous heart beat slightly faster as we whispered to each other.

"A bit?" she hissed. "Are you kidding me? This note has *stalker* written all over it."

"Do you have a stalker?"

"Some of my fans are pretty intense. What about you?"

"Me?"

She tapped the card. "This message could be for either of us. The flowers were delivered to the table, not to me. The maître d' has no idea how they got here."

It hadn't even occurred to me that I could be the target. "Maybe it's Tiffany?"

"I'm serious!" she replied, but I'd managed to lift that frown for a moment. That felt good.

"If the note is true," I added, "if they can really see us, they must be here right now."

"You think so?"

"If I was a creepy stalker, I'd want to know what you—er, or me—thought of the gift." Kelly liked to watch shows about creepy people, and I'd sat through innumerable hours on serial killers, sociopaths, and other unbalanced folk. There wasn't enough evidence to warrant calling the police, but there was more than enough for me to worry.

Stella released my hand and took out her phone. "We could video the restaurant and see who's here."

"I'm not sure the Ivy would like that."

"Then don't tell them. Pretend we're taking a selfie. Nobody's going to object to that."

I wasn't so sure, but we did it anyway. It was weird feeling her head on my shoulder. Some words formed in my brain with a warning tag. My mouth ignored the tag, and I turned to whisper in her ear.

"I'll protect you."

She turned and put her arm around me as if we were having an intimate chat. "I don't need protecting, Stuart. I can handle myself."

"But we'd work better together." The words sounded cheesy,

but I persisted. "We stay in touch until we've worked out who this is, okay?"

Our faces were close now. To anyone observing it'd look like the date was going really well. "That's sweet, but I'm tougher than I look."

"I work in risk management and there's no way I'm taking chances with your—"

The food arrived, and we sprang apart like a pair of teenagers caught just before a kiss. Stella and I argued through our smiles about what to do for the rest of the meal. She was playing things down while I was thinking about what happened to the victims in all those shows. Spoiler: It was never pretty.

When we came out of the Ivy to face the cameras afterward, I made sure to hold her hand.

"How'd it go?" asked Colin.

I answered before she had a chance, looking straight into the lens. "Let's just say that we'll be seeing a lot more of each other in the future."

Colin beamed at us. "That's wonderful!"

I beamed at Stella. "It really is."

Stella beamed at me a little too long, and squeezed my hand hard as she replied, "Yes. So wonderful."

CHAPTER 5
Stella

My phone buzzed early the next morning. And again. When it became clear it wouldn't stop until I replied, I groaned and found it. Vickie. Six messages. Figured she'd be an early riser.

I opened them, but didn't look: **I'm trying to sleep.**

She responded immediately: **You have a portmanteau!**

I frowned. **I have a what?**

Vickie: **A couple name!!! Check Twitter. Someone at the restaurant posted some cozy pictures of the two of you. And you had me thinking you didn't want to be there.**

I considered rolling over and going back to bed. I wondered if Stuart had been informed of this apparently exciting development or if he was blissfully sleeping late somewhere. No, I did not need to be thinking about where Stuart slept. We were friends. And only friends.

I wondered if his hair was spikier when he woke up or if it stayed perfectly in place. For that matter, I wondered what it looked like when it wasn't spiked but fresh out of the shower.

No, I did not. I did *not* wonder that.

But I checked Twitter.

Our couple name was a hashtag and there were, in fact, a lot of tweets—a disturbing amount—tagging us and Reachers and the *Oh, My Stars!* brand account. And—oh, goodie—my mom had retweeted one and added a kiss-face emoji to it. She would be insufferable.

My phone buzzed. Her, of course: **How's my favorite half of Stuella this morning?**

Stuart plus Stella. Stuella.

I put the pillow over my face. The phone buzzed again. Vickie this time: **You have to go out again and soon. It's great for softening up your image.**

And before I could protest that my image was fine by me as it was: **And Colin says donations to Reachers are already up 25 percent from last night.**

Maybe I could just live here, in this apartment, with a pillow over my head. That was a solid plan.

My phone rang. An actual ringtone. I picked it up and saw Stuart's name flash across. I couldn't leave him hanging. I picked up.

"Hey there," he said, "I just wanted to check in . . . I don't suppose you've been on social media yet today?"

"Vickie and my mother broke the news that we're now Stuella," I said. "We're to keep doing this—but we don't have to, you know. We could call it off."

Stuart was quiet for a long moment. "I keep thinking about those flowers and that note. I don't like the idea of you being on your own in London while there might be a stalker after you."

Oh, Stuart, I could transform into something and give anyone the slip, even you. Like I did the night we first met. I hadn't remembered that until just now, the weird, bulky man who may or may not have been following me after the Barnet event. Was that a coincidence? The thought of someone fixated on me—or Stuart, or me and Stuart—for months with us none the wiser chilled me more than the flowers had.

But I couldn't say any of that, could I? No, I couldn't. And even if I didn't need him to keep me safe, there was a sweetness to his worrying about it.

"I still think the stalker could be yours," I said.

"Then going out a few more times would help me out, too," Stuart says. "And Colin says . . ."

"Reachers donations are already up. I heard." This felt like something that could get out of hand. Something that, frankly, probably already was.

"We can keep it up, but if there are no more creepy notes or gifts we'll find a way to gracefully break it off, okay?" I suggested. "And in the meantime, if there are, we'll figure out who is behind this together."

"All right," Stuart said. "I can live with that. Where do you want to go next?"

The next few weeks passed in a blur of publicity stops and carefully plotted (by Vickie) excursions with Stuart. The first time we went to a theater in Regent's Park, and nothing strange happened, except that Stuart made me laugh so hard during intermission that I snorted like a pig and then he teased me about it and even though I felt like an idiot, I kept laughing. He'd snorted at me as he dropped me at my door.

I'd already begun to think about how I might disengage before things went too far and he got his feelings hurt. I wasn't the girl-friend type, especially not for someone as sweet as Stuart.

The third of our dates was at a café and interrupted by another creepy present delivery—a box of chocolates with another script note that said: *I am watching you and looking forward to eating you up.* Which, ew.

"Who could this be?" Stuart said, obviously frustrated, scanning the crowd around us. No one stood out.

"Vickie," I said, mostly joking, but then we each tilted our heads and considered.

"Too much risk for her, right?" Stuart said after a moment. "She'd be worried we'd call the whole thing off."

"True. She is Stuella's biggest fan."

"Besides Kelly," Stuart said. "Although she was grumbling about how I don't come by as often now that we're seeing each other."

He blushed and studied his plate, twisting pasta around a fork. I almost said that she'd be comforted when we stopped fake-dating, but I couldn't bring myself to.

We both received cards and letters along the same lines, always in public, making it impossible to tell who was behind it or whether one of us was being targeted more than the other. We were getting good at smiling for surreptitious cameras, pretending the gifts were delightful. I kept all of them in my London flat, which I'd decided to keep for my entire time in England.

I'd had to break it to Stuart that I was leaving London for a bit, though, and he had a deployment approaching anyway. It felt like a preview to a breakup. I was unaccountably sad as I packed up my suitcase for a tour of small English towns. Who knew when we'd see each other again? Maybe by that time, we'd have shaken off our stalker. Or they'd have moved on. Or gotten caught.

I could hope.

But, truth was, I already missed Stuart and I hadn't even left on my trip yet.

Stuart

I'd just flown back to the UK after helping a mountain rescue operation in Pakistan. Stranded villagers caught in a landslide. I'd basically been a fast-moving sniffer dog, aiding the team with detection and extraction. It had been a great success, the kind of thing that, while awful, feels unquestionably good to be able to help with. Colin had booked me into one of Heathrow's hotels after the return flight. I'd protested at the time but was glad of it now. My body ached, and traveling back to my flat suddenly seemed like a ridiculous idea. I'd worry about that tomorrow. For today, the only decision I wanted to make was whether to eat or sleep first. A shower would be good, too, but that could join the tomorrow jobs.

At some point I drifted off.

My phone woke me up. It was Stella's ring. I'd given her a special ringtone. Suddenly, I was wide awake. I grabbed for the phone, knocking it off the bedside table onto the floor. "Shit!" I tumbled after it, bringing the bedding with me. It took me eight rings to find the damn thing and answer. I was half on the floor, tangled in the sheets as I panted into the mouthpiece.

"Hi," said Stella. "Stuart, is that you?"

"Yes," I gasped. "It's me. Everything okay? Are you safe?"

"I'm safe."

"No more incidents?"

"Not a thing. You?"

"All quiet this end."

"That's good." There was a longer pause. "Listen, I know this is out of the blue, but I happen to be near the airport right now, and I was wondering if you'd like to catch up?"

I said yes, of course, and told her my hotel and room number. This was interesting. We'd only ever met before to try to draw out our stalker. She'd sounded a bit nervous. Was she planning to end our arrangement? If things had gone quiet, there was no reason to keep seeing each other. But she'd said catch up, not break up. Surely that meant something?

Stella arrived just as I was getting out of the shower. This meant that I either had to leave her out in the hall or answer the door in my towel. Neither option seemed appropriate. I decided on the latter.

"Hey," she said. Her eyes flicked down, then up. I blushed.

"Hi. Sorry, I'll only be a few minutes. You want to come in?"

"Sure."

"Make yourself comfortable," I told her as I grabbed my clothes and fled back to the bathroom. "I'll be right out."

I hadn't prepared for a date or even a hangout, so there were no worries about what to wear. I put on my only clean top and the jeans I'd been traveling in, and went back out to see her. She was standing by the wardrobe, looking at my McHeroface jacket. One of her hands was resting on the sleeve. She snatched it away as she heard me come out. What did that mean?

"Did you want to go out somewhere, maybe grab a drink?" I asked.

"So long as it's quiet." She turned to me but there was a slight frown on her face; then she grinned. "I was trying to work out what was different. It's your hair! I've never seen it down before."

"Oh, right. Sorry, I don't normally spike it when I'm not at work."

"That's okay. It looks nice down."

"Really?"

"Uh-huh." She met my eyes and my stomach did a little flip.

We left the hotel together, stepping out into a late-night drizzle. It was a bit weird. I wanted to hold her hand but we only tended to do that for the cameras. Neither of us was doing the public thing here and I didn't know quite how to behave. I decided to wait for a bit and see what happened, but I was quietly hopeful. You don't tell someone you like their hair if you're about to end a relationship, even if it is a fake one.

She ran a hand through her own hair. Was that a nervous gesture? "I know this whole thing has been really weird," she began, "but I'm glad that it was you, you know?"

I did not know. I wanted to know more.

"You're a good guy, Stuart. It's been fun hanging out."

"Thank you. It really has."

"Even though it's crazy what we've had to do, you've made it fun. These last few weeks, I actually missed you, you know?"

"Yeah."

"What I'm trying to say is . . ." There was a pause and her face froze. "Stuart, I think that's him."

"What?"

"The stalker. The stalker is right here!"

I followed her pointing finger to see the silhouette of a bulky man in a long coat lumbering toward us through the rain. "Don't worry," I said. "I'll talk to him."

"He looks dangerous."

"I'm an ace, remember?" I put my hands on her shoulders and looked into her eyes. It was time to be the hero, even if I didn't feel particularly heroic. "Believe in me, and it'll be okay."

She nodded as I stepped away from her and toward the man. Stella hadn't activated my ace before, but I knew this would be the time. She didn't need to pretend for the crowd, so that meant her affection would be real. And I would know for sure that she really liked me! All I had to do was prove myself equal to the man she thought I was.

The stalker was a lot closer now. There was something odd about him, but it was hard to make out in the poor light. He moved strangely, too, with a heavy, awkward gait. "Can I help you?" I asked.

He didn't answer, just continued to close the distance between us.

"Hey!" I said, louder this time. "I'm talking to you."

The man took another step and then swung. I jumped back, alarmed. I really haven't been in many fights. My training is all around first aid and rescue, not restraint. Without my powers I was as effective here as, well, an ordinary untrained man. But surely Stella would trigger my ace soon, and then I'd be more than a match for this guy, whoever he was.

"Last warning. I don't want any trouble," I added, but he didn't react to my words, just swung for me again. Another near miss. I swung back this time, my fist connecting just below his rib cage.

It was like hitting a wall. Literally. My knuckles made an unpleasant cracking sound and pain jolted through my wrist. And in that moment I knew I'd been wrong: Stella didn't believe in me. Not one bit. Before I could recover, he hit me in the stomach. The breath left my body and my feet left the floor. The next thing I knew I was lying on my side, half curled and helpless.

The man had to be some kind of ace. Even with my power, I'd be hard-pressed to beat him, and Stella had no chance. Luckily for me, there was no follow-up from the stalker. He was ignoring me now that I no longer stood between him and his real target: Stella. I rolled over so I could face her. It hurt to move. "Run," I wheezed.

But she did not run.

"I'm not leaving you." There was determination in her voice, nerves underscored by a kind of steel. The stalker stepped over me, his foot splashing rainwater in my face, and reached for her, and she . . .

Rippled.

That's the best word I can think of to describe it. The streetlights and the rain gave her a hazy aura as she kicked off her shoes. My dazed mind struggled to make sense of what I was seeing. Stella had started growing before my eyes. Changing. As if her shape had become loose and liquid. The fabric of her jeans tore as a second set of legs split off from the first, hooves sparking on the concrete as she adjusted her balance. I found myself looking up at the lower half of a horse, a muscular human torso sprouting from where the horse's head would normally be, a large bow in her hands, anger on her face. I had never seen anything like this before. She was incredible. Beautiful. And absolutely the last thing I was expecting.

The stalker was at least as confused as I was. He paused, and in that pause, Stella—or at least, the centaur that had taken her place—drew back the heavy bow and loosed an arrow. The stalker rocked from the impact, stumbling back a step as the arrow struck him squarely in the chest. A chip of something hard broke from the stalker's body and scratched my cheek. That seemed important, but I was feeling dizzy. A part of my brain informed me that I was going into shock.

The centaur fired again, this time targeting an ankle, then she spun and kicked out with her hind legs. The connection sounded like thunder and the stalker flew backward out of my line of sight to land with a crash across the street. She was about to leap forward after him when she suddenly seemed to notice me on the ground. The rage on her face vanished, replaced with concern.

I lifted a finger as if to speak but no words came out. What do you say when your date turns out to be a half horse? She was so powerful, so amazing. Stella was much more than I'd imagined. Frankly, it was too much to take in all at once. I flopped down in my puddle and passed out.

CHAPTER 6
Stella

I changed in front of Stuart. Brave Stuart who hadn't thought twice about jumping in to defend me, and who was currently flat on the sidewalk, passed out.

I hesitated, waiting for the attacker to crash back toward us. I'd make sure he didn't hurt Stuart again or die trying—the intense need to protect him an emotion I wasn't familiar with. My adrenaline had spiked. My heart thundered in my chest. I'd never been in a real fight before, not since some hair pulling in elementary school. It had come naturally—as naturally as pulling from the stars above to transform into Sagittarius's centaur. One of the most dangerous forms available to me.

But when that . . . thing—an ace or extremely strong joker of some kind; it had to be, didn't it?—hit Stuart and he folded in pain, I didn't hesitate at all.

No one knew about me. Not my mother. No one. Except now Stuart did.

He'd never look at me the same way again.

The figure ran off in the opposite direction. While I knew Stuart would probably be ticked off at me for not pursuing our stalker and letting him get away, I had a bigger worry. Stuart still wasn't moving.

This next bit would be tricky. I wouldn't be able to change again, not anytime soon. I would have to hope he (or she, I guess) wouldn't come back. I couldn't afford to wait, though; Stuart might need serious help. I could take him in my centaur form . . . try to find the nearest hospital. But that might well create even more problems for both of us. He was likely horrified enough about what I could do without us landing on the news.

So I searched inside myself and transformed. It felt like slipping on my skin and shrinking three sizes, a brief searing pain and then

I was me. But a big change like this would wipe me out and I'd need to sleep soon.

At least we were near Stuart's hotel. Shit. I realized I couldn't very well go in naked, or carry Stuart in my normal body. I should've stayed in centaur form. Too many years of secrecy had steered me wrong.

I'd have to try to wake him. I blessed my lucky stars that there weren't many people in sight and that the lip of a concrete curb wall hid us—for now—from those who were. I wanted to laugh when I thought of Vickie's reaction if we made the news like this.

Or maybe I wanted to cry. I crouched beside Stuart, his face so sweet and peaceful. My fingers hovered over his cheek and then I touched his skin. I felt it like tapping into an electrical current. Based on every movie I'd seen, you were supposed to slap or shake the person. I didn't do that. Instead I gently stroked his cheek and then again, and said, "Stuart, I need you to wake up. Come on, Stuart, wake up. I need you to be okay."

I knew I was this close to losing every shred of cool I had. What if he was hurt badly? Fear of an entirely different kind poured through my veins. An image of running through the night after my father died hit me, the blind panic and sorrow I'd felt. People you loved left. So it was safer to limit the number of them. Safer to make sure no one truly knew you.

I'd let Stuart into my heart without meaning to.

He blinked slowly, and then focused in on me. "Stella?" he said.

"Shhh." Joy that he was awake and panic that he knew what I could do mixed. "I need your shirt," I said. "I can get you inside and we can call you a doctor."

Stuart closed his eyes again, then opened them. He pressed himself up, not wanting to look at me, it seemed. He pulled his white T-shirt over his head, but stopped halfway through with a wince and a curse. "Can you . . ." he said.

"Of course," I said.

I reached over to help get it off, flinching when he gasped in pain. "Something's broken," he said grimly.

I should have acted faster. Then he wouldn't be hurt.

"I'm sorry," I said, whipping the shirt over my head. Thank everything, it hung to mid-thigh on me.

"He got away?" Stuart asked.

"He did."

"Because of me."

"No," I said, "I wanted to make sure you were all right. That was more important."

He still wasn't looking at me. "If you can help me get up," he said, and gestured with a tightness that looked wrong on him.

I did as he asked. He was steady enough on his feet. "Do you think you can get inside?" I asked him.

My purse was nearby and I went to find it. At least some stars were shining on me tonight—my phone was inside and unbusted. My shoes were just past it. I slipped them back on.

"I'll be fine," he said.

"I should probably go," I said. *Ask me to stay,* I thought. "I crash pretty hard after . . ." I change into a giant arrow-shooting centaur.

Stuart said, "That's all right."

Ask me to stay, and tell me I can go to sleep in your room.

But he gave me a brief wave and turned to hobble back inside the warm embrace of the lobby. I called a car and prayed I could stay awake until I got home.

Stuart knew my secret and I was clearly right. He'd never look at me the same way again.

Stuart

I lay in the hospital bed feeling sorry for myself despite the pain-killers. I'd been beaten up in front of Stella, who clearly didn't think anything of me at all. When she'd said she could look after herself I'd assumed it was bravado. But no, she'd been hiding an ace all this time, just like she'd been hiding her contempt. What a fool I'd been.

A doctor came in. She looked tired but mustered a smile for my benefit. "Good morning, Mr. Hill. I have your scans here."

"How bad is the break?"

"Oh, there's no break, just some heavy bruising." She held up the scan. "See?"

I could see the bones sitting as they should, undamaged. I'd told Stella I'd broken something. Now she'd think I was even more pathetic.

"Don't look so glum, Mr. Hill, this is good news. We'll have you out of here by the end of the day." She asked a few more questions, then added one more as she was leaving. "Are you up to having a visitor?"

"Yes."

"Very good. I'll send them through."

I wondered if Stella had come to check up on me. I hoped it was her, even as I hoped it wasn't. It was probably Colin though. Or Mum. A wave of fatigue swept over me that had nothing to do with my injuries.

The door swung open to admit neither of them. Instead, I saw Pygmalion standing there in a black shirt and trousers set off by a cherry waistcoat, cravat, and matching shoes. He gave me a flamboyant wave. I saw a bottle of red wine in his other hand. "My dear boy, how are you feeling?"

"Much better." I sat up straighter and immediately regretted it, my body protesting the sudden movement.

Pygmalion waved me back down. "No need to stand on ceremony. This isn't an official visit. I just happened to be in the area and thought I'd see how you were."

"How did you know I was here?"

"Being in the Silver Helix confers certain advantages." His voice dropped to a conspiratorial whisper. "I asked the boys to keep an eye out for you."

"Did they see who attacked us?"

"Oh, I don't mean literally. Your name was flagged when you were admitted here. Once I confirmed you were my Stuart Hill, I came as soon as I could. I must say, I am sorry to hear you were attacked. Did you get a look at your assailant?"

"Not a good one. Just a big man in a long coat. It was dark. He was tough, though." I held up a bandaged hand. "I made the mistake of punching him."

Pygmalion winced. "Leave it with me. I'll find out what I can about this mystery man."

"Really? Thank you."

"Think nothing of it. I did say I'd look after you."

"And you have." I sighed and dropped my gaze. "You were right about Stella. I should have listened."

"Ah, well, you wouldn't be the first young man to have been misled by a pretty face."

"I know it was all an act on her part but the person stalking her is real. I don't even know if she got home all right. Should I call her?"

Pygmalion came and patted my hand. "Not quite off her hook yet, I see. Do you really think a woman like that is in danger?"

An image of the snarling centaur flashed into my mind. "No."

"No indeed. She isn't interested in talking to the likes of us. If it is not of direct benefit to her, financial benefit, then you might as well try and talk to the moon." I nodded in miserable agreement. "More important, will it help your recovery to speak to her again?"

"I suppose not."

"Then, if you'll excuse the pun, make the most of this clean break. You're much better off without her."

"It doesn't feel that way."

"Not yet, dear boy, but it will. In the meantime you should try this Merlot—" He held out the bottle and winked at me. "—for medicinal purposes, of course."

"Thank you."

"That's all right. Women are fickle creatures, but you can always rely on a good friend and a bottle of wine."

I took the bottle and decided then and there that as soon as I got home, I was going to get very, very drunk.

Stella

Pretending everything was wonderful with my mom had gotten much harder—since she'd conveniently arrived here in England for a visit a week after Stuart got hurt. She'd been intending to come over, but her timing couldn't have been worse. At least I'd managed to get her to book the flat next door, but you'd never know we weren't sharing the place. She'd been a constant presence for the last two days.

"Now, when will I meet this Stuart of yours, my little stargazer?" she asked, winding a colorful floral scarf around her neck just so.

"He's really not mine," I said, not for the first time, and stared at my computer screen without taking anything on it in. My heart drummed a hint of panic. This was the first time she'd mentioned meeting him and something told me convincing her she definitely *did not* need to would prove impossible.

Speaking of Stuart, we'd exchanged some very brief texts since the incident. I'd wanted to go to the hospital and see him when I woke up, but the complete lack of encouragement persuaded me to stay home. And then he'd been discharged and his replies had turned monosyllabic. Vickie kept pressing for us to go out on another public date, but I kept refusing. Which is probably why she had summoned my mom.

I didn't know what to do. I had to see him again, if for no other reason than to make sure he would keep my secret. I thought I could still trust him . . . even if he'd blown me off so quickly that it confirmed my policy of secrecy had been a good one. I'd never make this mistake again.

"Honey," my mother said gently. "Trouble between you two?"

"What? Oh, no, I keep telling you," I said, "we're just friends. He's got a busy schedule right now."

"I thought you said he'd been injured?"

Of course she remembered *everything* I said on the subject. "He's feeling better."

"Good, then that's that."

This was a nightmare. Or . . . no, *this* was the nightmare. "Stuart, is this Stuart Hill, Hero?" I heard my mother say and looked over to confirm she was using my phone. She laughed at something. "I don't know if Stella told you I'm visiting her here—I'd love to meet you." She paused. I wanted to lunge for the phone or at least hear what Stuart was saying, but I stayed put. "Oh, no, I'd rather be able to really get to know you—and your family. They're from around here, aren't they? Maybe Stella and I could come for dinner? If you're sure it wouldn't be an imposition . . ."

"It is," I said. "We can just go out."

"No, that sounds perfect," she said. "Stella looks like she wants to speak with you."

She floated over, clearly pleased with herself, and passed me the phone. "We're going to dinner at Stuart's parents on Thursday."

Two days from now. I took the phone. "I'm so sorry," I said. "You really don't have to have us over." Though the idea of meeting the rest of his family was appealing. Even though it wouldn't matter, I reminded myself, because this farce was over.

"It's, ah, our pleasure. How are you?" he asked. He sounded nervous.

"I'm okay. How are *you*?" Before I could stop the words, I added, "I've been wondering. I'm sorry I didn't make it to the hospital."

"Oh, it's not that serious. I'm feeling better. Any other news?"

He meant from the stalker. So far things had been quiet. I didn't have much hope they'd stay that way. Not when the person had escalated to attacking us.

"Nothing to report," I said. My mother was watching this all closely. "I should go, but I look forward to Thursday and maybe we can talk then? Take care of yourself."

"All right," Stuart said. "You take care, too."

I hung up and braced. My mother clapped her hands together. "You *do* like him. I knew it. Well, this is exciting."

I supposed I could take comfort in the knowledge that nothing could be more disastrous than our last date. At least, so I hoped.

Stuart

I was miserable and hungover for a few days, but things slowly went back to normal. The bruising healed, I returned to work, the world went on turning. Luckily for me, Colin hadn't had any further brilliant ideas for fundraisers involving my love life. The whole bizarre thing seemed to be over.

Then Stella's mother called.

If it had been Stella herself I might have broken it off then and there, but I didn't have it in me to upset her mother, who seemed really nice. She wanted to meet us for dinner, and why wouldn't she? To Mrs. Sumner, our relationship was real. Rather than admit the truth, I'd agreed to dinner, which meant that Stella and I would have to pretend once more, this time to those we loved.

Before I knew it, I was standing in the dining room, listening to the sound of the clock ticking. Mum was more nervous than me. She kept fussing with the tablecloth while I put out the place-mats. "It's going to be cozy getting everyone around the table," she said. "I suppose you won't mind that, though."

"Mum!"

She ignored me and tutted to herself as Kelly arrived with a stack of bowls. "There aren't enough good bowls to go around. You and your father will have to make do with the breakfast set."

"Why do me and Dad get the crap ones?" Kelly protested.

"Because you broke two of them last Christmas, remember?"

"It wasn't my fault!"

"Yes it was, and mind your language. I don't want the Sumners thinking you've got a foul mouth."

Just as the two of them squared up to each other, the doorbell rang, and Mum's eyes went wild. "Stuart, get the door. Kelly, get your father down here, and for goodness' sake, be civil."

Kelly and I shared a look, then she headed for the stairs and I headed for the door. Stella's mum was on the other side, dressed in a floaty aquamarine dress with dangling sleeves and several long necklaces of silver. She was beaming at me. To my surprise, I felt my wild card ramp up. Seemed like she was a fan.

"You must be Stuart," she proclaimed, pulling me into a warm embrace. "I've heard so much about you."

Over her shoulder, I could see Stella. She was also more dressed up than I'd expected. No jeans this time. Maybe that was her mother's influence. The two of them looked like they were TV stars who'd walked onto the set of the wrong show. *Sorry,* she mouthed at me.

I just stared, caught amid too many feelings. Why did I still want to look at her all the time? Why did I want to be around her at all? More to the point, why was I putting everyone through this nonsense?

"This is lovely," said Stella's mum, kissing me on the cheek. "But might we come inside?"

I realized I'd been hugging her for far too long. Stella looked away as I stepped back, at least as embarrassed as I was. "Right. Yes. Please, come in, Mrs. Sumner."

"No, no, darling," she replied, resting a hand on my biceps, "you must call me Celeste."

Dinner was an odd affair. Mum apologized for everything, from dinner to the state of the nation, as if she were personally responsible for all of it. Kelly asked lots of questions about astrology and love, which Mum didn't like but couldn't easily stop, while Celeste flirted pretty equally with me and Dad. To my utmost surprise, Dad flirted back, seeming younger than I'd seen him in years. Stella and I said very little. There wasn't much to say, really. When tonight was over, I'd insist we stop the whole thing.

"Oh!" Mum declared in a voice strangled with horror. "I haven't put the crumble in. I'll do it now. So sorry."

"There's no rush with family," replied Celeste smoothly.

"More wine?" asked Dad.

"Yes please," replied Kelly and Celeste together.

"Stuart," said Stella. "Can you show me where the bathroom is?"

"It's just upstairs, first door on the left. You can't miss it . . ." I trailed off. She was giving me a hard look. Actually, everyone was: Celeste, Dad, even Kelly. I blushed immediately. *Oh. Right.* I stood up. "Let me show you."

The stairs creaked as we ascended them. I could hear her heart. It was beating very fast. She stopped abruptly on the landing and turned around so abruptly I nearly crashed into her. There wasn't room for two people to stand comfortably in the cramped space. I wanted to go back down a step almost as much as I wanted to go forward those last few inches. Pygmalion was right; I was still on the hook.

"I'm sorry," she said.

"That's okay," I replied automatically. It wasn't okay, though. Far from it.

"Listen, about that night: Nobody else knows about me, Stuart. *Nobody.*" With a pointed look down the stairs, she took my arm. "I need it to stay that way. Can I trust you?"

I looked at her. "You know you can."

Her whole body sagged with relief. "Thank you."

"That's okay. How long have you . . . you know?"

"Turned into a giant centaur?"

"Yeah."

"Did I freak you out when I changed?"

"Yes. No! I mean, I was surprised at first, but what you can do, Stella, it's . . . it's wonderful."

"You really mean that?"

"Of course I do. If you hadn't changed I don't know what would have happened. You saved me. I thought I'd be the one to save you that night but I couldn't even look after myself." I stopped talking. Something in the way she was looking at me had changed. Like she'd softened somehow. I wasn't sure exactly what was happening, but I didn't want it to stop. "Would you tell me more about it? About you?"

"Okay." She took a deep breath. "I first changed the night my dad died. My power's always tinged with grief because of that. I was sixteen, living in Hawaii, when the police knocked. Nobody saw it coming. 'An accident,' they said." Her mouth pressed into a hard line. "Still not sure I believe that. My mother fell apart right there on the floor at the door." She swallowed. "I had to get out of the house. The next thing I knew I was running under the stars. And then . . . I wasn't exactly me anymore. I was in the form of Leo, my birth sign."

"Wait. You can turn into a lion as well?"

"I can actually turn into all of the zodiac signs. Sounds stupid, I know."

"Turning into a lion sounds reasonable enough. I work for a charity that auctioned me off for a date, remember?"

She smiled. "And look how *that* turned out!"

I half smiled back. "How did it turn out, Stella? I'm asking for a friend."

"A bit messy but so much better than it should have been. My mother is infuriating, but I'm glad she called you. Otherwise we wouldn't be here." The little space between us seemed to have shrunk further. Her hand was still on my arm. I felt the other cup around the small of my back. "I didn't want anyone to see that side of me. I was ashamed of it. I thought your reaction the other night was . . . different than it apparently is. Turns out you don't make me feel like that."

"How do I make you feel?"

"Safe."

"Just safe?"

Her eyes sparkled mischievously and she brought her face to mine. "More than safe."

Was this happening? Were we about to kiss? She was so close it was hard to think straight. "But I didn't even keep you safe. I let you down. I'm a loser."

"That's not how I see you."

"It isn't?"

"No," she said firmly. "Trust me, I've dated my fair share of them. You're much better than that."

There was no space between our bodies now. I wrapped my arms around her and we kissed. It was as natural as breathing. I was acutely aware of the way her shape met mine. Supernaturally so. That was when it hit me.

I stopped kissing her. "It's you!"

She opened her eyes, bemused. "What's me?"

"I thought it was your mother activating my ace at the door, but it was you."

"If you say so."

"What's changed about me since that night with the stalker?"

She looked into my eyes, smiled. "I've had time to think. And seeing you get hurt, how I felt then, and tonight when I saw you . . . it clarified things."

I wasn't sure what to say to that, so I kissed her again. Time passed in a beautiful hazy way until my phone rang. I ignored it for the first few rings but then we both started laughing.

"Sorry," I said. "Let's ignore it."

"It's okay. We should probably be getting back to the others anyway."

I reluctantly let her go and braced myself for the relentless teasing awaiting us at the dinner table. My phone continued to ring. I began to worry. Maybe it was serious. I answered it and heard Colin on the other end.

"Evening, Hero. How are you and Stella doing?"

He probably felt me blush from there. "Pretty good actually. Hang on. How did you know we were—"

"Great, that's great. Perfect, in fact. I've had an idea for the two of you, my best one yet . . ."

Stella

Mom and I settled into a cab for the ride back. I'd put my foot down and refused Stuart's dad's offered ride home. We'd imposed on his family enough for one night.

Well, "imposed" might not be the right word. That had gone better than I'd ever have dared to imagine. I genuinely liked Stuart's parents, and it seemed mutual. And as for Stuart, I still worried I was a few years too old for him, and it felt strange having someone know the whole truth about me, and I'd never been in a relationship and so what if I wasn't good at it and the entire thing turned disastrous . . .

But these seemed like normal anxieties. And my feelings for Stuart were anything but normal for me. I felt like my heart was glowing inside my chest, visible from the stars themselves.

When we'd gotten back to the table, everyone had carefully grinned but not directly at us. I hadn't minded.

"That's quite the smile you're wearing," Mom said from the seat beside me, smug and extremely self-satisfied. She'd given both Stuart's parents a hug and a kiss on their cheeks as we left, and offered Kelly a personalized reading. "You're welcome."

"For . . . ?"

"Me pressing the dinner issue," Mom said. "Whatever was going on between you . . . seems like it's resolved? I like him."

"I'm glad. He's a great guy." My cheeks were blazing. My mom and I never talked about this kind of thing, because I never let her meet any of the hookups-only I'd been with in the past.

"I like him because he makes you happy," she said, and put her hand on my arm. "It really is all I want for you."

Happy? Was that the feeling in my chest? I guess it was.

I should have been worried about the families getting too close, about me and Stuart moving too fast, but somehow I wasn't. We'd had time to get to know each other during our fake relationship.

Colin had called Stuart with another big scheme, a last-minute charity appearance at an event at the British Museum, and I was looking forward to seeing the place. Who was I kidding? I was looking forward to seeing Stuart again.

So much so, I realized we'd forgotten to discuss the fact our stalker was still out there. We'd need to figure out how to proceed on that front, but I hadn't been lying when I said Stuart made me feel safe. The stalker hadn't gotten the better of us the first time they had attacked us directly. Now we were truly together.

It felt like nothing could touch us, and I couldn't help a shadow intruding on the bright light of the evening. That must be exactly what the stalker would hope we were thinking.

CHAPTER 7
Stuart

I was standing on the steps of the British Museum, waiting for Stella. A large crowd had already gathered. This was clearly a major event. Reachers banners hung from the pillars outside the main entrance, and I saw more than one camera crew filming the whole thing. Colin was clipping a microphone to my McHeroface jacket as he briefed me. Normally I hang on every word so I can brace myself for whatever he's got in store, but when Stella arrived I forgot Colin was even there.

I watched her being escorted over to us and felt the spark as our eyes met, a cocktail of emotions and a potent triggering of my ace. She quickly took the last few steps. I saw that moment of indecision that I felt, too, and then she was in my arms sharing a brief kiss.

The crowd cheered.

We had a competition for who could blush the most. It was too close for me to call. She stepped away but our fingers still touched and I smiled at her like an idiot. She smiled back. I almost didn't care about the hundreds of people watching us. Almost. What with Stella, Colin, and the few people in the crowd who believed in me, my senses were sharpened well beyond the range of a normal person. I became aware of a number of people interacting with their phones. Though it was impossible to tell exactly what they were doing, I knew the sound of the Reachers app better than anyone, and its distinctive beeps were sounding all around me.

"I missed you," said Stella.

"I missed you, too," I replied, but as I did so, I heard Stella's words a second time, whispered softly into a hundred sets of headphones. I frowned, pulled out my own phone, and fired up the app. A new banner immediately caught my eye:

Our Hero and Stella make history at the British Museum! Click here to join them and experience all the intimate details in real time!

I turned to glare at Colin. This was a new low, even for him. But to my surprise, I saw tears in his eyes. One of his hands rested across his heart as he looked at us. "Oh, you two are so adorable! Go on, lovebirds, in you go. Have a wonderful time."

A varied menu of insults came to mind, but given the microphone, the crowd, and Stella, there was no way I could use any of them. I forced myself to smile. Stella squeezed my hand and led me into the museum.

"Everything okay?" she asked.

"Sorry. Yes, everything's fine. More than fine actually."

And it was. We walked hand in hand through the British Museum followed at a respectful distance by a huge group of people eavesdropping through the wonders of modern technology. It was weird and normal all at the same time, and in the grandest setting for any of our dates yet. "You know," I said, "when this is all over, maybe we could go somewhere else, just the two of us."

"I'd like that."

"Aww," said the crowd.

Sometimes it's a curse having enhanced senses. I was able to catch way too much of the commentary going on behind us. Luckily Stella couldn't hear what they hoped we'd do next. After a turn of the Reading Room, we made our way into a section containing old Greek pottery and statues.

We were about halfway through when I heard an odd grinding noise from nearby. I turned to find the sound's origin. Next to me was a plinth with a statue of Aphrodite, the goddess of love, posed in a crouch. Its frozen expression of surprise met mine as it began to lean, then topple down toward me.

I don't know how many tons it weighed exactly, but a normal person would have had no chance of lifting it. For me it was just slim. There was no time to get clear, so I braced myself and leaned into it, catching the statue by the waist before it gained too much momentum.

The crowd gasped. Some screamed. Stella jumped back—I was glad of that—but then, somewhere nearby, there was a hiss of frustration.

"Oh, my God," said Stella. "Are you okay?"

"No," I grunted.

My arms and legs were starting to shake. I'd narrowly escaped death by blunt-force trauma, but being slowly crushed wasn't out of the question yet. I tried to push the statue upright, but it was too heavy. I tried to hold it where it was until help arrived, but it was too heavy even for that.

I glanced at Stella. Maybe if she changed into something strong we could lift it together. "Help," I gasped.

Stella

Stuart grimaced and I didn't know how long he could hold the statue before it crushed him. Members of the crowd were beginning to panic, jostling each other and crying out.

I could change, but there were two problems: (1) I worried even the brief time it would take wouldn't be fast enough for me to actually help Stuart, and—a far distant concern—(2) everyone would know my secret. Everyone.

For Stuart, I'd do it, but maybe there was a better way. I stepped in closer to him. "Stella—no—" he managed to get out.

I kept coming. "You got this," I said, and put my hand on his arm. "You got this."

I blinked as an older man left the crowd and came toward us, and who he was clicked. He was dressed in an over-the-top ye olde suite with a frilled collar and cuffs. Pygmalion.

"I'll help!" Pygmalion said. "Stella, I've got you!"

Something was off. He had a smug expression he barely concealed. Stuart grunted with effort beside me, and I dodged away from Pygmalion as he extended a hand toward the statue.

I spoke up louder. "Doesn't everyone agree Stuart's got this? I believe in you, Hero!"

Corny? Yes. But between me and the crowd, I did believe he had this. And I didn't trust Pygmalion's sudden entrance. He continued to gaze at me, and I saw the moment his lips twisted in displeasure. The exact same expression I'd seen before he stormed off from my reading.

It was the same moment that Stuart put forth an effort worthy of Hercules and pushed the statue back onto its plinth inch by slow inch. The crowd burst into applause and I went to his side. "You okay?"

"Yes, thanks to you," he said.

I started to explain my new theory on our stalker. "Stuart, I think—"

Pygmalion took another step toward us, then I turned my head to see the source of a crash behind us. An armless stone statue as big as the one Stuart had just saved himself from—and me, I realized; I was a target, too—stalked toward us across the floor.

"You should have listened to me, boy," Pygmalion said, adjusting his frilly cuffs. "A specimen of femininity this fine deserves a true hero. Someone to match her perfection."

Oh, no. He had to be joking. This dandy was suggesting we . . . as in me and *him* . . . should get together? There wasn't enough "nope" in the world. Though clearly he didn't care whether I wanted it or not.

"She has one," I said. Then, "Stuart, what's his ace power again?"

Another lurching statue appeared just behind Pygmalion. Stuart hardly needed to answer. "He's an animator—he's bringing the statues to life."

"You're both nothing next to me," Pygmalion said with a wild grin that was close to a snarl. "And I'll prove it."

"Everyone out!" Stuart shouted, but some people were crowding in closer with their phones held high. This had the makings of a disaster. "Pyg, you'll ruin yourself over this. Don't do this," Stuart said.

Trust Stuart to have a soft spot for the old guy. I didn't think he'd understood this was our stalker yet. Not fully. But I did. A man who saw a woman in these terms—as someone he deserved because he wanted her, because he thought he knew her without knowing anything but what she looked like—was capable of anything.

"Don't tell me what to do," Pygmalion said.

Stuart took a swing at him, which almost connected, but at the last moment an animated armless body lunged in between them to block it. Stuart took a quick step back. Pygmalion danced away with a mad cackle.

Meanwhile statues missing arms and other limbs crawled or stomped toward us. Even at Stuart's highest powers, he was going to need help.

"I hope you meant it when you said you didn't mind if your girlfriend turns into a giant centaur once in a while," I said.

"Are you kidding?" Stuart said. "I love everything about her."

Love, he'd said love.

Pygmalion snorted. "Love is what *I* felt, and she didn't want it. She should've come to me like Aphrodite."

The statue that had first fallen toward Stuart stretched and rose from its crouch behind us. "Now would be good," Stuart said.

"Hey," I said, "I love you, too."

And then I started to transform, people who hadn't fled yet taking pictures all the while. Cheers sounded and I wanted to tell everyone to get out of here.

When the transformation ended, I stomped and pulled my bow free, notching an arrow. "Everyone out!"

The crowd finally started to listen. And Pygmalion had an intense look of concentration on his face, spinning, working his arms like a master puppeteer as the statues came for us.

Stuart

Pygmalion was trying to kill me. I rolled the thought around in my head, trying to make it sound less absurd. Why? Why was he doing this? It made no sense. A number of statues were approaching us. Several lacked heads, arms, and in one case a leg. But they lurched and hopped as best they could, closing in around us. If I'd paid more attention at school I might have known who all the statues were supposed to be. But all I saw was an assortment of mostly naked, extremely heavy, and expensive things on the attack.

Aphrodite lunged for me first, the expression on her face shifting to match Pygmalion's anger. I stepped back and had time to watch her grasping at the space where I'd just stood. Between Stella and the crowd, my body was humming with power. And speed.

I stepped forward and pushed Aphrodite away from me, hard. She went stumbling away to crash into the far wall. Pygmalion made a gesture off to his right, and the lights in the room turned off, plunging us into darkness. Not complete darkness, though. There was still an ambient glow from the many phones being held up to record the fight. Although a large part of the crowd had rushed toward the exit, far too many had stayed, oblivious to the danger.

"Get back and give us more light," shouted Stella. Her voice was different in the centaur form, deeper, but it was still her.

One by one, the torches on the phones switched on, picking out Pygmalion and the other statues. I went after him immediately. Stone figures tried to stop me but I was faster. I ducked under one marble arm and sidestepped another, each movement bringing me closer to him. Gradually, his expression shifted from anger to alarm.

Though Pygmalion's ace was incredible, it did nothing to change him personally. We both knew that if I got to him, even for a moment, it would be over.

There was only a single, one-armed statue in my way now. I leapt past it, far faster than it could follow. Or so I thought. It caught me midair, hard fingers boring into my shoulder, so I was brought short in front of Pygmalion. I'd jumped slower than I'd expected, my ace fading as each member of the supportive crowd fled to safety. I grabbed the stone fingers in one hand, the thumb in the other, and tried to prise them apart. As we strained against each other, Pygmalion gestured, and the statue raised me up so my feet dangled above the ground. Another gesture and Aphrodite came bounding over, her feet thundering on the floor. "I'm going to enjoy this," whispered Pygmalion.

"It isn't too late," I replied, eyeing the approaching statue. "Nobody's been hurt. Stop now and you can avoid prison."

"Prison? My dear boy, the Silver Helix will never send me to prison. Nobody is going to take a hysterical woman's word over mine. And you won't be in a state to talk when I'm through with you."

"I won't need to," I said through gritted teeth. "You just told the internet what you're planning."

I looked down at the mic on my jacket. He did the same. An expression of shock, followed quickly by the purest rage, crossed his face. He raised a hand, clenched his fist, and Aphrodite copied the gesture, drawing back to hit me at full speed. "Stella is mine, you hear me? She is—"

His words cut off in a strangled cry as an arrow appeared in his outstretched fist, courtesy of the centaur. No longer actively controlled, Aphrodite froze mid-run and toppled forward. I twisted sideways to avoid the collision, pulling up my knees to get clear. It landed with a huge crash.

The remaining crowd cheered.

"Next shot won't be your hand," said Stella, lowering the angle of her notched arrow in a very deliberate way.

"Get back!" he screeched, and the statues pulled close to protect him, including the one carrying me. They formed a hard barrier between him and Stella, though they had to constantly adjust their position as she weaved back and forth, looking for an angle.

"Can you get free?" she asked.

I was about to answer no when I felt a shift. Someone in the crowd thought I could. With increased strength I pulled again to loosen the statue's grip. There was a crack, and the thumb came off in my hand. *Oops*, I thought as I landed in a crouch. I'd just broken a bit of history.

Stella took another shot. The statues lurched to get in the way and I took advantage of the moment to duck between the legs of a couple of them, bringing me inside the semicircle. Pygmalion noticed me and held out his unhurt hand. The statues twisted to grab for me but before they could, I threw the stone thumb. It hit Pygmalion square in the forehead, sending him staggering back. As I rushed forward, Stella leapt over the statues so that we both arrived at the same time. I pinned his arms behind his back and looked up at her. "You okay?"

"Yes. You?"

I nodded and saw her smile in the light of someone's torch.

"Oh, my sweet Stella . . ." began Pygmalion.

"Shut up," she replied, an arrow trained steadily at his face.

And he did.

Stella

I'll admit I was tempted to loose that arrow, for just a moment, but Pygmalion the prat wasn't worth giving up what Stuart and I had. Not to mention, he deserved real consequences. Like jail and public humiliation.

Stuart picked up Pygmalion and shouted, "Room with no statues?"

The crowd took his meaning. A security guard emerged and said, "This way."

I cantered along behind Stuart and a quiet, red-faced-with-embarrassment Pygmalion. The crowds parted for us, but they were still filming. I would be answering some questions soon. Very soon.

I wondered where Vickie was—she'd love that I finally needed her help.

The security guard unlocked a painted door at the end of the hall and ushered us into a closet/storage room, flipping on the lights. The fit was tight with my giant horse's body. The guard had handcuffs and once Stuart pressed Pygmalion back into a chair, the guard hurried in and fixed Pygmalion's wrists to the arms. Stuart took off his mic and squeezed it, crushing it to disable the signal.

"We should have been together," Pygmalion said to me, red-cheeked and still not getting it. "You were supposed to be mine. As perfect as a statue."

"Women aren't statues, you gross entitled prig," I said, stomping my hooves.

"That's right," Stuart added, a hand on my arm. "She was out of your league the whole time."

My eyes caught his. "I needed a hero."

The security guard sighed in a manner that reminded me that, even if they weren't listening in anymore, we still had an audience waiting to see what happened next. A big one.

The door banged open just then. "Stella!" Vickie said. And yes, Colin was right behind her. "Are you okay?" she demanded. "I mean, other than . . ." She gestured to my body.

"We're fine," I said. "But, ah, I'll need a changing room. And can you find me something to put on? I will need your help to figure out how to spin my being an ace. I also need to call my mother. Soon."

Stuart took off his jacket and handed it to me. "A start on the something to wear."

I took it with a grateful smile, holding his hand a few seconds longer than I needed to.

Vickie's phone rang and she passed it over to me. "Your mum," she said.

Of course. "Mom?" I said into it.

"Well, my Stella, I think you have many years of explaining to do, but I wanted to tell you . . ."

I braced.

"How proud I am of you. You were magnificent, darling."

My eyes started to sting. "You're not mad at me? For keeping it a secret?"

"My little stargazer, I could never be mad at you. I'm sorry you didn't feel like you could tell me."

Gratitude swelled inside me so that all I could do was say, "I should have told you."

"All's well that ends well, as they say. And it sounded like you and your hero are well on your way to a happy ending. I'll let you go now."

She hung up before I could thank her for all her meddling.

"Oh, my stars," Colin said, and I wondered why he was using the name of my column. He thrust his phone in front of Vickie and she blinked at it. She was taken aback for a moment, but then a genuine smile broke across her face. "I told you this would work."

She grabbed the phone and brandished it at me and Stuart.

People had donated half a million dollars to Reachers since the evening began. *Wow* hardly covered it. "I'd say this means your fan base is taking the news all right," Stuart said, smiling at me.

I gave him one back. "I think you mean *our* fan base."

EPILOGUE
Stuart

We were walking together in Trent Park. Just us. I was out of uniform and Stella was wearing a hoodie and, even if we were still recognizable, there was nobody in sight. It was wonderful and a little odd. I'd almost gotten used to having people watching us. "So," I asked, "what other things can you change into?"

"Stick around long enough and I'll show you."

"I'm not going anywhere."

She gave me an odd look. "Really?"

"Really."

"Even after you've met my mother?"

"If you can put up with mine, I can put up with yours."

She stopped walking and put her arms around me. "I think I can manage that."

I put my arms around her and we kissed. The tip of her nose was cold, but I didn't mind. "I love you, you know."

"I know." She gave me a cheeky grin. "Tell me again, just to be safe."

I cupped her face with my hands, looked her in the eye. "I love you, Stella Sumner."

"Good. Because I love you, too, Stuart Hill."

"I thought so but, um, it is nice to be reminded."

"Then I'll be sure to tell you again, from time to time."

We kissed some more. Actually, we kissed a lot. It was great. I hoped that wouldn't change anytime soon. As the sun began to set, I took her hand and we made our way out of the park. We didn't have to date now that Pygmalion was behind bars, but we wanted to anyway. I still couldn't get over the man being a stalker, but the public had grasped the idea very quickly. His career with the Helix was over, his reputation in tatters. I should have been happier about that, but I'd lost a childhood hero, and it stung.

Despite all of this, Colin's idea had worked. Reachers had done well out of our relationship, as had Stella's column. Even more unbelievable, it really had been the start of something beautiful. Her hero name was much cooler than mine: Stargaze, the news called her, and it stuck. I wasn't sure what was next along the road, but I was glad to be walking it with Stella.

"Did I mention that I love you?" I asked.

"It's been a while," she replied. "Better tell me again."

So I did.

2023

The Wolf and
the Butterfly

by David Anthony Durham

I yank my beanie down as far as I can. Who
knew Reno got this cold? It's the freaking desert, right? Everyone
here points out that it's *high* desert, but that hadn't seemed like
that big a distinction when I got here on a raging 103-degree late-
August day, the sun a ball of misery that scorched the very notion
of clouds from the sky. That's the Reno I arrived dressed for.
T-shirts and shorts jammed in a rucksack, cowboy hat on, hopes
and dreams written all over my lovestruck face. I might as well
have been chewing on a straw. I kinda mistook Reno for Vegas. It
wasn't the only mistake that landed me in the Biggest Little City
five months ago.

Like, thing one. Don't show up unannounced to surprise your
long-distance girlfriend when she's in her senior year in a city
she's enjoying on her own. Thing two. Don't expect she'll let you
crash in her apartment. Thing three. Don't think that her life is
going to always include you. That, actually, was a new realization.
Dropped on me a couple weeks ago, though it was in the works
since I got here.

Hanging a right onto California Avenue, I can smell the Bountiful Bean. That's where I work. Virtually no money involved. But all the coffee I can drink and dibs on the day-old baked goods. Living off caffeine and tips and sugar. That's a decent twenty-one-year-old life, right?

I pass the yellow house, the one with the chimes and the glass mosaic statue of a giant cactus peace sign. And the Doberman. What an annoying dog. Every time I walk by, the same stupid Doberman, wearing a white bandanna stained with drool around its neck, rushes up against the fence and goes freaking crazy. I hear it bark from inside the house, and then it slams through the dog door and begins its howling/growling/hound-from-hell imitation. It only does this with me. Other people? No problem. Me? Cerberus shows up. I kinda know why, but . . .

I snap around. Or, the *other* me snaps around, pulling me with it. The part of me I try to keep hidden. The wolf. It's faster than me, and because of it I see why we turned. The Doberman launches itself from atop a mound of hard snow blown up against the fence. It's over the chain link with ease. Lands on the sidewalk, skids on a patch of ice before finding its footing. Its eyes fix on mine. It surges toward me.

"No, no, no," I say. "You don't want to . . ."

The wolf in me rises so fast I can't do anything to hold it back. It runs up the vertebrae of my spine, leaps out of my back and over my head—a shadow I hope only I can see. Then the weird thing happens—the thing I try to avoid, to hide. I'm me, standing there about to wet myself. But I'm also a spectral wolf that surges toward the Doberman. I see through the wolf's eyes, feel the indignation in it, the rage at the Doberman's insult, the need to . . .

"Oh, God no, don't . . ."

The Doberman sees what's coming toward it. It slams on the brakes so fast it topples over itself. My wolf is on it. Bigger. Faster. Stronger. It crashes into the Doberman, locks its jaws on the dog's neck, and slams it to the pavement. Its eyes twist to take in the Doberman's whining fear, asking, *Do you see? Do you see now?*

The Doberman does. It goes limp. It whimpers. Its eyes staring into the wolf's. Into mine. I can understand them. They're saying, *Yes, I see. I see. Please, master, I see.*

It's not that either of them speaks English. Or that I speak dog. I don't mean that. It's just that I *know* what they're saying. Words lack clarity compared with the tremble in canine eyes.

It's what human eyes can see that I'm worried about, though. I call the wolf back. I retreat a few steps. That's one thing. Distance pulls on it. The farther it is from me, the greater the tension, like a rubber band stretched toward snapping.

The wolf loosens its jaws' grip. Then clamps down again. Just because it can. The Doberman squeals, which pleases the wolf. It lets go, stretches, and for a moment it refuses to come back to me. It stares down the street toward the mountains in the distance. It does this a lot, whenever there's an open view. Seems like it's wishing it could hit the road, head for the hills and beyond. I don't know. Life would be easier for both of us if we weren't connected in this weird way. Neither of us asked for it.

It lopes toward me, its eyes saying, *See? There's a way to deal with things.* It fades with each step, leaps toward me, and is vapor when it lands back within me, twirling around my spine and settling, satisfied.

I look around, sure everyone on the street has just witnessed canine murder. A cyclist rides toward me from across the street. He's wearing a skintight yellow cycling shirt and shorts like it's summer in the French countryside. His only concession to the Baltic weather is a thick hat with massive earflaps. "That was freaking weird," he says. "I thought you were dog meat, dude. That lady must have one hell of a dog whistle." He points.

To my relief, the Doberman is on its feet, looking only a little worse for wear, cowering beside a woman in a pink bathrobe. She does appear to have a dog whistle. She waves and sheepishly says, "Sorry if she scared you!" She looks down at her terrified, shivering dog. "Oh, Daisy, you gave yourself a fright!"

Daisy bolts for the house, the woman waving as she follows.

The cyclist shakes his head. "And they make fun of cat people."

As he pedals away, I breathe in a sigh of relief. Nobody saw what really happened. It must've looked weird—the Doberman squirming on the sidewalk—but my wolf seems to be invisible to others during the day. At night, it's a shadow darker than any black, with eyes that glow a cold white light. It's both part of me and separate at the same time. I'm pretty sure it would never hurt me, but I'm pretty sure that it *would* hurt others. That's why I try to keep it leashed.

The wolf and I met one wild night a few years back in San Antonio. The same night I met Dina. I was hanging with some stupid guys, and Dina—to teach us a lesson—took us to a dance club. DJ Tod in the house. Dina called his music "Seriously Psychedelic Deep House," but she didn't explain it beyond that. Turned out, he was this crazy ace whose power was in the bass drop of the music. He'd get the music rising, higher and higher, building in tension and energy until it felt like things were going to explode, and then, when the bass dropped into a cascade of sonic/auditory release, DJ Tod would transform the whole dancing crowd into different joker manifestations of themselves.

The first time it was terrifying. I and everyone around me were suddenly demons straight out of some medieval fever dream of hell. That was my first thought. But Dina was there beside me, a crimson-skinned, scaled, tailed version of herself, dancing like crazy. And then we changed again. And again and again. Demons, honey-faces, dough-people, animals, amorphous snail-like things, howling werewolves. Each time was comical, or grotesque, or just weird. But each time it was also beautiful. We were all still ourselves. The physical change didn't alter who we were inside, except to reveal how trivial our prejudices were. It also didn't hurt that each change included a wave of euphoria that I imagine is what an epic acid trip is like.

It was kinda deep.

Later that night, the wolf saved Dina when some assholes jumped us, beating on us because we still looked like jokers. The wolf was having none of it, and God I was grateful. It saved Dina, and that was the start of Dina and me as a couple.

After that night, Dina changed back to her normal self. I did, too, all except for the wolf. It stayed in me. I didn't tell Dina. She assumed the wolf was a part of that one night, and I let her assume that. I made sure to keep it locked down, or at least invisible. It made for some awkward moments, but I had dialed being awkward into a fine skill.

Sometimes at night I'd stare at myself—and it—in the mirror, wondering what it was, where it came from, what went on in the mind behind those canine eyes. I knew it was a wild card power, but just knowing that didn't help much. How was I supposed to live the rest of my life with it?

So I hid it. Mostly, it had hunkered quietly inside me. But it's been different since we got to Reno. It's getting more restless, like it's wondering what I'm doing with my life. And with *its* life, I guess.

The coffee shop is packed with customers. It's the kind of hipster spot that prides itself on being niche and unique, but it never lacks for customers. I slide past groups of college students then squeeze between two Silicon Valley techies talking in the line. One of the techies has bone-white skin and full green eyes. The other has a helmet of hair that looks like something off a Greek statue. A guy near the counter has a plume of feathers instead of a head. He's a regular. Loves to lurk and watch the room with the flat eyes he has at the tip of each feather. I used to worry about him until I got to know him. He's an artist who paints Technicolor mosaics of people's faces.

I slip around the counter. Merl is already back there. He looks like a pretty average college-aged white guy, disheveled mousy hair with no discernible styling to it. He wears the type of T-shirts stoned guys buy online, with jokes that are funny in the moment but don't hold up once the high is gone. Merl likes to call himself an ace. He has a small hole in the center of his palms that he can blow air out of. He claims he's powerful enough to blow a grown man clean over, but I've only ever seen him use it to froth warm milk. The customers seem to love it. I think it's gross. There's no way I'm drinking a latte with Merl's body air all up in it. Little too intimate for my taste.

I shove my bag into a cubby behind the counter and wash my hands. "What's up, Steamwand?" I call out to Merl.

"Come on, man! The name's Steamo."

For the life of me, I don't know why he thinks Steamo is better than Steamwand, but that's Merl. I blow air out from my puckered lips at him.

"You should respect a man's right to self-proclaim his identity," he says. "If you had an ace power, you'd understand where I'm coming from."

"Yeah, sure. Where's the boss?"

Merl holds up his hands and blows moist puffs of air at me. "In the hothouse."

I dodge his attack with ninja stealth and head for the back.

When I open the door to Laine's office a cloud of humidity hits me. It's like stepping out of the mall in Houston during the summer, minus the swarm of angry bloodsuckers. Laine's office is large, but it doesn't feel that way because of how absolutely stuffed with plants it is. Coffee bean plants to be precise. Laine's ace is manipulating microclimates. One of the café's biggest draws is that we grow all our own coffee right in the shop. Laine also made an arctic climate in one of the closets to substitute as our fridge. It saves a lot on the electric bill, but I have to shovel snow out of a closet at least twice a week.

Laine's hunched over her desk, writing something. She doesn't look up when I crack the door. "Bacho, my most marvelous employee," she says in her playful, impossible-to-place accent. No one on the crew knows where she is from and she refuses to tell us. There are some running bets. I have my money on Haiti. Merl says Panama. A customer once guessed Tasmania, but that seemed pretty random. She's definitely from *someplace*, though. Dark-brown skin, glittery lips, and hair that's pierced with an array of what look like pastel chopsticks. A style that's somehow classy, earthy, slightly dangerous, but also casual work chic with a touch of . . . well, *someplace else.*

"Today has been busy-busy, man," she says. "The cold weather driving people inside. That's the one good thing about it. Clock in and go help Merl up front."

I walk to the spot on the wall where the card puncher is hidden behind a bunch of leaves. I push the branches away and punch my card. Laine is one of those people who likes the quirkiness of using vintage stuff, even if it makes things just a little bit harder.

Before leaving, I pause at the door. "Hey, Laine?"

Though she's looking down, I can tell she smiles. "Yes, Bacho?"

"It's like . . . Baltic out there."

She lifts her head. Pushes her large glasses up her nose. They're way too big for her face, but they work on her. She's got the sexy-librarian look down. "Still a bit chilled, are you?"

"A bit."

"Should I warm you up?"

Just having her say it warms me up. I nod.

She purses her lips, holds them in a pucker for a few seconds, then blows me a kiss. It moves like a soft breeze through the air. By the time it hits my face it's a gentle pressure that floods my body with warmth. Now I'm in the tropics. Haiti, I'm sure of it! I'm not sure if this crosses some line about employer/employee protocol, but I'm all for it. I walk out the door knowing the warmth inside me will hum on for an hour or so.

Two hours later, I don't need Laine's kiss of warmth. The work is frantic enough, person after person, coffee after coffee, explanation after explanation. Why doesn't anybody *ever* know what they want? And after standing in line for ten minutes? Come on.

I slip a supersized mug—piping hot enough that I handle it with a towel—in front of an armadillo of a guy, his shoulders as bulky as plate armor. "Here you go," I say, cheery because it looks like he's the tail end of the rush. The man's scaled hands wrap around the cup. I start to warn him, but he looks like he could scoop molten metal with those hands.

As he lumbers out of the way, I see a young woman who'd been hidden behind him. She's looking at her phone, which gives me a moment to stare at her. She's take-your-breath-away striking. Her skin is obsidian black, so smooth it glistens. It looks like a solid shell, but her face is fully expressive. She smirks, blinks, quirks her lips at something. She has wide-set features, and her reddish-brown hair is short, tightly curled, and close cut. Something on the phone causes her to *tsk* and raise her arms slightly, which highlights that she has four slimmer arms poking through tiny armholes in her sweater. Oh, did I mention she has antennas growing from her forehead? And wings? She's got wings. I'm like . . . speechless. I'm sure she must be famous. I recognize her, but I'm not sure from where.

She says something.

And I, perfectly timed, super-smooth, ask, "Huh?"

"Do you mind if I put up this flyer?" She waves a printed flyer with one of her small arms. "It's about the Unity Alliance counter-rally next week. You know about it, right?"

I do. She's talking about an event sponsored by the university's POC, LGBTQIA, joker, and other diversity support groups. They've come together in response to a rally planned by a group called Tenth Pillars. Nobody knows exactly what Tenth Pillars stands for, but they pretty much have it in for anybody who's not their particular sort of red-hat-wearing, white-supremacist, sexist, anti-immigrant, joker-hating dude.

"Yeah, sure," I say. "I'm going." Which is true enough. Dina is one of the organizers and it seems like a good excuse to bump into her.

"Coolio. Also, I'll have a cappuccino."

"Ah. Okay." I start to turn away, but I have to ask. "Is that regular foam?"

"I dunno. What's the other option?"

"There's also . . ." I gesture at the board on the wall behind me. She squints. "The Steamo Speciale? What's that?"

And then, as if he'd been hovering right behind me, there's Merl. He leans on the counter, all smiles. "Check these." He holds up his hands. "Blowholes," he says, "hot and frothy from me to you. You game?"

The girl smiles. "Coolio. Sure." To me: "Give me the Steamo Speciale."

Merl high-fives her, then grabs a paper cup and Sharpie. "What's your name?"

"Adesina." She twirls away to pin her flyer on the corkboard.

Adesina. Of course! From the band competition in San Antonio! She was in one of the other bands. I never hung out with her or anything. I don't think I even spoke to her. She was a few years younger, and a lot of other distracting stuff happened that week. But yeah, it's totally her. In a way she looks the same, but at the same time she looks different. Or maybe it's the way I feel staring at her that's different.

Back at the counter, she asks, "Should I pay for it, or what?"

I ring her up. She tips the change into the tip jar. Looks at me. Winks. "That's for Steamo Speciale over there."

And I, perfectly timed and with no control of my mouth or awareness that I'm about to do it, say, "I think I remember you."

She cocks an eyebrow. "From . . . ?"

Over the sound of his frothing, Merl shouts, "You're totally a model, aren't you? I knew it the moment you walked in."

"Well, of course. *Vogue. Cosmo.* I've done them all." Adesina laughs, then feigns serious, drops her smile. "Oh, no! You didn't see the nudes, did you? God, I thought those had been buried! Where'd you see them? Please tell me it wasn't that spread in *Jokes on You.* I was going through a rough patch. Bills to pay. I mean, we've all had to *do things,* right?"

She looks straight at me as she says this. I'm tongue-tied. Brain-tied. "Ah . . ."

Adesina cracks up. "I'm kidding! God, your face! Who would have thought you could go so red? You're hilarious." To Merl she says, "No, I'm not a model. That way lies misery. I know that from experience. My mom's, I mean."

Merl slides her cappuccino to her with a flourish. He looks at me, at her, and points at the shape drawn in the foam. "Look, I made a heart." As he glides away, he adds, "So your mom is beautiful, too?"

What the hell is going on? When did Merl get, like . . . smooth, or something?

Adesina picks up the cup, cradles it, and takes a sip. "Yep," she says, "she's pretty definitely beautiful. In a different way, though." Looking at me again, she adds, "Now that I think about it, I remember you, too." With that she walks away, a bounce in her step that makes her hips—and her antennae and wings—sway.

I stand there, stunned. Was she flirting? Then I remember another thing about Adesina. I didn't speak to *her* in San Antonio, but I did talk with her mother, Michelle Pond. The Amazing Bubbles. Model-turned-superstar ace-hero world-saving Committee member. It was just a short conversation, her asking me about one of the weird little dramas that plagued the competition. I don't even remember what. I do remember how weird it was talking to someone so famous, powerful, and beautiful, though Adesina was right that they were very different variations on beauty. Bubbles = white-blond swimsuit-model ace beauty. Adesina = obsidian-black insectile butterfly joker beauty. At the moment, Bubbles's beauty kinda pales compared with her daughter's.

I turn around and see Merl leaning against the counter smirking at me. "Dude, if that's the best game you've got, I can see why your girlfriend dumped you."

Later, back at the bunga, I power up the ZSquare, load *Pantheon,* and sit wishing I hadn't drunk so much coffee at work. "Bunga" is short for "bungalow," which isn't a name I love. Feels perverse in some way I can't place. I share it with a roommate, a guy named Loulou. No, I've never asked why he's named Loulou. He's got the "masturbator" bedroom; I've got "the servant's quarters," which is a rectangular corridor with the washer and dryer in it. And a single mattress. It's dismal, but I was lucky to score even this considering how tight the rental market is in Reno. Loulou had just had some big fight with his last roommate and booted him. I'm not sure what that was about, but it worked out for me. Loulou even reduced the rent a little when he heard about Dina dumping me. He can be nice sometimes, though he can also be insulting in ways he doesn't seem to notice. That might be why he doesn't seem to have any friends.

The wolf hates the whole living arrangement. When I'm home, it's either pacing around inside me, or pacing around in the living room, or curled up and sulking on the couch. Most of all, though, it doesn't like Loulou. It seems to find pleasure in choosing to rest in spots where Loulou might sit. That's the main reason it's curled up on the couch now, invisible to anyone but me, daring Loulou to come home and make the mistake of sitting on it.

"Get it booted up, dude!" are the first words out of Loulou's mouth when he bangs through the door.

"Already booted," I say.

He pegs his skateboard while balancing a Sizzle Pie pizza box in his other hand. He's a thin, red-cheeked white guy with hair that looks like somebody left one of those old wet mops outside to freeze. I don't mean that he's a joker; he's a nat, but with weird hair. He calls himself an @truelocal. One hundred percent Battleborn. Reno-raised. He gripes about how much Reno has changed. Incomers from California, the tech bros, the university students, hikers and climbers, bikers and skiers, the artists. He likes to complain.

Loulou works at Sizzle Pie. Perk of the job is that he comes home with a box or two of pizza slices, a combination of legit end-of-night leftovers and slices he nabs from people's pans after they leave. We're not proud, and it completes my well-rounded diet. Coffee and pizza.

"Decent selection today," he says. "A slice of spicy bacon, a Mr. Mustard supreme, and a banana chutney. There are 'chovies, but those are mine. Let's do this!" He slides toward the kitchen with the pizza box spinning on a finger.

Sometimes it feels like part of how I pay the rent is by getting video-game-demolished by Loulou on a daily basis. *Joker Pantheon* is set in a universe in which the wild card virus was introduced to the ancient world instead of the mid-twentieth century. It's got these elaborate historical settings. The virus explains all the gods and monsters of mythology, and a bunch of horrendous historical figures, too. All the villains are jacks with serious powers. Loulou and I have been stuck on the same level for the past week.

The *Joker Pantheon* logo comes up. It's Zeus himself, the game designer, looking like a smiling Cthulhu, his many arms waggling, tapping away. They say he codes multiple layers of every game at the same time, doing the work of ten nats all at once. It's probably true, though there's also a rumor that he's not a coder at all, just a mascot to make the *Joker Pantheon* games seem more PC. It does make you wonder. If he wasn't a jack, would jokers support the game so much? The joker body count is off the charts.

Loulou comes back in, two slices of pizza layered across his palm. "Hey, you going to the rallies on campus this week? I might head down to the quad and check out the Tenth Pillars."

"Really? Why?"

"I saw a video they posted. I'm not like down with their message or anything, but those guys know how to get red-faced and hyperventilate. They get pretty hyped up. Might be fun to watch. Who knows what will happen? You want to check it out with me?"

"Nah," I say. "I might go to the other one."

"Yeah, could be cool to check out the jokers, too. Whatevs, man. Just entertain me! That's all I'm asking. Maybe I'll go with you." He shrugs. That, from what I've gathered, pretty much sums up his social consciousness. He turns and gets ready to plop down on the couch.

Eyes closed, unmoving, the wolf growls. It's a rumble I feel inside and outside, a vibration and a sound. I've no idea what Loulou feels or hears, but he freezes, his butt dangerously close to the canine jaws. I'd be alarmed, but I've seen this before. Loulou holds a partial squat for a moment, seems to think of something, snaps his fingers, and says, "Beer!" He leaps away.

It's a variation on the same thing every time. He comes close to sitting on the wolf, but he always manages to find something to do instead. Luckily, I'm spared finding out what would happen if ass met spectral canines. Loulou, a clueless nat who's at peace with the slacker mediocrity that is his life. It's weird, but I envy him for that. It's simpler.

— — —

A few days later, I am on the university campus, in the open area
in front of the Knowledge Center as folk gather for the Joker Alliance Rally. Nevada isn't exactly the most diverse state in the
Union, but you wouldn't know that from this crowd. There are
plenty of jokers in attendance, but also a mixture of white, Black,
and brown people, the openly straight, the openly gay, and the
openly proud of not fitting into any of the old categories. Big
speakers blare Joker Plague. A few dance. All the support groups
are here, with tables set up, banners announcing who they are,
lines at each of them to join up.

An enormous guy sits cross-legged in the center of the crowd.
He's shirtless, which seems crazy considering the chill, but there's
a reason for it. He takes pulls on a long bong, holds them for a few
seconds, and then exhales plumes of purple smoke through the
gill-like openings on his torso. Way more smoke comes out than
went in, clearly to the benefit of the enthusiastic crowd around
him. He's probably helping the general mood quite a bit.

Loulou said he might show up after he scoped the Tenth Pillars
event on the other side of campus, but I don't see him. I do spot
Dina, though. I pretend I don't see her cutting straight through the
crowd toward me. I plaster a clueless expression on my face and
gaze out over the crowd, bopping my head to the music.

Dina plants herself in front of me. Through clenched teeth, she
asks, "What. Are. You. Doing. Here?" God, she looks good. Which
is to say, she looks like she always did. Thin, her nose a little too
prominent. The wrinkle lines of her lips turned toward a frown.
Her gray eyes like two bright surprises.

"Me?" I smile, shrug. "I came for the event. Supporting the
peeps, right?" I bounce on my toes. "You taught me that."

"Seriously?" She frowns. She's got the best frown. "Bacho, come
on. You knew I'd be here. You said you'd give me space!"

I stretch out my arms. "There's lots of space."

Her smirk is withering.

I drop my arms. "I'm just saying. You do have space, Dina. I came for the event. I thought I might see you, but . . . I'm here to support everyone here, especially the jokers. You *did* teach me that, remember?"

That takes a bit of the edge off her. "Of course I remember. Obviously, you can be here. Just make sure it's about the event and not about me."

"It's about the event," I say.

"I hope so. It would suck if you got stalkerish." She inhales, looks over her shoulder. "Things are about to start. I gotta go."

"Sure. Go give 'em hell." Not sure why I said that. "Happy rallying!" Or that.

Dina shakes her head, but there's a hint of a smile at the edge of her lips. She backs away, holding her arms up like I'd just done. "Space, Bacho. Space." She turns and slips into the crowd, then joins the other organizers beside the stage.

God she's cute. Witheringly cute. Snarky cute. I know I have to give her space. I want to give her space. But only so that she'll not *need* me to give her space anymore.

When the speakers start, I try to pay attention, but my eyes keep wandering across the crowd to find Dina, part of a big group chatting away. A guy with a messy head of bleached-blond dreads leans over and says something. Dina laughs and touches his arm. Who is that guy? He's got a full beard! How old is he? Why is Dina touching his arm? And does the fact that I'm asking make me stalkerish?

Someone clears their throat behind me and says, "I think I know you from somewhere. Are you a model? I'm pretty sure I've seen you naked."

I turn around and the girl from the coffee shop, Adesina, is standing behind me, a wide grin on her face. Wow her teeth are perfect. She's got a new stud in her nose and she's wearing a black turtleneck and long camel-style coat. She looks sophisticated. I am suddenly very aware of my ratty Converse shoes and wrinkled windbreaker. She's staring at me. Oh, shit. How long have I been staring at her? I need a witty comeback.

"My mom used to take naked pictures of me."

She frowns.

"When I was a baby, I mean! I haven't posed naked since I was three or so."

"Clarification appreciated." Adesina laughs, and my embarrassment melts away in a rush of tingles.

I spot Loulou on the other side of the crowd. My hand starts to rise, but I stop it. I'm not embarrassed to be his roommate or anything, but we don't hang out much in public.

Adesina says, "Gotta love Purple Haze." She points toward the pot smoker joker in the crowd.

"You're Adesina, right?" I say her name slow and careful, like I'm remembering it as I say it. I feel the wolf perk its head up from its resting place inside me, curious about what's making my heart thump.

"So you really do remember me."

Oh, shit. Is it weird that I remember her name after all these years? I feel the panic come back. She's going to think I'm a creep. "I think you said . . . or maybe it was on your cup or something? I'm not sure. I'm just good with, like, names and stuff, and maybe I saw yours and thought it was cool so I remembered it."

"Well, which one is it? Are you good with names or did you think mine was particularly cool?" Adesina raises one eyebrow. Not a bad Dwayne the Rock Johnson impression, if that's what she's going for. She doubles over laughing. "You should see the look you're giving me! Like a confused gazelle. You're too funny. So you go to UNR?"

"Yeah," I say. "Part-time. Trying it out." That's true enough, but I don't mention that I've bailed on the two classes I was taking since things fell apart with Dina.

"Cool to see you here, Bacho."

She knows *my* name?

As if she heard the question, she says, "I mentioned you to my friend Ghost. She was in San Antonio and remembered you."

She mentioned me to a friend?

"Assholes," Adesina mutters. "I hope those guys aren't going to cause any trouble." She nods toward something on the other side of the crowd. It takes me a moment through the shadows cast by the setting sun, but I see them. Three red-hat-wearing guys, standing a little way from the main crowd, watching. They're supposed to stick to the other side of campus, but I guess there's nothing stopping them from listening.

Adesina perks up. "Oh look, the keynote speaker is starting!" She grabs my arm and turns me toward the stage.

Rosinante Perez steps up to the podium, notes in hand. She's a joker-ace activist. She has a huge social media following. Her nose is inverted into her face. Looks sort of like some bats I've seen photos of. It's useful, though. She can smell people's thoughts. It makes the folk she goes up against in debates and interviews really nervous. She says, "I want to start by thanking everyone who came today to show support for our cause. Give yourselves some appreciation." She pauses to clap. "Not everyone listening is down with the cause, though. I see some representatives of the hate have come to spy."

People point at the three guys. Heads turn to look at them. The guy in the center blows a kiss toward the crowd. The crowd starts to boo.

"No, no," Rosinante says. "Don't return the hate they give. It's good they're here. Maybe they'll learn something. Maybe they'll come to understand that their hate belongs in the past, and that we are the vanguard of the future! Maybe they'll see what we already know—that we've never had more momentum for women's, joker, LGBTQIA, Black, Latino, and Native American rights than in this moment! It's so beautiful to see all these different coalitions coming together to support one another. The love in this crowd is infectious!"

"She's good," Adesina says.

"Yeah."

The crowd erupts in chants and applause, waving their signs like crazy. Someone behind us plays a tune on a kazoo. Adesina turns to watch him. "That guy's not bad," she says. She nudges me. "Maybe we should start a band with him. The upright bass, right? You still play?"

"Not really. Do you?"

"Yep. And always will."

For a moment I'm distracted by the notion that Adesina thinks of me as someone to do something with in the future, and that she knows I played an instrument I haven't touched in a couple of years. Why did I ever stop playing? Doofus.

Rosinante speaks in bursts that I only catch parts of, but each time the crowd erupts. It's a back-and-forth exchange of energy that's infectious. Even I start shouting with the others. Adesina, too. Loulou has caught the vibe as well, it seems. He weaves through the crowd until he's near the podium. He looks entranced, like he's seeing the light.

The wolf grumbles at the very thought of him.

"We need to capitalize on this enthusiasm to lobby for real change in our government," Rosinante says. "That takes heart, dedication, and it takes putting our bodies and our wallets where our slogans are." She pauses a moment, like a thought she hadn't expected occurs to her. "Not everyone here does that." She leans forward on the podium, staring at someone I can't make out from where I'm standing. "Some of y'all are downright stingy," she says, an edge creeping into her voice.

The wolf stirs inside me. I feel it swell upward, settling roughly within my upper body. It's not trying to emerge, but easing into my head to better see through my eyes and listen through my ears.

Rosinante shakes her head like she's trying to clear it. "I mean, I understand. None of us are rich, right? I'm not trying . . ." She looks down at her notes, then back at whomever she started to address. She flings her notes away. "Actually, yeah, I am. I'm talking about you!" She points at someone. "Rich boy, you here for the cause, or to get into her pants?"

A murmur of confusion goes through the crowd. People look from one to another, trying to figure out where this sudden turn came from. Hushed conversations break out. I stand on tiptoes and realize she's talking to the blond dude next to Dina.

"Is she always this aggressive?" Adesina asks. "This doesn't seem right."

"I've never heard her speak in public," I say, "but I'm pretty sure it doesn't usually go like this. She seems so nice on Twitter."

Rosinante keeps talking, but she's already on to someone else. "And you—you whine and you whine about wanting change, but you won't put your money where your big mouth is. Stop being the pampered little child you are and start actually working for once. Do you have any idea how hard I work to make all your lives better? Most of you, though, don't do shit. You come out and wear T-shirts and paint your faces and wave slogans. Feels good, doesn't it? But are you doing it for the cause? Or are you doing it for your prick?"

Someone in the audience shouts, "Are you drunk or something?"

"You saying that because you think I'm an Indian?" Rosinante asks. "You are, aren't you? Shows what you know. I'm Latinx, stupid!"

"So you're lazy?" someone else shouts.

"No, she's a rapist!"

Rosinante explodes. "You're one to talk! You pretend to be cool with jokers, but they make you queasy. You think I'm disgusting, don't you? I can smell you like a book. That's my power, remember? I'm more ace than joker, you fucker!"

Wow, this has really gone off the rails. The wolf thrums within me, holding back the tremor of a growl. Whatever is happening, it doesn't like it one bit.

"Fuck you, Perez!" a deep gravelly voice yells up from the crowd. "You're lucky your nose is inside you or I'd break it!"

The crowd gets louder, more and more out of control. I turn to ask Adesina if she wants to leave, but suddenly I'm on my ass. A burly man with what must be twenty fingers on either hand stands over me. He's wearing a rainbow headband and tight gym clothing. "Why are you even here? You aren't even a joker! These aren't your people."

Adesina steps in between us. "Hey, he didn't do anything to you, fuckityface!"

"He needs to get rescued by an insect girl?"

Adesina leaps into the air. Her wings flare and she's hovering above him, spitting curses at him as he tries to grab her. He jumps but can't get very high. She dips down low enough for him to reach for her, rises, dips down, mocking him every time he misses.

Back on my feet, the wolf and I take in the scene. It's chaos. Fist-fights break out. Someone pushes over one of the big speakers, making an earsplitting screeching sound. Tables are flipped over. People shout curses at each other. The Tenth Pillar guys are in a brawl with a bunch of jokers. I see Loulou, but he's sort of just standing there, taking it all in. He's got a strange look on his face that I can't quite make out.

Where's Dina? For a few frantic seconds I don't see her anywhere. Then I do. She's arguing with the blond guy. She's right up in his face, angry like I've never seen her. He's red-faced and monstrous, and suddenly I'm sure he's about to hit her.

Help her! I think. *Help everyone!*

The wolf launches out of me. It stretches out and flies above the crowd, a growl propelling it. If it was just me, and if I controlled the wolf completely, I might do something horrible. I know it's wrong, but I think about sinking the wolf's teeth into that guy's shoulder, crunching down until the bones fracture. The thought horrifies me, but I still have it.

But the wolf has a mind of its own. It grows massive, large enough to fill the quad and hang over everyone. It makes itself so visible I know that others can see it. From nothing one moment to a mountainous black shadow of a wolf the next. I didn't know it could do that during the day! It cranks back its head and looks to the sky, opens its mouth, and howls with enough force to flatten the people below it and shatter some of the windows in the upper reaches of the Knowledge Center and the top level of the gym. It's a long, drawn-out, beautiful howl.

So much for my little secret.

At least, that's what I'm afraid of as the echoes of the howl slowly fade. Stunned faces beneath me stare up in shock and amazement. I'm there as the wolf looking down on them, and I'm also me, seeing the hulking shadow with its gleaming white eyes. The wolf blinks and vanishes, leaving people gasping beneath the red highlights of a sunset sky. Invisible, it floats back to me and dissolves into me.

"What just happened?" I ask.

Adesina stares at me. "I'm wondering the same thing," she says. Her eyes look unfocused. She shakes her head. "For a moment there I . . . God, I was so angry. I found a reason to hate everyone I saw. All that stuff I was saying . . . It's not like I don't, at some level, mean what I said to that guy. I just don't know why it all came out. These aren't people I want to attack. But I did. We all did." She looks at me again. "Except you. I was wrong about you. You're nothing like a confused gazelle."

For the second time, Dina makes a beeline for me. She slips through the milling, confused, but suddenly sad and apologetic crowd. "You did that, didn't you? Not the freaking weirdness but the . . ." She glances at Adesina. Lowers her voice. ". . . the wolf

part. How is that possible? You said it went away. Just like everyone else that night. That's what you said. And it wasn't like *that*
before." She stops. Looking from me to Adesina. "Who's she?"

Adesina says, "Anyone want to grab a coffee?"

A couple of hours later, Adesina and I part ways with Dina. The
three of us had an unexpected, strangely honest conversation. I
told Dina—and Adesina—everything I could about the wolf. As
soon as I started talking, the words poured out. Though we didn't
talk about it directly, it felt like we were talking about other stuff,
too, Dina and I untangling knots we hadn't even known were tied.
It didn't even seem strange that Adesina heard it all. She didn't act
like any of it was weird, so it wasn't. She didn't act like I was embarrassing myself by revealing so much, so I didn't feel like I was.

None of us could explain why things went so wrong at the rally,
but it had to be more than just the tension of the day. One of the
campus cops blamed it on Purple Haze, saying he passed some
bad weed to the audience. I doubted that. It seemed mostly likely
the Tenth Pillar guys somehow provoked it, but we couldn't connect the dots to land it on them. At least nobody really got hurt.
There was going to be a hefty bill for shattered glass, but according
to KUNR nobody could identify who or what did it. People
couldn't even agree on what the enormous shape actually was.

After leaving Dina, Adesina and I walk to her dorm. It's not a
long walk, but we stretch it out. Walking slow. Lingering at stop-
lights, not pushing the crosswalk button too quickly.

"I'm still pretty new to being on my own," she says, her words
exhaled as plumes of mist. "My mom's a pretty big personality, as
you know. Really protective. Which was good. I needed that when
I was younger, and I used to never want to be alone. I guess you
could say I've changed a lot over the last few years. Being on my
own has given me time to get to know myself. That make sense?"

"Yeah, totally." I nod, search for something more to say, but fail at it. Too full of nervous butterflies now that we're alone.

Adesina turns toward me. "Hey. Here's a thing. You ready?"

I swallow. "For what?"

"How about . . ." She rolls her eyes up in thought. "I got it! How about you relax and act normal. You are normal, right? I mean, except for the massive shadow wolf stuff."

I nod.

"Good. Then act like it. Pretend like we're friends. Like we like each other and we're not worried about impressing each other. Sound good?"

Not sure I can pull it off, but I say, "Yeah. Sounds good."

She squeezes my arm and tugs me into motion again. "So that was thing one. There's a second thing, but I think it'll help the first thing."

"A thing two?" I ask, and then immediately regret it. And then I don't regret it because Adesina smiles.

"Exactly. Thing two is that I'm in a show. *The Extravaganza!*" she announces with a flourish. "It's part of a drama class, but it's not just for people in the class. We're doing this weird collage of a bunch of different classic operas, Disney movies, musicals in general. The producer seems to consider them all artistic treasures. There's a *Jack and the Beanstalk* sequence, which is actually one of the best parts. The show runs through a bunch of different things, each annotated for a few brief highlights. And the actors in all the lead roles are jokers or . . ." She curtsies. ". . . jacks."

"Cool," I say.

"Not all the way cool, but we're working on it. It is kinda fun to change gears so much, and for the cast to be so diverse. But I've got issues with pretty much all the material. *Beauty and the Beast*? *Aladdin*? There are at least a few issues, in my humble opinion. And my role is in *Madama Butterfly*."

"Really," I ask, "what role?"

She play-punches my shoulder. At which point I understand how stupid that question was. Or funny? Yeah, let's go with funny.

"It moves fast," she continues. "You can't really get too bored. Most of the stories are Cro-Magnon enough that I'd hate them if we were doing an original version. Patriarchal. Racist. Sexist. Filled with Orientalist clichés. Token joker comic characters. That sort of thing. But our production is totally revising the plotlines. The director is kind of a theatrical cliché, but I like what he's letting us do."

"So . . . is there more to this thing two?"

She lights up. "Yes. You should be in it, too!" She leans in and clasps my arm. "No, listen. We need you. We have this one guy playing the Beast from *Beauty and the Beast* and also the Wolf from *Peter and the Wolf*. He's okay as the Beast, I guess. He looks the part. Big hairy dude. Eight feet tall. Scares little children. That sort of thing. He reminds me of a cop I knew in Jokertown, except that guy is super-nice and funny. This guy, though, is as wooden as Frankenstein's monster. Which would be fine if he was Frankenstein's monster. As the Wolf, though? No. You'd be way better. Can your wolf act?"

This is not something I've considered before.

She stops at the bottom of a long flight of stairs leading up to a complex of dormitory buildings. "And that is why you're going to audition for the Wolf part. It'll be fun. You'll be great at it! Or at least better than Calvin."

"I don't think—"

"Do you have a host of better things to do than spend evenings from six to nine hanging out with me and a fun, motley array of brilliant thespians? Not so much Calvin, but the rest of us. Hmm?" The enormity and variety of ways I don't have anything better to do than that is quite a lot to ponder. "Great! Can I see your phone?"

Once I've unlocked it and given it to her, she goes to work, tapping away. She hands my phone back. "There. All set. Text me to give me your number. I'll tell the producer about you, so you better actually show up." She nods and looks at me just long enough that I start to wonder if my nose is running or something. Finally, she smiles and says, "Thanks for the wolf-walk." Her wings flare and she's airborne, sailing up and over the steps. She lands lightly near one of the dormitory doors. Waves. Then she's gone.

I'm halfway home before it occurs to me that she didn't need me to walk her home. She didn't need me to, but she *wanted* me to.

For the rest of the walk, I barely notice the cold.

It's hard to tell what's more Reno: the glitzy casinos catering to nuevo artistic Northern Sierra aesthetic, or the stylized grit of the "preserved" tourist shops on Virginia Street. A few years back the city decided to employ homeless jokers instead of fighting to remove them. The idea was to create controlled seedy, the appearance of eclectic character, the insinuation of danger. Some of the jokers panhandle for the tourists. Others pretend to be drunk. There's always someone breaking into song, someone pushing a shopping cart laden with stuff. Twice hourly there's an across-the-street shouting match. After nine there's a graffiti ace who draws obscene murals all over the shops. The shop owners rush out yelling at him. Parents bring their kids to watch. Totally weird. All this and then the same actors give tourists dining recommendations and take selfies with them. At least the jokers make out well in tips.

Here I am about to audition for a big theatrical casino extravaganza, but it's my first time actually stepping foot inside a casino. One thing I've heard seems immediately true: Once you step into a casino, the outside world disappears. The carpet looks like it's from the seventies and has every bit of wear, spilled beverages, and grime accumulated over all that time. Neon signs flicker like they're about to go out. The gold plating is complete with nicks and bruises. It's a level of cheap chintz that would make Duncan Towers feel at home. Slot machines, beckoning beacons of flashing lights, sounds, voices that seem to speak directly to you. They have one for practically every famous joker. I pass two of Bubbles's slot machines—one where she's tall and skinny, and another one of her at full mass. It seems pretty insensitive to me.

I can smell hundreds of thousands of hours of smoking vapors filling every nook and cranny of the place. Escaping the smell is impossible. I feel like I'm choking. But there's a Reno casino and there's a Reno *tourist* casino. I'm in the latter. The air, they claim, is actually cleaner than outside. Some new ordinance requires the casinos to filter the air. The apparent smell of smoke is actually some sort of Ayurvedic cleaning formulation. The smell of sin and lung disease, but not the reality. The stains? Organic paint and compounds. The dings and apparent grime? All designed by a Lithuanian interior designer flown in at great expense. Maybe it's progress. Let Vegas be Vegas. Reno? It's a tech, university, artsy, quirky, outdoor town. With healthy casino options made to look unhealthy. Something like that.

And joker-ace extravaganzas!

"Bacho!" Adesina rushes over to meet me in the theater lobby, looking a bit too excited for my nervous liking. "Yay, you're here!"

The theater has a high curved ceiling and a massive stage. Beyond that, rows and rows of seats. Imagining how many people could fit in here does nothing to calm me down. The director sits a few rows into the stalls. Other actors are spread out in various small groups throughout the rest of the auditorium. I make out a tall hairy shape near the back that I'm guessing is the Beast and the current Wolf. As if this couldn't get worse. I'm going to try to steal this huge and probably angry man's role right in front of him. I scan over the rest of the crowd. Mostly jokers, some with more obvious wild cards than others. One guy is a good nine feet tall, most of which is legs, some of which is a beer gut spilling out from under his shirt. I'm guessing he's the Giant.

"Bacho, I'm so glad you could come!" a voice booms. "Adesina has said the best things about you." The speaker is a tall, slim guy in tight pink jeans and a striped tank top. He wears a handkerchief tied around his neck. His ears are long and pointy, like an elf, only bigger. "I'm Ronaldo Gutierrez," he adds, with a bow of his head. "The director."

"Nice to meet you. Thanks for—"

"What was that?" Ronaldo shouts.

"You've got to yell for him to hear you," Adesina whispers to me.

I start to gesture toward my ear. "But his ears are—"

Adesina yanks my hand down and finishes my sentence. "—not as effective as they look. Just make sure to project onstage."

"I said it's nice to meet you!" I yell. "Thank you for having me!" A few chuckles come up from the assembled actors. I might have overdone it.

"Yes, yes, of course. Let's get right to it." Ronaldo claps his hands. Then waits, staring at me. Everyone is staring at me.

"What do you want me to do? I haven't practiced lines or anything."

"Oh no no, none of that. The Wolf has no lines. I just want to see this wild card Adesina has told me so much about."

Adesina gives me a broad smile and a thumbs-up.

I swallow a lump in my throat. It's now or never. *Okay, Wolf, come on out,* I think.

This is the part that has me the most worried. I always have some amount of control over the wolf. But most of my efforts have been about keeping it down, not drawing it out. I can tell it hears me. Worse yet, I can tell it's amused.

Ronaldo clears his throat. He even manages to project that.

Wolf. Don't let me down, buddy. You want people to see you, right? Now's your chance.

That does it. It's toying with me a little, but yeah, it does want to be seen. I feel the rising sensation in me as the wolf leaps out.

The shadow above me grows until it is a hulking shape, spectral claws outstretched. My second set of eyes open far above my head. An audible gasp goes up from the actors.

"Well, that is certainly impressive," Ronaldo says. "Okay, now act. Do stealthy!"

"Stealthy?"

"Yes, yes. Like you're sneaking in the woods, stalking Peter. Where is Peter?" He casts around until he spots him. A small, spindly guy whom I'd say was a boy of ten, except that he sports an impressive handlebar mustache and is puffing on an e-cigarette. "Be stealthy, like you're stalking him. He's in the woods. A tasty morsel. You're hungry. Stalk him!"

Right. Stealthy stalking. What's that look like? I start to step across the stage, sneaky-like, miming the motions the spectral wolf mirrors above me. I'm going for menacingly wolfy, but I feel ridiculous. Like Wile E. Coyote.

There are a few titters in the audience. Someone whispers something I can't make out.

"Okay, okay," Ronaldo says. "We'll work on that. Now, more important, do menacing. Ferocious. A carnivore going in for the kill."

"You want me to . . . kill Peter?"

Peter says through a puff of vapor, "Do your best, kid. I'm all atremble."

More laughter.

"You're a wolf! Hunt!"

This time, I don't need to silently cajole my other half. It leaps out of me, in full wolf form, black enough for everyone to see. It runs a circle around the stage, slips into the shadows on one side, appears from the shadows on the other a moment later, twice the size it had been. It hunkers there, snout massive. Its tongue slides across its canines. Its eyes fix on Peter and glow.

Wow, the wolf is actually pretty—

The wolf leaps off the stage, hits the aisle with enough force and speed for its claws to carve grooves in the carpet. It rushes for Peter so fast it blurs. And then it's there, towering over Peter, paws slammed down on the seats to either side of him, jaws open, teeth inches from the actor's terrified face. The wolf growls. Peter, definitely atremble now, pees himself. The warm, rank scent of it hits the wolf's nose. The wolf snorts, blowing the e-cigarette out of Peter's fingers. There's a long silence. The wolf perches motionless above the actor until a single pair of hands begins to clap. Then it withdraws, going invisible as it slips back into me.

Ronaldo shouts, "Marvelous!"

The other actors stare at me. The Giant says, "Goddamn, kid."

"I'm sorry." I look sheepishly at the director. "I could tone it down. I . . . think."

"Sorry?" Ronaldo starts clapping again. "You've got nothing to be sorry about. Truly top-notch stuff. You, young man, have the makings of a great canine actor."

Soon the others—all except for Peter—join in the clapping.

Walking back after the audition, the evening is strangely warm, like we've stepped out into a sudden spring. I keep apologizing for terrifying that actor, but Adesina brushes it off. "Rowly was always a bit full of himself. He'll get over it. You were great! Ronaldo said so. There's some blocking work to be done, and you probably shouldn't make Rowly wet himself quite so much, but we have a few rehearsals to get it sorted out."

"I know, but what if something goes wrong? I don't really control the wolf. It might do something I don't want it to."

She stops walking, turns toward me, and looks at me with her perfect eyes. She smiles with one corner of her mouth. "I know you think that's true, but I'm not sure it is. You know what I think? I think the wolf is all you. All you, Bacho. Problem is you don't know yourself as well as you should. We should work on that. You know what else I think?"

"What?"

"*The Extravaganza* is going to be so much better with you in it. We'll have a ton of fun. You'll bring wolfy authenticity. And I'm going to be the most badass Madama Butterfly ever!"

She opens her wings and flaps them. They lift her into the sky. With the glow of the streetlight behind her, her wings are an iridescent mosaic, hues of blue, like living stained glass, her body a wonderful silhouette.

Before I can talk myself out of it, more smoothly and with no hesitation because I don't fight it, the wolf surges up. I extend my arms with it. The spectral wolf-me rises and catches Adesina. We pull her close; she pulls me close. I feel her human arms and the smaller insectile ones around me. She flaps her wings and we twirl, both of us under the lamplight on the quiet street.

I move in to kiss her, but at the last moment she pulls her head back. "As nice as this is," she says, "I'm not about to kiss a wolf. For that part, I'm going to need the human Bacho."

She looks down at me on the ground. "So . . . my place or yours?"

The next night, Adesina drags me out to a bar for a proper introduction to the rest of the cast. I was never a big bar guy in the first place, and up until this point I hadn't had anyone to go to any with in Reno. Loulou had dragged me out once to a dive bar called Bobby B's. It was so full of smoke—real Reno smoke—that I'd stumbled out coughing after a couple of minutes. I made up excuses any time Loulou invited me out after that. I think he got the message because he stopped asking after a while. Instead we played video games and ate pizza.

The bar I'm at now is nothing like Bobby B's. It's in the heart of Reno's Midtown. It's all sparkling yellow light, glass, tall metal stools in that industrial style that's so popular, warm jazz being played on an actual piano. Loulou would hate this place, but I feel bad because we had talked about finally beating Boss Croc in *Joker Pantheon* tonight. I shoot him a text letting him know where I am if he wants to swing by, though part of me hopes he won't show.

The rest of the cast is already lounging around a cushioned booth area in the back. They appear to be in various states of intoxication. The Giant, who is already drunk enough that he's slurring longer words, goes off on a long rant about how amazing my ace is. He tells me to call him Big G and insists on buying me a drink. If I'd known that "drink" was going to be a round of three giant-sized shots I might not have agreed. I'm not a big drinker, and my head starts to feel warm and fuzzy in no time.

There's also Minny, an exceptionally cute girl who looks right out of an illustrated Swiss children's book. She plays the American soldier, Pinkerton, in *Madama Butterfly*. She is shy at first, but after a few drinks she slips into a perfect Australian accent that has our table roaring. Calvin, the guy whose role I took over as the Wolf, doesn't look anything like a wolf. He's definitely a beast, though. Long snout, tusks, blood-red eyes. Scraggly tufts of fur clump on his gray skin. He's perfectly happy I stepped in as the Wolf. I also get my first real meeting with Rowly, the man playing Peter. It's awkward at first. Big G doesn't help by saying, "Watch out, Rowly, you don't want to get too full" or "Be careful, what goes in must come out" whenever he takes a sip of his drink.

I know I'm getting drunk when I realize my hand is resting on Adesina's leg. I'm not sure how long it's been there. She doesn't seem in a rush to move it. Instead she slides her hand into my lap and slips it between my thighs. She leans in and whispers, "I think we need to go to the bathroom."

"We do?"

She raises her eyebrows. "Yeah, I'm pretty sure of it." She scooches me out of my seat, grabs my hand, and pulls me weaving through the tables. She drags me to the end of the restroom corridor and pushes me against the wall. Her wings flare into a screen behind us. Her mouth meets mine so hard our teeth crash together. Then all I'm paying attention to is what her lips and tongue and all six of her arms are doing to me.

When she pulls back, smiling, she says, "Thanks. I needed some Bacho." She rolls her eyes to the side and slips away. "And also the little ladies' room."

A minute later, as we head back toward the group, I see Loulou. He stands near the entrance, his eyes roaming. He looks a little nervous. I wave. He sees me and waves back.

"Hey," I say, all smiles when I reach him. "Loulou, meet Adesina. Adesina, Loulou."

Adesina smiles and reaches out a hand, dainty. "Charmed, I'm sure." She is so cute. My God, I'm lucky.

Loulou is stunned speechless by her. His eyes bounce from her face to her wings, to her extra arms. He hesitantly takes her outstretched hand, but lets it go a second later. "You're a . . . Adesina?"

She nods, wonderfully tipsy. "I am an Adesina! And you are the roommate, he of pizza and video-game dominance. Your fame precedes you."

He's speechless again. I suspect Loulou doesn't have much experience with girls, certainly not with someone as stunning as Adesina. She isn't the least bit offended, just smiles and says, "Come join us." She moves away.

Loulou's eyes follow her. His body doesn't. "Those are your actor friends?" he asks, taking in the entire crew at the long table. "You didn't say there were jokers."

"Oh. Well, yeah, they mostly are. They're cool, though. They won't mind that you're just a nat." I play-punch his arm.

Loulou focuses on me. "You drunk or something?"

"I've had a few."

"Yeah, I can tell. You look happy. It's a weird look on you."

"Of course I am! I've got a girl. Did you see her?"

"You said her mother was Bubbles."

"That's right. And I've got some new friends."

"She *does not* look like Bubbles."

"And . . ." I raise my chin and enunciate. ". . . I'm an actor. A man of the arts. Long live the theater!" Loulou doesn't find this as amusing as I do. "Seriously, the show is cool. You should see it. It's a joker version of old classics and stuff. Anyway, come on. Let me introduce you."

Loulou thinks about it for a moment. Though it's hot in the bar, he scrunches down in his winter coat like he's cold. "Nah. I was just passing by. Going to meet some friends."

"You have friends?" I say, grinning. I'm hilarious.

He stares at me, seems on the verge of saying something, but instead turns and pushes through the door, leaving me standing in the blast of cold air that enters as he exits.

It ends up being a great night, which Adesina and I conclude at her place. Grumpy Loulou is very much forgotten.

The next rehearsal, however, doesn't go quite as swimmingly as Adesina hoped. *Her* part is awesome. She flits around the stage, light and angelic with her amazing blue wings, flowing robes of white and pink silk trailing after her in the air. It's definitely cultural appropriation, but she makes appropriation look really good. She delivers her lines with soft precision, a musicality to her voice. The way Minny watches Adesina move around the stage you could be forgiven for thinking she was actually in love with her. Or maybe she is. That's possible, too.

My part, though? Utter failure during what isn't even the big scare scene, just the one where I spy on Rowly as he picks berries. I sneak up behind him, raise my arms, and summon the wolf. I feel it surge up out of me, but after that nothing happens. No second pair of eyes opening. No new wolf senses flooding my brain. He comes out and towers over me, but instead of doing any of the things he's supposed to, he crosses his arms, turns his head, lifts his chin, and goes into a huff. He won't do any of the things I ask him to, no matter how many times Ronaldo reiterates his very clearly projected directions.

I'm still confused about the whole thing the next evening as I finish up my shift at the Bountiful Bean. We've just closed, and the front of the store is empty besides me, Merl, and Adesina, who came to talk things over. "Hi," I say, sitting down across from her at one of the small round tables. I slip her a coffee. "Your Steamo Speciale."

She points at my black coffee. "I don't understand why you never let Merl froth yours."

"Because it's gross," I say. "I don't understand why you do it."

"I dunno. There is just another layer to the taste when he does it. Almost . . . earthy."

"Yeah, definitely a pass. Earthy?"

"Hey, I can hear you," Merl says while he mops.

Adesina and I sit for a moment. The attempts at levity aside, my non-performance last night is the elephant in the room. "Adesina," I begin, "I don't—"

"You," she interrupts, "had a bad night. It happens to everyone. You should be glad it happened when it did."

"I should be glad?"

"Definitely. Stage fright happens to everyone. It's having it at the worst time possible that's bad. You didn't. It was just a stupid dress rehearsal. You can work on it. Figure out what went wrong and fix it before there's an audience to deal with." She takes a sip of her coffee, leans closer, and whispers, "I think you're still nervous about people knowing you're an ace."

"Don't say that here." I glance over at Merl. "They'd just make fun of me. Anyway, I'm not an ace."

"What do you call it, then? Have you thought about what you and your wolf can do?"

"Fail tremendously in public," I say. "Or hurt somebody."

"Or do a lot of good."

I shake my head. "Since yesterday it's gone still. It won't respond when I call it. It's pissed at me or something. I don't even know why. Adesina, it's not . . . *me*. It comes out when it wants to. Becomes visible when it wants to. Ignores anything I ask it when it wants to. More and more, I'm realizing I can't control it."

"Maybe it's not about controlling it. Have you asked what it wants?"

"To be a pain in the ass."

"You see a pain in the ass; I see a part of you. If the wolf is a problem, it's also an answer. I get that you didn't ask for it, and that it complicates your life. I definitely get that." She tweaks an antenna and flutters her wings. "I've got some experience with this sort of thing."

"Yeah, but you're crazy cute and you can fly. I've got a seriously problematic dog."

"I am crazy cute and I can fly, yes," she says. "I love what I am, but I didn't always. I didn't ask for this, either. And . . . some of it was really hard. More than you can imagine. I think the problem is that because you don't know who the wolf is, you don't know who you are, either."

From the silence after this, someone else speaks.

"Who is this beautiful young woman distracting you from your work?" It's Laine. She's got her bag and her hat on, an indication she's on the way out. No coat, but walking with her own climate she doesn't need one.

"Adesina, this is Laine," I say. "My boss."

"I'm sorry if I'm keeping him."

"Not at all, child. Bacho works hard enough. He deserves some time off, especially with good company. Adesina, where are you from?"

"New York. I'm here for the university."

"New York?" Laine stares at Adesina for a long moment, then says, "No, that's not right."

That seems a bit out of character for Laine. Then it gets stranger. Laine says something to Adesina in a language I've never heard before, full of round vowels and long rolling words. Adesina sits up straight and nearly slips off the stool. Her eyes go blank, like she's not seeing with them and like she's not even in the room. Laine touches her shoulder and says something else, softly.

This time, Adesina answers. Her voice is hesitant. Full of pauses, but she strings together a collection of words that sound like the same language. For the next few minutes they carry on a conversation that has nothing to do with me.

Eventually, Laine squeezes Adesina's hand and says, "You should come. Think about it. Call me here if you want to. Anytime."

After Laine leaves, I ask, "What just happened? What language were you speaking?"

Adesina smirks, reluctant for a moment, then spills. "Swahili."

"Swahili?"

"It's been a long time. I didn't know I remembered it, but . . . well, I guess it's still in me." After another pause: "I'm African. I was born in the People's Paradise of Africa."

"Oh," I say. I'm not the most globally aware, but even I know some crazy stuff went down over there a few years ago. Stuff with the Committee and child soldiers and weird experiments.

"I was young," Adesina says. "It's in the past, and I don't talk about it much. I'm here now. That's what matters, right?"

I nod. "How did Laine know?"

"Something in my accent, she said."

"Wait, Laine was speaking Swahili? She's from Africa?"

"Kenya. She invited me to come to a dinner group she hosts. Some African professors. A few students. I said I'd think about it."

"Whoa. I guess that's a mystery solved. Africa. I was sure it was Haiti." Adesina looks perplexed. I ask, "You have an accent?"

"Apparently. To some. That's weird to hear, actually. When I was younger—after being adopted and coming to the States—I became American fast. Lots of American slang. *Totes* and *kewl* and stuff like that. It wasn't that I didn't like myself or anything, or was ashamed of where I came from. I've always been pretty . . . okay in my skin, right? But it was kinda that the more I sounded super-American, the more I could leave the bad things of the People's Paradise behind me. There was a lot to leave behind."

"When did Bubbles come into it?"

"Mom and I had a connection. It's a long story. Point is she saved me, adopted me, gave me a new start. She loved me, and I loved her. Still do. I confused her a little bit when I moved out here, but I just wanted to see what it was like to walk on my own for a bit."

Merl's finished mopping and he walks over to our table. "You all want to do something?"

Adesina stands up. She starts to put on her coat, which requires slipping her wings through slits for them and snapping the body into place. "We," she says, "have plans. We're going to Bacho's. We'll curl up and watch a movie we've both seen before and don't really care about seeing again. If you know what I mean. We definitely won't talk about serious things for the rest of the night. We actually might not talk much at all. Right, Bacho?"

This is news to me, but I say, "Sounds perfect. Except, let's go to your place?"

Merl looks genuinely put out. He blinks and says, "I'm a little bit jealous."

Adesina pinches his cheek. "You should be. Also, Bacho's an ace. That flyer for *The Extravaganza*? He's in the show. Come check it out."

As Merl sputters, Adesina grabs my hand and pulls me toward the door.

I wait until I know Loulou will be at work for a few hours. He and I have been mostly avoiding each other anyway, but I need to have the apartment all to myself and the wolf. I wish Adesina was here to do this with me, but she insisted this was something I needed to do on my own. I know she's right. What I don't know is whether or not I can do anything to prevent the failure that's careening toward me.

I sit cross-legged on the floor in the living room. I close my eyes and call to the wolf, asking it to come out. I can tell it hears me calling it. I'm both the one calling and the one resisting the call. Will I ever get used to this? I don't know, but it's time to try.

Come on, I think, *let's have it out. I'm here. All right? You've got my attention.*

When it moves, it's abrupt. It doesn't climb up my spine like it usually does. Instead, the wolf just steps out of my chest. It leaps onto the couch, sits on its haunches, and stares at me. It's not exactly the alpha wolf that attacked the Doberman. Or the surly semi-sleeping mutt that hopes Loulou will sit on it. It's not the massive shadow that towered over the rally, or the werewolf that made Rowly pee himself. This one is a lean, shaggy canine, spectral in that it glimmers with an uncanny energy, and yet is as grounded in flesh as I've ever seen it.

"We have to figure some stuff out," I say. "You have to start listening to me."

The wolf cocks an eyebrow, a gesture that reads clear as day to me. It's a sneer.

"You think I should listen to you. Fine. What do you want?"

The wolf closes its eyes. After a moment, I do the same.

An image emerges out of my eyelids. Tufts of sagebrush dotted across high desert hills, rising into mountains, rock features like enormous spearheads slammed upward from beneath the earth, creviced with highlights and shadows. I smell the pine trees from the higher slopes. Above it all, a wide-open, clear sky that's aglow with orange at the horizon, with the promise of stars just visible in the deepening dark at the crest of sky.

It's beautiful.

Then I'm in motion. The ground scrolls beneath me, each step a leap that's like flying. Myriad smells burst against my face. I inhale them, know them, want to explore each and every one of them. But not as much as I want to hunt, to be high in the silent night, scraping against the stars, warm blood in my teeth, tearing skin and fur, gnawing on bone. Howling and hearing my kind howl back.

I open my eyes. The images and sensations and smells vanish. The wolf looks at me. It tilts its head slightly. "You want to go into the wild?" I ask. "You want me to take you there?"

The wolf bridges the space between us and nuzzles against the side of my face.

"Right. You want to go for a walk. Why did I never think of that?"

The wolf takes a step back, indignity radiating off it.

"I'm kidding. I get it." And I do. I understand what he craves because I crave it, too. All those high wilds and the hunt and night and the universe to be found there. I want that, too. It feels like I've always wanted it. I was just too dense to know it. I lean forward and reach out to touch the canine face. "I'll take you. But can it be a deal? If you help me out with this play, I'll take you."

It slams its weight into me, nearly making me crash over. For a moment, I clenched its astral fur in my fingers. Its pushing changes and it slips into my body, through my skin. It curls up deep within me, but different from before. It feels like a campfire inside me now, filling me with warmth.

Adesina sits in a chair backstage sipping a cup of ice water. She's the picture of controlled calm in her customized silk kimono. Her wings are visible, but they're pulled in and incorporated into intricate loops and rolls that make them seem like some artistic elaboration on her kimono. She wears a wig of long, straight silver hair over her short hair. Her makeup is elaborately perfect: lipstick and eyeshadow, sparkling rouge highlights on her cheeks. All the classic touches, with one major difference: Her skin is her true black. No whiteface for this butterfly. Adesina has flipped that notion of beauty on its head. She's good at things like that.

Me? Not so much controlled calm going on here. I pace, knowing that each second brings me closer to stepping onto that stage. It doesn't help that the music from the *Beanstalk* number is doing my head in. Why did I agree to this?

Adesina stands up, takes my hands, and stills me. Looking into her eyes, I have my answer. I agreed to this because she asked me. Pretty good reason, really. She says, "Bacho, all you have to do is trust yourself." She moves her hands to either side of my face, cradling it and looking up at me. Her touch seems to quiet the dissonance in my head. She pops up onto the tips of her toes and kisses me. When she pulls away, my head moves with her, desperate for it to last longer. "And I need to get into position."

Oh, right. I'm on soon, but that's *after* the Madama Butterfly sequence.

Big G pushes through the curtain to the stage, an enormous club balanced on his shoulder. He looks at me and Adesina and raises an eyebrow. He snorts, grabs a towel to dab his sweaty face with. Others rush in behind him. Fairy-tale characters. Ducks. Woodland creatures. A muscle-bound princess. A gingerbread joker. A witch on a floating skateboard. The *Jack and the Beanstalk* sequence is quite a mash-up. They're talking a mile a minute, ecstatic, hugging and high-fiving. I guess it went well.

"Adesina, you're on in twenty!" Ronaldo shouts.

Minny's Pinkerton rushes over to stand beside Adesina, humming with energy in her crisp officer's suit.

"It's crazy out there," Big G says. "The place is packed. Everyone dressed up. All sorts of people. Jokers, nats, and everything in between. And you're never going to believe this! We've got international celebrities in the house." He pauses for dramatic effect, a wonderfully goofy expression on his face.

"Out with it," Adesina says.

"Ten seconds!" Ronaldo shouts.

"Bubbles and Rustbelt are out there! I mean, talk about a dream. I've had a crush on Bubbles since forever. And she clapped. Even blew a bubble at me!"

"Bubbles?" Adesina looks suddenly pale. "Why is she here? I didn't tell her anything."

Big G shrugs. "Guess the word got out."

Minny, who had been smiling ear to ear, squints one eye. "What do you mean you didn't tell—"

"Five seconds. Adesina . . ."

It's my turn to be supportive. "Adesina, just go perform! You're awesome. She's awesome. Go make her proud."

"Annnnnnnd go!"

Adesina has just enough time to smile at me before she's ushered through the curtains. Her appearance onstage is announced with a roar of applause. There's even an actual roar, but I guess that sort of thing is to be expected with an audience as diverse as this one. The crowd noise slowly dies down when Puccini's music kicks in.

With Rowly and a few others, I watch what I can from the left wing. Sure enough, Bubbles and Rustbelt are a few rows back in the stalls. Rusty wears a tailored tuxedo, sports a rainbow bow tie, and sits in an aisle seat with his legs stretched out in a manner that doesn't look the least bit comfortable. He doesn't seem to care, though. His metallic face looks on the verge of tears. Bubbles is more composed, but just as entranced. She's as model-beautiful as ever, in a dark-red gown with her blond hair flowing down over her shoulders.

Looking across those ranks of faces, sizes, shapes, colors, and features, I see Merl and a few other folk from the Bountiful Bean. And Dina, sitting with the dude I presume to be her new boyfriend. Laine is up on the mezzanine level with several people I now figure are her African friends, the ones Adesina has been meeting up with. Just below them in the rear stalls, I spot someone else. Loulou. When I first mentioned Adesina and the show he'd seemed interested, but since that weird night at the bar he'd mostly dropped it. I'm surprised he showed. He's in a cluster of guys. Nats by the look of them. They're the only ones not focused on the stage. They look around like they're more interested in the audience than the show itself. Maybe that's what Loulou's problem was. He'd told his new friends he had an in with Bubbles's daughter. He probably bragged about her being a mini Bubbles before he knew she was a jack starring in a joker-led production.

I catch the best part of Adesina's sequence: the suicide scene. Only, it's not like the original, and it doesn't end in a suicide. It starts off with Minny's Pinkerton trying hard to appear callous as she rejects Madama Butterfly, but with Minny's doll eyes and rosy cheeks her actions never quite match the expression on her face. That's by design, of course, as part of the point is that it's absurd that anyone wouldn't love Adesina's Madama. Minny brushes Adesina aside and stalks off on her tiny legs, doing the best she can to be a jerky soldier-guy. Adesina swoons about the stage in a dance of misery and rejection. She draws a knife from the folds of her kimono and waves it as she twirls across the stage. The intensity of the music increases.

Adesina stops center stage and holds the knife high. She turns the blade in her hands and moves to sink it into her abdomen. She stops as if she's halted by the audible gasp from the audience. She cocks her head to the side, studies the knife, and then shakes her head. She discards the blade with a casual flick of the wrist. The music changes. A drum rhythm emerges. It doesn't overpower the Puccini but gives it a different backbone. It fuels Adesina's dance. She's not swooning anymore, not weak or fragile. She steps hard, confident, planting her feet and moving her arms with a flowing, military crispness. She tugs at the ribbons securing her wings and tosses them out over the audience. As they descend, Adesina's wings flare out, the gorgeous mosaic of shades of blue lit from behind. She lifts into the air and flies over the audience, rising and falling. She swoops over the mezzanine, reaching out and touching hands with Laine and her friends in the process. They're on their feet, clapping and calling out, dancing. This Madama Butterfly doesn't die; she soars.

"Bacho, you're up next!"

Crap. How am I going to follow that?

Maybe it's having just watched Adesina.

Maybe it's the energy in the auditorium.

Maybe it's that in the stage lights I can't see the audience.

Maybe it's that I'm a natural actor?

Probably not that.

Whatever it is, once I'm onstage, I actually feel good. I'm in sync with my role, the stage, and the other actors. When I summon the wolf it appears, slipping out of me to stalk Rowly. When the spectral shadow of the wolf looming over me becomes visible to the crowd, someone shouts, "Whoa! Bacho, are you fucking kidding me?" I recognize the voice. It's Merl.

Eventually, I'm chasing Rowly around the stage. Either he's become a much better actor or he doesn't quite trust my control. The look of terror on his face is very convincing. The crowd makes all the right sounds at the right moments, the *ooo*s and *aaa*s, the laughter. The wave of gasps that rushes through the audience when I howl into the rafters makes my heart race. I'm in a zone I never knew existed. I strut around the stage, hamming it up for the crowd, improvising as I stalk, pounce, and fumble in my pursuits of poor Peter. The best parts are when I really let the wolf out, stretching it high to tower over Rowly, twisting at weird angles to keep things fresh. It's not all stuff I rehearsed, but it feels right. The crowd goes crazy. They love me.

I sneak a grin at Rowly when I'm turned away from them. He shakes his head and scowls a little. "Show-off."

I do feel like a show-off, but so what? I've never shown off in my life. But the real thrill is that I'm showing my wild card. That feels better than I could've imagined.

We get to the part where Rowly shoots a cork in the wolf's shadow butt with his air rifle, making it yelp and jump. It's the sequence's turning point, when the hunter becomes the hunted, which leads to the two reaching an eventual truce in which nobody ends up eaten or caged. And no ducks get swallowed whole in our version. For this part I stand still, letting the wolf do most of the running around. Out in the dark audience someone shouts something that I can't make out. There's a grumbled response, but I'm not really paying attention. I'm watching the wolf, amazed that it's so into the acting.

"You're supposed to run," Rowly says. He's walked up behind me. He's smiling, but not in a friendly way.

I mouth, *What?* and gesture toward the wolf. "You're supposed to be—"

"Okay, suit yourself." Rowly hefts the rifle up, aims, and shoots. At me!

The cork bullet bounces off my forehead. It hurts. That could take an eye out! I'm about to say this, but Rowly swings the rifle around like he's going to smack me with it. His face is twisted with an anger I don't understand. I turn and run. Just a few steps and something catches my foot and I sprawl out, landing hard on my chest and sliding across the slick wood.

Flipping over, I see what I tripped on: the rifle. Rowly must have tossed it at me. He stalks toward me, yelling something. None of this is in the script, but neither is the grimace on his face, or the fact that he's unzipping his trousers. "You thought making me piss myself was funny, didn't you? Got a big thrill out of it. Make fun of the small guy, the guy who looks like a kid, right? Well, screw that, and screw your stupid ace."

He reaches in to pull himself out, and I realize what he's intending. I scramble back, trying to get to my feet while avoiding the stream of urine he lets loose.

"Are you crazy? Rowly, we're onstage!"

The wolf swipes him on the shoulder, just forcefully enough to spin him and his pee around.

Thanks, wolf.

I'm up and running. Utterly confused, disbelieving. There's an audience out there that just saw what happened. At least, that's what I think until the lights on the stage go down, and the house lights go up. I freeze, horrified by what's now brightly lit. Nobody in the audience is paying attention to me and Rowly. What they're doing is rioting.

The crowd that was jubilant a few moments ago is a raging mob. Yelling. Shoving. Punching one another. Throwing things. It's like the rally all over again, except worse. A man near the front grabs another by his coat and yells, "Stop looking at my wife, you joker trash!" He slams the guy's head against the edge of the stage. Somebody else hurls one of the overflow chairs right into the middle of the stalls. Even the cast is fighting. Big G roars on to the stage, wrestling with Calvin as the muscle-bound princess throws punches at both of them. Ronaldo is yelling at the top of his voice, not actually hitting anyone but casting withering looks with abandon.

It's complete chaos. I stand there watching it, helpless, confused. It doesn't help that I'm seeing the whole scene in double vision. I see with my eyes, and I see through the wolf's. But as my eyes jump from one shocked scene to another, the wolf scans with a different intensity. It's not looking at everything. It's looking through the confusion *for* something.

Through my eyes, I see Rustbelt walking with his arms spread wide in a calming gesture. "Come on now," he says. "Let's not fight. No, no, no, no fighting! Don't punch that lady!"

Through the wolf's eyes, I see Loulou. I don't know why the

wolf has picked him out of all the chaos, but even to me it's weird that he's such a still point among all the motion. He just sits there, the same strange expression on his face that I saw on it at the rally. While he's motionless, the guys around him are in full-on brawls. They've donned red hats and they're bashing the crap out of anybody they can get their hands on. Of course. They're Tenth Pillars.

Bubbles races through the crowd. I assume she's trying to calm things, but it's more like she's crashing into fights, getting punched and kicked, growing thicker and fatter in the process. Okay, good. That's part of how Michelle Pond becomes Bubbles. I've seen her power in action before. Maybe she can fix whatever is going on.

"Bacho!" It's Merl, clawing through the scrum toward the stage. When he's near, I reach out a hand to pull him up, but a brute of a guy in a red hat slams into him. The two go down, wrestling on the floor. The guy pins Merl, cocks back his fist to punch him, but Merl's hand—which has been clawing at the guy to no effect—opens. He sends a blast of air into the guy's face forceful enough to knock his head back, lift his body, and send his stupid red baseball hat swirling toward the ceiling.

Merl gets to his feet, looks at me, and says, "What assholes! Aren't they assholes?" Then something occurs to him. "That was Steamopower! Didn't I tell you?"

I don't get to answer. There's something big coming my way.

Bubbles. She's way heavier than before, her dress stretched taut over rolls of flesh. She shouts, "You wanna hit me? Do it! Hit me good, you little beanpole!"

I try to back away, but she's at full charge and I don't have a chance. I'm also not about to hit her. The wolf materializes with a claw outstretched and smacks her hard enough to spin her around. It's just what she wanted. She leaps off the stage, gaining girth in midair. She crashes down in the stalls, crushing seats—and unfortunate people—beneath her. That'll give her bubble supply a boost.

She gets to her feet and lets loose a barrage of gooey bubbles. They float over the crowd, dropping down slowly. As soon as someone touches one, it slips around them. She's trapping them, but it's not exactly in a nice way. Once trapped, the people inside lash out, trying to break the bubble. But everything they try bounces back on them. They're trapped, but trapped with themselves and beating the crap out of themselves. Adesina flies around after her, calling to her and trying to get in the way, but Bubbles shoots around her.

The wolf moves. It leaps off the stage and bounds in spectral form, passing through the crowd. It heads straight for Loulou. As it reaches him, it materializes, becomes solid in the werewolf form that terrorized Rowly. It grabs Loulou around the torso, claws digging in enough that Loulou screams. It leaps up to the mezzanine, roaring to clear people out of the way. It works. It throws Loulou against a pillar, traps him, and moves in. The wolf's eyes close and don't open. It's shutting me out.

I run from the stage. Leap down and shove my way to the nearest exit. Out into the corridor and up the stairs. People curse me, punch and pull my hair, but I keep moving. I have to stop whatever the wolf is about to do. I'm winded by the time I get to the mezzanine level and squirm through the fleeing crowd into the seats. I see them.

Loulou lies panting against the pillar, the wolf hulking over him. Sweat stains the front of his white T-shirt, red seeping through some of the places the wolf's claws grabbed him.

"I said I give up!" Loulou pleads. "I'm not doing it anymore. They can arrest me or whatever. Just don't kill me!"

"Stop!" I say in the most commanding voice I can muster.

The wolf turns and looks at me. Just like that, I can see through its eyes again. It's like the wolf pulls me into it instead of me pulling it back into me. This is what it wants—for me to see what it's about to do, for me to do it *with* him.

We lunge at Loulou. Our jaws bite down on his head. I'm afraid I'm going to feel my friend's skull crushed by my teeth, but that's not exactly what happens. His physical head is pinned in our physical jaws, but our wolf teeth sink deep into something that isn't Loulou's physical body. We bite into the energy inside of him. I feel his essence leaking like blood in our jaws. With it comes a barrage of memories and emotions. Loulou's life screams into me. I taste all of him, all he's seen and thought and wanted and feared, with blasts of specific moments: Loulou curled into a ball as his father batters his mother, Loulou in the bleachers watching two football teams brawl, Loulou standing at the side of a city street as a driver plows into a crowd of peaceful protestors, Loulou alone in his apartment, alone again and again and again, Loulou meeting the red hats and finally finding people who embraced the animus he gave off. There's so much loneliness and despair in him, so much self-doubt and uncertainty and need for acceptance. It's an overload of all things Loulou, depths in him that I'd never considered.

It overwhelms me, but still the wolf and I chew and tear and swallow. We're spectral hunters feeding on spectral flesh. On his soul, because I have no other word for it.

Reno city jail. I'd not expected to ever see the inside of it, but here I am, in a cell crammed with people from the auditorium riot. A few of the other cast members are in with me. Calvin is pressed into one corner, shoulders hunched like he's ashamed of his bulk. Big G is in the next cell over. I can see his long shins jutting through the bars. Two Tenth Pillar guys sit across from me, both of them glaring at me. Beside me, Rowly mumbles under his breath and through his swollen lips. He calls them pimply assholes. He impugns their mothers' virtue. He sketches out the breadth of their collective massive fucking stupidity. They don't say a word. He's the only one talking, but nobody shuts him up. Most of us agree, and the red hats are outnumbered. If this were a cage match, they wouldn't come out of it well.

But nobody's got any fight in them anymore. That bloomed, exploded, and died in the auditorium. It began to evaporate the moment we attacked Loulou. When the wolf had enough, it let me pull back. It faded into me and went still, leaving me alone with what we'd done. Loulou slumped against the pillar. Alive but motionless, bruised and bloody. He stared straight ahead, eyes vacant. A stream of drool slipped from the corner of his mouth. He didn't seem to notice. By the look of him, he wasn't noticing anything anymore.

Some people fought on for a while, but for most the hatred and rage faded, leaving battered confusion, shame, apologies. Murmurs and questions, people asking for help or offering it. The red hats tried to fight their way out, but others grabbed and detained them. Rustbelt called for calm from the stage. Bubbles joined him, speaking in a firm but comforting tone that was the opposite of how she'd been just moments before. Then the police showed up in force and there was all the new hostility and confusion they brought with them. They leaned right into making arrests, me included.

I spilled the beans pretty quickly. I told the cops everything: about the wolf, about attacking Loulou, about pushing into his mind and devouring it. All those memories. All the moments that twisted him. Some of the memories were starting to fade, which I was glad of, but the things I'd learned about him seemed like they were going to stick. His ace power became the curse of his life. Loulou had never really been a bad person, but the prejudice and anger that radiated from him poisoned every interaction he had. That's why he had no friends. I understood now that the wolf had shielded me from the effects of Loulou's ace. I probably shouldn't have blabbed so much, but the guilt made it pour out of me. For all I knew, he was a vegetable, a mindless shell of himself. Maybe he always would be.

If that was the wolf's fault, it was my fault, too. I'd take what punishment was coming. If I got locked up, so be it. At least the wolf would be locked up, too.

"Hey, wolf-boy," one of the red hats says, "is it true? You got some dog in you that attacked our boy?"

"Damn near killed him," another says.

"Might die yet," the third adds.

"Even if he doesn't," the first guy says, "mind-fucking someone like that . . . that's a life sentence. The rest of us just scraped a little. But you? You're carrying a load weight. Get ready to be a bitch for your Black and brown brothers."

Rowly turns toward me. "Can you eat their minds, too?"

Before I can answer, there's movement and voices in the corridor. Two cops. They call my name. They get me to stick my hands through a slot in the bars. Cuff me.

The chief red hat laughs. "Told ya! Didn't I tell ya?"

"Too fucking right!" another says.

One of the cops shoves me into motion. Neither explains where they're taking me. Maybe it doesn't matter. Whatever has to happen has to happen.

The red hats keep it up. "Bend over, spread your cheeks, and cough."

"Welcome to life as a bitch!"

The Tenth Pillars start to howl like wolves.

When one of the cops opens the door and leads me into the room, I'm expecting more cops, lawyers, or something. I'm not expecting . . .

"Adesina!"

She bolts up from where she's sitting and runs to me. She hugs me, kisses me, her hands moving over me checking for injuries. Finding none, she pulls back and punches me in the arm. "Don't ever go running off like that again. I was worried about you!" Then she grabs me again, all six arms pulling me in. It feels so good to be within that embrace, though I'm not feeling like I deserve it.

Beyond her, Bubbles and Rustbelt sit at a table, watching. To the cop, Bubbles says, "Can you take off the handcuffs, please? And give us a moment. Your supervisor agreed to that."

The cop mumbles something I can't make out, but he uncuffs me and then steps out and shuts the door. The way it clicks makes it feel like he's locking us all in.

"Come sit," Bubbles says.

Adesina and I do. Bubbles is back to normal size. She's still wearing the dress from the show, but she's wrapped in a sweater now, looking tousled but composed. "Bacho. So you're the boyfriend that I didn't know about. It seems odd to say nice to meet you, considering the circumstances."

"I didn't want to meet you . . ." I trail off, unsure of what I'm starting to say.

Bubbles cocks an eyebrow. "Is that a complete sentence?"

"I mean I didn't want to meet you like . . . *this*."

"Golly, we wanted to surprise the kiddo," Rustbelt says, motioning to Adesina, "but we didn't expect all this, either."

Bubbles smiles. "Bacho, we're going to have a lot to talk about, but before all that I want you to know that I am glad to meet you. I know we met briefly in San Antonio, but this is a pretty different circumstance. From what Adesina has been telling me, you're someone she cares about. I understand that my daughter's privacy matters to her, but I'm trying to get her to understand that sharing with me matters, too."

Adesina rolls her eyes. "Mom, I know that. I would've invited you to a performance once I knew how it was going."

"It was one heck of a show," Rustbelt says. "Before it got weird, I mean." He looks puzzled. "I'm not sure I understand theater."

Bubbles stays focused on me. "Bacho, we don't know exactly what went on in that auditorium, but we understand that your roommate and his power caused it. And about the Tenth Pillar guys wanting a big chaotic scene. Seems like they befriended Lou-lou and then used him. He was the fuel driving the chaos in there, right?"

I nod.

"And from what you told the cops, you're the one who put an end to it."

I close my eyes and nod again. Put an end to Loulou . . . "I didn't mean to. It was me and it wasn't me. It's hard to explain."

"I explained to them," Adesina says. "As well as I could, at least."

"Like I told the cops, I accept responsibility. What happens to me doesn't matter."

"Ah, yes it does!" Adesina says.

I slip my hand away from Adesina's. "Not after what I did. I took his mind away. His memories. Everything about him. I might as well have killed him. I destroyed him."

"No, you didn't, son!" Rustbelt says.

Bubbles squints at me. "Wait. Did the cops not tell you? He's in the hospital, but your roommate is getting better."

"What?" I manage to ask.

Adesina answers. "He started talking again a few hours ago! The doctors say it is like amnesia. He's going to recover, Bacho. I'm sure of it."

I look from face to face, disbelieving. "I thought we'd eaten his soul."

Rustbelt grimaces. "You should probably stop saying things like that."

"Definitely," Bubbles says. "There may still be an arraignment and trial, but a trial for exactly what we'll have to wait and see on. Adesina is right, though. Your friend is doing a lot better than it first seemed. If he gets better, the real thing that you and your wolf did was stop a horrible situation from getting a lot worse. Some-one could've been killed in there, but that didn't happen because of you."

Rustbelt grins. "That's why we're here to bust you out, kid."

Adesina slips close to me, arms pulling me in again. "He means bail you out. You and the wolf." She growls close to my cheek, teeth bared. "We're going to unleash the wolf."

"Okay." Bubbles rises. "Let's give these two a moment." She heads for the door.

Rustbelt follows, but not without giving me a thumbs-up as he exits.

Adesina laughs. "I love my mom, and I love making her uncomfortable. Not a lot of things do that to her, superhero and all. Also . . ." She flares her wings, hiding us from anyone who might open the door. ". . . I might love you, and the wolf, too."

"Are you sure about this?" Merl asks. "I don't want to be the one who has to file the missing hiker report. Those things never end well."

We're pulled over on a side road off a lonely stretch of highway east of Reno. Merl leans against his beat-up green Gremlin, a car he drives with pride for how heinously ugly it is. A plus of the desert climate: Cars don't rust and can keep going if you maintain them. A downside of the desert climate: Cars don't rust and can keep going if you maintain them.

I swing my pack onto my back and start tugging on the straps. "I'll be fine. It's just a few days."

"Why here, though?" He gestures at the landscape. Scraggy high-desert terrain off to the west. Hills rising into mountains to the east. "Are you having a crisis or something? Should I be intervening? You know you can't skip out on bail, right? You've got court dates com—"

"Merl, I'm okay. We just need some time. Me and the wolf. We made a deal."

"Okay, but if you don't come back I'm going to be the first to comfort Adesina, if you know what I mean."

"I love you, too, man." I punch him in the shoulder. "She's going to pick me up here in a week. So trust me. I'll come back."

"Is she going to fly you?"

I smile. "She doesn't have a car, so I guess so."

"You lucky fuck. How did you even—"

"I'll see you in a few days. Go on. Go froth some milk, Steamo."

Before Merl's Gremlin is back to the main road, the wolf is out of me. It's not watching the road like I am, but looks the other way, taking in the mountains.

My thoughts are still back in Reno. So much happened in the days after the *Extravaganza* riot. Lawsuits thrown around. Press all over the place. National attention thanks to Bubbles and Rustbelt. The Tenth Pillar guys folded under questioning, admitting the plan was theirs. They were hoping to use Loulou's power to start some sort of an anti-joker/anti-diversity revolution, with ever-bigger riots planned. Concerts. Football games. Political conventions. A session of Congress. Idiots.

As for Loulou, there's good news and bad news. On the bad side, he's confessed to inciting both riots, and to conspiring to start more. There's going to be a trial. It's just taking a while to figure out the details of the charges against him. More keep popping up. He's going to be dealing with it for a long time.

On the better-news side, he's been steadily recovering. I visited him while he was still in the hospital. He was complaining that they should let him go home. He's fine, he says. Just a few scratches. He remembers some of what happened that night, enough to admit that he was there to cause the riot, but he's lost some things, too. He doesn't remember the moment the wolf attacked him, and he seems to have lost some of the worst memories we tore out of him. I started to describe a few things, but he looked at me like I was crazy and told me to stop. He said, "Those don't sound like things I *want* to remember." I couldn't dispute that. Each passing day made his memories fainter in me. I remembered the horror of having them, but not the specifics, not the vividness of them. Maybe I'd lose them completely, too.

So that's where I left things with Loulou. Both of us happy to forget some things, both of us waiting on the courts. I might be in less legal jeopardy than I thought, but that stuff is going to play out for a while. There's so much information to gather and so many interviews to conduct, it's going to be weeks before I'm back in court. In the meantime, I'm out on bail and free to move around what I've learned is the most mountainous state in the lower forty-eight. Who knew?

The wolf looks at me. I realize that I've underestimated it in ways that are still occurring to me. It's not some dumb brute. Sure, it doesn't suffer errant Dobermans and doesn't always listen to me, but on the things that really matter I should be listening to it more. It must've known what it was doing with Loulou—taking the worst of his memories, knowing he'd be left better for it. There was a lot more to this wolf than I'd thought.

"We're really doing this?" I ask.

The judgment in its eyes and the side lean of its head are crystal clear. We had a deal. I knew the terms.

"Fine." I shrug off the pack and find a crevice in the boulders. I stuff the pack into hiding. When I'm pretty sure I've got my bearings to find it again, I walk back to the wolf. "It's your show. Now what?"

In answer, it leaps to one side. It dips its head down, dashes toward me. Its spectral teeth nip my trouser legs, giving them a tug, and then it prances away. It's all pretty weird. It's like it's . . . happy. I'm still not at peace with it, but that's the point of this. Alone time, me and the wolf. Here's hoping we can work out a way to share whatever it is we share.

It cuts away from the hiking trail and heads across the scrub, toward the hills. As I follow, I inhale the scent of the recent rain and the sparse green vegetation that's responded to it. There's so much more life here than I knew. I can smell it now. The things that have passed beneath me, on the sand, beneath it, the creatures in the distance, how near or far: It all makes sense to me, excites me. The mountains step back toward the horizon, great shapes climbing over each other, each layer its own earth hue, each a promise to be explored. It's beautiful.

Up ahead of me, the wolf kicks up its pace. And so do I.

GEORGE R. R. MARTIN is the #1 *New York Times* bestselling author of many novels, including those of the acclaimed series A Song of Ice and Fire—*A Game of Thrones, A Clash of Kings, A Storm of Swords, A Feast for Crows,* and *A Dance with Dragons*—as well as related works such as *Fire & Blood, A Knight of the Seven Kingdoms, The World of Ice & Fire,* and *The Rise of the Dragon* (the last two with Elio M. García Jr. and Linda Antonsson). Other novels and collections include *Tuf Voyaging, Fevre Dream, The Armageddon Rag, Dying of the Light, Windhaven* (with Lisa Tuttle), and *Dreamsongs Volumes I* and *II.* As a writer-producer, he has worked on *The Twilight Zone, Beauty and the Beast,* and various feature films and pilots that were never made. He lives with his lovely wife, Parris, in Santa Fe, New Mexico.

georgerrmartin.com
Facebook.com/GeorgeRRMartinofficial
X: @GRRMspeaking

About the Type

This book was set in Palatino, a typeface designed by the German typographer Hermann Zapf (b. 1918). It was named after the Renaissance calligrapher Giovanbattista Palatino. Zapf designed it between 1948 and 1952, and it was his first typeface to be introduced in America. It is a face of unusual elegance.

GEORGE R. R. MARTIN PRESENTS
WILD CARDS

An alien virus
ravages the world, its
results as random as a hand
of cards. Those infected either
draw the black queen and die, draw
an ace and receive superpowers,
or draw the joker and are
bizarrely mutated.

**Welcome to the
world of the
everyday
superhero.**

VISIT
GeorgeRRMartin.com
or WildCardsWorld.com
for more information.

BANTAM

Available wherever books are sold